LORD OF GOBLINS

IV

BY
MICHIEL WERBROUCK & HADI Y. BENDAKJI

Lord of Goblins
Volume 4

Copyright © 2024 Michiel Werbrouck & Hadi Y. Bendakji

ISBN (print): 979-8-88993-045-7
ISBN (e-book): 979-8-88993-044-0

Written by Michiel Werbrouck & Hadi Y. Bendakji
Edited by Joi Massat

Published 2025 by MoonQuill
www.moonquill.com

TABLE OF CONTENTS

GLOSSARY

Lev/Gherm: Assassinated during his victory speech. Lev was forcibly torn from his world during his moment of triumph, but death was not the end. He now finds himself in the body of a greyborn bogey named Gherm. Now in a new land, Lev must find a way to survive and—just maybe—thrive.

A white being trapped at the depths of the monster caverns had forged a contract with Lev, granting him Ainshard's key. Owing to his achievements and those of his men, he has ascended to a prominent position within Bogey society. He might have lost the position of High Chief to Vyrga, but as Chief of Commerce, he still plays a prominent role in guiding goblinkind into a better future.

Ghorza: Gherm's older sister. She and Gherm are greyborns, which makes them slaves according to the bogeys' primitive society. Having lost her parents at a young age, Ghorza cares deeply for her brother, Gherm, and works hard to keep him safe and fed. She's wary of Lev and wonders how much of her brother is left. In Gherm's absence, she became close friends with a trio of peculiar greyborn girls: Abelarda, Reeza, and Lore. She decided to live on her own, away from Lev, and later invited Thorst to move in when his house burned down.

Abelarda: Ghorza's friend and Volker's older sister. She is a straightforward person, unafraid to voice her opinions, and she naturally assumes the role of leader within her circle of friends. While she values her friendship with Ghorza, she is not fond of Volker's involvement with Lev. She sports a head of dyed blonde hair.

Reeza: The youngest member of Abelarda and Ghorza's circle of friends. Her kindness and calm demeanour charms children and wildlife alike. In times of tension, her presence comforts others. She has chosen to dye her hair brown.

Lore: A member of Abelarda and Ghorza's circle of friends. She comes from a family of smugglers. She has an exceptional knack for manoeuvring undetected. She is recognized by her dyed black hair.

Volker: Lev's second-in-command. He is the youngest son from a family of potters. Endlessly loyal to Lev, his honest nature and work ethic shine through despite his timid personality. He's proved himself as a capable leader and combatant who can hold his own in Lev's absence.

Rak: One of the biggest, baddest greyborn around. Even as a child, Rak was always stronger than his peers. Forced to turn to crime to save his mother, his strength, charisma, and loyalty to his men allowed him to take over the mining quarters and southern living quarters in the slums. He supported Lev during the elections instead of taking part himself, as he had no interest in politics. He helped lead Pàrras' defenders against Lachas' bereke.

Hem/Hemgall: One of the few truly loyal members of Rak's gang. He likes to keep things simple and respects men who can take risks for their ambitions. Besides that, he can hold his liquor. Despite his lingering caution, the loss of most of Vyrga's sons has prompted Hemgall to begin repairing their strained relationship.

Vyrga: Considered to be the Lord of Wretches and King of the Immoral, his actions know no bounds. He is no priest nor poet, neither a warrior nor noble. He is a greyborn, but not just any greyborn; a leader with the blood of nobles in his veins. He cares not for the consequences, as long as he gets his way. Against all odds, he won the election against Lev, earning the title of High Chief of the city. However, his fortunes quickly turned when he lost Ludger to the bereke, leaving only Bolo by his side.

Gelmar: Gelmar, the eldest and first child to follow Vyrga, held a unique place in his mentor's heart, serving not only as a son but also as a companion. His arrogance, coupled with his steadfast conviction that he was destined to succeed Ainshard, led to feelings of deep betrayal when Vyrga did not consider him a viable successor.

Fuelled by resentment, Gelmar hatched a plot to amass followers and instigate a coup. However, his plans were thwarted when Vyrga discovered his treachery and sent him into battle against Lev. Unfortunately, Gelmar met a tragic end. Defeated, he was subsequently slain by his own followers.

Heimo: Serving as one of Vyrga's trusted commanders, he holds the distinction of being the youngest among the protégés raised by Vyrga. His potential surpassed that of his comrades, hinting at a future where he could have reigned supreme. However, his somewhat unnerving demeanour made him inaccessible to others. Among Vyrga's commanders, he formed friendships only with Bolo and especially Gelmar. He harbours an intense loathing for Lev, who he perceives as having humiliated Gelmar through death.

Without Vyrga's restraint and fuelled by a potent mixture of rage and a drug procured from Bodobert, he killed Oswald. During his remorseful episodes, he was manipulated by Bodobert into overthrowing the chief retainer—installed by the Jiira to govern—and his followers.

His aim was to elevate the status of greyborns and bolster goblinkind's resilience against the looming threat of Brizilum. In a turn of events, he defected to the side of the Jiira who betrayed Bulgu and was on the verge of killing his other brothers, when Vyrga dealt him a fatal blow. His death was not unremarkable—due to the consumption of various potions prior to his demise, he emitted a dazzling blue light before erupting into blue flames. This was followed by a brilliant flash and a shockwave that left everyone unconscious. Upon awakening, Vyrga and the others discovered his body had vanished.

Os/Oswald: Serving as one of Vyrga's Commanders, he is also one of the children raised by Vyrga, demonstrating unparalleled loyalty among his peers. Known for his rigid, upright nature, his unwavering devotion has earned him the nickname 'Vyrga's Hound.' Given his steadfast disciplined disposition, he is considered the most probable candidate to succeed Vyrga in the unfortunate event of his passing. He was betrayed and killed by Heimo.

Ludger: One of Vyrga's adopted children and the biological elder brother of Bolo. Despite being obnoxious, quick-tempered, and generally unlikable, he harbours a deep affection for his brother and remains dutifully loyal. His flaws are mitigated to some extent by his exceptional combat skills, particularly his mastery with the spear. He carries a distinct distaste for Heimo and Gelmar.

He regularly shaves his head as a response to Hemgall's childhood teasing about his 'rat tail.' Nowadays, Hemgall teases him about his short stature. During Lachas' invasion, he prevented a suicidal charge aimed at Bolo but lost his life in the process.

Bolo: One of Vyrga's adopted children and the younger brother of Ludger. Though his intimidating stature and assertive demeanour may suggest otherwise, he possesses a surprisingly gentle soul. Nevertheless, he won't hesitate to fight when it comes to safeguarding his kin. He is among the rare few of Vyrga's adopted children who formed a true bond with Heimo, treating him as a real brother. The death of Ludger distressed him greatly.

Bulgu: As the expedition's leader and the youngest heir of the Jiira chief, he is recognized for his ambition rather than his leadership. His glaring flaws—notably his greed, ineptitude, and lofty aspirations—coupled with an utter disregard for others' lives, render him universally unpopular. He spearheaded the expedition with the objective of procuring a weapon believed to have been once wielded by Ainshard and held the conviction that such an accomplishment would validate his claim to the Jiira throne.

After the expedition reached the safety of the bogey caverns, he surprised everyone by saying there would be an even bigger expedition. His advisors were so upset with this decision that they decided to poison him, starting a civil war between the bogeys and goblins.

Rapha: The leader of the harem guard. She is an exile from the Ajiin, a clan renowned for its formidable warriors. Following her father's reckless deeds which resulted in his death, she and her family faced exile from their clan. Her paternal uncle, seeking to make amends for his brother's missteps, joined their exile, only to be killed in a confrontation with a Jiira warband. In the ensuing chaos, she was separated from her mother and sister, ultimately finding herself as part of Bulgu's harem guard.

Yet, in spite of these adversities, she clung to her dream of becoming a shieldmaiden. Her life took another twist when she was kidnapped, and a spiderling crushed her left arm. Thinking her life was ending, she was offered a lifeline by Lev, who promised to heal her arm on the condition that she'd join his crew. Accepting his proposal, she pledged herself as his shieldmaiden, thereby realising her long-held dream.

Ruune: An integral part of the harem guard. She stands as Rapha's right-hand woman and closest confidant. Embodying a rowdy and boisterous spirit, she is known for her unfiltered emotional transparency, always wearing her heart on her sleeve. When Rapha was presumed dead, she temporarily stepped up to lead the harem guard. However, upon discovering that Rapha was alive, she was filled with joy and promptly returned the leadership role back to her.

Gul: A cherished childhood friend of Volker and an established member of Lev's faction. He used his persuasive abilities to coax Volker into joining their ranks, steering him away from a career as a potter. Known for his sharp wit and sarcastic humour, he carries a determined and stubborn disposition.

He survived the hiveling onslaught when they attacked the bogey outpost on the second floor of the monster caverns. He suffered from altitude sickness after climbing Sinner's Reach but refused to rest, unwilling to delay the exodus. He died upon reaching the outskirts of Pàrras.

Molg: One of Lev's followers. He admires Lev and is loyal to a fault. Instead of following Volker during Lev's presumed death, he went with Jem who he trusted more than Lev's protegee. He suffered severe wounds inflicted by the hivelings and died a painful death in a healing tent, passing away before Lev and Volker could even see him.

Jem: Lev's third-in-command; a seasoned, middle-aged Greyborn who has served under various groups, typically shifting allegiances whenever their leaders meet their end. His considerable experience as both a combatant and a leader are commendable, yet he opts to sidestep conflicts and adamantly declines any offers to ascend to leadership upon the death of a group's figurehead. When it was presumed that Lev had died and Volker assumed control, he decided to leave, taking half of Lev's group with him to form a temporary gang until they could find a better arrangement. Upon hearing news of Lev's return, Jem promptly reconnected with his former group. He held on until they reached Pàrras, where he died in a healing tent at the encampment just outside the city.

Shahn: Born to Kafar Ramun, he is a dignified Darg hailing from the thriving state of Edoros. Despite his relative youth, he commands the Dargs under Bulgu's rule. His past is marked by a stint as a gladiator in Brizilum and, earlier still, a seafaring life that mirrored his father's own maritime beginnings. He made a deal with Vyrga to aid him in his ambitions. The minority faction wanted him as their representative, but he refused to engage with the political establishment.

Varra: One of the Dargs dispatched to participate in Bulgu's expedition. Nursing a soft spot for Volker, she makes a point to safeguard him at all costs. As is typical among mercenary Dargs, she is a proficient warrior, and her combat prowess is further enhanced by the Brizilum-crafted armour and weapons she wields.

When it was believed she was the last darg alive in the expedition, Bulgu arranged for her to meet her end, ensuring she couldn't inform other dargs if she reached the surface. Fortunately, she survived. Pressured by the situation, Bulgu eventually permitted her to use a shrine to return to the surface.

Gozzag: He is the revered leader of the Deka dispatched to support Bulgu in the expedition. His age and accumulated experiences have shaped him into a wise leader who commands respect from his men. Following the expedition, he became the leader of the Dragma, a haven for all Deka and other survivors of the expedition who shared their hatred towards the Jiira. During the civil war, he struck a deal with Lev to offer assistance in the fight against Barra, the now deceased Jiira war chief.

Ban: Serving as Gozzag's right-hand man and trusted confidant, he blends a firm determination with a congenial and easy-going personality. He's a man of action, never shying away from a confrontation, be it a physical fight or a spirited drinking contest. After the expedition, he followed Gozzag.

Grasha: A deka mercenary with a troubled past. Having little affection for his fellow deka and only bonding with a few, such as Gozzag and Ban, he chose to join Lev's exodus and eventually found himself in Pàrras. During Lev's search for the birdfolk and Ainshard's old trade route, he was often paired with Raban. His horn was broken by a behemoth—but thankfully, it grew back.

Thorst: A gifted green bogey. He transitioned from serving as a guard to supervising greyborn miners and is recognized as Kul's protégé. Generally exhibiting an easy-going demeanour, his attitude shifts when it involves Ghorza, for whom he harbours romantic feelings. After settling in Pàrras, he joined and eventually led the city's guards. When his house burned down in an accident at a nearby smithy, he moved in with Ghorza.

Kathaga: As a Priestess of Zeja, she was sought out by Lev for Zeja's blessing. Unbeknownst to Lev, Kathaga would masquerade as a mere temple servant before revealing her true identity as the priestess. Her knowledge extends beyond Lev's expectations, to the point where even his true name isn't concealed from her. Ultimately, she bestowed Zeja's blessing upon Lev's army in anticipation of their impending clash with Gelmar's forces. Operating under Zeja's direction, she masterminded Heimo's betrayal and downfall, the ascensions of both Lev and Vyrga, as well as the demise of Vyrga's father, who was the former chief retainer. Her influence grew after the exodus.

Kul: An old, pale-green bogey overseer. Once considered to be one of the best warriors of the bogey race, he fell from grace after failing to protect a noble's son during a rebellion against the Jiira. He was a good friend of Gat, Gherm, and Ghorza's father, and decided to take care of them in order to repay his debt to him. After settling in Pàrras, he joined the city guards and uncovered a drug smuggling operation orchestrated by the dargs.

Rogg: A bogey herbalist and witchdoctor who is neither skilled enough to treat commoner and noble bogeys, nor kind enough to charge greyborns a fair price for his services. He met his end in the bogey outpost on the second floor of the monster caverns due to an influx of hivelings swarming the upper levels. Despite his connections affording him a safer hideout, he sacrificed this advantage for his son and sole apprentice, Hermut.

Barra: Bulgu's older brother who, unbeknownst to Bulgu, assumed the role of war chief during the time of the expedition. He shares his brother's greed and arrogance but excels on the battlefield. However, following his ambush and subsequent demise at the hands of a group of Dragma horsemen, Raban assumed the position of war chief to maintain morale among Barra's troops.

Raban: Barra's deputy and the voice of reason during the campaign against the bogeys. His experience as a mercenary made him a highly skilled combatant but did not earn him much support, as mercenary work is viewed unfavourably in Jiira society. His familiarity with bogeys, gleaned from leading past cavern expeditions, also played a role in his selection.

A formidable fighter and an open-minded intellectual, he holds little regard for taboos and has a distaste for Jiira traditions and customs. He empathises with other goblinoids due to his experiences. Captured by the bogeys, he negotiated a deal with Lev to secure his and his men's freedom in exchange for his service. He also served alongside Grasha when the time came to search for the masked ones.

Meinrad: A highly respected member of the blue bogeys. Despite his strict adherence to the laws, he is considered a voice of reason and tolerance. He supported Reingard and Bodobert in their youth and helped them rise to power in hopes of improving bogey society as a whole, but he was eventually disgusted by how corrupt they had become and became their foe, especially Reingard for his treatment of Vyrga and his mother. He supported Lev's idea of forming a council and persuaded many blue bogeys to join the cause.

Eleric: An escaped slave who leapt off a waterfall to flee captivity. He was eventually found by goblinoids and escorted to Pàrras. There, he was assigned as Lev's steward. He was astonished by the ancient city and its residents, many of whom belonged to so-called 'barbaric races' yet had successfully revived it.

Servius: A darg merchant who saw potential in Pàrras and managed to become a member of the council. Due to his experience, his standing among the merchants, and his ability to speak many languages, he represents the dargs on the council and acts as a mediator between the city and outsiders.

Lachas: He served as a double agent for both Jotul and the Coalition. He and his men were among Jotul's earliest recruits and was known for his silver tongue and cunning. After betraying Jotul, he led his soldiers on what would become their final mission: investigating Pàrras and its denizens. Deceived by Meinrad, he entered the city with his elite retinue, leaving his men and the accompanying Coalition forces without leadership. He was ultimately killed within the city, his betrayal and overconfidence sealing his fate.

Egon: The Blood Lord, Bringer of War, Father of Warriors, and The Crimson One. Egon was one of Ainshard's guides and continues to wield influence beyond his seal through his champion, Jotul. She, like her predecessors, serves him begrudgingly, fully aware that his power will eventually drive her mad.

After the fall of Ainshard's empire, Egon abandoned the use of Chosen Ones and outsiders, believing their interference disrupts the natural evolution of civilization and brings about ruin. Determined not to repeat the mistakes of the past, he seeks to avoid the actions that led to the guides being sealed.

Jotul: The War Queen, Prophetess of the War God, the Bloodbringer, and the Mad One. Her father once ruled over the bereke, but the nobles who formed the Coalition betrayed him, leading to the hunting and downfall of her family.

With Vilde's help, she escaped the purge and, under the blessing of the Crimson One, found refuge in the lands of the Korrigal. There, she was adopted and trained by the father of Vreskiven and Baldem. In time, she raised an army composed of both Korrigal and bereke, leading a revolution to reclaim her birthright.

Vilde: She once served Jotul's father, holding back the Coalition's forces long enough for Jotul to escape. During her time of need, when she was forced to lay low while hiding from the Coalition and believed she had failed her charge, Egon approached her. She became one of his most devoted believers. Now Jotul's enforcer, she is feared for her sadistic nature, showing no mercy to her enemies or the foes of her faith. Her only kindness is reserved for her followers and Jotul. She holds deep disdain for Vreskiven and Baldem.

Vreskiven: Baldem and Jotul's brother. He is a fierce warrior renowned for his straightforwardness, pride, and foul temper. While his loyalty and brotherly devotion to Jotul are beyond question, he makes no effort to hide his disdain for the Crimson One and his followers, particularly Vilde. He lost his left eye in a battle with his uncle.

Baldem: Vreskiven and Jotul's brother. He is known for his good humour, keen observation, and love for animals untouched by the Guides. While he often jokes—usually at his brother's expense—he serves as the voice of reason and is one of the few who can calm both Vreskiven and Jotul. He lost his right tusk in a fight with his father.

Maria: Raised along with Lev and Brutus in the orphanage, she's strong-willed and hard-headed. Leaving Eurasia behind at the young age of 18, she relocated to its adversary, The Empire, where she painstakingly climbed the ranks. In time, she penetrated the Empire's inner circle and reached out to Lev, promising him vital insights into the Empire's internal operations.

With her assistance, Lev managed to infiltrate the Empire, becoming one of the emperor's trusted aides. She also aided Brutus—under the alias of Fynn—and Maik to infiltrate the Empire, helping them to secure roles as logistics managers.

Brutus: Lev's childhood best friend. Despite his large size and intimidating, scarred visage, he has a kind heart and can be shy during social gatherings. Now known as Fynn, he is part of the espionage mission into the Empire.

Maik: An imperial war veteran who served in the neutral zone. He's a spy working for Eurasia who helped Lev infiltrate the Empire.

Moritz: Moritz was a member of the bloodhounds, an order established by the imperials that is specialised in espionage. His hideout in zone five was flushed out by the Technocracy, and the Empire doesn't know he had been captured. Lev had assumed his identity to infiltrate the Empire.

Lucian Ruxgan: One of the emperor's eyes. He is a nonchalant, self-indulgent man whose actions as his family's representative would have driven it further into ruin. However, under pressure from Maria, he appointed Lev as his retainer during the selection, a decision that ultimately saved his family from decline.

Bogeys: A goblinoid race known for being physically weak, but intelligent. The typical lifespan of a bogey is sixty years, and they tend to produce less offspring than other goblinoids. Within the intricate web of bogey society, the roles are colour-marked: green-skinned bogeys are categorised as commoners, blue-skinned ones hold positions akin to nobles, and unfortunately, grey-skinned bogeys are confined to the status of slaves. With the defeat of the Jiira, and the rise of many greyborn figures during the civil war, this hierarchy has been greatly diminished.

Greyborns: Bogeys born with dark grey skin, silver hair, and yellow eyes. The greyborn are slaves among slaves, as the tribe they belonged to was a victim of war between the goblin Jiira and kobold Kur. Although it was once an honour to be greyborn, a failed coup by greyborn elitists centuries ago has long besmirched their reputation.

Goblins: As the most numerous and ancient goblinoid species, they stand a tad taller than most bogeys, boasting robust resilience and adaptability to various environments. Their physical prowess is offset by their limited magical capabilities and relatively short lifespans, typically not exceeding that of bogeys. Due to their distinctive looks, aggressive disposition, and impulsiveness, they often find themselves unfairly stereotyped as violent, unintelligent brutes—a stereotype many male goblins inadvertently perpetuate. Female goblins, on the other hand, tend to display fewer of these perceived negative traits.

Dekas: A species of large red goblinoids, these individuals are distinguished by a single horn protruding from their forehead. Their impressive size, formidable strength, and intimidating appearance make them a terrifying presence on the battlefield. However, what often surprises others is their intelligence and keen logistical skills, which defy common perceptions. Additionally, they demonstrate exceptional horsemanship, with many among their ranks choosing to serve as mercenaries.

Dargs: A fascinating species of purple goblinoids, Dargs are known for their long hair and elongated ears. Despite their graceful appearances, they are formidable warriors and skilled sailors, traits that often surprise those deceived by their elegant exteriors. Primarily residing off the mainland in the prosperous state of Edoros, the Dargs experienced a substantial setback when they lost to Brizilum, subsequently becoming its vassal. This change in status led to many Dargs being subjugated as slaves and gladiators.

Burgas: Belonging to the goblinoid species, the Burgas would bear resemblance to goblins, if not for their increased size, pronounced tails, and more robust jaws. Although they may not possess the intellectual prowess of other goblinoids, they compensate for this with their exceptional senses and superior tracking skills, rendering them ideal scouts and hunters. Renowned for their outstanding honour, Burgas are exceptionally loyal; under normal circumstances, they would scarcely ever forsake their comrades.

Bugbears: A species of large, yellow goblinoids, known for their notable physical strength but less so for their intellectual capacities. Their natural aggression often overshadows their conversational skills, rendering them less appealing partners for dialogue.

Avians: A moniker used for the race of birdfolk discovered and rescued by Lev from Behemoths during his search for the masked beings that attacked his group upon their first arrival in Pàrras. Unlike their distant relatives, they were not subjected to Kram's experiments and despise him so deeply that his name is considered taboo among their kind. They have managed to preserve their identity and culture.

When Lev invited the freed avians to Pàrras, only a portion chose to follow him.

Merits: Merits serve as a form of lead-based currency. Intentionally dull in appearance, they are primarily used to compensate greyborns for their work. Enforced by the upper class, this near-valueless medium of exchange was designed to limit the greyborns' access to high-quality resources and equipment.

Chosen Ones: Deemed as the reincarnations of gods or their divine champions, Chosen Ones are distinguished figures within the mortal realm. Not only do they retain their past memories, but they also command powers that exceed natural limitations. These capabilities can span from extraordinary strength to the more profound, reality-altering abilities.

Lost Souls: A reincarnated or transmigrated individual that retains their memory, but unlike a chosen one, doesn't have extraordinary abilities. Most of them die in obscurity but a few, using their past life's knowledge and experience, rise to become legends.

The Expedition: An annual event mandated by the Jiira, the expedition serves to harvest refined haze crystals and excavate treasures hailing from Ainshard's era and the age of the gods. Owing to the unique nature of this expedition, Lev and his men found themselves forced to participate, necessitating a truce with Vyrga.

This year's expedition was further distinguished by the unprecedented involvement of Bulgu, a Jiira prince, who brought along with him a cadre of slaves and mercenaries from various goblinoid races. Under the ostensible leadership of Bulgu, the group confronted a relentless struggle as they battled their way to the lower floors, their journey plagued by limited opportunities for rest.

The Cycle: The cyclical process of life and death as understood in bogey mythology. The Cycle is represented by four distinct facets: life, death, the afterlife, and reincarnation.

Cyfrac Oil: Cyfracs are a rare family of plants, found on the fifth floor and below, that resemble a red-coloured rye and are easily combustible. Their oil has many uses, from ceremonies to smithing, but is most valued by shamans and witch doctors because its flames spread fast and last a long time.

Bluecatcher Mushrooms: A giant, blue, carnivorous species found on or below the second floor of the monster cavern. The mushroom uses its sticky sap to catch prey before encapsulating it for digestion—the sap also works well as an adhesive for wood, leather, and cloth.

Haze Crystals: A special crystal that can store immense amounts of magical energy. This makes it a great alchemical reagent, and essential for making focus tools for shamans. Before refinement, they are highly corrosive towards creatures with low magical resistance. It is rare to find them outside of the bogey and monster caverns where they naturally grow.

The Ancient Shrines: Mystical constructions originating from the era of Ainshard, if not earlier. These shrines possess the power to teleport small bands of individuals to corresponding shrines elsewhere. Upon the Jiira's first exploration of the caverns, sacred sites above the third floor were demolished, deemed by the Jiira as symbols of heretical worship. The survival of the remaining shrines was a fortunate accident. A pioneering group from an expeditionary force rediscovered their teleportation ability when they were seeking refuge from peril while laden with treasure.

Killigs: An order of great holy warriors who served as Ainshard's elite troops. They were all the same height, about twice that of a goblin, so goblinoids eventually started measuring things relative to their height.

Corpse-eaters: A species of carnivorous, black-scaled lizards with striking emerald eyes. These creatures display a preference for scavenging on carcasses over actively hunting prey, earning them their distinct name. Characterised by their prolific reproduction, they are a ubiquitous presence across the vast expanse of the cavern.

Bogey Caverns: A section of a mysterious cavern abundant in haze crystals, artefacts from the age of the gods, and treacherous beasts. The bogey caverns are situated in the upper regions of the cavern, encompassing the entrance and first floor, which are under bogey control and serve as their living quarters.

Monster Caverns: An alternative designation for the caverns inhabited by the enslaved bogeys. This term references the lower floors, areas not under Bogey dominion. In contrast, the zones under Bogey control are referred to as the Bogey Caverns.

Hivelings: Giant, ant-like creatures that inhabit the monster caverns. They left the bogeys alone to begin with, but years of bogey invasions into hiveling territory turned the hivelings aggressive. They come in various sizes and shapes. The smallest are the workers, with the largest being the warriors.

Spiderlings: Brownish-green spider-like hivelings that dwell on the lower floors of the monster caverns. They're known to favour ambushes over direct confrontations. Their yellow blood has paralysing properties.

Sky Devils: A race of giant, migratory, jellyfish-like creatures that float through the night skies and shelter themselves during the day. Predatory by nature, they feed on magical energy to sustain their bodies and relentlessly pursue any high concentration of energy, including living beings. To protect themselves from sunlight, they form a hard outer layer known as morning shells. At night, their bodies emit a luminous glow.

Sky devils are equipped with tentacles containing hundreds, if not thousands, of venomous needles. They instinctively fire these needles at the first sign of a threat. The tentacles are unique in that they do not degrade in sunlight and can still shoot needles even after being severed.

Behemoths: A race of towering, muscular deerfolk, nearly as tall as trees, with arms that reach their knees. They inhabit the dense forests between Pàrras and bereke lands and are known for their primitive, aggressive, and fiercely territorial nature. These formidable beings attack or attempt to capture any intruders on sight. They possess the ability to wield magical energy, even imbuing their weapons with it to enhance their lethality.

Ainshard: Ainshard the Great, also known as The Enlightened One, is believed to have been a goblin who conquered all the people of the forest and established a great kingdom centuries ago. The land under his control encompassed the central and western parts of the continent and was home to hundreds of tribes of bogeys, goblins, kobolds, and various other species. He's worshipped by many goblinoids, and in the eyes of the Jiira and some bogeys, he's the *only* being deserving of worship.

Jom: Revered as the father of all and the world's guardian against creatures of the void, he is a deity familiar to goblin-kind, often credited with the creation of the goblinoid races. Although his popularity has waned among most goblinoids—particularly those who lean towards Ainshard over him and his pantheon—he still commands the faith of certain races, including the bogeys. He fell victim to The Void Walker in a brutal clash, but Zeja, in an act of divine intervention, resurrected him. Under her leadership and alongside the other gods, he managed to triumph over his nemesis.

Maga: The goddess of love and fertility, she presides over her priests and priestesses who officiate marriage ceremonies and provide stress relief to followers. Naturally, such services require a generous donation.

Zeja: Born from a droplet of Jom's blood, she initially took the form of a young girl characterised by white hair and red eyes. Embarking on a quest to the underworld, she collected fragments of Jom's soul and negotiated with Dorn, the god of death, to reassemble these pieces into a singular soul, thereby resurrecting Jom. Blessed by Jom, she led the pantheon into battle against the entity known as The Void Walker, repelling it back into the abyss. This victory secured her ascension as the goddess of war.

Jorm: Zeja's son and the god of defensive wars and ranged weaponry, he may be classified as a minor deity by many, yet he enjoys significant popularity among the greyborns.

Dorn: As the god of death, he oversees the souls of the departed in the underworld. He arbitrates whether souls should be reforged for another opportunity—at life or to join the gods' table—or sent into The Cycle of reincarnation for rebirth.

Tanach: As the god of slumber and dreams, he is often perceived as indolent, forever asleep. In truth, his sleep is not without purpose. He vigilantly monitors the dreams of others, purging them of any demonic influence.

Mal: The goddess of deception, she commands a following of cultists and is known for dispatching demons to possess individuals during their most vulnerable moments. Once ensnared, these victims are manipulated into committing unthinkable deeds under her influence.

The Void Walker: An enigmatic force that once sought global domination. The Void Walker clashed and overcame Jom, the father of all, and could have vanquished his kin if not for Zeja's intervention. After resurrecting Jom, Zeja marshalled her armies and brought about the demise of the Void Walker.

The State of Edoros: A once-powerful city-state that remains prosperous, situated on an island to the north-east of the continent, bordering the White Sea. It is the heartland of the Darg and their largest settlement. Despite their fall to the Brizilum, becoming a vassal state in the process, the Darg retain their pride as exceptional seamen, traders, and warriors, continuing to regard themselves as the undisputed masters of the White Sea.

Pàrras/The Frontier City: the ancient name for the ruined city that Lev and his companions uncovered. It used to be overrun with Kram's failed experiments: a hostile group of bird-like creatures that turned to ash upon death, but they disappeared upon the exodus' arrival. The domain the city is situated in is referred to as the frontier.

The Jiira Tribe: A goblin tribe founded after Ainshard's empire collapsed. They are aggressive and arrogant, given their heritage, but their cultural and technological advantages among the goblinoids are disappearing at a steady pace. They were severely weakened after the civil war against the bogeys and Jiira traitors. Their future on the continent is now uncertain, with the Kur's superior forces ready to crush what remains of them.

The Kur Tribe: A tribe of Kobolds that fought with the Jiira for domination over the region. Not much is known about them among the bogeys.

The Brizilum Republic: A great republic situated in the eastern half of the continent. They're expansionists who seek to engulf all their rivals, converting them into vassals.

The Coalition: The ruling faction of the bereke who oppose Jotul. They are composed of the bereke nobles who betrayed her father and orchestrated the destruction of her family, the Coalition wields significant influence. They have allied themselves with Brizilum—the bereke's former enemy—and leveraged this partnership in a desperate attempt to hamper Jotul's growth.

The Neutral Zone: The only unclaimed zone on Earth with resource-filled, fertile lands. It is the main theatre of war between the Eurasian and Imperial Armies.

The Technocracy of Eurasia: The Technocracy is one of the world's few superstates. The Technocracy and its United Council rule over Eurasia with an iron grip. The Technocracy is the largest continental superstate on Earth, spanning over most parts of Europe and Asia.

The Empire: The oldest nemesis of Eurasia, ruled by the Emperor of the West. The emperor's realm spans over North and Central America. Unlike Eurasia, they're highly advanced both in civilian and military technology.

CHAPTER 1

A BIRD'S PREY

Far from the turmoil of Pàrras, the city reclaimed by the goblinoids, a battle was about to ensue. Days away from the city of Briecka, the earth rumbled under the feet of the Coalition's forces. They marched forward to reinforce the recently liberated city. They marched forward against Jotul, the Mad One. Unbeknownst to them, they were being watched by the same enemy they sought to destroy.

"Seems the Coalition spared no expense on this little attempt of theirs," Jotul commented whilst checking the javelins attached to the right side of her beast's saddle. "Too bad they fell for our trap."

"Indeed. Just as planned, the Coalition dogs snuck through a mountain pass in order to arrive early. Our men are ready and awaiting your orders."

Jotul grinned. "Let me guess—We should thank Lachas for that? He knew the area like the back of his hand. It would be a shame if he *forgot* to mention all the nearby blind spots, especially the hills overseeing the surrounding woods."

Commander Alram reluctantly nodded, causing the bereke to groan.

Maybe I shouldn't have offed him so early. That weasel was pretty reliable. Oh well... War spares no man.

She looked at the sky and whistled.

A silver-feathered falcon answered her call, and once it landed on her gloved hand, the giant bird stared at her with its ruby-red eyes as if demanding something.

"I know what you want." She rubbed its neck. "Though you don't deserve it, do you?"

The creature cried out in indignation and ruffled its feathers. Jotul giggled at the bird's antics and brought out a piece of cured meat, quickly appeasing the falcon.

"Now, why didn't you warn me about those vermin coming early and playing in our lawn?" she asked while gently rubbing its head.

It poked her hand away, spread its wings, and shrieked.

Jotul shook her head. "I'm not blaming you, just asking."

She nodded in understanding when the falcon tucked its wings and let out a few whistles. "That's reasonable. I should've assigned more eyes over here, but how could I have known the lunatics would ever grow a pair and risk crossing the mountains in this cold?"

Her discussion with the creature carried on. This hadn't been the first time she'd talked to her birds, yet Alram still awkwardly eyed the other scouts.

"Will you and your brethren remain our eyes in the sky?"

The falcon let out a loud cry and flew away.

Jotul turned to the scouts. "Have you counted the enemy's forces? How much are we facing today?"

Alram reached for his rucksack and pulled out a piece of parchment. "The attack party mostly consists of mercenaries, specifically the Blood Bears and the Melgren of Beynidar. In short, they hired second-rate scouts. It would've been quite bloody if we'd had to fight the Prowling Wolves instead of these dime-a-dozen sellswords."

"So we're still in trouble," Jotul muttered. "They may be second-rate, but they're still mercenaries. They'll never be persuaded to back down peacefully with the Coalition's coin waiting for them."

Alram nodded. "You're right, it won't be easy. The Blood Bears have deep ties with many of the Coalition's nobles; it'd be unwise to betray their wealthiest employer. The same applies to the Melgren of Beynidar."

"And who's leading this merry band?"

"It's Lord Hakan."

Jotul tilted her head in bewilderment. She believed she had a firm grasp on all of the noble houses, especially her father's traitorous entourage, yet the man's name hadn't rung any bells.

In the plight of his liege's struggles, Alram began to explain. "He isn't exactly well-known. His family had the thankless job of guarding the southern borders for generations and were rewarded with poverty. The territory they gained is surrounded by mountain bandits. You can't exactly build your estate if it's ransacked every couple of months."

With a mischievous smile on her face, Jotul gazed at the approaching army. "If he's so underappreciated, then there's a possibility of turning him to our side. We could even sow discord among their ranks."

Alram chuckled.

Jotul's smile dwindled. "What's so funny?"

"Much like the mercenaries, Hakan would never join us. Instead of coin, he's devoted to the way of Drevulka."

Jotul pondered for a while before facing Alram. "That old crone of honour and loyalty? People still idolise her?"

He frowned. "Down in the south, they still appreciate the old guardians."

Jotul couldn't help but facepalm. "So he prefers to die for whatever stupid cause they put in his mind rather than surrender."

Alram rubbed his chin. "Correct. Drevulka aside, Hakan's clan is known for their eternal loyalty to some of the most prominent families on the Coalition's council. A wiser bet would be his second-in-command, Stig. However, convincing him to defect would still prove troublesome, since his father placed him under Hakan."

Jotul rubbed her forehead. "Great. Just great. We got an indoctrinated idiot for an opponent and his nepotistic lackey." She took a deep breath and straightened her back. "Make preparations to head out. Delegate some of your men to act as messengers for our other forces. I'll send one of my birds to inform Vreskiven, Baldem, and Vilde."

Alram gave a salute upon receiving his orders. "Anything else?"

"As a courtesy, make sure to send a messenger before the battle. Maybe that Hakan will surprise us and see reason."

He cursed under his breath. *Knowing that old bastard, whoever we send is likely a dead man.* He shrugged. *I'll just send Svein. A recoverable loss.*

* * *

Jotul and her forces laid in ambush on the verdant hills, waiting for Hakan and his men to appear.

The Coalition army warily emerged out of the mountains, and once they made their way into the woods proper, they encountered a curious sight. Svein stood there, shivering as he cursed Alram in his heart, with a white flag in his hands.

As Alram had expected, Hakan hadn't deigned the thought of parleying with the followers of the Mad God. Before Svein could escape, an iron bolt pierced the back of his skull. To add insult to injury, Hakan had used a crossbow popular for hunting wild pigs.

Jotul's left eye twitched at the utter disrespect, and she bared her teeth. *You just signed your death, old fool.*

The Mad One raised her spear in the sky and her beast roared. "Let's show these sods what a real battle is like!"

She summoned the Crimson One's might, engulfing her forces in a red glow. Soon after, the battle began.

Enok, Jotul's steed, raced down the hill to feast on the blood of its enemies.

Hakan wasn't fazed by the approaching force, raising his iron-tipped spear in response. "Seems the harlot of war has decided to show her ugly face. Brothers, break their spirits with our shield walls!" he commanded.

With the sound of horns blaring through the trees, Hakan's warriors stood shoulder to shoulder, their shields overlapping and weapons bared, while the archers and crossbowmen moved to the rear, protected by the mercenary troops. All were ready to meet the coming storm.

Jotul scanned the wall of flesh and shield and found no modifications or deviancies. Their shield wall was as standard as it could be. "An amateur," she scoffed. "We're not like the bandits who dwell within your borders."

She grabbed a straight horn from her steed's utility belt, and its shrill call echoed throughout the battlefield.

As the sound of the horn filled Hakan's ears, his years of experience screamed of an ambush. He was wary of his surroundings, expecting hidden forces to emerge from nearby in hopes of flanking his troops once they were locked in combat with Jotul.

Then he saw flashes of light from the corners of his eyes before screams erupted from the back of his army.

The rear formations had been cut off by a rain of fire. Hakan noticed broken containers near the flames, indicating the use of tar, but something else caught his attention.

"Is that... barley?" Hakan muttered, seeing large golden wheels rolling from the forest line towards the fire.

The giant pitch-covered bales were immediately set alight, completely blocking their escape route.

Hakan's lungs forced him to cough, desperate to expel the smoke that ensued. His watery eyes could barely glimpse a cloud of dust charging down the hills, approaching the now-panicking rear. His eyes widened when he realised what Jotul was up to.

When one of the shamans tried dousing the flames, the water caused the tar to explode, spreading the inferno.

"No, you fools! You'll burn us alive! Focus your magic on the enemy!" Hakan hollered in a frenzy.

His startled messengers raised haze rods that glowed green, catching the attention of the Coalition's magic users before pointing them towards the rear.

Feeling the magic in the air, Jotul now knew the position of the enemy's magicians. A savage grin crept upon her lips.

With the blessing of the Crimson One, her men were bestowed with magical attunement, making them glow with an eerie crimson aura. Their minds were now synced with only one goal: kill until they physically couldn't kill anymore.

Despite the scorching heat and heavy smoke, the Blood Bears and the Melgren hadn't abandoned their posts. Years of fighting against the Crimson One's cronies had taught them that keeping their cool was the best way to ensure their survival. That mental fortitude was shaken when they heard the bleating of rams. The two mercenary captains had the same thought. *The Korrigal...*

The mercenaries shared a historical bond, with the founders being brothers, and that resulted in a friendly rivalry with each band trying to upstage the other. Yet, this time, the Melgren captain had no qualms about letting the Blood Bears take the brunt of Jotul's cavalry.

As the ground vibrated under his feet, he silently watched his long-time rival lead his men further into the smoke. With one hand on his sword, he raised the other high, rallying the archers and crossbowmen to prepare for his signal.

The sound of hooves grew louder, and no matter how much saliva his nervous nausea produced, the Melgren captain's mouth still felt dry. He heard a clatter and noticed a crossbowman fumbling with his weapon. When the man steadied himself, he kept his finger close to the trigger. Part of the captain wanted to reprimand the man, but the other part understood how he felt.

We just need to wait for the signal... No sooner had he thought that, the signal came, it was the screams of the Blood Bears.

He dropped his hand, and with that, arrows and bolts showered the battlefield, followed by the occasional magical spell.

He raised his sword towards the screams and shouted, "Release everything you have! If we have to die, we'll drag these bastards with us to the abyss!"

The soldiers complied. A flurry of projectiles flew into the aether, and the men were rewarded with the pained cries of the infernal beasts.

The captain knew their attacks weren't enough, and when the first korrigal emerged from the smoke, he harnessed the magical energies into his body and leapt at the tusked one, slicing the rider's neck in one fell swoop.

Seeing their captain take action the roused Melgren chanted Beynidar's name as they faced off against Jotul's cavalry, whilst Hakan's men provided ranged support.

They exploited whatever wounds the Blood Bears left on the riders.

One soldier stabbed a ram's already-injured knee, holding it down long enough for his brethren to slit its throat. Some even received fatal injuries but kept clinging to the rams and stabbing them until they were stomped to death.

The korrigal were horrified when they found a surviving Blood Bear hiding in the flames of all places. His eye had been reduced to a crispy, shrivelled grape, and his skin had sloughed off of his body, but that wasn't enough to stop him from decapitating his captain's killer.

The mercenaries' spears became pincushions on which the rams corpses laid, and their blades became the needles.

A ram bleated in pain as a downed soldier managed to stab it in the underbelly before succumbing to his wounds. It lashed out in fury as it crushed his skull under its hooves.

Its rider gently rubbed its blood-soaked fur before returning his attention to the battlefield. An arrow whizzed past, almost puncturing the wet cloth covering his face.

Similar scenarios could be seen throughout the battlefield. As the smoke thickened, the archers' accuracy decreased, and it became difficult to breathe.

The Melgrin struggled. Their bodies bled and writhed, fighting blood loss and suffocation, until they could no longer function.

"This was your plan after all..." the Melgren captain managed to croak as he coughed up blood. He laid cold on the ground, dark spots obscuring his blurry vision. The only thing he could make it out was the hazy form of a korrigal with one tusk and his ram munching on the captain's severed arm.

"I'm afraid so. If things were different and the stakes weren't high, I would've wanted our fight to be more honourable."

The captain chuckled. "Honourable, my ass."

The korrigal clicked his tongue. "Can't deny that. The name's Baldem. Tell me yours, and I'll at least—"

The captain spat on his face, and with his last act of defiance, his eyes began to dim.

Baldem wiped the spit off of his face and rode away on his ram. The battle wasn't over.

Having witnessed the destruction of their rear formation left the army with a sense of foreboding dread. Even half-blinded by the hellish smog, Hakan bore the misfortune of seeing the collapse of his own cohort. What were once valiant soldiers, defenders of their realm, were reduced to skittish children, trembling in their own boots.

He knew any words of reassurance, rallying cries to calm their trembling knees and blubbering prayers, would fall on deaf ears. For their foe had arrived.

Kill! Kill! Kill! the Crimson One growled in Jotul's mind.

She licked her lips, her eyes narrowing in jubilation. *With pleasure.*

Even when mired with fear, Hakan's men instinctively raised their shields, hoping to impede her rampaging beast.

As Enok approached, the first line of defence steeled their agitated hearts. Their clammy hands numbly gripped their spears too hard, hoping against all odds to repel Jotul's monstrous steed and the encroaching horde behind her.

Once Enok was within reach, the soldiers let out a boisterous cry in defiance, thrusting their weapons at the giant ram. Most of their spears only left a few scrapes on the beast before horns met metal and flesh, sending all in Enok's way hurling into the air.

Hakan's shamans were stunned as their compatriots rained down onto the underbrush. They were then met with the butcher herself as her bloodthirsty forces made their way through the gap.

A sanguinous edge, thrice her blade's length, erupted from Jotul's spatha. What was once cold metal now seemed alive.

"M-Monsters," a shaman stuttered before his head twirled into the sky, leaving a fountain of blood on its way.

"Sharp as ever," Jotul praised as she swung her blade clean.

As the shaman's head rolled onto the ground, with his last seconds of life he saw Jotul mowing through his brethren. *Why did Master Hakan take us to this forsaken place?*

I don't want to die he—

His skull cracked on a jagged rock before he could finish his last thought.

Jotul's relentless carnage made Hakan's stomach drop. His eyes kept darting, praying his soldiers would retain their positions until their opponent tired themselves out.

I know them well—they will hold. They were trained to hold their ground, he thought to himself as he began to nervously pat his equally stressed horse. His heart wrenched whenever a man died, every lost soul was a lifetime's investment of magical training gone, but the payoff made it a sacrifice he was willing to make.

The Crimson One's blessing promised its wielders great strength and endurance, but it didn't make them invincible, instead, it dulled their minds and fueled their hubris. Jotul's men began to slip, their bodies tired and they slowly succumbed to their wounds. None of those weaknesses seemed to affect Jotul, but he could sense the magical energy around her wane.

Hakan licked his lips. He tightened his grip around his spear as he waited for when the magical energy around Jotul was its weakest, that was when he'd aim for her head.

His hopes were dashed once he heard a familiar shrill voice.

"Retreat! Retreat!" Stig yelled once Jotul's forces had finished eating through a third of their forces.

"No..." Hakan muttered.

All it takes is one man to break an army. That was the first lesson Hakan learned on the battlefield. One becomes two, two becomes four, and more become emboldened to abandon their post.

His body felt numb, and his breathing faltered as the shield wall crumbled. His soldiers weren't able to react fast enough to close the gaps.

One of the deserters ran towards Hakan. His despair gave way to fury, and he swiftly gouged the cur's neck.

"Come back here, you damn coward!" he yelled.

"Shove it!" Stig growled before running deeper into the woods, avoiding artillery shots, courtesy of his former allies.

Just as he neared the tree line, a single bolt shot by Hakan himself shallowly pierced the deserter in the shoulder, but Stig didn't bat an eye. His mind had but a single thought—survive.

Another round of adrenaline kicked into Stig's system. *What was I thinking, fighting against her? Inheritance be damned! If Father wants her gone, he can challenge her himself!*

Running, he manoeuvred through the undergrowth, pushing his way through shrubs and thistles until he tripped on a root. With a loud yelp, he fell headfirst onto a patch of moist soil, thanking his stars it was free of manure.

When Stig stood up, he found himself in a grove. His eyes wandered around the clearing, expecting to be attacked, until he noticed that the sounds of battle had dimmed.

He finally felt safe enough to catch his breath and jubilantly proclaimed, "I'm finally safe!"

His smile faltered when he heard a branch snap. When he spun around, it was only a hare. The curious creature was twitching its nose as it stared at the noble brat.

Stig was indignant when he found that his lip was quivering from such an encounter. He threw a rock at the rodent, sending it scampering away. Making his way out of the grove and further away from the battlefield, he hoped that would be the last surprise of the day.

Sadly, that didn't last long.

He pushed another branch away and stopped dead in his tracks. He'd found an army led by a middle-aged woman of his kind. The mask covering her mouth made her identity all too apparent.

Vilde?! his mind cried.

It didn't take long for Stig to realise he'd walked right back into the meat grinder. His eyes couldn't process seeing such an infamous figure in his lifetime. From her short greying hair to the predatory glint in her narrow emerald-green eyes, he could see her thirst hadn't been satisfied just yet.

"Hello, rodent," Vilde rasped.

Stig's face grew pallid. "Lady Fate, you've got to be kidding me…"

He slowly backed away, desperately scanning for a new escape route.

"Did you really think we'd let you leave this early?" Vilde cackled. "I haven't had this much fun in a while!"

Her laughter sent a shiver down Stig's spine. His legs almost gave out when he saw her lick her lips in delight. More blood for the Crimson Lord.

Wasting no time, he tossed his blade aside. "I—no—*we* surrender. Your god forbids harming unarmed foes, right?"

Vilde's face soured. "Correct."

Does this mean I'll live? Stig thought.

The last embers of hope snuffed out when she smiled once more. "But there's an exception for rats and pests. You know what that means, don't you?"

Stig's foot kicked off the ground, and he scrambled towards the grove.

Just as he started his final step into the clearing, he felt a cold edge followed by a searing pain in his back.

Vilde gleefully yanked the chain on her infamous bladed whip, causing Stig to fall backwards.

"Someone help me! No! No! I don't want to die!" he yelped.

His screams echoed throughout the battlefield. Even Hakan could hear his woes.

There was no remorse on Hakan's face. Instead, his teeth ground more and more at the humiliating sight of his panicking men. Thanks to his second-in-command's retreat, the entire formation was now in disarray, if intact at all.

Hakan spat in the direction of Stig's wails. "Whatever you're going through, you deserve worse." His eyes focussed on the approaching crimson wave of enemies. "No matter. Victory was never my goal to begin with."

With a delighted smile and his spear raised high, he greeted the incoming tide. His legs squeezed the sides of his armoured horse as he leaned forward. Having been trained for combat, the horse knew its fate. It, along with its brethren, let out a boisterous neigh and raced towards the Mad One's forces.

At first, Jotul was confused by Hakan's actions, but decided to meet him directly. It's *likely he knows he won't be spared after what he did, so it makes sense he wants to end his final moments with glory.*

The surrounding madness seemed to halt in the riders' eyes. Gone were the sounds of clashing steel and the cries of men. The stage was set, and the spotlight focussed on Hakan and Jotul.

With haste, the commanders approached each other, the ground trembling underneath their trotting steeds.

Hakan lowered his spear and pointed it at his foe. Jotul responded by raising her shield. *Only a fool would meet a charging spear head-on.*

As the winds tickled her ears and caused her long ponytail to dance, she could feel the heart of her crimson ram beating with excitement, much like hers. The Crimson One filled her veins with euphoria in preparation for this climactic clash.

But suddenly, her lord screeched in her mind. *Avoid him at all costs! This isn't his last stand, it's a suicide attack!*

His warning sent a chill down Jotul's spine, and her eyes widened when she noticed Hakan's chestplate glowing.

But it was too late to turn back now. Collision was imminent.

Jotul sneered and held her javelin high above her head. "Die, you sneaky bastard!" With bestial rage, she launched the javelin at Hakan.

Seems this is how I'll die. He smiled. *At least I'll rid our Coalition of your curse.*

Resigned to his fate, he closed his eyes and waited. But reality surprised him. With a painful neigh, his horse reared, and his body tumbled on the ground.

His men tried their best to halt their horses in order to avoid trampling their commander. Alas, their formation was too rigid, too close. The end result was a terrible crash.

Hakan wailed in agony when a horse crashed down upon him, most of its weight landing on his chest. The glowing plate groaned from the pressure and slowly crushed his insides. His heart was pierced by his own ribs before metal followed suit.

Blood gushed from his orifices, and he felt the world slow to a crawl.

Black spots filled his bloodied vision, followed by a bright light. In its destruction, Hakan's armour had activated its main function too early.

With the light engulfing his surroundings, Hakan gazed at his dead steed. The javelin was lodged into its forehead like some twisted horn.

His mauled heart wrenched at the sight; the horse had been a gift from his deceased wife.

Black veins now joined the spots in his vision, filling him with even more despair. *What a pitiful way to die.*

In his last moments, as the world around him grew darker, Hakan found the source of his demise cackling in front of him. *Damn you, Jotul! At least we'll rot in the underworld together.*

The idea of his opponent accompanying him lifted his mood.

Slowly finding his peace again, Hakan watched Jotul dismount her steed and take cover behind it.

Hah. As if that will help, Hakan mocked. He couldn't move, and even if he could have, he no longer had the strength to utter any words, nor could he hear anything.

A pity. I would've liked to hear her wails, he thought as the light of his armour brightened yet.

Taking cover won't delay the inevita—wait. That's not fair!

Though Hakan's vision went dark, and he could only barely make out shapes and shadows, he could still sense the crimson energy surrounding Jotul and her mount, forming a protective shell in the process. It was coming from the beast itself.

This isn't fair... This isn't fair at all, Hakan wailed in his mind before getting engulfed by the ever-increasing light.

A tremendous explosion followed.

* * *

With Hakan's death, the battle was over, and even the staunchest of his soldiers had attempted to flee. In the hollow remains of Jotul's onslaught, her birds were singing their wretched songs, ready to feed on the unburied cadavers.

Jotul joined in with a merry tune as she admired her feathered fiends nibbling on whatever remained of Hakan's burnt chunks.

Her face creased to a frown once she heard a horn blow in the distance. There were three figures approaching Jotul: Vilde, Vreskiven, and Baldem.

"How many did we lose?" Jotul asked without delay.

"Eight hundred soldiers died, while a thousand were injured. Thankfully, only two hundred suffered from heavy injuries," Vreskiven answered, having always had an eye for such details.

Jotul ran her hand through her hair, feeling a headache build up. After all, loyal men didn't grow on trees. "And the enemy?"

Vilde grinned. "More than a thousand dead with a couple hundred captured. They'll make a worthy sacrifice, especially those troublesome mercenaries."

Vreskiven gritted his teeth and glared at Vilde. "We're not sacrificing our captives. That's beyond stupid! We could exchange the important ones for ransom and use the others for labour."

Vilde shifted her gaze towards the one-eyed korrigal and sneered. "Don't even think about taking our lord's tribute. His blessing and powers are what brought us this great victory!"

Vreskiven rolled his eye. "Don't insult our efforts. It's thanks to our ambush, our tactics, our numbers."

"Those numbers are made up of good men and women who made the right choice of dedicating themselves to our cause. Why don't you do the same?" she snidely remarked.

Vreskiven clicked his tongue. "Because your cause is a double-edged sword, and the inner edge is sharper. Unlike us, they don't know of the horrors done in their lord's name. Those who do and still follow him are nothing more than bloodthirsty maniacs."

Vilde's face contorted in rage. She jabbed her finger at the much taller korrigal's chest and yelled, "you have no idea what you're talking about, you stupid boar!"

He shoved her away, almost throwing her on the ground. "I know more than you, you ugly bastard!"

Both of them kept adding fuel to the fire as their argument raged on.

This scenario had become common enough for Jotul's usual response: ignore them until they calm down.

Baldem patted Jotul on the shoulder. His face was a mask of worry. "You alright, Jotul? Enok seems exhausted."

"Don't worry." She faced her now-sleeping steed. There was a gentle but morose smile on her lips. "He ensured my safety."

Baldem rubbed Enok's head. "He's a good companion. He's always had your back since he was a small hogget." Baldem eyed the arguing pair and frowned, their screaming had risen to a crescendo. "A heavy sleeper too. With those two louts arguing like a married couple, I'd prefer to be asleep right now as well."

Jotul laughed. "I can definitely agree with that."

Baldem grinned. "Who wouldn't."

"More importantly, how many enemies escaped?" she asked as she eyed Vilde. "Can't trust Vilde's numbers—you know how she is."

"Heh, you're right. Alram's on the case. All I know is that Hakan's elite troops are no more. The rest? Many of them are still on the loose, especially Stig's ilk and the surviving mercenaries."

Jotul tilted her head. "Weren't the Blood Bears and the Melgren of Beynidar known for never breaking a contract?"

Baldem shrugged. "The veterans fought to their last breath to let some of their greenhorns escape. Even if some of the older members flee, the guy who pays them is dead, so can you blame them for escaping an unpaid death?"

She gave a nonchalant shrug. "They could always get their money from the rest of the Coalition."

Silence ensued for a moment, followed by a fit of laughter from the two.

"Good one," Baldem replied. "We both know that the other noble bastards would just say it's not their problem. Besides, nobody would fight for a lost cause. We just wiped out the last people who would."

Jotul sighed. "A shame if you ask me. We'd have made better use of them, but it's their creed to stay faithful until the end."

Baldem gave her a silent nod. "Now, what should we do about the runaways? Our rams are too tired after the battle and horses don't fare well in thick woods."

"If Alram's hunting them down, we have nothing to worry about."

Baldem's expression soured. "Can't we leave them to the threats lurking there? It's better for those damn deer freaks to kill them than kill our men chasing cowards. Enough of us died because of them."

Jotul looked at the skies and whistled. It didn't take long for her falcon to answer her call.

Once it landed on her stretched arm, she answered her brother. "We don't have much choice. They'll likely make contact with another threat."

"The goblins living in that ruined city?"

"Who else? They can't be underestimated."

Baldem chuckled. "You're pulling my leg, aren't you? Goblins lost their edge a long time ago. Heck, they're almost as bad as us korrigal at magic! Do you think they can wield whatever power you fear in that husk of a city?"

With no reply from his adopted sister, Baldem's smile faded. "You're going to do that trick of yours again? Then that means you're serious."

Jotul didn't reply. Instead, she closed her eyes and calmed her mind. A brief imperceptible surge of energy surrounded her in the form of a spire.

A pulse was released, taking with it a stream of red threads. Wherever the pulse went, the threads followed and stopped at nothing until they made contact with a multitude of crimson-eyed birds.

Jotul opened her eyes, and instead of seeing remnants of the battle, she was on top of a metal spike. A part of a building overlooking an entire city.

No matter how many times she spied on the goblinoids, she always found herself enamoured by their newfound home.

Tall, black buildings reached to the sky, glowing under the sunlight in an ethereal tone, yet somehow, the light's reflection wasn't blinding.

Wherever Jotul looked, the obsidian-like city felt as if it was moulded by hand. From the structures and the roads down to its waterways. Even the statues and murals speaking of times yore had a sense of forgotten excellence that can hardly be copied by modern hands. And all of it was once host to a source of great magical might, now inert.

It all felt magnificent albeit unnatural, with the only mortal touches being left by the current residents of this ancient sprawling city and their efforts towards its slow revival.

Goblinoids of all shapes and sizes were spread throughout the city, from the ones she knew—such as the common goblins, the seafaring dargs, and the rare deka—to an unknown race with grey-skin. Her heart raced in their presence and her blood started to boil. Jotul took a deep breath to calm her nerves and searched for a distraction from these invasive emotions. It didn't take her long to find it.

"Are those bird people daoine sgòthan?" Jotul exclaimed aloud, as she spotted yet another race wandering around the city. This even caught the attention of the arguing duo.

Baldem scratched his head. "Daoine what?"

"Daoine sgòthan are the masked folk, you dumb fool. That's what they call themselves," Vreskiven growled.

Baldem scratched his bald head. "Those masked chicken tribes that live in hovels inside forests and marshes? I thought they call themselves clann nan speuran."

"They're more like flightless crows," Vilde corrected. "Which makes their name even more ironic. Before you ask what it means, let's not bother Jotul anymore for now. We can discuss their naming later."

Jotul nodded in appreciation before returning her view to the city—through the sight of one of her birds, to be exact.

She grinned appreciatively. *Another one of my lord's gifts.*

Jotul observed the city from atop what seemed to be a grand hall.

Though the sight of so many goblinoids fascinated her, it also confirmed her suspicions and reminded her of the great threat they faced should they leave the goblins unchecked. She could even feel her master's anxiousness.

"Ainshard," she uttered, catching her companions off guard.

"Ainshard? That nightmarish monster from the old tales? What about him?" Baldem hissed in uncharacteristic hostility.

Jotul wasn't surprised. Ainshard's hatred was well-earned, but she had to admit that the architecture of his cities was a sight to behold.

She took a deep breath. "We've all heard tales of the goblin emperor. He built a vast empire spanning most of the continent."

Baldem shrugged. "Yes, but he's a myth. Even if he was real, he's a tyrant whose empire ended in ruins. There's barely anything of his legacy left, barring some large goblinoid tribes in the far south and the east."

"Seems their race is making a comeback in this city," she replied. Her sight switched from bird to bird as they shared their vision. "They're not wasting any time in rebuilding that damned city. Their battlement repairs aren't shoddy either."

Baldem rubbed his chin. "We could nip the goblinoids in the bud before they grow, but crossing those damn woods would be quite a hassle, let alone mountains. Wagons aren't exactly forest-friendly, and the damned Coalition won't make things easier."

"It's doable. We can start small and send raid parties to harass them, like we sent Lachas. We'll pick their settlements off one by one and watch the rest fall apart," Jotul replied.

Vilde crossed her arms. "I'm not a fan of that approach. The important part is that they settled in one of those accursed cities, and if they manage to uncover any of Ainshard's secrets or take control of any of his absurd facilities, it'll prove quite troubling."

Jotul gave a short nod. "Indeed. They'd be a bigger problem if they join either the Coalition or our little war as an independent third party. Many of the escapees and deserters are already heading towards their territories. We have to deal with them before they make contact."

"And the goblins?" Vreskiven asked.

"We'll deal with—"

A sharp pain in Jotul's chest cut her words short. The bird atop the hall had been shot through the heart with an arrow.

When she switched views and faced the attacker, she saw a long-haired grey goblin glaring at her from far below.

Without a word, the goblin released another arrow and pierced the second bird's head.

This hadn't been the only time. Throughout the city and beyond, many had either captured her birds out of interest or killed them outright.

With each death, she felt a wave of excruciating pain; one so great that if her three compatriots hadn't held her this time, she would've been force fed a mouthful of dirt.

"Are you okay?!"

"What happened?"

"Cut the connection, Jotul!"

All their shouts fell on deaf ears as she stayed focused on one image in particular.

Inside a house near the centre of the city, one of her last birds was being choked by a short grey goblin wearing an ornate tunic.

His condescending grin stretched from ear to ear.

"You really thought we'd be a bunch of blind fools, didn't you?"

How... How did they know?

"I guess I know what you want to ask, but I'm not obligated to reply. Just know one thing." His gleeful face twisted into a furious sneer. "We don't take kindly to spies."

That was the last thing Jotul saw before the goblin snapped the bird's neck. Unable to handle the pressure anymore, she collapsed.

Jotul's birds panicked. Even though she had collapsed, she hadn't broken their connection, sending them into chaos.

CHAPTER 2

A CAGED BIRD

Lev gazed at the crow in his grip. His eyes studied the energy from the magic coating dissipating from the small corpse.

Any other bogey would have been baffled by the bizarre nature of the energy, but Lev found it familiar—sickeningly so. "You know what, Gherm?"

Let me guess, you hate magic?

Lev stifled a smile. "I do, but I hate these so-called Guides even more. For beings that were supposedly sealed away, they've sure been coming out of the woodworks. Now we have a third one spying on us, so what could they be planning this time?"

Gherm pondered for a moment. *I have no idea. But don't you think killing their bird might cause trouble down the road? Especially with their patience running thin.*

"You mean Farald's cheap play?" Lev could feel Gherm's confusion echoing through their connection.

Cheap play? What in the name of the gods do you mean by cheap play? Gherm questioned, annoyance evident in his tone.

Lev's lips curled into a smile, but there was no joy on his face, only frustration. *"What else would you call it? We both know we've been had, and the Guides' message was clear, but there are better ways to throw a threat. I don't know what their true goal is, but I think we have more time than what they had us believe."*

Lev felt Gherm's surprise. *So it was just an act? Then what about their contract with you? Isn't your soul going to be annihilated if you don't keep your end of the bargain?*

Lev scanned the area for any additional undesirable magical signatures before replying.

"One of the things I figured out was that we never agreed on a time limit for the contract, Gherm. Those same higher powers would strike them down if they tried anything funny, and there are many things that never made sense 'til now."

I wouldn't put my trust in that, Lev. I might have never met Farald, but from what I've seen from that mental hellscape that you consider your last meeting, we can't ignore the contract, nor can we work against our Ainshardian benefactors. Besides, it makes sense they're spying on us, all things considered.

Lev knew Gherm was right; The deal was built on shaky foundations and there was no amicability between both sides. "Alright, Gherm, I see your point."

Although... I do agree that many strange things happened. The masked bird-like creatures. The disappearance of the mysterious orb that powered this place...

"Indeed," Lev answered out loud. "The Guides are what led us here, and from what we've seen so far, they're not sealed. At least not fully, otherwise the contract would've been moot." Lev looked at the feathered cadaver in his palms. "Judging from our little friend here, the hivelings aren't the only thing under their control. Even the local wildlife can't be trusted."

His ears twitched as he heard the panicked cries of birds echoing throughout the city.

Then he stuck his head out a window. His eyes narrowed as various species with glaring red eyes circled above Pàrras's sky. To his surprise, they simultaneously let out one last ominous shriek before plummeting down towards certain death.

"They're killing themselves?!" he hissed before deftly closing the window frames and holding them tight. A sickening crunch reverberated outside as the birds smashed into the wooden covers, gushing the crevices with their blood.

Once the madness was over, Lev slowly opened the dinged frame, causing bloody chunks to fall down the window sill onto the street below. He made sure to add the dead crow to the mix.

Not wasting a moment, Lev grabbed his glaive and was ready to depart, but just before he made his way down the stairs, he paused as his instincts brought his attention to his old shield.

He eyed the symbol of Zeja, its lustrous red still shining on the scarred wood, and sighed. It hadn't seen much use since the war with the Jiira. With the arrival of darg merchants there was no need for tools made of cumbersome, yet fragile, stoneworks and outdated metallurgy techniques, so most of their old equipment was decommissioned, recycled, or given to pioneers.

He grabbed a hold of it and made his way down the stairs. With the shield raised above his head, he rushed out of his house, ignoring the three corpse-eaters tugging on the dead crow's head and wings, and made his way to the council.

Lev slowed down as several birds collided with the shield. He trudged carefully, trying not to step on the warm bodies or bump into panicking onlookers who were trying to claw their way into the nearby houses, many of which were the families and servants of the councilmen.

"Cleaning all of this will be a hassle," he grumbled before catching sight of a corpse-eater emerging from a nearby drain.

Joy filled its eyes once it sighted the lifeless feast of birds. It let out a loud shriek, and more of its kind converged into the vicinity.

As the corpse-eaters became a tide, the crowd became even more frantic. Arguments broke out and shoving and pushing became the norm as the masses tried to either break into the nearby homes or grip onto their pillars, hoping to climb and reach a high enough elevation to escape from the scaly menace. A few guards tried to retain order, only to be trampled by goblinoids and corpse-eaters alike. Lev clenched his teeth. As much as he wanted to help, he needed to find a way to the council.

He kept manoeuvring through streets and alleyways, yet he somehow found himself stuck in a crowd and dragged into a large foyer.

"Fancy seeing you here, Lev." The disgruntled voice had cut through the masses and caught Lev's attention. It was Vyrga's.

Before Lev could form a reply, a third party joined the discussion.

"What in the world is happening? Why is everyone, especially you two, in my house?!" Gerwyn demanded, shivering. His eyes darted around the building hysterically.

Vyrga menacingly towered over the angsty blue bogey. "I often wonder if it was Ainshard who made the blues dull-minded. His runes tell me your wage would be much better spent on Orva."

Surprised by Vyrga's hostile demeanour, Gerwyn took a deep breath. "My apologies. Please take my situation into regard. After a painstaking handling of parchment, you decide to take a nap until suddenly, you hear the manic cries of birds followed by loud screams, all while you sense a wave of malicious energy. The moment you run downstairs to check what's going on—"

"—you open the door only to find a crowd of people eagerly trying to rush inside," Lev completed.

Gerwyn snapped his fingers. "Exactly! So excuse my conduct, but can someone please explain what's happening outside?"

"We were being spied on by the birds," Vyrga answered.

Gerwyn's eyes widened.

Lev's ears twitched as whispers began to emerge from the crowd. He pointed inside towards the staircase. "Let's discuss this somewhere more private."

They fought their way through the people towards the stairwell and began their climb. As they made their way up, Lev happened upon Lord Albrecht attempting to assuage the fears of the people. The two exchanged nods before Lev continued his way up to the fourth floor and found it just as busy.

"Don't let anyone near the door," Gerwyn ordered his office guard, who was struggling to push back the influx of panicked goblinoids, and peculiarly enough, avians.

Once the guard gave an affirmative, he proceeded to lock the door.

Inside his office, Gerwyn threw a barrage of questions. "How did you find out? Where did the birds come from? Why are they spying on us?"

Vyrga cleared his throat. "While I was taking a short break from all the arduous council work, something about them piqued my interest. Those birds rarely ate or drank anything. They prioritised observing the city above all else. Once I approached one to figure out why, I noticed a thin line of magical energy stretching from the bird into the far north."

"Have you informed anyone of this?"

"That we were being studied by small animals? I'm sure you can imagine the political fallout that would cause, especially without proof. Some might even excuse the birds' magic as some instinctive ability."

Gerwyn snorted in derision. "If only magic was that easy," he argued. "Most creatures that can instinctively use magic do it on a pretty basic level. The only exceptions are hivelings and sky devils, and that's only because they're naturally adapted to handle complex forms of magic."

"Can we imitate such a technique?" Lev inquired. "Can we create a link with trained dogs and birds? That'll help a lot with scouting missions."

Gerwyn shook his head. "We have our hands full researching the shrines and how to make new ones. Even if that weren't the case, communication through magic isn't easy. Us shamans have a hard time comprehending it, let alone using it. With the exception of some outliers such as Orva and I who have extremely high magical affinity," he scoffed. "Most shamans call upon the spirits to guide their magical energies, not animals."

"What about outliers such as yourself?" Vyrga asked with a hint of mockery.

Gerwyn let out a long sigh and rubbed his forehead. "A few years ago, my colleagues and I tried to form a connection with the hivelings in order to pacify them. Can you guess what happened?"

"It failed," Vyrga remarked.

Gerwyn couldn't help but chuckle. "That seems the obvious conclusion, but no. It worked but fried the minds of our two brightest shamans. All for a minute or two of telepathic control. It's worthless."

Both Lev and Vyrga thought otherwise.

Despite the negative effects, it's still a viable option in dire scenarios, Lev surmised.

Sometimes sacrifices need to be made for the greater good, Vyrga concluded.

Before they could discuss the concept in more depth, a tingling sensation went up Lev's spine. When he looked at his two companions, they were in the same boat.

Gerwyn was the first to break the silence. "What the hell is that?!"

he shouted, running towards the window and gazing at the sky. Lev and Vyrga followed.

Everyone on the street, even magically inept races such as the deka, could sense the oppressive magical energy gathering in the sky, manifesting as a foreboding crimson fog.

"It's the same energy that controlled the birds," Vyrga muttered.

Suddenly a chilling feminine voice creeped into their minds.

Everyone but Lev gasped at the bizarre phenomenon. It was a form of communication that many had never experienced before.

As the voice spoke, they could feel its hatred coursing through their bodies. *It seems you are far more capable than I assumed, but no matter. Goblinkind won't rise again. In this era, it shall be the bereke and korrigal who dominate, not the followers of an outsider.*

Out of the blue, the dead birds that were still intact twitched and rose up, startling goblinoids, avians, and corpse-eaters alike. The black lizards abandoned their meals and fled into the sewers.

When the animated birds flew again, they soared towards the red haze in a V-shaped formation.

"Tha mi air cluinntinn mu dheidhinn seo! Is e fearg Egon a th' ann! Ruith a-steach do na taighean!" one of the masked avians yelled.

When others saw them running back into a house, they followed suit. Not long after, the soaring birds turned and plunged, beak-first, into the homes.

Call this retaliation for attacking my messengers. This is my formal declaration of war, the voice gleefully announced, echoing for the last time.

"Duck!" Lev yelled before locking the shutters and jumping away from the window. Gerwyn's ceiling shook from the aerial bombardment as screams filled the city.

Everyone took cover and clenched their teeth as the building shook, praying for the hellish scene to end.

Eventually, their prayers came true. The bombardment was over.

Lev carefully approached the window. His hand slowly unchained the lock sealing the wooden frames. Then he found the streets devoid of life. Only the bludgeoned corpses of the smashed birds and those who hadn't managed to get inside remained. The voice's magic had disappeared as well.

He spat on the ground below him. "We need to head to the council immediately."

Vyrga and Gerwyn silently nodded.

* * *

"This is outrageous!"

"Will we be alright?"

"Where did these bastards come from?!"

Cries and yells filled the Grand Halls, Pàrras's administration complex.

Meinrad ground his teeth harder and harder every time his fellow leaders acted like little kids. *What came over me to accept this shitty position? The more I stay here with these buffoons, the more I lose hope in Pàrras's future.*

"Silence!" he shouted. His voice echoed throughout the building and quieted all of the overgrown children who called themselves representatives of the people.

"Stop this meaningless prattle!" he jeered. "Whatever did... *that* already delivered its message and left. If it was able to do more, it would've done so already."

A green bogey stood up. "You saw what it did, Meinrad! It rained corpses and blood! Do we really need to fight that?"

"We all heard the voice. The bereke will come whether we want them to or not," Servius muttered.

"Scout the enemy," Lev ordered. "Servius, use your connections to learn their numbers, strengths, weaknesses, then prepare to fend them off. Follow that up with a swift counterattack and you'll have a crippled enemy that can't retaliate in the future." His voice caught everyone's attention. He then glanced at the man beside him. "Vyrga and I already sent our best men to gather information."

Vyrga nodded. There was an excited grin on his face. "Indeed. Once we get our hands on the reports, we should target the enemy's supply lines to weaken them. We'll engage them in a series of short skirmishes in the woods surrounding the lands to avoid structural damage to our outposts and casualties, both soldier and civilian."

"We already mapped out most of the region over the months. We know where to hit them if they step into our territory, we just need to figure out which road they'd take," Lev added.

"During the counterattack, we should assess if it's possible to siege and conquer their cities and use them as a buffer," Vyrga said, a glint in his eyes. "After all, why should we fight them on our lands when they can bloody themselves trying to reclaim theirs?"

Seeing the two rivals excitedly discussing strategies, Meinrad couldn't help but nod in satisfaction. *At least those two can agree on something.*

"Splendid idea, my lord!" a certain pink-wearing buffoon yelled. Vyrga's face soured. It didn't take long for Lev's to follow suit.

Bodobert, as usual, didn't seem to mind. Instead of shutting up, he puffed out his chest, causing his gut to bounce, jingling the bells attached to his outfit. He raised his fist high in the air. "We'll not only teach those tall wretches and their master their place but take everything they own as compensation!"

What Meinrad could perceive were the dumbest specimens in the entire city hollered in affirmation to Bodobert's words. Every time, he wondered what came over the citizens to elect such individuals into positions of power. He of all people knew Bodobert was more than he seemed, but he still kept getting surprised by his antics.

what's been said. As much as I'd like to take revenge on the bereke, there's a more pressing matter we need to address first." He glanced at Lev and Vyrga.

"What are you on about now, Bodobert?" Vyrga shouted. "Don't you think you've mocked us enough with your presence already?!"

Lev leaned over to the high chief's ear, whose veins bulged.

"Don't let him get the better of you, or you'll only entertain him further," Lev whispered.

"A festival is in order first, don't you agree, Lev?" Bodobert continued.

Had it been said during his previous echo-chamber warmongering, no one would've paid mind to little Bodobert. This time, however, the fallen noble had returned to his old sharpness, if only for a brief moment.

Lev's eyes widened as he noticed a familiar gleam in Bodobert's eyes. "A festival?"

"Our citizens are in disarray, with many of them not even stepping outside due to fear of another aerial attack," Bodobert clarified. He chuckled, louder this time. "Those wretched birds sure shook them to the core.

Vyrga clicked his tongue. He rose from his chair and glared down at the strangely dressed bogey. "How long will all of you take part in this farce? A festival? Now?"

Bodobert submissively lowered his head and muttered, "Forgive me, my lord. It was a mere suggestion to appease our people! It will distract them while we make the necessary preparations for war."

Lev restrained Vyrga as he felt his rage build up. "He's right, Vyrga."

"You're playing games too now? And here I thought we finally understood each other."

Lev shook his head. "I understand you, but I also take Bodobert's point. We can't leave our HQ in chaos and expect it to remain intact while we're fighting the bereke."

Bodobert frowned. "HQ?"

"Our city," he corrected.

Vyrga shook off Lev's hand and walked past him, towards the hall's exit. "I hope you're right, Lev, because it'll be your head if you're not."

Lev looked down. *Yup, that's the Vyrga I remember.*

The one and only, Gherm added with a metaphysical sigh.

"Well, then!" Bodobert's eyes had returned to their usual dullness, devoid of intelligence. The lunatic had returned. "Another group of cavern survivors arrived this week, mainly dargs. So why don't we organise a festival for them and our people?"

"Whatever you say, Bodobert. Whatever you say," Lev said as he stepped out of the Grand Halls.

With the ruckus over and Lev and Vyrga's absence, no one dared to interfere with Bodobert, at least this once. His suggestion came shortly before a holiday for dargs. It was time for the darg festival, and afterwards, inevitable war.

CHAPTER 3

PILLARS OF EUPHORIA

In the darkening hours of dusk, fires danced in the city and the sound of drums filled the air. From atop the city wall, Lev and Volker looked down at the gathered crowd awaiting Lev's command.

"It's finally time," Volker said.

"I guess it is," Lev muttered. He gave Volker a glance and extended his hand. "Pass it over."

"Understood."

Without wasting a second, Volker took a stout horn from his belt. Once it reached Lev's hands, he blew the horn. Its sound echoed throughout the city as the crowd cheered.

The darg festival had begun.

Lev peered down at the jubilant crowd, almost cracking a smile from seeing them able to display such joy despite facing countless harrowing events, but then he directed his vision to the distant woods.

We really shouldn't be wasting our time like this, especially now.

But... Bodobert is right. He took a deep breath and shook his head. The sight of children being chased by a greyborn priest wearing a red and white sash—an emblem of religious men who handled the orphanages—had finally made his smile come to full bloom.

Lev and Volker descended the wall's staircase. At the bottom, an unusual gathering of faction leaders waited for him.

While the populace was rejoicing in their fleeting moment of festivity, these leaders of the Frontier would briefly discuss how to deal with the bereke menace, away from the prying eyes of their opponents in the council.

After all, this wasn't the time to quarrel. Such complacency would crush all of their ambitions.

Ever since Pàrras's refounding, Lev had caught everyone's interest with his novel strategies. In the eyes of both ally and foe, many of his ideas were practical, albeit unorthodox.

One in particular had fascinated a certain green bogey.

"That's a marvellous idea!" Hiltrude had cried during one of Lev's workshops.

She had gawked at Lev with a radiant smile. "I like the idea of hiding strategic depots beforehand. That's less work for my department. The last thing we need is an entire army of wagons to build."

"That'd be a boon," Lev had pointed out. "We still need enough wagons for our soldiers, though, otherwise they'd have to make do with what's on hand. If there are no depots in sight, we can't have our men face the enemy bare-handed on an empty stomach."

It was strange, working with tested and proven strategies from his world, but it felt good, nonetheless.

"Lev!" Vyrga yelled.

"Uh, what? Sorry I wasn't following."

"So as I was saying, from what we've heard from our bereke captives, the enemy specialises in mobility and offensives. It'll be a disaster if her raid parties catch us off guard," Vyrga explained.

"If we move fast enough, I doubt they would be able to do anything," Rak responded. "Cursed birds or not, they don't know the layout of the land as much as we do. We might be newcomers, but we thoroughly scouted the area beforehand."

Rak shrugged. "Besides, didn't our new darg friends tell us something weird happened to her army? They stopped most of their hunting parties and closed in on themselves, not even allowing a single merchant group near their camps. Furthermore, her birds' eyes stopped shining red and most fell dead to the ground. I believe we have enough time to set up the depots."

"At least the ones close to our base," Lev muttered.

Vyrga shook his head. "I stand with my prior words of bringing the fight to their lands and advise against fighting them near the settlements. Recent events are still on our people's minds. The last thing we need is a repeat of the bereke forces landing on our doorstep."

"There's also another reason that'd make things hard," Lev added.

It didn't take long for his fellow council members to guess what.

Hemgall shook his head. "Constructing in a forest will be an issue. We'll need to clear a lot of roots if we want to dig the depot's foundation."

Lev nodded. "Even with magic, it'll be hard to dig through the forest floor. We might also have to deal with wildlife smelling the depots' contents and breaching them, or worse, leading the enemy towards them."

Vyrga sighed. "This is quite the conundrum. According to our captives, the path they took previously to get here is full of hostile wildlife, and to add salt to the wound, the scouts just spotted migrating swarms of sky devils. Stragglers, according to the natives."

He sneered. "The accursed beasts will further hamper our efforts, if not outright cripple them. We might need to simplify our demands on logistics."

"But winter's over!" Hiltrude and Gerwyn yelped, shocked about the sudden migration.

Lev found two dumbfounded expressions staring back at him. "You didn't know? The scouts reported the damned creatures' arrival near the farming settlements over a week ago."

Gerwyn shrugged. "I was busy studying the old runes Lev's expedition party found. After all, they brought us here."

"I'm surprised nobody informed me about this," Hiltrude said.

Hemgall chuckled. "It ain't even a secret. You two really need to get better informants."

She huffed in indignation. "In case you've forgotten, I'm one of the best traders among bogeykind. I've already invested a lot when it comes to gathering information."

"Maybe they didn't think the sky devils were worthy news. They're not heading anywhere near the city, and the settlements would likely hunker down to prevent any casualties," Rak concluded.

Wincing, Volker couldn't help but scratch his head. "Many are worried. News of the sky devils was bad enough. Now we have the birds bombarding our homes and an approaching, invading army. One that can spy on us using those same birds."

He inspected the plaza, which was now brimming with all the colours of the goblinoid races. "I wonder if Bodo's right about this festival. Will it really calm the people?"

Hemgall rolled his eyes. "Who knows."

"One thing about this whole ordeal does bother me," Vyrga started.

"From what I know, there's no rule that they can't control other creatures. Let alone that red eyes are the only sign. I'm sure many among the council think the same."

With a deep frown and steely gaze, Lev studied the surrounding locals. Despite their attempts to act normal, tension hid under their wavering smiles as they drank their imported darg wine and sang songs of joy and prosperity.

He shook his head. "Things will erupt if we mishandle the situation, so it might be best to tackle the issue with clear minds. To ensure that, the festival needs to be perfect."

Everyone went silent as they pondered the future of the city.

With a loud cough, Gerwyn grabbed everyone's attention. "While I understand the need to be cautious, I doubt their control extends beyond birds. I recommend we announce this to the masses to ease their worries. I'd even do it myself."

"If you're wrong, the consequences would be dire," Vyrga warned, but Gerwyn was adamant.

"If they are able to control more, then the blame will fall on me and me alone."

Hiltrude blinked. Her eyes were wide, staring at the blue-skinned shaman as if he'd just grown another head. "If we face defeat because of some squirrel or corpse-eater spying on us, you'll be lucky if all the people demand is for you to step down."

Gerwyn nodded. "They'd demand blood, I'm fully aware. But luckily for me, there weren't any corpse-eaters before we arrived," he replied in an attempt to brighten the mood.

Hiltrude blankly stared at him. Gerwyn, irked by the bemused frown on her face, replied with a deep sigh.

She shrugged. "It's your head on the chopping block."

He scoffed in response. "You'll be praising this head when it turns out I'm right."

"Don't count your chickens before they hatch," Rak cautioned. "Even if it's just birds, they're still a nuisance. They're quick and nimble and can observe almost anything from above. We still need to find an effective way to deal with them."

As the group walked around a corner toward the festival, a corpse-eater ran towards them carrying a bird's still-bleeding head.

Right before it bumped into Vyrga, it took a step back, and decided it was wise to run to the side instead.

Vyrga's eyes narrowed at the lizard-like creature as it ran down a drain with its dinner in its mouth.

"If only we could somehow use our own pests to deal with the bereke."

"They seem to like bird meat. I've even seen some corpse-eaters hunting living birds," Hemgall pointed out.

Vyrga sneered as he saw a few more fighting over a bird's corpse in a nearby alley. "They're still unreliable and disease-ridden vermin. Not only would they make bad bird hunters, I'm sure their population will spike thanks to all the corpses. The only good thing about them is that they keep the rats at bay."

"Do they? You're still here," Hemgall said with a smug grin. The resulting sneer made him beam from ear to ear.

Volker saw others poking out of a drain. "We may have to inspect the sewage system again or smoke them out somehow. After we deal with the bereke army, of course."

To the surprise of many, Lev slowed down and stopped in his tracks. "We'll deal with all of our problems eventually, Volk. For now, enjoy the festival and rest well. I need to go back to the wall."

Rak tilted his head. "For someone advocating to tackle our problems with a clear head, shouldn't you also be taking a break? It'd be fun to have you around for once."

"He's right, Lev. It's a waste for you to accompany us this far and just leave," Hemgall added while pointing at the festival grounds.

Lev shook his head. "Take it as my way to relax. I'll join later, though. Enjoy the show while it lasts. Zeja's realm awaits us afterwards."

Hemgall chuckled. "Your loss. More beer and those fancy darg wines for me!"

Vyrga groaned. "I would've done the same. Sadly enough, as High Chief, I have an obligation to attend."

Lev waved the others goodbye. "Let's continue this discussion tomorrow."

"Agreed," all of them replied in unison.

"I need a drink, let's go to the town square!" Hemgall started off.

"Is the gods' nectar all you think about?" Vyrga scoffed, causing chuckles.

* * *

Once Lev was back on the city wall where he had announced the start of the festival not long ago, Gherm resurfaced for much-needed reflection on the Frontier's perilous situation.

The bereke are strong, Lev. Are you sure we can defeat them? Gherm said with a hint of doubt in his ethereal voice.

"We'll divide and conquer, like we've done from the start," Lev replied. "They're strong and, if the voice we heard is right, have the backing of the korrigal."

Gherm sounded pensive. *How can we conquer what can't be divided? It's like you said earlier, they've got eyes seemingly everywhere.*

"True. But those eyes can't be everywhere, no matter how numerous they may be. If we cause enough mayhem, we'll slowly draw their aides out and then converge on their whereabouts."

It won't be easy with those birds, Gherm noted.

"There are no problems that can't be solved, Gherm. We'll figure out their weaknesses and strike them when they least expect it," Lev assured him with a smirk.

But her birds would—

Lev's eyes grew intense, as if he were staring into Gherm's. "What did I just tell you?"

"We'll find a way to mess with their senses. They didn't fly to their deaths just to haunt us, not at first. When all the birds fell the first time, it seemed as if they lost their... connection to whatever was controlling them right after we killed a few of those kin."

Gherm's voice was just as intense. *Do you think our shamans could tamper with the birds' magic?*

A smile creeped onto Lev's face, one all too familiar to Gherm. "Now we're talking."

* * *

Lev looked down from atop the city's wall.

Screams of joy filled the area as children ran amok, their bodies covered in paint.

The girls were painted blue and the boys red. Such was the custom of his darg allies.

"It'll take weeks for the paint to come off," Lev surmised before his eyes went wide.

Are they stealing apples? And who said dancing near the firepit was okay? Thank goodness the body paint isn't flammable.

"What are they doing now?" Lev asked as he looked at the town square from the western side. The only things he could make out were distant pots and vases being broken by the children.

"They're using slings. I would've preferred a crossbow," he mumbled.

From what Volker heard from Shahn, his people were notorious slingers, Gherm dryly commented.

"Duly noted." Lev went silent for a moment before turning away. "Also, my apologies for disappointing you and the others. Though I truly want to turn this place into a paradise for everyone, I got carried away by its mysteries."

Actions speak louder than words. You've proven that to me in the caverns, Gherm answered, a smile in his voice.

Something tells me you won't lose the elections again.

Lev shook his head. "Honestly, I'm sure I'll make similar blunders in the future. It's a part of sentient creatures to be greedy. Greed and ambition are what allow species to strive."

Gherm's smile left. *One day you might go off the deep end, but for now, we must look at tomorrow,* he added, and the words echoed into nothingness.

"Exactly, my friend."

Volker was stunned. He'd made his way back to the city wall and up the steps, only to see Lev talking at an empty parapet next to him. "Sir, are you coming down now? I think we gave you enough time by yourself, and the others are waiting."

Lev simply walked past him, only stopping once he reached the base of the stairs. "You're right. Let's go and join the party."

* * *

Lev found the festival's more adult-centred events less intriguing than those meant for children.

They were common events he'd seen hundreds of times in his past life. Music, drinking, and a few athletics.

Some men were throwing a boulder with a cloth sling while others were jumping over wooden barricades or throwing spears at faraway targets. There was also a competition using a board game similar to backgammon.

It was no wonder Vyrga won the musical event while Lev and Rak won many of the drinking and athletic ones, but what shocked the crowd even more was Ghorza winning the board game event with Hemgall in second place.

"Is it so shocking that I won?" Ghorza asked Lev with a medallion swaying around her neck.

"Not as much as Hemgall coming in second place in something other than a drinking contest. Who knew he had a brain?" Vyrga uttered. He held an elaborate blue flute in his hand, his prize for winning the music competition.

"Very funny," Hemgall growled.

He turned towards Lev, Volker, and Rak with a grin on his face. "Can you believe this bastard thinks I'm a dimwit?"

Vyrga's eyes flared. "Who are you calling a bastard... bastard!"

Another form appeared from behind Hem's muscular frame. "Hem, don't start another fight! You just tried to wrestle two bug-bears! Bugbears!" Orva whined.

"And I'd have won if I were sober enough!" Hemgall roared.

Vyrga's eyes went wide. "Y-You were sober when you won that board game contest, right?"

"Sober? Ha! Drank a few barrels before I joined the others. Who's a dimwit now, huh?"

Orva replied with a firm facepalm before dragging Hemgall back to his sleeping quarters. "Enjoy the festivities, guys, I need to take care of this big intoxicated baby before he tries anything."

Hemgall's face turned red. "You know what? You can all bite the dust for all I care, especially you, Vyrga!"

"Go to bed, little baby," Vyrga scoffed.

Rak rubbed his forehead. "I'll cheer him up later. Nothing a few drinks won't fix."

Gerwyn let out a tired groan. "Maybe I should get some rest as well. We've got a big day tomorrow. The council will be a mess once we formulate our plans."

Ghorza turned to Volker with a bright smile. "Are you guys coming to the main event? The girls are already waiting for us."

"Is my sister there?" Volker asked.

She nodded. "I met with her earlier. She was consoling your dad for all that broken earthenware thanks to the slings. I think it's weird for the dargs to fill them with wrapped sweets, but what do I know?"

"No wonder so many kids participated," Volker muttered.

"Anyways, we need to go before the drums ro—"

A hammering of drums filled the city.

Thorst stormed over, wide eyed and grabbed Ghorza's hand. "We're late!"

Ghorza turned towards Lev and Volker and shouted, "I'll meet you there," before continuing on her way.

"As High Chief, I am obligated to attend the trial. Seems I'll bid you farewell," Vyrga said. "Remember to begin preparations once the festivities end tomorrow. This was a needed inconvenience but an inconvenience nonetheless."

"Do you want to see the main event?" Lev said to Volker. "I've been thinking of heading home, since it'd be better if we prepared first thing tomorrow."

Volker shook his head. "This is the adulthood ceremony. It'd be a shame if you didn't congratulate the victors, sir. Many kids look up to you."

"Then we better make haste."

* * *

The duo jogged their way through a dense crowd, towards the outskirts of the city. On top of two nearby hills were two makeshift shrines. Stopping before the hills, Lev and Volker saw more than a hundred youths of all species gathered around seven dargs. At the dargs' head was Shahn, who wore a two-faced mask, with one half resembling a full moon and the other side black, representing a new moon.

The dargs, both male and female, wore ornate robes and jewellery along with hats like conical eggs.

Once everyone had taken their seats, with the chiefs and their helpers in the centre of the youths, the dargs started humming. They sang in their ancient tongue of a tale from the faraway city-state of Edoros.

As the song progressed, the young ones looked at the cloudy sky and danced. Their figures kept twirling 'til the moon showed its face through the night sky.

"In the name of Lel," they announced in unison before bowing.

Shahn gazed at the crowd, then turned his attention to the youths.

"An old cycle goes, and a new cycle comes. We're gathered here under the grace of the night mother. Lel welcomes these young boys and girls into adulthood," he announced. He pointed at the two shrines. "But adulthood isn't something that should come so easily. As the mother of all dargs, the stars, and the moon proclaimed, it should be earned." His face shifted into a smile. "Are all of you ready for the trial ahead?"

The young ones replied with cheers and squawks of approval.

Grinning at their enthusiasm, Shahn clapped. The other dargs began wrapping pieces of cloth around the youths' arms. They were evenly split between fifty white cloths and fifty green ones.

More dargs appeared near the shrines and hung two banners with the same colours as the two cloths.

"In each shrine, there are ten urns. The goal is to take six of your opponent's urns and place them in your shrine. Keep in mind that the team that breaks more than four urns loses. Understood?"

All of the youths looked at each other in confusion. Several even began debating what the point of this trial was, and what it had to do with adulthood. Some of Orva's shamans came to translate the rules to the more confused avians who still hadn't caught on to the basics of the goblinoid languages.

"Now, go to your hills, and when the drums play, let the trial begin!"

With the children scrambling to their respective hills, the rest joined the spectators.

Shahn tried his best to hide his embarrassment once he met Lev and the others.

"Well, that last part was rough. Can't believe the other dargs dragged me into this," he muttered, sitting down between Lev and

Volker. "Still," he said, "I wouldn't blame them. After we were transported here to fight in the expedition, I thought I'd never see another lunar festival in my life. It was always one of my people's most favourite holidays."

"I'm surprised Servius wasn't pulled in," Lev replied.

Shahn shrugged. "Gods know where he went. He must've had something dire to take care of."

"That's not an issue," Lev continued. "Let's see how the kids will do."

The drums thundered once more, and the game began.

At first, Lev had imagined a childish squabble would ensue, but what happened exceeded his expectations. *This is more intriguing than I thought.*

He slowly straightened. His eyes were glued to the children's rudimentary display of tactics.

The white team riskily left only three individuals to guard their shrine whilst forty charged towards the others' hill. Seven of them were attempting to sneak their way around the green team's hill and climb from the other side.

"I see you like the white team," a familiar voice commented. A human sat down next to Lev, earning weary gazes from nearby goblinoids. "Sorry I'm late. I've been smoothing things over with the bereke captives. Some of them tried to break out once they saw the birds."

"I wonder if those bereke are the same ones we'll face," Lev said. "They seemed to be in distress when the birds assaulted our streets. Wouldn't they rejoice knowing their allies are on their way?"

Eleric shrugged. "I don't know. They refuse to tell me their leaders' names. They don't seem to know much about anything."

"I'll keep that in mind."

"Now." Eleric grinned. "What is it you like about the white team?"

"They're interesting," Lev answered. "Though the green team aren't slouches either."

From the green team, forty children ran down the hill. Twenty were in the centre whilst the other twenty split into teams of ten and covered the sides.

"Who do you think will win? Brains or brawn?"

Eleric laughed. "Who knows. It depends on their leadership, if they have any."

"Seems they do," Volker interrupted. He pointed at a child from the white team. "Look at him! He's giving orders to the others."

Lev let out a loud whistle. "Bravo!"

The white team stopped their charge halfway down the hill and prepared to meet the green team, who, despite the momentary confusion, hadn't stopped their sprint.

"The greens are doomed," Lev concluded. "If possible, never face an uphill battle."

He was right. Tired and fatigued, the formation of the greens quickly dispersed and collapsed under the whites' assault. The last ten members of the green team who were stationed up the hill were stunned by the sight. They didn't notice the seven whites stealing their urns until it was too late.

The white team had won.

"So what's the punishment for the green team?"

"In ancient times, the losers were to receive ten lashes per member—" Shahn started.

"You are not lashing children under my watch," Lev warned.

Shahn raised his hands in surrender. "Easy there. I said in ancient times. We don't perform such archaic practices anymore."

"Good thing you stopped such inane acts, or you would have dealt with me," Eleric said.

"Calm down," Shahn pleaded. "Those were dark times that my people left behind. I assure you the punishment is much more reasonable nowadays."

"What is it, then? Are they still considered kids until they win next year?" Lev asked.

As Shahn was about to answer, Elric interrupted him. "The losers will still become adults, but they'll get colour-marked."

"How do you know?" Volker asked.

Eleric chuckled. "I always went to the darg isles during this festival. Considering all the improvisation I've seen in this version, it might be the strangest one I've attended so far. Though it has to be one of my favourites."

Shahn sighed. "Well, he answered your question. The losers will have to wear one of the most shameful colours of all for four days."

"Bright pink?" Lev guessed wrong, judging from Shahn's expression.

"Of course not! It's orange!" Shahn yelled. "Why you'd think pink is a shameful colour is beyond me." He pointed at his skin. "It's the closest to purple, the most royal colour of all."

"And orange is shameful?" Lev asked, bemused.

Shahn huffed. "The only good orange is the fruit. Everything else is terrible, especially the poisonous insects and toxic mushrooms."

And so, the festival came to a close.

The white team gathered around the pillar established in the centre of town square and had their first drink of beer as adults while the green team was painted orange.

Such was the way of the dargs.

CHAPTER 4

VICIOUS DIPLOMACY

"I hate this!" Orva yelled at the top of her lungs, tightly grabbing onto Hemgall as they sat on top of a galloping horse.

Under Hemgall's equestrianism, the creature had barely shown any of its usual grace and majesty, leading to a very bumpy ride.

I could've been back at my office researching the appropriate runes to fix Pàrras's foundries, but no! Maga had to stab me in the rump, making me participate in this madness! Orva cried to herself. The goddess of love was at it again.

It'd only been a few days since the festival, and Orva was already craving its warmth. Despite Lev's insistence on gathering more information, the council had chosen Rak to lead an attack on the bereke the moment the scouts identified enemy forces near the Frontier's furthest farming settlements.

The scouts hadn't been able to get close enough to assess the situation, not that any of that mattered to Orva. Relieving the pain from arching her legs for hours was a far greater priority. The council's squabbling was something she could reflect upon in the comfort of a tent.

"I told you that you wouldn't like this," Hemgall reminded her.

"Well, you should've told me how long we'd ride for!" Orva argued as she almost lost her grip on Hemgall's waist. "These past few days have been a lot of waking up and getting on a horse you can't even ride. I'm not even allowed a proper breakfast!"

She sighed. "At least we'll pilfer more of the bereke tools. That should serve as decent compensation. Their runes are more advanced than ours, I'm sure they'll help in my current projects."

"Isn't Gerwyn also researching them?"

"Hemgall, quit while you can! I'm *not* counting that blue buffoon in my equations."

"Alright, alright. But couldn't you have delegated some other shaman to ride with me rather than yourself? Heck, Gerwyn could have—" Orva tightly squeezed Hemgall's sides, almost causing him to let go of the reins.

"What gives?! Are you trying to kill us?" Hemgall complained.

Orva huffed. "Better to plunge myself alone into the behemoth forest than have that old weasel even dream of taking my position!"

After hearing that, Hemgall couldn't help but laugh. "I wouldn't call him old. The man's not as bad as you think. He's grumpy, but he's not half the menace that Hermut's late dad was. Although, I do miss ol' Rogg, now that I'm thinking about it."

"You say that because you never had him as a mentor," Orva muttered under her breath.

Hearing about Hermut instantly made her turn her head to the only darg in the group. It was Servius. The middle-aged goblinoid had lost his pomp after the first day of horseback hell.

She remembered Hermut's advice. If only Servius had listened and bought that blend of herbs to help against nausea. He'd arrogantly scoffed about horses being nothing compared to the rough Edoraian seas.

Orva bit her lip after seeing the dishevelled purple-skinned sap clinging to Rak for dear life.

She couldn't help but turn away when she noticed that he

wouldn't be able to hold back the urge to vomit much longer. Moments later, Rak's furious shouts confirmed she was right.

I hope that councilman's a better translator than he looks. Otherwise, Rak wasted a bag of haze crystals on vomit.

Her thoughts were interrupted when Hem's horse jumped over a log, smacking her headfirst into Hem's back.

"I hate horses," Orva loudly hissed. Luckily, Grasha was nearby and had seen her earlier predicament.

He laughed. "With that attitude, I bet they probably hate you too, m'lady shaman. It's not their fault that you're all amateurs," he added with a grin.

Orva sneered. "I hope a behemoth eats you and your dumb horse!"

"As if some dumb deer man could catch me. Simmer down, lass. We're almost there. We'll meet up with the scouts we sent ahead in a short while. Enjoy the ride 'til then!"

She had a lot of words to say to the deka, but Grasha's horse had already sped past them.

"At least the bastard's enjoying himself for once," she grumbled.

Hemgall smiled. "His mood's been getting better ever since we settled in Pàrras. He finally found a place where he belongs."

"Hmph. He was grumpy during the last campaign too."

Hemgall softly chuckled. "So would I if I had to search for a bunch of bird people in some accursed forest. I'm glad you all managed to get away from the behemoths last time."

Orva sighed. "Point taken. Though where we're going isn't gonna be much better."

"If we stumble upon those antlered beasts again, they'll be much easier to handle with you around. Once we get back, tell me what you want to eat and I'll make it," Hemgall promised the shaman. Orva's giddy smile was the only answer he needed.

It quickly turned into a frown as a large overhanging branch came into view. "Branch!" she warned.

Hemgall ducked his head, narrowly avoiding it. "Thanks."

"Now you're the one trying to kill us. Just keep your eyes on the road."

This time, Hemgall stayed silent and did as he was told for the remainder of the trip.

Not long after, Rak abruptly halted up ahead and commanded everyone to stop.

He and Grasha jumped off their horses, and from the nearby shrubbery, one of their scouts emerged.

Unlike the horses of the more experienced riders, it took some effort for Hemgall's steed to comply. Once he'd gotten it under control and descended, he wasted no time lowering Orva down.

After she gave him an appreciative nod, the two joined the others.

There's the expression we know and love, Orva thought after seeing Grasha's scowl. All traces of his earlier jovial mood were void now.

"Let me guess. The enemy found out," Hemgall said as several goblinoids gathered around the scout.

To Hemgall's surprise, the scout shook his head. "They're doing our jobs for us," he answered.

"What?"

"Two days ago, a group of armed bereke came and set up camp around our settlements. I think they were preparing to burn and pillage the farms in order to starve Pàrras bit by bit before their main forces arrive."

"Continue," Rak said.

"We monitored the situation closely and came to a surprising conclusion. The bereke are killing each other.

"Just as one group of bereke were about to start their raid, another group intervened and promptly slaughtered them."

Hemgall frowned as he crossed his arms. "They slaughtered their own kind? That doesn't make sense."

Rak shook his head. "I think we're dealing with two separate groups here."

"Why would there be two groups?" Orva chimed in.

"When they besieged Pàrras, brief as it was, they didn't have those birds with them. If they'd utilised them, I'm sure they'd have seen through Vyrga's plans."

Hemgall facepalmed. "Right, they would've seen our ambush from miles away. I knew something was amiss."

Rak paced around. "That and our bereke captives seemed to dread those birds, even though the voice attributed them to the bereke... and korrigal."

"Some of the material I found in the library mentioned them," Orva said. "They were better known as the tusked ones back in Ainshard's day. They clashed with Ainshard not long before his fall.

"Seems like they've regained some of their old strength," she surmised.

"There's one more thing," the scout interjected.

"The farming settlement did get pillaged in the end. My guess is that the victors had to resupply after the infighting. They seem to have left now, though."

Rak mounted his horse. "Lead the way to the settlement. We need to check for survivors."

* * *

Once they'd left the forest, twirls of black smoke greeted them from behind a few distant hills.

Rak gritted his teeth. "I hope they spared some of our people. Damn savages."

"Faster!" Rak yelled as he cued his horse with his legs.

The others could only watch as Rak sped past the scout, leaving a cloud of dust behind him.

Once they'd approached the settlement's perimeter, their horses panicked.

Seeing the desecrated remains of cattle was enough to fray the docile beasts' nerves. It took great effort for everyone to calm them down so that they wouldn't flee.

"Looks like we'll have to approach on foot from here. I don't blame the horses," Hemgall said as he covered his nose. The stench of burnt flesh was overpowering.

After they tied the horses to the fences of a field which had once housed cattle, they ventured deeper into the settlement.

The trail they followed was bloody, as if something, or someone, had been dragged into the centre.

What they saw next reminded Hemgall of the previous bereke raids. Charred cadavers littered the scene. And those were the lucky ones.

Orva covered her mouth, resisting the urge to vomit at the *artistic* liberties the bereke took with the deaths of their victims. Servius, on the other hand, liberated his guts on the accursed soil.

Looking at the sight, no one could blame him. Some corpses were flayed, their skin stretched so far that it could be used as tarps. Others had their broken limbs intertwined with bronze wheels, their faces displaying the agony they endured in their last moments of life.

Among the burnt corpses, Rak noticed the remains of a mother and her child, their white bones shining through molten flesh. He could see stab wounds where the flesh hadn't fully burnt away. "They spared no one, not even the children."

He turned towards the scout, who'd barely managed to retain his lunch. "Looks like the bereke are still as vicious. Birds or not, infighting or unity."

Rak's grip around his axe tightened, threatening to bend the metal that made its pole. "They died with no one to save them."

Hemgall patted his shoulder. "Rak, it's the bereke's fault, not yours."

To Hemgall's surprise, Rak slapped his hand away. "While they were slaughtered, we worried about who'd win the drinking games during the festival." Rak shivered. "To think we slept with full bellies..."

Hemgall grabbed him by both shoulders. "Regret at this moment won't change anything, Rak. We didn't know they would arrive this soon. More importantly, we need to decide what we'll do, here and now."

Before Rak could answer, his ears twitched. He wasn't the only one, as some of the men began looking around.

Once he looked towards the sky, a soft chuckle escaped his lips. "Do you see that, Hemgall?"

"What? I see nothing. You alright, man?" Hem answered, but then it hit him. Shrill cries and a slight magical signal rang in the back of his head.

Rak sneered. "It's the same feeling we had in the city. One of that *thing's* pesky birds. A falcon, don't you see?!"

He lifted up his battle-axe with crazed eyes. "Zeja's calling for retribution! They're close!"

"Rak's right," Hemgall told the others. "It's the same energy as the birds that attacked the city."

"It's over there!" Orva pointed towards a speck with a suspicious red glint.

With his axe pointed towards the heavens, Rak declared his stance. "A head for a head! If they want vicious diplomacy, they'll get it!"

With their weapons raised, Rak's men roared at his declaration.

He cocked his head at the scout who reported on the bereke. "You. You noticed them first, and I'm sure you can track those spawn of Mal again. Count their heads and report back as soon as possible."

The scout took a step back. "A-Are you sure, Rak? I get your anger, but the situation is dire. My mission includes reporting my findings to the council. I should leave. We should leave."

Rak grabbed the scout by his collar and raised him until their eyes met. "Count. The. Heads."

He threw the scout next to one of the burnt cadavers before continuing. "Unless you want to give them the chance to burn yet another settlement. In that case, I'll gladly inform the council of your cowardice."

* * *

As the falcon soared through the sky, it observed the battle below with keen interest. It didn't want to miss a single second of it, as it was sure its master wouldn't reward it otherwise.

It'd gotten used to battles of all kinds. From flawless victories to Pyrrhic dramas. And each time it observed them, a reward of sorts awaited. The feathered creature's stomach growled as it anticipated its bounty.

Would it be a piece of tender meat this time? Perhaps a feast of rodents? As it pondered this, it noticed a grey goblinoid peeking from behind a nearby bush. The falcon squawked as it sensed familiarity. The goblinoid below it had also been ordered to observe. Would the grey creature also be rewarded? To what degree, it pondered.

Then something dawned upon the bird. Observation didn't necessarily equate to a reward. Spotting anomalies, however, would.

It flew back towards its master with promising intel. This intruder mustn't be allowed to observe. This anomaly must be dealt with swiftly lest a meagre meal await its beak.

* * *

"How many?" Rak growled.

"I don't know. They're moving too fast and... dying too fast," the scout replied, not daring to meet Rak's bloodthirsty eyes.

"Useless," Rak scoffed before peering at the sky. "At least their bird's gone."

Rak ploughed his axe into the ground in front of him and sat upon its knob. "If they're dying too fast, then that means they're getting exhausted."

"Which means we have a chance at revenge."

He glanced at his men and, from their looks, knew retreat wasn't an option. They too demanded recompense for the horrors the bereke had inflicted. Many had lost family members in the previous raids.

Blood demanded blood, something Rak knew all too well.

"Hem, you with me?"

Hemgall split his double-headed axe into two. The runes on its hilt glowed a soft purplish hue. "Always."

"Are you sure, Hem? If we report back to the Frontier, I'm sure Lev will—" Orva stopped once she saw there was no emotion in Rak's eyes.

Hem knelt in front of her. "Orva, when Rak's like this, nothing will get through to him. That, and I feel as much hatred for them as he does."

"But retreating is the only sensible thing we can do! Even if they're exhausted, I'm sure they'd rather kill goblinoids than their own!" Orva insisted.

"I know. But who will avenge our people then? Many of them were part of the exodus. They put their faith in us and Pàrras to protect them and their future, and in return, worked hard to supply us with food, cattle, and liquor."

Hemgall stood again. "If we don't wipe out the bereke now, then when will we repay our debt to the poor souls who died at their hands? How many of our men, especially Rak's, would keep their sanity knowing that they let the killers of their kin go scot-free."

Orva nodded as she realised Hemgall's stubbornness matched Rak's. She couldn't blame the two; their perseverance had probably been the main reason they'd survived in the caverns. "Then I'll support you from the back. Just because I wanted to play it safe doesn't mean I don't want to tear those bastards a new one," she said with newfound determination in her voice.

"And I'll translate your choice words to their accursed tongue," Servius added.

Rak flashed a vicious grin. "That's more like it!

He turned to his soldiers and raised his axe high. "Men! Prepare to charge! Whatever it takes, we'll expel these vermin from our lands! Make it known that Parras is not a force to be trifled with!"

Rak's men met his command with a boisterous cheer.

"Let's bleed those bastards dry 'til the last drop!" Rak announced before charging towards the sound of metal against metal. Towards the battlefield where brothers killed brothers.

Once the enemy was in sight, Rak and Hemgall exchanged nods before splitting their army into a two-pronged formation. And sure enough, just as the scout had told him, the battle was nearing its end, with one side of the bereke finishing off the remainder of the other.

As the goblinoids charged closer, the bereke's dreams of mead and battle tales evaporated. What came instead was a wave of panic.

Many yelped before taking up their weapons once more. They grumbled as they resumed a defensive stance with their shields raised high.

"Keep the bonfire burning, men!" a bald-and-bearded bereke instructed as the bird on his shoulder gulped down a piece of mutton. "We'll need to burn a lot of bodies after this!"

The commander petted his falcon. "Aren't you a beaut. And to think I doubted you minutes ago."

And to think you've got more fat than I, the falcon remarked internally as it peered at the commander's voluptuous proportions.

"Well, up you go again! Can't leave the she-boss waiting, can we, now?" He waved the bird off and it promptly flew away north. "Jotul will like this... development."

Once Rak's horned formation had almost encircled the bereke line, Rak raised his hand, causing his men to stop their charge.

The bereke commander approached the front of the shield wall, motioning for his men to make room. "What do we have here, more worthless meat to grind?"

"Only meat that needs to be ground up is yours," Rak spat after Servius's translation. "Orva, now!"

With a wave of her staff, Orva launched a volley of stone spikes at the first row of bereke shield bearers, killing most of them in an instant. Many bereke gasped at the surprising display of magic.

Shortly after, Rak gestured for his men to charge at the weakened bereke. Where there'd once been mockery now reigned supreme fear.

The commander's voice trembled as he stumbled back through the line of shield bearers. "Fall back to the hills! We'll make our stand there!"

"They're retreating to the hills," Servius informed Rak, "probably so their shamans can shower us with mana-imbued projectiles."

After pulling his axe out from a skull he'd split, Rak glanced at Orva, who was herself busy forming a massive ball of lighting energy.

Once it was fully charged, she launched the ball ahead of the fleeing bereke, creating a wall of pure electricity which blocked their path.

A few unlucky souls were caught inside the barrier and were fried to a crisp.

Several of the bereke shamans tried breaking through the barrier, but alas, their mana pools had already been exhausted by the infighting.

With a single swing of his axe, Rak cleaved another soldier in half before reforming his horned formation with the remainder of his men.

A spear flew past Hemgall, cutting through the tip of his right ear before whizzing behind him and hitting one of his men in the gut. "You damn bastards!" Hemgall roared before blocking another two with his axes.

Hemgall fused his axes back into a greataxe, just in time to block a third spear aimed at his chest. It flew vertically, arcing towards one of the bereke. After a sickening noise confirmed another kill, Hemgall rushed at his remaining opponents.

Once he'd gotten close enough to the spear wielders, he split his axes yet again and cleaved one of their arms off effortlessly. The remaining two knew what was best for them and fled through a momentary gap in the electric barrier.

"Orva, how long can you keep it up?" Rak shouted over the wails of the dying and wounded.

"A few more minutes at most. Finish off their shamans! They're trying to pool their mana together to break through." Another wave of energy surged from her staff and flew towards the barrier to reinforce it.

Rak nodded at Hemgall, and the two charged towards the shamans.

"Faster!" the bereke yelped in their foreign tongue just as they gathered a ball of mana strong enough to create a wide-enough gap for them and their commander to flee through.

"I don't think so, bereke scum!" Rak screamed at the top of his lungs, throwing his axe at one of the shamans.

Blood splattered from the artery he'd hit, and the shaman protecting the others fell to his knees, gurgling curses at Rak before losing consciousness.

It took a few seconds for Rak's bloodthirst to subside. His eyes focussed as he surveyed his surroundings and, sure enough, found the enemy commander. A pool of urine drenched his padded pants. Where there'd once been fear now dripped... piss.

After Rak ordered a few of his men to guard the remainder of the bereke forces, the others finished off the last of the shield bearers at the front.

Once most of the bereke forces were wiped out, he approached the commander with Servius in tow.

Rak grinned and whispered something into Servius's ear. As he did so, his eyes darted every now and then to the commander.

"What's he saying?!" the commander demanded with bated breath.

"Now, what's your life worth?" Servius translated.

CHAPTER 5

SAVAGE MONSTERS

After the battle, the surviving bereke were dragged back to the settlement, where their bone-chilling screams filled the air, especially the commander's.

"Enough! I told you what I know!" he screamed from inside a hut on the outskirts, one of the few structures that were barely scathed by the flames.

Earlier, even after his defeat and subsequent capture, the commander had tried to salvage what little was left of his pride via threats and curses. Not that Rak or any of his men could understand him, let alone care. They knew that once the time came, the interrogators—trained by Lev himself—would make the bastard and his men squeal like pigs.

Hemgall was glad that Rak had taken Lev's suggestion and brought them along; over the next few hours, they served his purposes well, since after each interrogation, the goblinoids' knowledge about the bereke grew.

With the help of Servius translating their confessions, the goblinoids learned the reason why the bereke had fought each other, and who their leader was.

Once they confirmed what they needed to know, Servius immediately ushered the bereke commander, Rak, and the rest of the squad leaders a few paces outside of the settlement.

Rak began. "Let me get this straight. So there's this woman named Jotul who has a civil war on her hands, and yet, thanks to her stupid god, she thinks Pàrras is a bigger threat? All because we're somehow inheritors of Ainshard?" he asked Servius with wide eyes. When he received a nod, he rubbed his forehead in a mixture of disbelief and astonishment.

"And we're going to take this lizardshit's word for it?" he asked in frustration. He looked down at the battered form of the bereke commander. The shivering oaf was mumbling under his breath. "What is he even saying?"

Servius shook his head. "He's praying to his god, Jotul's God, for salvation. The few mercenaries who dared to enlist know him as the Crimson One. But I doubt that war god cares about a mere commander in particular, especially one that surrendered to his enemies. Lev's men did a number on the miserable wretch, but he'll be alright in a week or two. After isolating them and separately interrogating the remainder of his men, we confirmed the validity of the information he gave us."

With a deep scowl, Rak turned his attention to Servius. "What do you mean, he'll be alright in a week or two? After all he's done, we should skin him alive in front of his men right here and now!"

"Be reasonable, Rak. I feel your pain and mourn our losses, but we need information to prevent further skirmishes on the Frontier," Servius answered.

"Then we'll keep them here and bleed them out of everything they know," Rak countered.

"That wouldn't work. The more we linger here, the more danger we're exposed to. Scouts couldn't find that damned falcon; reinforcements are probably on their way already."

Rak took out his axe, startling everyone. The distressed commander took a few step backs while tugging on his restraints. Before he could even attempt to run, Rak threw him on the ground and pinned him underneath his foot.

"What do you think you're doing, Rak?" Orva yelled.

"Ending this here and now. We can interrogate the rest further, but this bald pig is the one who ordered the massacre. His sins will be redeemed through death."

Just as he was about to bring down his axe and sever the panicking commander's neck from his torso, Hemgall grabbed the axe by the back of its head. Blood dripped from his hand as Rak stared daggers at him.

Hemgall didn't budge. Instead, he looked Rak straight in the eye and said, "I know how you feel, Rak. They have to be punished for what they've done, and I'd be a liar if I said I didn't want to be the executioner."

"Then why?"

"I hate to say it, but we need to keep this slimeball alive. At least 'til Lev can wring him dry."

"We can make it work without him! If he was so important for Jotul's plans, she wouldn't have sent him here!" Rak argued.

"Yet it's still better to use him. The more we know about Jotul's forces and their hierarchy, the better we can plan ahead. Knowing at least how to decipher the enemy's signals and messages would be a godsend by itself. More of our people would be safer if we knew how the enemy thinks."

Rak growled but couldn't argue with Hemgall's logic. After a moment of silence, Hemgall let go of the axe and Rak hooked it onto a notch on his belt.

He gave the bereke commander a kick to the gut and turned away, towards the woods.

"Hey! What was that for?" Servius yelled.

Rak shrugged. "Have Orva heal him. Once she's done, chain the pig's legs and keep him out of my sight. I can't stand being here any longer."

With that, he walked back into the settlement.

"He took it well," Grasha mused, to Servius's irritation.

"You call that well?"

Grasha chuckled. "For Rak? Very. Not that I blame him. I want to skin these bereke alive and hang them on skewers. I'm sure the behemoths and the other wildlife would love a hearty winter meal."

"Savage monsters," Servius muttered under his breath.

"What's that?"

"Nothing. We need to hurry and pack up. Orva, please tend to our *guest*."

Hearing his words, she couldn't help but groan. "Maybe having Gerwyn wouldn't have been a bad idea after all. At least I wouldn't be the one getting my hands dirty."

Surprised that she didn't hear even a chuckle from Hemgall, Orva bit her lip and gave him a worried pat on the back. He gave her a slight smile and waited for her to be done healing the commander before they too stepped toward the huts.

When the two came back, they were greeted by the sight of their forces preparing to march. With a heavy, morose mood, everyone was ready to depart from this accursed place.

Hemgall hoped that things wouldn't escalate. Even the most forgiving fool in Pàrras wouldn't deign to think of letting the captured bereke off this easily, much less their commander.

This made the task of deciding who'd escort the war criminals a headache and a half.

"The only choice I can think of is giving the bald pig to Grasha, but what should I do with the rest?" Hemgall grumbled.

"You could hand them over to Lev's men," Orva advised.

A flashback of Lev interrogating Raban surged through Hemgall's head. "Normally, I'd agree with you, but which group do you think put the most effort in establishing the settlements and bonding with their residents? Disciplined or not, I doubt they're a good choice this time."

"If they're so blinded by hatred, the interrogators would've tortured Lachas' bereke worse."

"Who do you think will take care of our prisoners when we go back to Pàrras?"

"Then I've got nothing," Orva admitted with a shrug.

They jeered at the bereke commander and his men while they were dragged out of the hut and chained together.

The captives yelped and knelt, covering their heads with their tied hands, when a few of the men began pelting them with rocks. One of the captives in the back stumbled, causing a chain reaction that toppled the others as well. In a surprising turn of events, Rak was the first to intervene. Thanks to him, it ended before the bereke received any considerable injuries.

Hemgall clicked his tongue after counting the perpetrators.

I was gonna entrust the bereke to some of those idiots. Now I have to figure out their replacements!

He threw his arms out and hissed, "Fuck it! Let's leave it to chance!"

Orva nodded. "Can't be helped. Can you help me up the horse?"

"Yeah, sure." Hemgall smiled.

He grabbed Orva's hand and held her tightly as she placed a foot on the stirrup, then heaved her up on his steed.

Not long after, the prisoner guards were allocated, and it was time to return home.

"I can't believe you gave me the fattest one," Grasha complained.

"I'm sure you can handle it," Hemgall said with a grin, much to Grasha's bemusement.

"For now, but once the cloth I placed in his mouth falls, my ears will be berated by bereke profanities."

Hemgall turned towards the hog-tied commander. He was dangling on the back of Grasha's saddle, wriggling like a worm trying to escape.

"We can't help it, Grasha. You're the best horse rider."

Grasha huffed indignantly. "You mean the best horse rider in Pàrras."

"Can't deny that," Hemgall said. "Just keep him safe and I'll pay you back. Gonna serve you some of the good stuff once we're back."

Grasha couldn't help but shudder at the offer. "Hem, your good stuff is that mushroom froth your people call *ale*. It's not."

"It's the last of its kind! The last barrels we brought from the caverns are being consumed as we speak!" Hemgall argued.

"Rarity doesn't make it any more precious. Get me some tried-and-true crimson ale when we're back and I'll call it even."

Hemgall nodded in agreement before speeding to the front of the formation to consult Rak.

"Any information from the scouts about Jotul's forces?" he inquired. Rak shook his head.

Hemgall sighed. "So we're blind. Great. The bereke we fought can't be the only ones. Other settlements are at risk, or worse, already burnt down."

"I'm sure we'll be spilling blood soon," Rak hissed. "I can sense it in my gut, Hem. The moment we let that bird escape was the moment we brought danger upon ourselves and the Frontier lands. Next time, we won't face exhausted goons.

"We'll have to fight a much greater force. Jotul's main army."

"Rak's right," Servius affirmed. "One of the things we found out during interrogation is that Jotul has an entire army of not only bereke, but korrigal as well. As someone who traded with them, I can assure you that they're a big threat, especially when riding their war rams. We better get out of here before that glorified seagull leads them towards us."

"You're scared of guys who ride oversized wool balls?" Hem jested.

"Those *wool balls* can rip your flesh and have horns that are as good at bludgeoning as any hammer. Our captives told me Jotul got one as well. I bet many opponents were trampled under her steed's hooves."

"Carnivorous sheep... Got it. Can't we still outrun them?"

Servius let out a mirthless laugh. "Good luck with that. Their rams might not be as fast as horses, but that doesn't stop the korrigal from hunting faster prey. Whether it's on the open plains or in mountainous terrain, you can run from the korrigal, but they'll still get you in the end. Heck, they'll probably track you 'til the edge of the world."

"What about weaknesses?" Rak asked.

Servius pondered for a moment. "I've never seen a korrigal using magic before. Not even runes."

"So they're inept at magic?" Orva questioned. She'd been intrigued after hearing Servius talking about the tusked ones. Most of the records she and her fellow shamans recovered in Pàrras were far too derogatory to be taken in earnest.

"Likely. They compensate for the lack of runes with fine craftsmanship and an ingenuity that I've only seen from you bogeys, especially Lev."

Hemgall shrugged. "That's something, at least."

"I guess," Rak mumbled before addressing Orva. "We'll be counting you from now on. Are you up to the task?"

She gave him a quizzical look. "Are you really asking me that?"

Just when Rak was about to reply, a horn could be heard in the distance, then was abruptly silenced.

Rak's grip tightened around his reins. He exchanged looks with Hemgall and the two nodded.

"Get into forma—"

Before he could finish, the woods ahead of the group were engulfed in a torrent of flames.

He quickly grabbed Servius and jumped off his mount. Rak's horse fell into the flames while Hemgall's stopped in its tracks and reared up in fear.

Shutting her eyes, Orva tightened her grip around Hemgall's waist, holding on for dear life, while he struggled to control his maddened steed.

What followed were the screams of horses and men alike, and a now-familiar smell of burnt flesh.

"What's happening?!" Orva yelled.

"I guess we're not the only ones who know how to play with fire! The bastards got us," Hemgall hissed once he'd regained control.

A shrill horn sounded from the nearby woods. Orva recognised it wasn't one of their own.

Hemgall brandished his axe. "I wish I could tell you to keep your eyes closed, but that's not a luxury we can afford. The bastards are coming."

As if to confirm his words, korrigal riders emerged from the woods, sitting atop their rams.

With their enemy quickly approaching them, the goblinoids' training kicked in.

Rak took out his axe and solemnly faced his enemies.

Servius gasped. "You're facing them on foot?!"

"Do I have any other choice? The moment I try to climb a horse is the moment my head falls off my shoulders. If you think you can negotiate with them, go ahead and try."

Servius sighed, tossed aside his robes, and took out his sword.

Rak stared at him and his weapon, a steel xiphos. He hadn't anticipated the darg translator to have such seasoned form.

"Edorai trading isn't a job for the weak," Servius admonished, but Rak took no offence. Instead, he savagely grinned, knowing there was no need to hold back now for Servius's sake.

"Grasha! Keep our bald *guest* from the korrigal! Their leader might go after you."

Grasha chuckled. "As if I'll let some sheepfuckers win against me! For famous cavalrymen, their form sure is sloppy."

But his excitement turned to worry once he spotted barrels being loaded into a strange apparatus several metres off. It shuttled them into a pipe aimed their way. He charged past Rak and threw a cavalry spear at one of the barrels. What followed were an explosion and the surprised screams and bleating of sheep.

When Rak turned around, he found a few korrigal and their rams running away from a burning amalgamation of bronze, leather, and shattered glass. Near the broken glass lay Grasha's spear, covered in a burning black ooze.

"Thanks," Rak told the now-listless deka.

"You're welcome." Grasha helplessly gazed at his burning spear. It had been a pricey weapon made of Brizilum steel and enhanced with weight-reduction runes, courtesy of Pàrras's shamans. "I had a loan on that," he mumbled as his weapon began to melt.

A crossbow bolt flew past his face. He turned his attention to the attacker and found it was one of the vengeful korrigal, who had gone from operating the contraption to reloading some form of crossbow similar to the ones used by the bogeys. Grasha was sure the korrigal's next shot wouldn't miss its mark.

In newfound fury, Grasha grabbed his trusty axe and, with a mighty roar, sped towards the korrigal.

Knowing that there wasn't enough time to run away, the korrigal raised his crossbow the moment he'd secured the bolt, only for his head to fly off his shoulders before his finger could find its way on the trigger.

Yet Grasha wasn't done. He grabbed a pike aimed at his horse and rode forwards, pushing its wielder onto the ground before crushing him under his steed's hooves.

A korrigal tried to attack from behind, only to receive a kick to the skull from Grasha's horse.

Seeing their unmounted brethren struggling against the deka, a few korrigal riders came to their aid.

Grasha hooked the axe in his belt and, with deft movements, flipped his newly acquired pike to face the riders head-on. As his horse picked up momentum, he held the pike under his armpit and skewered the first korrigal in the chest.

The pike's handle shattered from the force, yet Grasha didn't recoil one inch. Before the other korrigal could react, he took out his axe and began his next onslaught.

Unlike Grasha, Rak and Servius weren't faring as well. The two had managed to take down a number of korrigal, yet their enraged mounts had gotten relentless.

"When will they stop?" Servius cried before deflecting the horns of a ram with his xiphos.

Rak didn't reply. Instead, he held a ram by its horns as it fervently tried to bite his throat.

With a mighty heave, he slammed the ram sideways onto the ground. As it tried to get up, he dug his axe halfway through the beast's throat and kept cleaving at its neck until it stopped thrashing.

As he was getting up, Rak's ears twitched at a loud bleat. He jumped to the side, nearly avoiding getting entangled within the beast's horns.

The ram took a sharp turn before he tackled it once more to the ground.

"Can't deny these creatures are hard to kill!" Rak yelled as the frenzied beast tried biting his head off. Using both arms, he managed to keep its mouth shut. A few moments of struggle later, the ram slammed him against a nearby tree.

His grip loosened, Rak couldn't retain his control. The horned creature pushed him to the ground, but just as it was about to rip open his guts, a stone spike pierced its head.

After a short pause, the ram fell on top of Rak, almost crushing him under its weight. With a heave, he pushed the beast aside and got to his feet.

"You're welcome!" Orva yelled before returning her attention to the foes in front of her and Hemgall. Both of them were still on top of his steed.

The two had fallen into a rhythm. While Hemgall blocked any approaching foes with his axe, Orva rained magical death upon them.

With their tenth korrigal struck down, Orva noticed how helpless the tusked ones were against magic. Despite their bravado, some became hesitant whenever she pointed at them with her staff.

Shouldn't they have fought against that Coalition the captives kept talking about? How are they unable to hold their ground against magic users, especially a bogey shaman?

Orva's eyes widened as she came to a realisation. She turned her attention to Hemgall, who was holding off two korrigal with his split axes. "I have an idea to save everyone, but it's risky. I have to layer three spells."

Hemgall shuddered. "Who are you trying to kill, the enemy or us? You've told me that layering spells is dangerous. Heck, layering two to make that lightning wall took a lot out of you."

"Don't worry. The staff isn't a normal focus, it has fail-safes built in it. We need to do this."

"It's still dangerous," Hemgall insisted, but to his frustration, Orva refused to budge.

"Look around you. The alternative is almost everyone except us, Grasha, and Rak dies. If you don't trust me, all of those good men will die."

Hemgall sneered as he deflected another slash with an axe.

"Fine! I don't like it, but I trust you on this."

Orva smiled. "Thank you." She took a deep breath and began gathering magical energy into her staff.

Unlike with normal magic, where the energy gathered around the haze crystal in the focus, Hemgall felt the energy twirling around the entirety of Orva's staff. It swept its way to the bottom of the staff and climbed through the runes until it condensed at the top.

Hemgall would have wanted to invest more time into watching the spectacular display, but the korrigal couldn't help but barge in.

The moment they noticed all of the goblinoids taking a surprised look at the shaman, they knew something bad was about to happen. As if their ancestors descended from the Sky Horde to warn them, even they felt a chill on their magically inept skin.

With many korrigal approaching to stop Orva, Hemgall tightened his legs around his steed, making it grunt.

He gently patted its neck. "I'm sorry, but we need to hold on if we want to live. If we survive this, I'll make sure to slip in some mushroom ale with your hay."

As if understanding his words, the horse huffed in excitement. It was one of the few creatures, aside from Hemgall, that enjoyed that concoction.

Just as another korrigal approached the duo with his hammer raised high, a spear pierced through the back of his knee, followed by a swift decapitation. Hemgall nodded in appreciation as one of Rak's riders galloped past him.

"Looks like even the boss's right hand is watching our backs," the rider called out.

Soon a boom erupted, and when Hemgall looked, he saw Grasha had blown up another one of the korrigal's fire-spewing contraptions. Its hose had been aimed at him and Orva.

Seeing how everyone was not only fending off the korrigal but also driving them back, Hemgall smiled. *Maybe... maybe this will work in the end. Once Orva's spell works, we'll be—*

With the sound of another shrill horn, Hemgall's hopes shattered.

It'd come from a large mounted korrigal force led by two threatening members of their kind: a one-eyed bereke with long hair and a bald one missing a tusk. Hemgall would soon know them to be Vreskiven and Baldem.

Run, his instincts screamed upon seeing the approaching horde, but he couldn't disrupt Orva, not at this moment.

Some of the foolhardier of Rak's men faced the two. They didn't stand a chance, and the horde passed through them without much effort.

In a hint of irony, one of Rak's men, a greyborn, attempted to headbutt the much larger korrigal. Vreskiven responded with a grin and headbutted the man right back, crushing the greyborn's skull.

"Pathetic," huffed Vreskiven before speeding towards Hemgall and Orva.

In response, Hemgall placed the reins in his mouth and readied his split axes.

While Rak was dealing with Baldem, Hemgall would have to defend Orva against the menace that was Vreskiven with his horned steed.

Hemgall was outmatched in both equestrianism and combat experience, yet knew he couldn't back down with the shaman this close to finishing her spell.

This isn't fair. This isn't a fight at all! Hemgall wanted to cry after blocking the first blow of many.

Unlike the close-quarter brawlers he was used to, Vreskiven fought elusively. He always kept a short distance away from Hemgall and only charged ahead when he detected a blind spot. Try as he might, Hemgall's axe couldn't hit the korrigal.

Hemgall blocked another blow from Vreskiven's spear, but this time, his horse's legs almost gave in.

Hemgall spat out his reins and yelled, "I thought korrigal were warriors! If you're man enough, fight me head-on!".

Vreskiven let out a bored yawn. "Shut up, grey goblin. Unlike us, you have magic on your side. You're unworthy of my axe."

Hearing a clang, he turned around to check on Baldem. His nose scrunched in annoyance. Baldem had gotten off of his mount, enjoying his fight with Rak.

Raising his spear, Vreskiven turned his attention back to Hemgall. "I guess it's time to end this before my bald buffoon of a brother finds a way to ruin things. Good luck in whatever afterlife you find yourself in. The warrior life doesn't suit you."

At his command, his ram kicked up the dirt as it charged. Hemgall braced himself with shaking hands for an impact that never came.

Vreskiven had changed his pace at the very last second to avoid a spear from Grasha, yet the deka wasn't done just yet. The moment Vreskiven's ram tried to manoeuvre around Grasha's horse, it took a kick to its side from the mighty steed.

What followed was a thrust that grazed Vreskiven's cheek. He'd only managed to deflect Grasha's attack by taking out his steel axe in the nick of time.

Grasha grinned. "Instead of attacking an amateur, why don't you go after someone your own level?"

Vreskiven grimaced. "And you think you're up to it, you red, one-horned freak?"

"I'm a deka, sheep rider," Grasha shot back.

The air was electrifying. The moment the two stared each other in the eye, they knew the world wasn't built with the both of them in mind.

With his axe raised high, Vreskiven sped towards Grasha. "I'll gladly tear you limb from limb."

Grasha responded in kind. The ground rumbled under the hooves of their mounts as the poised riders readied their weapons for their clash.

Grasha unexpectedly stopped his steed and boasted, "I hate to disappoint you, but time's up!"

Before Vreskiven could comprehend Grasha's words, an immense emerald glow shone from Orva's staff as more of its light dug its way into the ground.

Giving him no chance to escape its range, thorny roots shot out of the soil and attempted to drag him deep into the earth along with his fellow korrigal.

His ram shrieked, trying to escape the tangled thorns to no avail.

"The name's Grasha, sheep rider. Remember it in your next life," he said to the half-consumed Vreskiven, but then the roots froze. The spell had abruptly ended.

Shocked, Grasha turned to Orva and found her unconscious. Hemgall dismounted his horse and laid her in front of him before pulling out a horn and signalling their retreat.

Shit. Grasha aimed his spear at Vreskiven, but a crossbow bolt flew past him, then another. A squad of korrigal was shooting at him from a distance while more of their forces came to rescue their trapped kin.

"I guess the gods favour you, so count yourself lucky, tusked pig!" Grasha screamed before he too retreated.

"I'll kill you, red one! I'll drag your rotten festering corpse to the depths of the abyss!" Vreskiven responded in kind as he struggled to free himself from the roots.

The surviving goblinoids escaped, and the korrigal didn't give chase. Not all of their brethren were as lucky as Vreskiven, with some of them having been fully swallowed by the earth.

This would later be known as the first true confrontation between Pàrras and the full force of the Mad One.

CHAPTER 6

DELEGATION

"So, if what you're saying is true," Lev started while he organised a stack of maps, "then the darg merchants from Brizilum are up to something."

"Something shady," Kul added.

Lev glanced at the old bogey. "Right, something shady."

Kul readjusted himself in his chair. "You of all people should know where that leads to."

Lev put the now-tidy stack away in one of his office drawers before seating himself opposite Kul. "I do, but I also know what'll happen if this war ends badly."

Kul abruptly stood up, but Lev motioned for him to sit down again.

"I get what you're saying, Kul, but I need to know exactly what these merchants are importing before I can do anything. You know how the council is these days."

Lev sighed. "Can't get anything new through their dense skulls. At least they're collectively focussed on something for once instead of just quibbling."

Well, two years ago you were still a child as well. Until those rocks knocked some sense into ya, Kul remarked internally before stroking his grey beard, pondering his next words. "I overheard the merchants. They were cautious about whatever it was they were selling."

"Yes, shady merchants," Lev replied, his eyes already darting towards the next pile of unorganised documents. "How cautious are we talking here? Is someone's head going to roll if word gets out?"

"With all respect, Lev, you don't seem to be listening to me."

Lev looked up from his documents and stared Kul in the eyes. "I am, but it's like I said. My resources are stretched thin. First, they want my interrogators to go to the edge of the Frontier, now they want me to make additional battle plans for each possible outcome."

Kul slammed both hands on Lev's desk. "But this is also a priority!"

Seeing Kul's crinkled eyes and the new dent in his desk, Lev devised a better way. "How about this? The council knows your loyalty lies with the Frontier and its people and respects your humble service as one of Pàrras's guards."

Kul's eyes lit up. "And?"

"And... I can try to convince them to give you the resources you need to investigate this merchant issue more thoroughly."

Lev stood up and walked towards one of his office's windows. "Look outside, Kul. What do you see?"

Once Kul joined him, he peered outside and saw several of the birdfolk being chased away by an angry blue bogey. "A fallen noble chasing away avian kids?"

"Yes, but you're missing a critical detail here. Take in the entire view."

Kul looked left and right, up and down, before noticing a few idle guards watching the young avians as they were whipped with the blue bogey's stick. "The guards... they're doing nothing. He's assaulting those children!"

"Correct. Pàrras, no, the entire Frontier is so young and fragile that we don't even have proper laws yet, not a lot of them. We've been so focussed on rebuilding the city, keeping invaders at bay and the populace happy enough, that we've forgotten about injustice."

Kul turned to face Lev. "So you did listen to what I said! The merchants are criminals, at least I think they are. They remind me of how Vyrga used his noble connections to make it even harder for his rivals to get surface world materials like wood and food into the caverns."

"Correct. For now, though, you'll have to wait until the next council session."

Kul firmly grabbed his hand and shook it. "I won't forget this, Lev. I was afraid you'd changed with your new position, but I'm glad to see the boy who stood up against Vyrga's thugs is still in there."

Lev pointed back towards his desk. "That boy never left, he only got more responsibilities—"

The office door swung open, and Bodobert's merry bells jingled as he smugly dropped another stack of documents on Lev's desk before leaving again without a word. He hadn't even regarded Eleric, who was standing outside the door and waiting for this meeting to conclude.

"—and less sleep."

Lev walked back to his desk, took a piece of parchment from the stack Bodobert dropped, and read it. "Great, the people are worried about the bereke captives Rak brought in. A wonderful combination with the already mounting issues we have with the birdfolk in the northern district."

He put the parchment back before turning his attention again to Kul. "Seems like things will boil over in the slums without a Chief of... Justice."

"Chief of Justice?"

"Your new position will need a name. Don't think we have a chief yet that handles unrest. Vyrga and I have been doing most of that."

Kul huffed in confusion. "My new position? Didn't you just say you were only going to give me resources, as in manpower?"

Lev smirked as he came to a realisation. "I did, but now I have a proper reason for the council, one which happens to be more logical if I promote you."

* * *

"Delegation!" Lev shouted from atop a pedestal. Men and women from all the goblinoid factions had gathered to hear his impromptu proposal.

"Delegation?" Hiltrude asked.

"Exactly! The act of empowering some to act for others," Lev explained as he looked around the oval council room.

Vyrga eyed Lev. "And who do you wish to empower?"

"Kul."

One look at Vyrga showed he wasn't amused by the prospect. He'd had many arduous encounters with the former overseer. Similar dissatisfaction could be seen on many of the blue bogeys' faces.

"That old overseer from the cavern days?" one from Gerwyn's faction asked.

"Correct. He's serving as one of Pàrras's guards and makes sure the streets are safe during the night."

"Which is why"—Lev raised his hands, building anticipation—"I wish to promote him to a previously non-existent position."

He pointed an index finger towards the ceiling. "Chief of Justice!"

"Don't be ridiculous, Lev!" Vyrga bellowed. "Don't you think we have more pressing matters?" The other council members nodded. "And why Kul? The old man doesn't need more stress in his twilight years!"

Lev shook his finger with a mischievous grin. "Vyrga, he's as sharp as ever. In fact, he's found a festering wound in Pàrras's social body."

Vyrga's eyebrows shot up like lightning. "You're being melodramatic, surely."

"I wish I were, but he's told me about a concerning development regarding our influx of foreign merchants. Those from Edorai in particular."

"The dargs?" Vyrga huffed but motioned for Lev to continue.

"I'm afraid so. He witnessed several of them trading suspected black-market wares."

Vyrga rubbed his temples. "I understand the old bogey's concerns, but now I'm starting to doubt your priorities."

"Well, I'm the Chief of Commerce," Lev replied matter-of-factly.

A darg argued, "What does giving an old man a judicial position have to do with commerce? It seems like he's out to get my people instead. Despite our contributions to Pàrras, many bogeys believe we're bad for their business. I wouldn't be surprised if Hiltrude put him up to this," he added, much to Servius's scorn.

"How dare you!" Hiltrude protested as she stood up from her seat and venomously stared at the darg.

The two began hurling insults at each other, and just when the chaos seemed like it would spread to the other factions, Vyrga intervened. "Enough!"

This silenced the two, along with their followers.

He was causing chaos on purpose, Vyrga surmised. *Seems whatever Kul uncovered would foil some of the merchants' plans.*

With an expressionless face, he turned his attention to Lev. "Explain yourself. How do Kul's discoveries involve you?"

"Illegal trade, especially contraband, negatively affects commerce far worse than you all think. Those goods can't be taxed without our government understanding the issue, much less controlled."

"A minor concern for the time being," the same darg scoffed.

"For now. But the sooner we handle this, the better. Time is on our side."

Murmurs filled the oval room before Meinrad stood up and walked towards the front.

"Lev's within his rights to bring this egregious development to the council's ears."

Vyrga was silent, as were the other faction leaders.

Eventually, he spoke. "I say aye. If anyone disagrees, then let it be heard with a nay, loud and clear."

Servius gave his affirmation while the room remained silent.

Meinrad looked at Lev with an understanding glint in his eyes. "Looks like you're in the clear, then."

Lev leaned inward. "Sure does."

* * *

The next morning, a scroll sporting a wax stamp of the eye of Zeja had arrived, one addressed to Kul.

A pot of soup simmered, made with spices and mushrooms he'd bought from the market. He took it from the fireplace, brought it with him to his kitchen table, and grunted. "What's this?"

Once he filled a bowl and sat down, he broke open the scroll's wax seal and pulled out its contents.

At first, Kul was excited. But with each word concerning his new responsibilities, his initial excitement turned more and more into a frown. "These youngsters always overcomplicate things."

He read one of the job rules aloud. "Justice can only be conducted when there's sufficient proof."

Kul shook his head. "I know injustice when I see it. The cavern taught me that well enough. So did my years as a warrior."

With a spoonful of mushrooms in his mouth, he continued to the next rule. "The council needs full transparency."

He almost wanted to agree before reading the disclaimer below it:

"Each case must be presented to the council, and if the assembly is in agreement, only then may it be prosecuted."

Kul almost choked on a stem before he realised something. There were quite a few prominent dargs in the council, most of them traders who had arrived months after the exodus.

With his meal swimming in his stomach, he grabbed a piece of cloth and began cleaning the table while he pondered the final rule.

"Since your first case concerns the darg merchants specifically, please attend the next commerce session. I will be present as well.

"Your friend, Lev," Kul read aloud before tucking the scroll in a cabinet. "I hope my old bones are up for the job.

"Well, I brought it on myself. Can't quit now."

And with that, Kul donned his guard attire, a simple grey tunic, and walked out of his front door.

He shielded his eyes from the sun's rays with his hand. "Looks like it'll be a beautiful day."

As he took his usual route to the guard barracks, greeting familiar faces on the way, he spotted the same blue bogey he'd seen at Lev's office yesterday murmuring to himself.

Bodobert, he recalled. Even if Kul never had much contact with the man, whether it was during the cavern days or now in Pàrras, everyone knew of the clown on the council.

Although he couldn't understand much, the ex-noble certainly didn't look happy.

"Everything alright?" Kul asked him.

Bodobert turned around with a glare. "I would be if those beak-blighted youths didn't ruin my morning.

"They oughta be punished for their mischief. But you know how it is. Feathers seek dust."

Something in his words caught Kul's attention. "Dust?"

"Haze dust. They're always on that stuff, snorting it like it's Jom's breath."

Without wasting a word, Kul started sprinting towards the Grand Halls. *That's it!*

CHAPTER 7

THE PLAN

"This isn't enough," Lev muttered.

He stood over a large table in the war room, overlooking a detailed map showing their territories, settlements, and Crimson Lord-blessed enemies. All of their forces and buildings were represented by wooden figurines, courtesy of Vyrga.

Other than Lev, only Rak, Volker, Hemgall, Bolo, and Vyrga himself were still present. Shahn and Raban had already left.

After this war is over, we need to thank the scouts and the shamans for their hard work, Lev remarked to himself after taking another look at the detailed map. Almost everything had been accounted for. It contained information from both their scouting efforts and documents uncovered from the city's ancient library.

"If only we had the same gifts as our enemies, things would've been easier," Vyrga dryly said before placing a figurine representing an outpost near an old mountain road from Ainshard's time. While it was dangerous due to the presence of sky devils this time of the year, it was large enough for an army and led straight from the bereke land into the Frontier's heartland.

Lev said, "Why else do you think I opted to build a fort along the largest river? Even if they don't take the route facing it, we can still use the boats the dargs brought to evacuate any farmers we have left in the settlements. This would allow us to respond immediately to Jotul's forces."

Vyrga chided, "Let's hope that stone monstrosity of a fort proves itself useful. Even if we ignore the ludicrous costs, the manpower needed for such a project could have been used to build a dozen smaller ones out of wood. We'd have covered more ground and bled the bereke dry as they encroach upon our lands."

Lev shook his head. "I considered that, and the outcome would've been disastrous. All of our intel shows that the enemy are siege experts. Unless we want to offer the lives of our men on a platter, bringing the fight to a single heavily-fortified location with advantageous terrain is our best option."

Volker placed some wooden outposts and relay stations around the forest. The glum look on his face spoke for itself.

"Anything wrong, Volk?" Hemgall asked, yet Volker was hesitant to speak his mind.

"Go on," Lev told him. "Maybe you'll enlighten us."

Volker sighed. "I doubt it, sir."

"Still, anything could help."

"We're being too reactive, and Jotul is used to that. Now that the Coalition prisoners know we're fighting Jotul, they're singing like corpse-eaters after a massacre, hoping we can crush or weaken her. But from what the bereke we captured who fought Jotul tell us, her forces are not only good at sieges, but they excel at breaking all forms of defences, especially since her generals tend to attack different fronts with specialised forces."

Volker divided the pieces representing Jotul's army. He pushed away most of the figures before placing two pieces representing korrigal in the north and a bereke figure in the south, which was Jotul—a wooden bereke with a crown. He followed by surrounding it with a plethora of goblinoid figures.

"She's not the only one who can divide and conquer. We should leave a token force to distract her minions while we strike at her. When the rest of her army hears the news from her birds, they'll abandon their goals and come to her aid."

Bolo shook his head. "I mean no offence, and I know it's a sound plan, but it's not going to work the way you expect it to. We won't be able to hide a large army from her little feathered rats. We need to drag her deep into our lands so that even if she's informed, she has no way out."

"I have to agree with Bolo for once," Rak scoffed. "I don't see the korrigal falling for your plan. They'd either try to capture Pàrras and use it as a bargaining chip in case we capture Jotul alive or burn the city to the ground if we kill her."

After hearing everyone's arguments, Volker deflated like a balloon.

Lev gave him a reassuring smile. "Hey, don't lose confidence. You gave us a good plan, but it needs some minor tweaks."

He moved Pàrras's pieces and had the majority of their forces surround the korrigal and the other bereke, leaving a token force to face off against Jotul near the stone fort.

"What if we deal with her generals first and only lure Jotul afterwards?"

"So you're saying you want to deal with Jotul yourself?" Vyrga asked, frowning.

"Indeed," Lev smugly replied.

Vyrga crossed his arms. "I refuse. If your irksome Chief of Justice fails, you need to be the one to keep an eye on the darg merchants. Try as they might to supply us for the war effort, we can't trust them after their latest debacle in the council."

"You of all people should know that Kul will deal with it," Lev bit back. "Even back when he was a mere overseer, he didn't leave a single stone unturned. Now that there's no one to chain him, we have nothing to worry about."

Vyrga rolled his eyes. "How wonderful. But we're going to need more boats from the same merchants if we want to evacuate faster. Did you think about that as well when you approved Kul's mission?"

Lev sighed. "You're right. I'll wait until enough boats arrive. After that, though, I won't hold him back."

With his little debate done, Lev turned his attention back to the map. "Now, going back to our main topic, we need to find a way to deal with the birds. Reducing their numbers will make things much easier. The obvious options are trapping the things and finishing them off, but that'd be taxing for the scouts alone."

"Without that Crimson One's influence, aren't they just normal birds?" Hemgall asked. "Some fancy bait is all we need. We'd leave a box full of the good stuff, cover it with pitch, and set it on fire when it's full of birds."

"How simpleminded. From what we've seen during her spying, she has a multitude of species under her control," Vyrga said. "If they act naturally, they wouldn't approach each other without the Crimson One's influence. It'd also be expensive to bait them all, and we're not made of money."

Hemgall crossed his arms. "It's easy. Your lackeys placed a giant golden statue *in your glory* in the Grand Halls, right? We just need to melt that ugly thing and have the dargs, untrustworthy as they turned out to be, deal with it. Once the war's over, maybe we could deal with the rat the statue's based on."

Vyrga scoffed and turned his attention back to Lev. "Another issue is that Jotul, or rather the Crimson One, would know when and where the birds die."

After Lev contemplated Vyrga's words, a large grin sprouted on his face. "We can trick them."

"What?"

"Bait the enemy. Falsify defensive positions. Have them focus on the wrong locations. They'll catch on eventually, but until then, we can use all these tactics and more to make Jotul bleed."

"That could work," Vyrga begrudgingly admitted.

"It will, and the distractions will help us deal with the other threats."

"Like the korrigal," Hemgall said, then went on yapping. "Those tusked warriors shouldn't be underestimated, especially the one named Vreskiven and his brother. We only managed to escape thanks to Orva."

Lev looked at him. "How is she? I couldn't check on her due to the never-ending pile of documents piled up on my desk."

Hemgall gave him a reassuring nod. "She says she's fine. I would have been there, but she decided I should focus on the war. I'd give her a week or so until she's fully recovered."

"I'm glad that she's better. We need every man and woman in the field, so I wish her a safe recovery."

Hemgall snickered. "If you want to send her back to war, you better give us an army of shamans as well. I can't think of another way to fight those tusked ones."

Lev playfully threw a few shaman figures towards Hemgall. "Take as many as you need, but leave a few for our second-biggest threat."

"Of course. Knowing you, Jotul won't know what hit her." Hemgall replied with a grin.

Lev responded with a sly smile of his own. "I never said they'll be for Jotul."

"What?"

Lev grabbed another bereke figure and placed it next to Jotul on the map.

"I see you've put a collar on the figure. How fitting," Vyrga said after studying the figurine.

"Vilde is known as the hound of the Crimson One, after all," Lev replied.

"Excuse me, sir," Volker said. "How is Vilde such a big threat? From what we've gathered, her army's the weakest of the three. They mostly act as Jotul's inquisitors."

"Never underestimate your enemies. That's the worst mistake you could ever make in battle," Lev warned his protégé.

"But they're nothing more than fanatics! Armed fanatics, sure, but still a barely coherent mob in the end," Volker blurted.

"Say, Volker, do you remember how we started out?"

"What do you mean, sir?"

"Back when we were in the cavern, how did things go?"

Volker nervously turned to Vyrga. Despite the irritation on his face, Vyrga begrudgingly gave him a nod to proceed.

"You protected people, including me, from thugs by making a deal with Rak which improved all of our lives. We wouldn't have lasted long on the expedition without your equipment and training. We also wouldn't have lasted long against..." He stopped. He turned his eyes to a disgruntled Vyrga and gulped.

"Oh, continue. Please share with us more of your completely un-biased view of past events," Vyrga remarked, his calm words barely hiding the icy tone beneath them.

"Gelmar," Lev continued in Volker's stead. Vyrga stared daggers at him, but he continued, "You say without my training, you wouldn't have lasted against Gelmar, but that's not the full picture. Without Kathaga's blessing, many of our men wouldn't have had the grit to become such an effective force."

Volker shook his head. "There were still elements at play, sir."

"There were, but we can't ignore the boost in morale from hearing the goddess of war is on your side. That, along with our tricks, played its part in allowing a mob of barely trained miners to beat a large group made of experienced killers."

"I understand, sir."

Lev smiled. "Good. Now guess why Vilde is dangerous. The bereke commander told us everything we needed to know about her past."

"She's a fallen warrior who failed her duty and was given a chance by a mad god. He, along with the daughter of her former sire, became her salvation. She's ready to cleanse the lands of her master's enemies. She forged an army of believers, an army to not only bring salvation to their lands but expand its borders."

Lev slammed the bereke figurine near Pàrras, startling his second-in-command.

"Rabid fanatics are a tactician's worst nightmare. They always flip the chessboard with their sheer resolve. They'll never tire, never fear, and never hunger until every speck of dust that insulted their reason for existence is wiped off the face of the world."

Volker shuddered. "But it's not possible... Even if their resolve doesn't break, their bodies will if they're as reckless as that."

Lev grimaced. "They can always rest when their enemies are wiped out, and as for food? If they can't find it in our settlements like they did previously, the dead are a good source of meat."

"Y-You don't mean..." Volker began.

Lev eyed Volker. "Ask the captives. The ones who fought against Jotul. They might hate us, but they'll wholeheartedly share their grievances, especially when it comes to Vilde."

Volker's face turned pale as he shuddered in disgust. He turned towards Vilde's figure and stared at it in a new and unsettling light. "That's monstrous."

"Most rabid dogs are like that," Vyrga proclaimed. "Even our kind isn't safe from fanatical zealots. During the height of the last generation's rebellion, zealots took control of the temple of Zeja and riled the people up to commit atrocities against the Jiira. Cannibalism being the least of their crimes."

Seeing the fear in Volker's eyes brought a malicious grin to his face, but a cough from Lev made him calm down.

"Though some good happened," Vyrga continued. The elders say Zeja herself chose Kathaga. Her first act as the head priestess was to cleanse the temple of the wretches and demand a ceasefire from the nobles. If it weren't for her, who knows if the Jiira would have allowed for Zeja's worship to continue."

"I see..." Volker meekly answered.

"I hope this drilled into your head why we need to annihilate her forces. Zealots are abominations and we should take all precautions against any of her dirty tricks, especially poisoning our water supplies," Vyrga stated before placing a few soldier tokens near significant streams and rivers.

Vyrga tightened his fist around Vilde's figurine. "They'll use every dirty trick known to bogeykind and justify it in the name of their god. Nothing is sacred in their hands. We have to annihilate them before they annihilate us."

"But wouldn't Jotul's forces be the same? She's their god's champion," Volker asked.

Vyrga chuckled, then shook his head. "And Zeja chose Kathaga and Lev. Gods aren't stupid, boy. They just know how to use desperate people. Even if they're not as loyal to the cause, I doubt a war god would leave their champion with just grovelers and sycophants."

"And the lackeys of nobles would help. Not everyone believes in her cause so they're likely using her as she's using them. And if the Crimson One and Jotul are as mad as they say, things will be better for us," Lev assured. "Going up against a sound mind, now, that would be a different tale."

Hemgall let out a loud yawn and headed to the exit, "I think my head will pop if I stay here much longer, so if you'll excuse me, I'll be on my way to the tavern."

Lev stretched his arms. "You're not wrong. It's getting late, and we've spent enough time in this cramped room. It's better to freshen up and continue our work tomorrow. Maybe, by some miracle, we'll come up with a way to increase our odds."

He turned his attention to Vyrga. "Do you agree?"

Vyrga closed his eyes and grunted. "Dismissed."

Not long after, everyone emptied the room, and after a short detour to check on Ghorza, Lev went to his home.

Night fell. Just as he was about to head to sleep, he felt Gherm's presence.

This will be a hard war, Lev. Do you think things will work out? Gherm asked him.

Lev stared at the ceiling for a while before he answered. *We'll try our best to make sure they do, but in war, nothing is guaranteed. Even an empire can find itself having a hard time against mere rebels, so who knows which way the wind will blow. I just know that I won't let the Crimson One waste our efforts. His minions won't touch a hair on our people.*

Sensing his words satisfied Gherm, Lev smiled and slowly closed his eyes.

When he opened them again, he found himself floating above a white plane that stretched into infinity, with nothing in sight in all directions.

His eyes widened when he spotted a few greyborn children playfully running below him. When he looked up, he saw an eerily familiar massive orb descending towards the children. Materials floated within the translucent orb, much like in the one he'd seen in Pàrras when they'd first discovered the city.

A giant lightning bolt streaked down from the orb and struck near the children. Instead of inducing fear, it only attracted the kids. A boy jumped towards the orb, yearning to touch it.

Then a weird but familiar feeling overcame Lev. He tried to resist looking at the orb, but his head was held in place by an unseen force.

Once the orb had lowered itself close enough, the other kids formed a ring around the boy. He was now nearly able to reach it with his fingertips. "Almost!" the boy exclaimed, and the others giggled in anticipation.

As soon as his fingers touched its surface, their giggles turned to bone-chilling screams and the orb exploded into blinding white light. Even though Lev couldn't see what was happening, he could still hear screams, and before long, sickening screeches.

The light quickly shrank into a singular point, before that too dissipated into nothingness. As Lev regained his bearings, he saw what had become of the children. Where there'd once been greyborns now stood the race that had declared war on all of goblinkind. The bereke.

Lev felt their hatred as they pierced him with their gazes. He knew they wanted to hurt him, kill him.

CHAPTER 8

UNVEILED ORIGINS

Stunned in horror, Lev stared at the nascent bereke as they took their first fumbling steps.

This is just a dream, those children never existed, Lev reaffirmed to calm himself down.

He couldn't feel his body anymore, he wasn't even sure he had one. He was just an observer and this dream, or whatever it was, would force him to watch until the end.

Once Lev accepted his predicament, any confusion, anger, and sorrow dwindled and were replaced by a calmness, one so tranquil that it overpowered all.

The world around Lev started to mould around him once more, and his vision darkened.

A flash of brilliant colours filled his vision. Once the light subsided, he found himself overlooking a large forest clearing. Within, he saw clay huts, simple tilled fields, and scattered stone tools. Lev knew it to be a goblinoid village once he saw their familiar short, green ears.

He spotted a young goblin cooking some meat on a skewer using a miniscule flame fuelled by a charcoal kiln. It was like watching a movie, but at the same time, he existed in the moment. He felt he was a part of this world as much as it was a part of him.

A trail of purple light stretched towards where the forest line came nearest to the kiln.

Where the light ended, a tall and slender goblin man wearing a fur mantle materialised. He walked out of the forest towards the boy.

"Hey!" an older goblin yelled. "Who are you? I haven't seen you around here before."

The towering goblin merely glanced at what Lev presumed was the boy's father and continued walking towards the boy staring at him with confusion.

"Ainshard! Go inside, now!" his father yelled in desperation.

As Ainshard was about to make a run for it, time froze in place, with only the tall goblin able to move about as he pleased.

He approached the father and leaned in to whisper something.

Lev couldn't hear what was said, nor could he see the tall goblin's mouth, as it was covered by his spindly fingers.

If only I could move!

Time resumed, and the father's eyes glazed over as he responded with a soft mutter. "I see. So that's how it is. Okay.

"Ainshard, you can come out now. He's just a traveller. Why don't you help me with the kiln, boy."

Ainshard peeked from behind the wooden door of their hut. "A-Are you sure? He doesn't look friendly at all."

"Yes. Yes, I'm sure. Come out and help your father."

"O-Okay."

Ainshard walked towards his dad, who'd already taken a piece of hot charcoal from the kiln. It was in his hand. He was merrily swinging it around, causing bits and pieces of it to fall off. "The traveller told me something amazing. Yes, truly amazing," he added as the charcoal burnt his flesh.

Ainshard took a step back. "B-But Dad, you told me to go inside."

He looked around but couldn't see the tall goblin anymore. "Where's that tall man?"

"We need to be quick, boy, he's on his way! They don't visit us that often, so we have to make haste! Yes, make haste, just like he told me."

"The traveller's coming back?" Ainshard asked, taking another step back. "Why aren't you letting go of the charcoal? Throw it away, it's hurting you!"

His father shook his head and flashed a mischievous grin. "Oh no. Someone else, someone great. Yes, that's what he told me!"

"Dad, can I go back inside? I'll get the ointment for your wounds."

Instead of maintaining its joyous facade, Ainshard's father's face contorted in a fit of sorrow and rage.

"NOW! NOW! NOW! NOW!" he screeched as he charged towards Ainshard with the charcoal clenched in his hand. "NOW!"

Ainshard ran as fast as he could, but his father's speed was overpowering. He hadn't expected him to be this fast.

With a lunge, the old goblin threw Ainshard to the ground and held him by the throat.

Ainshard's mouth was forcibly opened with one hand while his father spooned the charcoal fragments in with the other. Had Lev's emotions not been tampered with, he'd have screamed in sync with the boy.

Ainshard began to convulse, his eyes rolling back in his head, while his father grinned in maddened glee. Eventually, his smile waned and was replaced with a baffled look.

"Ainshard! What's happening?!" his father yelled, having come back to his senses.

"Ainswald, everything okay back there? Ainshard fooling around again?" a middle-aged female goblin asked from a few killigs away.

Once she'd gotten close enough to see what had transpired, she dropped her washing basket. "What happened to your boy?! Someone help!"

The other goblins noticed the commotion and came running.

Now Ainswald held his son in his arms. The boy's convulsions worsened before suddenly halting.

"What's happening?!" the father exclaimed, his voice swelled with desperation and regret.

With a cough, coals were spat from Ainshard's mouth. He started to breathe again.

As soon as Ainswald felt his son's lungs fill with air again, tears filled his vision. "Ainshard! What did I do to you... how could I..."

He looked around at the crowd inside the hut and found disgusted expressions staring right back. He whimpered, "I was adding wood to the kiln, and before I knew it, I was holding charcoal and..."

"I swear, I don't know what came over me!" Ainswald hollered. "It felt like I wasn't in control anymore!"

"Liar! You hurt that poor boy! Have you truly gone mad this time?!" the middle-aged woman yelled. "You're sick, Ainswald! Sick!"

"Poor Ainswald's gone mad. The greyborns enslaving his wife must've broken him," a younger woman murmured.

"Didn't he only have one son? How could he do such a thing?" an elder added.

Ainshard gasped. "Where... am I?"

He looked left and right, and screamed in fear, causing his father to jump back in shock.

"This can't be real!" Ainshard yelled in a tongue his father couldn't understand. "My mouth! It hurts so much—water! Get me water!"

Lev wanted to observe Ainshard further, but before he knew it, he'd floated above a mountain range. He squinted his non-existent eyes, confused, as the mountains felt familiar. Then it clicked that they resembled Sinner's Reach, albeit with six giant towers instead of its rocky fingers. Giant orbs hovered above the towers.

Lev was dragged past the towers and lowered to what had to be one of the largest entrances to the bogey caverns. Instead of Jiira sentry towers in front of a gaping hole, he saw an unfamiliar ornate gate.

When he flew through the entrance, he found a huge underground city. Its buildings were made of moulded stone. Several ziggurats lay within each residential ring and contained the same runes he'd seen on the shrines and Pàrras's monoliths. What surprised Lev the most, however, was that both bogeys and hivelings filled the streets in uncanny harmony.

Lev gawked at the sight of a female greyborn, lavishly adorned with jewellery, lying on a sedan carried by a warrior hiveling. By her side were two blue bogeys in servant attire tending to her needs.

He wanted to rub his eyes in disbelief, not that he had eyes.

Lev saw greyborn youths zipping past him on winged hivelings. "Are you gonna let me win this one too?" a greyborn boy at the front of the hiveling formation yelled.

"It's not my fault my hiveling's so slow," a greyborn girl responded. She gently brushed its head and chided, "I shouldn't have fed you all those treats."

Her hiveling chirped with satisfaction.

"More treats? You can have them if we win for once!"

Lev flew towards one of the orbs, which powered a giant shrine in the innermost ring of the city. Groups of greyborns gathered on its platform before being transported away. There was no shaman in sight aiding them; they seemed to have innate control over the shrine and its destination. He surmised these shrines linked to all parts of this lost greyborn civilization, be they underground or aboveground.

A time lapse played in front of Lev's eyes, and he saw the city expand beyond the caverns. He saw places turn from luscious valleys to sprawling industrial cities.

He saw war, slavery, much like he'd seen in this life and his past one.

Lev witnessed a legion of greyborns heading north, into unknown lands. In front was their slave army. The slaves mindlessly shuffled about, their rune-engraved collars having stripped them of their free will.

Time flew at an incredible pace, and Lev saw how one by one the mighty greyborn cities fell into chaos. What started as minor rebellions and riots caused by unaligned, desperate resistance movements eventually turned into precise assaults on small greyborn forts. With each victory, alliances sprouted between the once-divided forces as they upped the stakes.

Before Lev now stood an army composed of various races, mainly goblinoids, but also what he guessed were korrigal and kobolds. He watched as they gathered in front of Sinner's Reach. Leading them all was a goblin wearing a silk mouth veil.

Lev spotted several burn marks near his mouth and nostrils once the wind briefly blew the veil aside.

"We stand at the precipice of salvation. My masters need but a few more days to complete their side of the agreement," the veiled goblin announced, his words followed by the cheers of his comrades.

"May Ainshard's forces be victorious and our freedom come with it!" a bald, red-bearded blue bogey boisterously added, fist raised in the air.

From behind him, a female green bogey stepped out. Her white hair waved by his shoulder. "Father, we should deliver the final blow now. We've laid siege to the grey sinners' capital for months. Show your masters that Ainshard can accomplish anything with his own willpower."

The veiled goblin shook his head. "Not this time, Zeja. The masters will make sure we won't even need to conquer the other strongholds."

"But—"

Zeja wanted to protest but stopped once the muscled blue bogey stepped in between them, his wide frame blocking her view. "Your father may be Ainshard, but that doesn't make you his equal. Listen to him for once. His eyes have seen more than ours or the sinners' ever will."

She pouted. "Whatever you say, oh great general Jom, fist of Ainshard."

Lev looked at Sinner's Reach and its outstretched palm and saw the same ornate door blocking Ainshard's path. This time, however, the door had cracks all over the place, with massive boulders lying at its base. Moreover, the towers acting as the mountain's fingers were now slowly crumbling, and the orbs atop them spawned bolts of lightning that hit the tower's foundation at random intervals. Slowly but surely transforming the molten stone into the fingers of the present Sinner's Reach.

After days had passed, with the sun and moon zipping past the horizon, Lev saw movement in the massive door. It opened up just enough for a mass of greyborns carrying white banners to pass through.

"They're finally here to repent for their sins!" Jom bellowed as he brandished his huge steel swords. "With blood."

He glanced at Zeja's tent. "If Ainshard's right, hijacking their oh-so-precious towers is just the start. We'll see several suns on the horizon any moment now."

Zeja yawned as she slid her tent's flap aside. "Yeah, yeah. In the east and west, I know. Too bad we won't be able to fight the sinners anymore. All it took was a couple months of sitting idle on our asses to have those *masters* of his do the fun bit."

Jom laughed as he walked towards her. "That's right, they'll be gone long before they can reorganise their armies! But we can't miss what your father has worked for decades to achieve, can we? Now, cheer up and dress yourself, young lady."

"Fine. Where is he, anyway? Mother should be here any moment now."

"He's waiting for you outside his war tent. The other generals are there as well. As for Andrava, I hope she's in the approaching crowd of sinners, like we planned for."

"Aren't you coming?" Zeja asked as she tied her hair in a ponytail.

"Nah, Ainshard told me to supervise the pillaging of the mountain. See it as a reward for all our strife."

"Sinner's Reach."

Jom frowned. "What do you mean?"

Zeja pointed at the towers in the far distance as a bolt of lightning hit the mountains' palm. "That's what my father calls it, right? The place where the sinners reached for the heavens with those accursed towers of theirs."

"Heh," Jom scoffed. "Won't do them any good now. What are those orbs for, anyway?"

Zeja shrugged. "Don't know, but the *great* Ainshard told us not to destroy them, so they must be just as important to our cause as theirs."

* * *

As she approached Ainshard, Zeja couldn't help seeing the crimson-eyed bird on his arm, but she decided not to inquire about it. It'd always been a mystery, to her and everyone else, how her father could communicate with beasts. He never shared the secret behind his miracles.

Once the two were together, Zeja tried to kneel, but Ainshard held her shoulder in place.

"It's no time to kneel; we have to greet your mother and her escorts. Then we'll head to the city."

Zeja, stunned, turned her head towards Sinner's Reach. "What about the plan?"

"It shall still commence, but our masters have told me that she opened the gates once most of her kind sealed themselves in the underground capital. We'll give the greyborns one last gift before they're gone."

Once again, Lev's vision shifted, and he bore witness to what happened next.

The once-glorious city was ransacked by Ainshard's vengeful army as they scoured and looted each residential ring. A scant remainder of armed greyborns hastily destroyed as many shrines and relics as they could in a last-ditch attempt to keep their technology from Ainshard's reach.

Entire ziggurats caved in on themselves, and the cries and curses of the greyborns who refused to hide echoed throughout the cavern: a mix of sorrow, pain, and hatred mainly aimed at the traitors who chose to follow Ainshard's wife outside.

Once the pillaging was done and the army had retreated back to the surface, it was time to initiate the final step in Ainshard's plan.

His army moved to a mountain a distance away from the city to witness the master's miracle. Jubilation was the only thing on everyone's mind as they prepared to enter a new era.

"Are you sure you don't want to join us? The view would be better from atop the plateau," Zeja asked Jom, who was drinking ale with a kobold, a fellow general who'd sworn his men to Ainshard's cause.

"Nah, kid. I've had my fun in the city. Now's the time for drinks and games. Can't say the same about your mother and her lackeys."

Zeja's brow furrowed. "She made things easier. Without her, we would've lost more good men to those wretched sinners."

"Andrava's a wretched sinner, kid, remember that," Jom said before taking a swig of his ale. "And I'm sure even though she realised the mistakes of her kind, she and her followers aren't happy that they doomed their kin. What kind of monster would? She'd be more hated if she got out of her tent and happily stood with you and your father to witness his miracle."

"But…"

"Save it, Zeja. Let's not sour everyone's moods. You go join your father. He's been waiting for this day long enough."

With a huff, she walked until she reached a plateau on the mountain's summit. There she saw five tall goblins clad in ornate armour, four uncomfortably close to her father, their eyes glued to the city, while one with a red plume on his helmet looked away in what she perceived as a mix of shame and disgust. She hadn't seen them before, and neither did she know why they were standing next to her father.

Something about them felt wrong. Their forms kept twisting and shifting like smoke burning from wet wood, and their expressions spanned the full emotional spectrum. Their features were made anew every time she laid eyes on them, and the gaping holes that were their eyes held the secrets of life yet none of its joy.

Throughout all her life and all the battles she'd faced, Zeja was never the type to submit to fear. Yet for the first time, a primal horror filled her, and she instinctively took a step back. If Ainshard hadn't lunged forwards to catch her hand, she would've fallen to her death.

He pulled her back from the ledge and hugged her.

"What…"

"It's okay," Ainshard whispered to calm her down. Suddenly he looked up and ahead. "It's starting," he muttered.

She pushed him away and irreverently yelled, "What are they, Ainshard?!"

He turned his gaze towards the city.

Before she could protest, Zeja's ears twitched. She felt magic building up to a heretofore-unknown degree, and heard distant wails from the east and west. She turned towards Sinner's Reach, only to witness droplets of light pouring on the city.

And sure enough, just like Jom told her, something similar happened in the eastern and western mountain regions. Even though these rain clouds were distant blobs, they had an undeniable glow not unlike the sun's.

During the shining rain, Sinner's Reach trembled as if it were moaning in pain. Flocks of hivelings flew in terror from every possible exit, trying to get as far away as they could from their home.

Suddenly, the droplets of light stopped, and so did the wails and the trembling. An eerie silence engulfed Sinner's Reach before a tremendous pillar of light, reaching all the way to the throes of the heavens, engulfed the hand and the city within it, followed by a heart-wrenching scream. She saw the towers melt as their orbs were engulfed by the light.

Finally, Ainshard answered her question. "They are our guiding light in this cruel world."

Zeja stood silent before falling to her knees, unable to process the horror that she'd witnessed.

Lev could do nothing but watch the horrendous spectacle.

The odd goblins around Ainshard departed not long after the light show ended. Ainshard ordered his men to march back to the eviscerated city. They were hesitant at first, since some of the hivelings were already returning. Nonetheless, they believed in their leader.

As the army cautiously made its way through the broken gates of the city, Andrava and the rest of the defecting greyborns immediately used their magic to calm down the hivelings. Seeing no intact shrine in the city, the army descended through the cavern. Once they reached the second floor, they spotted a few wailing warrior hivelings.

Zeja approached one and looked into its compound eyes. The creature bent lower to the ground when she tried to touch its head. Once she felt it was comfortable enough, she gently rubbed her hand over its hard exoskeleton.

Even though the army had brought fresh panic to the giant ants, they didn't attack the invaders unless provoked.

"Hey Zeja, this one wants us to follow!" Jom shouted as he motioned towards a hiveling drone nudging him forwards with its antennae.

The sole drone led them to the third floor, where other hivelings of various sizes had gathered a pile of crystals emitting light.

"That's strange," Jom said as they watched from afar. "The sinners never had those. Why do I feel magical energy coming from those stones, and why... am I crying?" A tear streamed down his face. Zeja wasn't feeling any better, nor did any of the turncoat bogeys.

When she approached the crystals and tried to pick one up with her trembling hand, the hiveling drone rubbed against her, as if it were seeking solace for a great sin. But when a goblin tried to take one, all of the hivelings furiously clicked their mandibles.

"Hey, calm down!" Zeja urged the hiveling next to her. She patted it on the head, unable to comprehend how the fearsome mounts of her enemies were reduced to such a pitiful state.

Once Ainshard and his shaking wife approached the crystals, the hivelings became even more agitated.

Both Jom and Zeja, along with their respective men, saluted their leader.

"Report the situation," he commanded.

"Seems that not even bodies were left after the miracle," Jom said. "It's... creepy. Horrible, even. Should we check the other floors?"

"The sinners had to go for the sake of us all. And yes. They've left many important relics necessary to rebuild civilization."

Jom scratched his head. "I don't quite understand. Most sinner tools won't work without magical energy. You know that well."

Instead of responding, Ainshard brought out a calming rod, a device used to subdue hivelings. It had a modified hilt, yet even with the modifications, Jom knew it would never work in Ainshard's hands, chosen one or not. Only bogeys with an affinity for magic could use the runes, and the sinners were best at it.

Jom was shocked when Ainshard picked up one of the glowing crystals and his skin sizzled. He didn't mind. He smashed the crystal into smaller fragments and placed one into the hilt of the rod, which brought the device to life.

The hivelings had seen enough and let out a shrill cry. Before they could attack, Ainshard activated the rod, and the infuriated ants plopped on the ground, wailing in anguish.

"What in the world just happened?" Jom asked, wide-eyed.

"I merely used the gift our masters bestowed upon us. These crystals shall be the fuel of the new era."

At his words, Andrava fainted.

Everyone rushed to her side to support her, and Ainshard instructed the deserters to escort her back to the surface, where she and her grey kin would be looked after by the detachment force he'd left behind.

Over time, as they organised more expeditions into the sinner caverns, they made three major discoveries about their new crystalline fuel source.

The first being all the crystals. The lower they descended through the caverns, the more they found. If left alone for weeks, they could regenerate. And a few hivelings had started to swallow the crystals. Upon dissecting them, the expeditions found a noncorrosive version of the rock in the creatures' abdomens.

Lev helplessly watched as Ainshard used his newfound resources to lay the foundation of his empire by building an outpost in a valley on the other side of Sinner's Reach. He watched as the outpost turned into a village, and before long, a sprawling city built with recovered greyborn technology.

Pàrras.

He concluded that the same outcome that befell Sinner's Reach must have transpired in all of the major greyborn cities. Only a few could've survived the massacre.

From his new seat of power, Ainshard declared himself "God Emperor of the Goblinoids" and gave each of his masters the title of Guide.

He ordered the capture of the remaining greyborns and sent them to the caverns in Sinner's Reach so that they could work on his projects, which made the races allied with him wary.

In but a few short years, he began his conquest of the continent, pointing his blade at those he once called friends. The biggest suspected reason for his callous nature was the loss of his wife, who Lev saw hang herself after Ainshard's ascension.

Lev couldn't blame her. Andrava had sold her people for a man she loved, only for him to crush her kind and use them as fuel for his ambitions. He had repeated the same sins he had accused her people of: enslaving the races, such as the avians, that refused to participate in the war.

Many uprisings came, one a rebellion staged by Jom's own daughter, Mal, who led the kobolds against Ainshard before being crushed by his Guides.

Yet with all the massacres and bloodshed, Ainshard turned a blind eye to one thing. When Sinner's Reach had been engulfed with light, the Guides neglected to mention that something else had arisen from its deepest depths: a new race. From the greyborn bodies and the souls of those who were deemed worthy by the Guides were born the bereke.

After Lev witnessed the first bereke emerge from the caverns, the world began to shake and wake him up with a jolt.

He almost jumped out of his bed, panting and covered with cold sweat. He took a deep breath to calm himself.

There's no way, Lev internally growled.

Yet it felt all too real. It was too detailed to be a figment of my imagination.

With that thought and another breath, he turned to the closest haze crystal in the room, which powered a lamp on his desk.

Lev? What happened? W-What are these new memories?! Ghern yelled in his mind.

What's wrong, master? Why are you agitated? Glaive asked.

Ignoring the worried Gherm and the glaive, Lev hurriedly took the haze crystal from the lamp and held it in his sweaty palms. He braced himself before trying to establish a mental connection with it.

When he felt no response, he chuckled.

What did I expect? That was so absurd it had to be just a dream. There's no way a mineral could have been a—

He dropped the haze crystal from his shaking hands when an unintelligible pulse came through. Lev couldn't make proper words out of it, only knowing that it was an echo of an amalgamation of emotions.

His doubts were resolved. Lev was hit by a cascade of emotions and let out a deafening scream.

CHAPTER 9
CHIEF OF JUSTICE

Kul couldn't sleep after what had happened the other day. He stayed up all night at home, leaning against a newly furnished desk.

He had told Lev how the birdfolk were indulging in a new drug based on haze crystals, but... the response wasn't what he'd hoped for. Or expected, for that matter.

He could still hear Lev saying, "There's been a development, Kul."

"A development! By Mal's buttocks!" he shouted. "First he arranges a ceremony in front of the entire council assembly for my new position."

"Then he gives me the command over Pàrras's guards, and now... he tells me to wait!"

Even though Kul felt his anger was justified, he knew why Lev had instructed him to halt his investigation into the darg merchants. Even though the drug was destructive to the city's social body, the darg merchants had also supplied the vastly superior weapons and resources they needed to beat back Jotul's forces.

He too had heard the horror stories about the korrigal ambush and knew just as well as any soul in Pàrras with half a brain that interrupting the dargs now would only mean trouble for the entire Frontier.

His fingers kept tapping on the desk as he looked down on whatever measly notes he'd gather for his investigation. His gold pouch sat near the edge of the desk.

But something wasn't right—call it a gut feeling, if you will. Why would the darg merchants compromise the Frontier's stability while simultaneously supplying them with the materials they needed to secure the realm?

He grabbed a gold coin from his pouch and chuckled. It had a regal-looking human on it.

"I wonder how you Brizilum folks handle those merchants. Conquered or not, they're a part of your republic, after all."

Upon his realisation, the coin fell from his hand.

Even though Kul knew he wasn't the best man for the job, he had a premonition of how this situation might go.

"Brizilum!" he thought aloud. Shortly after, a few bangs through his thin walls confirmed he'd disturbed his neighbours with his nocturnal yelling.

"Sorry," he whispered in response, and the banging stopped.

Think, Kul, think. If I'm right and Brizilum wants the merchants to destroy Pàrras, then why did they help Pàrras?

They helped to form the trading guilds… they rebuilt the plaza and its fountains, helping it become the city's main market square, where, even if you leave out Hiltrude's group, the darg merchants own most of the shops.

They—

Kul's eyes widened.

—are still earning a lot of haze crystals and gold, even now.

It made sense. Whether there's war or peace doesn't matter when your coffers are full either way. But Brizilum couldn't benefit from their underground activities, could they?

Sure, the dargs sourced their wares from the wealthy ports of Brizilum and sold them in lands where they were worth their weight in gold, but Brizilum would take a portion of the profits. The same couldn't be said for foreign activities. Brizilum couldn't tax the activities in Pàrras like the blue nobles taxed surface imports to the caverns.

I need to talk to Lev tomorrow, Kul concluded as he saw the sun slowly rising.

* * *

"You look tired, Lev."

Lev had been pacing around his office for the past hour without saying a word to Eleric. From the window back to his desk, and from his desk back to the window.

Eleric wondered what was eating at his boss. Was it the war? The council? Perhaps a combination of the two, or maybe something entirely out of scope.

"It's because I am," Lev murmured as he continued his pacing.

This was getting on Eleric's nerves. He blocked Lev's path to his desk, something he felt he should've done much earlier. "May I speak candidly, sir?"

Lev stared at him with heavy bags under his eyes, hoping to grasp his intentions, before giving him a nod. "Go ahead."

"If you're concerned about the war, then you should bring your vexation to the council's attention."

"Hmm," Lev started, but he couldn't form a proper reply, even though he knew he could shrug Eleric off and claim the council wouldn't listen to him anyway. *Even if they listened, what difference would it make now?*

Settlements would still be pillaged, battles would still be fought. It wouldn't alleviate Lev's ever-compounding worries.

As he prepared to shove Eleric's arm away, his *fellow* human unexpectedly asked another question.

"Is it Brizilum?"

Lev froze. His mind had been so occupied with current affairs, especially his latest revelation, that he'd forgotten about Brizilum.

"I overheard you talking to Kul. What he described sounds eerily familiar to what happened in Edorai."

"The darg homeland? What about it." Lev raised his eyebrows.

"There's something you need to know before I can elaborate." Eleric motioned towards Lev's chair. "Take a seat. You've been walking back and forth long enough."

As Lev did so, Eleric grabbed a spare chair and placed it next to his.

"Isn't this a bit cramped? I can barely move my legs with you next to me," Lev whined as he tried to wiggle his legs.

"I don't want to catch anyone's attention. Someone might overhear us just like I did."

Eleric let out a deep sigh. This was going to take him way back in time.

"As you know, I hadn't always been a Brizilum slave. My family was of notable nobility once."

Lev smiled as he pointed at Eleric's hands. "Anyone would've guessed that. You were a servant judging by the lack of scars and calluses, right?"

Eleric nodded. "Yes, but that doesn't explain my family's origins."

"It does. The dargs told me bits and pieces about Brizilum customs. Only valuable slaves get positions closest to their masters. I bet you had your own room, which gave you a degree of privacy."

Eleric gasped.

"How did you know? Is it that obvious?"

Lev chuckled. "I guess not everyone would've been that precise in guesstimating your past, but I have my methods."

Brizilum reminded Lev of the Roman Empire from his world. The customs, attire, and social code were similar enough for him to connect the dots. After all, the patricians of ancient Rome were their own worst enemy. Everyone could become a slave. Even if your family were affluent, only some held positions of power.

In Roman society, respect was worth more than gold. Lev figured it'd be the same for the Brizilum Republic.

"Say, Eleric. Was your family in debt before their fall?"

The human shook his head. "No, it was because we were too rich."

"When Brizilum discovered Edorai, they made sure to export as much of their vastly superior wares as possible to the darg markets."

"Let me guess, the dargs ate it like hot cookies."

Now it was Eleric's turn to frown. "What's a cookie?"

"Never mind. I meant indulged," Lev clarified.

Eleric laughed nervously. "Yes, that they did. Being a culture of sailors and merchants, they knew Brizilum's aim, but their hubris made them think they could turn the situation to their advantage, so they played along. It was a better option than going to war."

He continued, "My family was once part of a powerful tribe, before the construction of the great citadel. When we were conquered by the first Brizilum settlers, they offered us citizenship and riches in exchange for a peaceful transfer of our lands."

Lev unlocked his ankles. "Makes sense. They didn't have a standing army back then, right?"

Eleric nodded. "Correct. They couldn't afford conflict, especially not with a stronger tribe that knew the land."

Lev fidgeted in his chair, eager to hear what happened next. If he remembered correctly, many barbarians had envied the Roman way of life. It'd make sense that they'd want to be a part of a richer, more refined culture.

"Well, as many rich families did, we moved to Edorai to profit from the dargs and their thirst for the material world, but..." Eleric hesitated.

"But what?" Lev asked, urging his aide to continue his story.

Eleric nervously scratched his head. "But while my family was wealthy, we held no power in office. Policies changed, and the most skilled dargs were eventually recognised for the wealth they contributed by distributing our wares overseas to less-developed peoples."

Lev's eyes gleamed in understanding. The gold rush couldn't have lasted long. After a few short years, prices would've adjusted to Brizilum's own internal market. Profit margins would've been too slim to maintain a life of luxury.

"As opportunities dried out, my family slowly withered into obscurity."

Eleric paused, unsure how to proceed with his history.

"I was the first to offer myself up. A prominent trading guild promised they'd treat my family well if I sold myself to a nobleman."

He pushed his hair off his shoulders. "I think Brizilum is trying the same thing here, although I don't think they'll assimilate your kind like they did the dargs."

"I think that..." Eleric pursed his lips. "I think that Brizilum is using the profit to build something."

"Like what?" Lev asked with prying eyes.

"Were it not Brizilum, I'd have guessed something less cynical," Eleric said.

Lev clenched his jaw. "It's their armies, isn't it?"

"Correct. We can't be too careful, Lev. You can't mention this to anyone. Act aloof for now until you're certain we can handle this," Eleric advised.

The Chief of Commerce grimaced. "We'll need the support of the council for that..."

* * *

A few hours of poor sleep and a hasty breakfast later, Kul waited in front of Lev's office. He saw Eleric going in and out several times before he asked the human when he'd be able to talk to the Chief of Commerce.

"Soon," Eleric cordially replied.

Several hours afterward, he sat across from Lev. "You could've just told me to come back later, you know. I'd have been able to sleep longer! Eat longer!"

Lev was flabbergasted by Kul's reaction. "I haven't seen you this grumpy since announcing my allegiance to Rak's gang back in the day. What's on your mind? The merchants?"

Kul rolled his eyes. "Yes! The merchants. If that's what you want to call those criminals."

Lev sipped from a mug filled with a steaming hot black liquid. "Well, those criminals are just about to finish their boat shipments. Heh, that's a fun way of saying it."

"Saying what?" Kul asked, his tone lacking any form of enthusiasm.

"Boat... shipments. Get it?"

Kul's eyes rolled once more.

Even though his ears heard Lev, his nose was busy sniffing the strange nutty and smoky scent coming out of his mug.

"What's wrong, Kul? Finally understanding why I have you on hold?"

"No, I've just never seen you drink something like... that. What is it?" Kul asked, his eyes glued on Lev's beverage.

Lev took a sip. "A new drink from Brizilum. I forgot what they call it, but I call it coffee."

Kul raised an eyebrow. "And what does it do? Is it based on haze?"

Lev chuckled. "No, it's based on a bean they cultivate over there. They actually have nice weather there all year round, unlike our harsh behemoth-filled winters."

"They roast its beans and then grind them into fine particles before steeping them in hot water. I do prefer iced coffee, though. Man, I miss iced coffee…"

Kul's eyes widened. "Iced what? Never mind. Don't you see what's going on?! Brizilum is everywhere yet nowhere. They use those dargs as proxies and label them as harmless merchants. They're wolves among sheep!"

With a wave of his hand, Lev dismissed Kul's theories. "Aren't you taking it too far, Kul? I see your concerns, but all I've gotten from you so far is the whining of a certain unlikeable blue bogey and a couple of birdfolk messing around."

As Kul was about to protest, Lev stopped him with a raised index finger. "And that isn't enough to convince the big man himself, let alone the council."

"You mean Vyrga? When did you start caring so much for that vile man and his adopted rascals."

Lev finished his mug. "Ever since he became High Chief. And it's rascal now, singular. The others died untimely deaths not too long ago, if you recall."

"Right," Kul muttered. "Hemgall doesn't count, so only Bolo remains, right?"

"Correct."

"Alright, alright. I get it. I'll halt my activities until we're in the clear to hunt the merchants and interrogate them," Kul said, defeated.

With slumped shoulders, he walked towards the door. "But can I say one last thing before I leave?"

"Go ahead."

He looked Lev in the eyes and declared, "If I find evidence that is so glaringly obvious, so painfully direct that I have to take action, then I will proceed with it myself. The council can demote me, for all I care."

He straightened his back with newfound resolve. "I only accepted this position to take care of the issue, remember that."

Lev smiled. "If the council tries anything, I'll have your back the same way you had mine and Ghorza's."

"You better have the back of your people when I do," Kul told him before walking out of the door.

Once Kul left, Lev dropped his smile and sighed.

"You're not the only one who's trying to protect this city."

* * *

Even though he'd been appointed Chief of Justice, Kul still took pleasure in patrolling the streets at night. It wasn't like he could do much besides his old duty at this point, at least until the council allowed him to do his job. The full moon illuminated the cobblestoned streets as Kul walked past the various landmarks of Pàrras.

He hummed an old overseer's work song to himself as he climbed the staircase that led to the plaza now serving as Pàrras's main market square. Its beautiful restored fountains were a sight to behold once he'd conquered the last step of the seemingly never-ending staircase. He took a short break to catch his breath before cursing. "Why'd Ainshard's people have to make it this long... didn't they have old people back in their day?"

Like usual, a scant remainder of bugbears and merchants was moving containers filled with merchandise back to their respective warehouses. Kul didn't pay them much mind these days; he wasn't worried about the bogey merchants. Heck, most of the nobles who'd converted to rich merchants had stopped their whining and accepted their new place in society.

Kul took one of the branching streets that led around the upper section of Pàrras until he arrived at the administration district. The splendour of the towering Grand Halls and their haze crystal lanterns was a stark contrast to the not-so-illuminated streets of the slums.

Speaking of the slums, it was time for him to check on the bird-folk. After all, it was in those dark alleys that Kul had noticed a feathered silhouette dancing through the moon's rays a few nights ago.

I still need to build a better case against the dargs, he noted before he arrived in the northern district. A few alleys and glares from avians later, he saw that same silhouette dancing yet again through the streets.

"Can't blame him for dancing his sorrows away. They were promised a home and were thrown away like trash," Kul remarked as he followed the avian to the jovial doors of the Heart of Edorai: a pub renowned among merchants of the purple variety.

"Here we are again," he muttered. He'd seen a sign of underground activity in the vicinity of this establishment, something he hoped to witness now.

He took in his surroundings, but didn't see the figure he'd followed here anymore. Not until he heard the clank of the pub's door closing.

Bingo.

As much as he'd wanted to go inside, he knew it'd only draw unwanted attention to him, especially now with his new title. The dargs in the council had been eyeing him suspiciously ever since.

If they want my head, I won't make it easy for them.

He sat on a nearby bench and keenly observed the pub. As the hours passed, boredom settled in.

Kul yawned. "Looks like they're taking it slow these days. Can't blame 'em."

Just as he was about to leave, the same figure reappeared in the pub's doorway. Light illuminated his feathers from behind, and Kul could see that the avian now carried a translucent bag of blue powder.

Knowing what was best for him, he moved himself to a better position, behind the cover of a few empty liquor crates, and observed from afar.

"Next time you better pay up front, piss beak, or the jig is up."

The avian nodded as he closed the door behind him.

"If you don't, there'll be more than coin to pay!" the muffled voice of the darg sounded from inside.

With trembling hands, the avian opened the bag and lined up the powder on a windowsill. The shaking intensified as the bird snorted the blue powder and his eyes glowed a faint blue.

As soon as all of the powder had entered his nares, the shaking subsided and the creature danced his way back home in a state of ignorant bliss.

With careful steps, Kul followed the creature back to his home in the slums. Once they were far enough from the pub, he spoke up. "Need coin? I can provide it."

The avian's feathers ruffled in shock before he glanced at the old bogey and calmed down. "M-Money? Y-Yes please, kind sir."

Kul was surprised the creature had learnt the common tongue. *Was it out of necessity? Probably.*

Language aside, had Kul been dressed in his guard attire, the avian would've made a run for it, but without it, he looked like any old bogey: ancient and harmless.

"But you'll have to do something for me in return. Nothing unordinary, just a small favour," Kul added.

The next night, he observed the pub from the same spot as the avian approached its entrance. Once he opened the door, a deep voice responded. "Here so soon again? Didn't I tell you no dust without up-front payment, piss beak?"

"I-I've got your payment right here, sir darg."

"Well, look what we've got here. Finally, an avian customer worthy of our esteemed wares."

A few praises from the darg later, and the avian was back outside with Kul. Once both of them had walked far enough away, the creature handed the bag to him.

"C-Can I keep some of it?" he asked with probing eyes behind his mask.

"No. Giving this to you would only benefit those bastards. Take this instead."

The masked creature inspected the piece of parchment handed over to him. "I-Is this money?"

"No, it's better. It's an employment voucher for the guardsmen of Pàrras. A good job will keep you away from trouble."

It finally dawned on the avian to whom he was talking to.

As the creature disappeared into the cover of night, Kul nodded to himself. *Better to use the common tongue for work than buying drugs.*

* * *

"This is outrageous!" Servius claimed after Meinrad had presented the bag of haze dust to the entire assembly.

"We'll be sending the guards to investigate the Heart of Edorai," Lev announced.

"I won't deny his claims, but the actions of one darg establishment shouldn't dictate the laws of the Frontier! We merchants have provided all the resources the Frontier lands need to rebuild for over a year now!" Servius cried out.

Kul jumped from his seat and sneered, "Then why didn't you do anything about it? The Heart of Edorai has many darg merchants, I'm sure at least one of you knows about its dark side."

Meinrad waved off both Kul and Servius. "Gentlemen, let's stop this quibbling.

"Kul presented evidence, that much is true; this matter will be handled thoroughly."

Lev nodded. "I'll personally look into it with the High Chief to check its validity."

Another darg started, "But—"

"But nothing. Let's drop this discussion and focus on the original intent of this meeting," Lev said.

Meinrad opened a piece of parchment on the flat pedestal. "In front of you you'll find the war room's plans. Read these carefully and discuss your verdict among your faction members."

"Voting will start next session. We will meet back in the oval room. Everyone's dismissed."

With that, Meinrad left the room, Lev and Vyrga in tow.

Kul sighed in relief. *They took it quite well, all things considered. I'd expected full-blown war like the horror stories I heard during the first elections.*

Can't believe they actually threw pots and chairs at each other. The council sure acts like a bunch of hivelings when livid.

As Kul walked towards the exit of the Grand Halls, a darg rushed next to him and whispered into his ear, "Stop while you still can, bogey."

He didn't recognize the darg, but from the emblem on his coat, he surmised he was a member of Hiltrude's merchant faction.

** * **

A cloaked darg walked into the Heart of Edorai. "One of your finest wines, please."

"Coming right up, sir." A slender darg eyed the sliver of council attire underneath the cloak.

As the bartender presented a bottle of wine, he subtly leaned in and muttered, "Are we full or half-full today?"

"Worse, empty," the hooded darg grumbled.

The bartender nodded before placing the bottle of wine back in its rack. "Then empty it shall remain, good sir."

The cloaked figure stopped in its tracks just as it was about to open the door. "And empty it shall remain until I bring word."

"Understood."

CHAPTER 10

VOLKARRA

Much like every morning, Volker walked on top of the city walls; from the northern gates all the way to the southern gates and back.

It'd become a ritual for him to walk and watch as every day, around a dozen migrants and refugees from war-torn lands arrived in the city.

Most of the time they were goblins from the northern tribes, but also, surprisingly, there were those who came from Jiira lands. Many of the latter came by darg ship after hearing that the city was a new promised land for goblinoids. He knew little about their situation nowadays.

Whispers of exhausted refugees hinted at another Kur incursion, and with their valuable haze miners gone and a hiveling outbreak at their doorstep, defending their borders would prove more difficult than ever for the Jiira. They might even have to rely on outsiders for aid.

He'd seen kids packed against each other in shoddy wagons as their cattle, and sometimes their parents, pulled them forwards. From where did they hail? Why had they come here out of all the places they could've gone to?

Sure, the Frontier proved to be stable for the time being, but Volker knew he and the others lived in a beautiful yet empty castle. To the outside world, it felt like a fairy tale. A rejuvenated goblinoid city, from Ainshard's time!

He stared at the empty horizon and the rising sun.

Will today be different? he wondered, but of course, he wouldn't know unless he made sure to be there every day to check the influx of souls and scrutinise them for even remote familiarity.

Just as he reached the southern gates and turned around to make his way back, a distant horn made him turn right back to the south.

Volker recognized its baritone note all too well. It was that of the sentry towers and could only mean one thing: foreigners.

"Looks like today's bunch is here," he murmured as he leaned on a parapet.

Distant figures appeared over the hills, accompanied by a few guards from the tower. Volker counted their heads, then gasped. The mass of figures didn't stop at ten. In fact, he counted well past a hundred.

Once they'd gotten close enough, he recognized the different races. *Dargs, goblins, deka...*

"Deka?" he thought out loud. He hadn't seen many deka migrants, let alone refugees. The deka homeland was one of the few relatively peaceful places left on the continent. They'd curried enough favour from surrounding factions by fighting for them in various wars, and in return, were granted luxuries other races could only dream of.

He remembered that many of his former comrades from the Vengeful Souls, along with Varra, had been escorted back to deka lands. "Can it be?"

Volker skipped down the gates' staircase and reached the mass. He scrutinised each head as they poured through the open gates. Sure enough, he found Gozzag and Ban among them.

Joy filled his being as he ran towards them.

"Oh!" Gozzag gasped when he recognized the young greyborn's tall frame making its way through the crowd.

"Volker!" Ban added.

"Gozzag! Ban! You've finally made it!" Volker yelled, getting a look from the puzzled guards.

"Calm down, kid!" Gozzag smiled. "We're here, alright. Do you know a place where we can eat something warm and drink to our hearts' content? It's been a long journey, so I'd prefer to catch up with a satisfied stomach."

"Sure do! I know one right around the c—" Volker stopped as he recognized another face. This time, a keenly familiar purple one.

Tears filled his eyes. "Varra... Is that you?"

His lips quivered as he slowly walked away from his two deka friends and pushed bystanders aside to make a path towards the darg girl he hoped would be Varra.

Her head was covered by her Edoraian helmet, and her hair wasn't as short as Varra's. No, in fact it was long, reaching down her shoulders.

Zeja, I prayed for her recovery. Please let it be truly her this time.

In the past months, he'd seen more darg girls who looked like Varra than he could count. But no awkward misunderstanding had withered his resolve. No, they had only strengthened it. After all, if Pàrras attracted this many races, then surely one day...

"Varra!" Volker shouted over the crowd.

The darg girl removed her helmet before raising her head and said softly, "Volker?"

It'd been a year since they last saw each other. Through that year, she'd had no choice but to go with Ban and Gozzag to recover, unable to help during the rebellion against their goblin overlords. From the moment she was able to move, she'd kept searching for him. Volker had gone through a lot during that time but so had she.

As the two united in embrace, tears flowed down both their cheeks.

Volker ran his fingers through her long hair. "What happened to your practical cut?"

Varra laughed and responded with a snarky, "What happened to your tattered clothes? I mean... look at you!

"And here I thought you couldn't grow taller!"

Volker blushed. "Yeah, a lot happened."

He shook his head. "More importantly, you're healed!"

Varra wiped the tears from her and then Volker's eyes. "Took me long enough, didn't it."

The greyborn boy laughed awkwardly. "Sure did, but that doesn't matter anymore. With you, Gozzag, and Ban, I have all the strength I need."

"For what?" Varra asked with a concerned look.

"I'll tell you soon. Come, let's join the other two. We've got a lot to catch up on."

* * *

"I thought you said it was right around the corner, Volk," Ban admonished his greyborn friend.

Gozzag patted Volker on the shoulder and frowned. "Come on, now, Ban, don't sour the mood. It's time for drinks and boisterous talk, not the whining of an old hag!"

"Right, sorry," Ban replied as he caressed the back of his head. They turned a corner and stopped. "So, this... Heart of Edorai? Is it any good, Volk?"

Volker eyed Varra. "I figured Varra wanted a taste of her homeland after all this time."

His nose wrinkled. "I mean, after all those deka customs, I wouldn't blame her for wanting a palate cleansing."

"Hey! You haven't even tried our cuisine!" Ban chided.

"Well, Grasha was once on cooking duty and—"

"Let me rephrase it," Ban interjected. "You haven't *properly* tried our cuisine. Grasha's a good fighter, but he's a bad cook."

Embarrassed, Volker scratched his head. "Sorry if I was being rude. It's just that, from what I understand, she's been with you all this time. Not sure if you guys have the darg specialities she craves."

"They certainly did not. Good thinking, Volk!" Varra smugly added as she entered the pub.

"Then the two of you should prepare to be disappointed because they love fish and the sea is a long distance away," Ban grumbled. "Damned dargs, I at least hope they got good liquor there. Nectar, I tell you! Nectar's what I need." He too entered the curious establishment.

"Don't mind him too much, kid, he hates travelling even though it's part of the job," Gozzag clarified.

Volker was puzzled. Ban had been the one to introduce him to outside-world concepts like the late druids and Brizilum's conquests. "I thought he liked travelling?"

He'd even replayed Ban's stories in his head before bed. Epic tales of goblinoids aiding pink-skin tribes in their fight against the all-but-in-name empire breathing down all of their necks. Sadly, the deka were mostly hired by nefarious entities like the Jiira and the Brizilum Republic.

So many heroes and legendary battles...

"Oh, that he did. But it's been a while since we've lent our wrinkled mercenary hands and battle-hardened weapons to others. He's grown complacent."

Gozzag patted his belly. "And it looks like I've grown fat. Looks like these will be my last beers for a while."

Volker laughed and entered the pub with Gozzag.

He'd also heard many tales about the Heart of Edorai. Stories of epic brawls between first-rate merchants in their drunken stupors, but also tales of more nefarious activities, like trafficking the infamous haze dust.

Anyway, this wasn't the time to worry about rumours. It was time to catch up and get some much-needed answers to questions that had festered in his head for a whole year.

Varra pointed at a round table in the corner. "This looks comfy. Let's sit here?"

"But we'll get served faster at the bar," Ban complained before being smacked on the back by Gozzag.

Then Gozzag cleared his throat. "What my dear friend was trying to say is that he'd love to sit in the corner with us and wait patiently for his drink."

Ban complained with a guttural groan, and all four were seated.

Volker ordered a bottle of the finest darg wine for Varra and him while the two deka attempted to order niche deka drinks such as crimson ale. They contented themselves with a pint of Brizilum ale after hearing "this is a darg establishment, gentlemen" from the purple-skinned waiter.

"So tell me, Volker, is there work for us in... what's this city called anyway?"

"Pàrras, and yes, there sure is. We're recruiting more men for the war."

"War," Varra gasped. "I thought that was a rumour. Are the goblinoids really at war again with each other?"

"No, this time we're united against someone else entirely," Volker clarified.

He eyed everyone before asking, "Have you ever heard of the bereke?"

"Ears as long as you bogeys? Tall and slender warriors from the woods? Personalities as rotten as this poor excuse for ale?" Gozzag asked with a raised eyebrow.

Volker nodded.

"I heard they had a civil war among themselves," Ban snarled. "Serves them right, damned wretches. They never accept mercenaries outside of their own race. Too prideful." He took a swig from his mug.

"Anyway." Ban set it on the round table with a soft thud. "Let's get back to business."

Gozzag glanced at his compatriot. "When we asked for work, we were serious, Volk. Life's been tough without the Jiira employing us. Sure, we fucked up protecting them twice, but at least the pay was reliable. Well, until Bulgu's advisors decided to blame his death on us and force us to work for free."

Volker could certainly see that. He wasn't sure just how much they'd been paid during the expedition, but it must've been good enough to justify the risks, though he hadn't seen a lot of deka fall during the expedition. He only knew that a certain Drogg from Lev's vanguard had fallen when they were separated. He also knew that Drogg was a pompous lunatic who thought himself invincible.

"Yeah," Ban said, "haven't done much fightin' lately and it's not just us. Most deka are sitting pretty back home, doing nothing but adding pounds to their soft bellies."

Gozzag clicked his tongue. "It's true, Volker, the deka are struggling to make ends meet, and with no one to fight for, we either grow weaker by the day or have to resort to unsavoury acts such as banditry to make ends meet. Our reputation is already in the gutter without some scummy raiders pillaging our old clients."

Volker spun the wine in his glass. "Like I said, there's enough work here. We could use your mercenaries.

"Besides." He grabbed a purse filled to the brim with haze crystals and pulled it open. "Pàrras has made all of us much wealthier."

"I've noticed," Gozzag said as he glanced at one of the darg waiters. "Coin follows purple, or is it the other way?"

Varra lowered her gaze. "We're not all like them. Some of us want to fight without a purse at the end of the road."

With both mugs empty and the answers they needed, Gozzag and Ban stood up from their ornate wooden chairs. "Drinks are on us," Ban said as he pressed a couple Brizilum coins near Volker's purse. "We'll tell the others about the war and send news back home. I'm sure they'll be pumped for it."

After his old deka friends had left, Volker shifted his feet. He and Varra now sat in private and could talk about anything.

But neither Volker nor Varra could talk. They blushed as their eyes briefly met.

It was Volker who finally spoke up. "May I ask why you decided to stay with the deka? Didn't you want to go back to Brizilum where your people are?"

"I did, and I had a chance when they sent one of their envoys to Brizilum to report the expedition's losses, but..."

A tear rolled down her cheek. "They didn't want me back."

"Do you know why?"

Volker shook his head. "No, please do tell."

"The deka envoy told me I was a failed product, according to one of the Brizilum commanders. They lent us to the Jiira as a sign of goodwill, and in return we failed to protect one of their princes and fought on the side of the rebels."

She took a deep breath before continuing. "You know that us dargs can only trade outside of Brizilum. And even if we do, we still need to pay a percentage back to Brizilum's merchant guilds.

"My family were once sailors, but they only transported the merchants and never entertained the thought of trading themselves."

"Thus, they never build a network of trade families to exchange ideas with, causing us to fall behind."

"But since they ensure their own safety along with the safety of their cargo," Volker said, "wouldn't your family already have established goodwill with the merchants?"

Varra shook her head. "Not enough to protect them from Brizilum. When they absorbed Edorai, only the largest trading guilds and those who already sold themselves to the humans kept their ships. The only way to survive was to enlist as a mercenary or become a gladiator."

Volker gulped. He'd never heard this story before. During the expedition, they'd been too busy surviving, and when they did have time, they talked about happy memories and cultural differences. Her past was never a subject, nor did Volker inquire about it out of respect. Both of them knew just how hard life could be.

"So I stayed behind and improved my skills as soon as I was able to wield a sword again." She clenched her fists. "It's a good thing I wasn't allowed back into their ranks. At least now I can fight for whoever I want. If there's a place for me..."

She looked to Volker for an answer, but his understanding eyes were all she needed. She'd seen that look before, after each battle with the hivelings. No matter how many men Volker had lost, his confident gaze had kept her on the right path.

"Volker, I want to fight for you. I want to fight for a new life here, in Pàrras."

He nodded. "Before you pledge your allegiance to the Frontier, I need to tell you something else."

She smiled. "Go ahead."

"Shahn's here. You should talk to him about this as well."

* * *

"Do you two claim to have a mercenary force at the ready?" a council member asked. Several had gathered to meet the two deka standing at the opposite site of a half-moon table.

"Correct, about two hundred strong," Gozzag replied.

"Say, how tall are these Grand Halls?" Ban asked as he scratched his head. He couldn't see where the arches above them ended when they were walking to the meeting room.

Servius laughed. "Even we haven't had the time to measure their height, my friend. Their craftsmanship hails from Ainshard's time."

"Impressive," Gozzag added. "Throughout my years of fighting in so many cities and temples, I've never seen something like this."

Vyrga motioned towards the door. "Leave us now. We need to discuss your proposal and payment."

A few moments after the two had left, Lev walked in and took a seat. "When are they coming? I heard deka mercenaries arrived from Volker."

"You're late. They've already left," Vyrga snarled. "Out of all people, I least expected you to slack off, especially now."

Lev rubbed his neck. "I know and I apologise. I've been having some wild dreams as of late."

Vyrga clicked his tongue. "Whatever. I vote that we take these extra warriors and pay them their weight in haze crystals. Half now, the other after the war is settled."

"I agree," Lev murmured, knowing he couldn't argue with him after displaying such nonchalance.

Considering his history with the Vengeful Souls and knowing how much of an advantage Gozzag and his men brought to the table, he would have come to the same conclusion if he'd come to the Grand Halls earlier.

"Then let's put it in writing," Vyrga said as he passed a piece of parchment to Lev. One by one, the present council members scribbled their crude signatures to approve. Not a single one voted against Vyrga's proposal. They needed every man, be they red, purple or green.

CHAPTER 11

IGNITION

Leaves rustled in the dark hours of the night as the bereke hammered stakes in the ground for their tents.

Aside from the clanging of their hammers down the hill, Vilde could hear the howling of beasts in the distance. Not that it bothered her; she revelled in the fear hidden in their cries, and once she took a deep whiff of nature's bounty, a wide smile crept on her chapped lips.

They know what's coming. Shouldn't have expected less from the children of nature. Even beasts understand the fate of my master's enemies. Then her expression twisted into one of murderous glee. *Soon, in his holy name, we'll rid these lands of all who dare corrupt it. Ainshard's s ill-begotten spawn won't have their way.*

Her piercing green eyes scoured the land, and to her satisfaction, saw no signs of danger. What greeted her sight were the finished tents bearing the banners of her master. Near them were covered wagons, filled with barrels of poison and tar.

She turned to the western sky and knelt in prayer. With weapon in hand, she bowed towards a lone crimson star. "With your glory, they shall perish. With your might, they shall submit. With your fire, they shall be cleansed. Oh, Crimson One, may their hour of reckoning be at hand. Let there never be another Ainshard again."

A squawk interrupted her prayer. On instinct, Vilde pointed her whip in its direction, only to receive a bemused look from a red-eyed bird sitting on a tree branch.

She let out a self-deprecating chuckle. "Apologies. Old habits die hard."

She gently ran her finger along the bird's beak. "Even if the heretical goblinoids tried to attack us, you would've already warned us and informed Jotul."

The bird nodded its head and haughtily flapped its wings, receiving another laugh from the old veteran.

Vilde chuckled. "You're a prideful one, aren't you? I'll make sure to throw more offerings to thank the Crimson One for sending you with us."

With a delighted whistle, the bird flew away, leaving the bereke commander alone atop the hill.

Vilde stretched her body and. with a twist of her feet, walked back to the camp.

It was a hive of activity, from servants taking stock and cooking meals to soldiers guarding the perimeter and preparing to defend against potential night raids.

She approached a few of her more paranoid men as they tirelessly set up additional barricades and traps. The palisades now surrounded most of their encampment.

"Stand down," she ordered. "That's enough defences. His eyes protect us."

"But the palisades—"

"Our camp is surrounded by mountains, and you've already covered the important paths. Unless they can fly over the mountains, there's no way they could reach us unnoticed," she added.

Most of the men complied, with the exception of one: a young nobleman barely into his twenties. He was part of the *reinforcements* sent by the nobles who swore allegiance to Jotul. He hesitantly approached her, piquing Vilde's interest, and she smiled.

He performed the customary salute, two firm thumps on his chest with his left hand. Once Vilde gave a nod of approval, he gathered his courage and cleared his throat before letting out his worries.

"With no disrespect to your wisdom or our lord's abilities, what stops them from hiding in some of the caves atop the mountains? For all we know, they've already crawled into them during the day to avoid the sky devils and are biding their time to ambush us."

The amusement on her face gave way to befuddlement. "And you think that the eyes of the Crimson One are blind? That they wouldn't have spotted the goblinoids?"

The young man gasped. "N-No, I only speak of erring on the side of caution. Unexpected development or not, it was foolish of us to take a passage that has those magical leeches flying above it in the first place!"

"What you presume is foolish was a calculated risk. The only sky devils up there at this time of the year are stragglers, and if they had detected our enemies, they wouldn't have kept themselves to the peaks. We'd have been in danger as well."

"How would you know?"

Annoyed, she took a few steps towards the man, startling him.

She grabbed him by his robe and sneered. "If anyone knows the sky devils, it's me. I've confronted those wretched jellyfish on multiple occasions."

"B-But..."

"If you don't want to die for wasting my time, get out of my sight," she hissed before tossing him aside.

With a shrill shriek, he fell on the ground, shocking those nearby before they erupted into a fit of laughter.

"Yeah, laugh it off," the man grumbled once he got off the ground.

He patted the dirt off his clothes and inwardly cursed his lessers for not giving him the respect he deserved.

A veteran said, "You bet we will," earning another laugh from his colleagues.

"My father will know of this!" he whined, much to Vilde's irritation. She showed her bladed whip and a sinister grin, the sight of which alarmed the noble youth to no end.

"Threats? In my army? Seems like your precious father forgot to teach you some discipline. It's nothing some character building can't fix."

A few of his personal servants tried to come to his aid, but a glare from her was all it took to give them a change of heart.

"Keep an eye on them," Vilde commanded one of her men.

He saluted. "As you wish, captain."

The noble found no mirth nor resentment on his older compatriot's face, only pity.

"Now. Let's begin, shall we?" Vilde said after throwing the young noble a xiphos.

Seeing no way out, he shakily grabbed the weapon and gulped.

What did I do to deserve this? A whimper escaped his lips.

It didn't take long for the supposed character building to conclude. Afterwards, Vilde walked through the flaps of her linen tent ready to sleep in full armour while the bloodied nobleman was dragged by his servants to the healers.

She grabbed a jug of wine from a bedside stand. After she wet her parched throat, she lay down, but try as she might, she couldn't sleep.

Worries gnawed at her mind.

Lachas and the Coalition, fools or not, many of them weren't new to combat, and still... the goblins took them out. The sneaky bastards also discovered my lord's birds and killed them with ease.

She sat up and took another swig from the jug before returning it to the nightstand.

With her eyes fixed on the ceiling of her tent, and numerous failed attempts at figuring out how to reduce their army's losses in the upcoming battles, her frown deepened. "We know too little about the heretics. This won't be an easy fight, especially when we siege their city," she muttered to herself.

"But we shall prevail. The Crimson One will never allow the vile things to rebuild Ainshard's empire. Though I bet they'll still play dirty to even the score..."

After a few moments brooding about it, her eyes narrowed, and her nose scrunched up.

"Thinking about this won't help me win the war," she grumbled before getting up and grabbing her whip. "It's better if I check with the men, at least the ones on duty."

Halfway out, her ears twitched and she stopped in her tracks. Her eyes widened when magical energy began coursing through the ground.

"Shit!" she cursed before rushing towards the exit as the ground sank under her feet. She reinforced her legs with magical energy and lunged out of the collapsing tent before it could drag her with it to the depths of the earth.

After a roll, she stood up and observed the chaos. To her horror, most of the tents were sinking into the ground, burying many soldiers alive.

To end the madness, she gathered magical energy around her foot. With a single stomp, the flow of the magic was disrupted, returning the earth to normal.

"Prepare for battle!" she yelled as she rallied the shaken men to face the unknown threat.

With the spell having done its work, tunnels erupted from two opposite mountain walls, making way for an army of goblinoids.

"Commander!" one of her men screamed. He rushed towards her, followed by two of her heralds.

"Please forgive us! There weren't any caves earlier, we would've—"

"Save it. The goblinoids played us well. Instead of grovelling like a bunch of dogs, raise your blades and face the enemy! Retribution for the Crimson One!"

"Retribution for the Crimson One!" the trio screamed before relaying her orders.

With order restored and her men ready for the charging goblinoids, Vilde brought her sight to the goblinoid force closest to her. A female goblin was leading the charge. From her chain mail armour, Vilde guessed that she was a leading figure for the enemy force, if not their commander.

"Don't think you've won yet, you green scum. In the name of my master, I'll make sure you'll pay for this humiliation."

* * *

Like a pack of wolves, Rapha and her battle maidens rushed out of the caves and lunged at the bereke remnants. The enemy met the goblinoids' zeal in kind.

With a battle cry in his strange tongue, a bereke thrust his spear at Rapha, only to be surprised by how easily she deflected it with her buckler before she jabbed her new steel blade down his throat. Both gifts from the dargs.

Without a second of respite, she slightly leaned her body to the right, avoiding an incoming axe. The bereke, not even trying to regain his momentum, sloppily swung his axe back in hopes of at least grazing her but failed.

Unlike her opponent, Rapha tempered herself with the fundamentals of her art. Perception, distance, and footwork were the key aspects of battle for any good swordswoman.

Frustrated, the axeman reinforced his body with magical energy and charged ahead, ready to finish her off with a terrible cleave—only for his attack to miss, giving Rapha a chance to bash him in the mouth with the sharpened edge of her shield, cleaving his face into a perpetual grin.

Yet that wasn't enough to take the magically empowered bereke down. But stabbing the stunned axeman through the ear was. She moved away before the destabilised magic caused his body to blow.

This was her sixth foe and seemed to be the last for now.

Finally having some form of reprieve, she took a look across the battlefield.

While the losses weren't low, Rapha's maidens were faring better than expected against the bereke.

The enemy wasn't adapting well to fighting on two fronts, especially against two forces with different tactics.

In contrast to Volker's highly disciplined troops, moving in unison as an impenetrable wall of shields and spears, Rapha and her maidens were closer to wild jackals as they drew their swords against the enemies of Pàrras.

Not all bereke donned their gear after the shamans sank the earth, and now they had to contend with at least three to five maidens each.

Whenever the maidens gave their shamans an opening, the bereke were either hindered by the earth or bombarded with spikes. The highest-priority targets were those who had protective runes on their armour, not unlike the late Lachas.

Using magical energy during the night in the presence of sky devils was a risk not lost on the goblinoids, but consequences be damned. It would be more foolish to hold out against such an enemy.

If they hadn't sunk the earth as their first move, the price of victory would have been dire.

The sight of the powerful bereke barely holding their ground against the formerly menial harem guards brought a proud smile to Rapha's face.

It might not have been the path she originally wanted, nor close to the path of a proper shield maiden, but she'd take a sword and buckler anytime if it meant death for her enemy.

Pàrras already had horsemen, magic users, scouts, and organised armies, but they needed an elite force that could make their enemy bleed up close, and that's what she and her maidens would do.

Rapha's revelry didn't last long. A chill went up her spine and, following her instincts, she threw her body on the ground, narrowly avoiding an incoming whip laced with blades.

To her surprise, the whip changed direction midway and flew back at her, forcing her to roll out of its path.

According to the information from the council's war department, there was only one person in Jotul's army who used such an impractical thing on a battlefield.

I've finally dragged her out.

Rapha blew her horn, informing the entire force that their target took the bait.

Grinning, she sped towards the enemy commander.

Fittingly for a relic, Vilde's whip was faster than any whip had the right to be. But to Rapha's trained eye, even if Vilde drastically changed the whip's angle using her magic, her attacks were still predictable.

Strike after strike, she blocked the whip with her buckler, and any bereke who tried coming to their commander's aid was intercepted by her sisters.

Seeing that her attacks had no effect, Vilde pulled her weapon back and sneered at Rapha's audacity. "You want to fight up close? Fine."

With those words, her whip began to glow as she cracked it once again.

Rapha's eyes widened. The whip uncoiled into eight tails, all coming in to attack her from different angles. *Her weapon can do that?! That wasn't in the reports!*

She deftly dodged four of the malicious lashes and blocked two more, only for the remaining two to cut through her chain mail.

Seeing her pesky foe finally bleed made Vilde grin.

Rapha hissed from the pain. No matter how much it stung, she needed to keep her eyes on Vilde and her whip.

With a quick jump to her left, she missed six of the tails as they struck her earlier position, ducking just as the last two almost took out her eyes.

As soon as she stood up, Vilde struck again, one lashing across her back.

Bleeding, Rapha tried her best to protect herself from the bereke woman's onslaught, but she kept receiving nicks and cuts from the whip's vicious tails. If it weren't for her new armour, she'd have already been at death's door.

In a fortunate turn, she found herself near the remnants of a ruined tent, one whose main beam had avoided sinking into the ground. She wasted no time hiding inside, but she would have no chance to counterattack from the cover.

"Scurrying around won't save you, you little green rat!" Vilde screamed as she furiously lashed at the demolished pavilion, knocking a burning brazier over onto the tent.

Once the cloth caught fire, Rapha used the smoke to slip out and escape her opponent's pursuit.

Blinded by the smoke, Vilde whipped wildly at her surroundings.

Rapha's heart pumped. Deep down she knew that this was the best chance she had to strike at her formidable opponent, but a distraction was needed to catch Vilde's attention.

To her delight, a distraction arrived.

With a loud cry, Ruune ran towards Vilde. When she responded with her whip, Ruune grabbed a bejewelled bereke youth and used him as a meat shield. Vilde didn't have enough time to change all of the trajectories; only seven out of the eight whip blades struck true.

The young man's screams were cut short when the seventh found its way deep through his throat.

It's now or never! Rapha lunged forwards.

Vilde hissed at her blunder and, seeing the charging Rapha and Ruune, spun her whip to get the two to back off.

Yet they didn't relent. Vilde had experience dealing with multiple foes, but the goblins were tricky. And it was obvious to her that while Ruune wasn't as skilled as Rapha, she made up for it with her tenacity.

When avoiding one of the whip blades became impossible, Ruune took the blow to her thicker armour in stride. Her steel helmet further reduced her weak points.

Adding to Vilde's chagrin, Rapha weaved and blocked the four bladed tails that came her way and even managed to close the distance further.

Vilde took in her situation, along with the continuing decimation of her forces, and the end result dawned on her. *I've lost. Oh, Crimson One, I have shamed you and your champion...*

But. She turned her head to the sky and smiled as if to greet the encroaching sky devils. *Fret not; I'll drag Ainshard's vermin to the afterlife with me.*

Vilde's glowing body and maniacal grin caused Rapha to gasp. Before making a run for it, she yelled, "Ruune, move! She's going to blow herself up!"

"You don't have to tell me twice," Ruune screamed.

I'll leave the rest to you, Jotul. May our master grant you victory over the wretches and the Coalition. Those were Vilde's last thoughts before dying in a blaze of glory.

Rapha and Ruune barely escaped the intense blast. Rapha coughed violently as she rubbed her eyes to clear them of the rubble's dust. With Vilde gone, she turned her attention to her foe's subordinates battling all around them and was stunned.

Instead of surrendering after the death of their leader and at the sight of the approaching sky devils, the bereke were spurred onwards. They'd rather follow their commander and die with dignity than surrender to the vile goblinoids.

"They're mad," Rapha proclaimed when she saw the bereke's newfound zeal.

"What did you expect from a people that love to explode? Their leader even sped up our plan for us!"

Rapha couldn't deny Ruune's words. Another reason they wantonly used magic was to attract the sky devils in case the bereke proved too strong for them to handle. While they knew from the captives that Vilde's men weren't the cream of the crop, Volker had proposed to use those damnable jellyfish if things went awry and a lot of the bereke forces knew how to reinforce themselves.

Horns erupted throughout the battlefield.

"C'mon! Volker's men are already blowing the retreat horns," Ruune urged.

Rapha was about to nod but shuddered. "Wait. Is it me, or are most of the sky devils heading directly towards us?"

At those words, Ruune's eyes widened. She grabbed Rapha's hand before running towards the tunnel they came out from. "How much magic did she have?! Her blast caught the damn jellyfishes' attention!"

As they ran, shocked screams and blaring explosions were heard everywhere. Every bereke who knew magic sacrificed themselves to hasten the arrival of the sky devils lured by the residual magical energy.

As the two rushed to the nearest tunnel, they watched in horror as the glowing monstrosities descended on friends and foes alike.

Many of the shamans wanted to help but couldn't do anything without compromising the escape routes. During the entire battle, they were ordered to stay close to the tunnels in case they had to draw the sky devils away from their main forces. With the vile creatures' magic, however, there was no telling if they would attempt to break through the shamans and block the caverns.

Just as the two goblins were near their salvation, a sky devil closed in on them and wrapped its tentacle around Ruune's foot. Rapha crashed into her, toppling the two to the floor. Its thin needles made their way through the steel mesh of Ruune's leggings, drawing out a scream as their poison entered her veins.

Rapha wasted no time chopping off the tentacle with her xiphos. When the detached appendage instinctively shot out more of its needles, she gritted her teeth and blocked them with her buckler. She deflected the worst of them, but a few pierced her chain mail.

Weakness wormed its way through her body, yet she still tried to drag Ruune away and escape, pushing and cutting away nearing tentacles with her sword, thus activating even more thorns.

In the end, her shaking knees gave; she fell on the rocky ground with Ruune by her side. Some of her battle maidens behind her screamed before their voices turned to inaudible noise.

Is this how we'll die? she contemplated as the mass of the glowing abominations came near.

But it paused. The closest sky devil turned away before, suddenly, a flask hit it and erupted in flames.

The blaze caused the sky devil merely to twitch before flying back the way it came.

More sky devils reached towards the two girls with their tentacles but were repelled by two deka and a female darg.

Volker threw another firebomb at one of the vermin and yelled, "Varra, we'll push back the one in the centre while Gozzag and Ban will deal with the rest!"

With xiphos and shield in hand, Varra complied and tore at the sky devil's tentacles. None of its needles pierced her skin, as her superior Brizilum armour offered much better protection against them.

Gozzag and Ban weren't slouches either. Their gallant form was reminiscent of the expedition days as they ripped and slashed at the accursed flying jellyfish.

In her hazy vision, Rapha saw a sky devil split in two under Ban's axe whilst Gozzag baited two more away from his companion.

As the field cleared, her vision became spottier. She saw Varra grab Ruune and hold her in what Lev called a fireman's carry.

"Var... ra..." she muttered.

In the corner of her blurry eyes, she caught sight of another sky devil gone aflame before two grey arms dragged her through the tunnel.

"Leave things to us, Rapha," the greyborn said. "We couldn't make it before you fought Vilde, but we can at least keep you safe. You did great out there."

"You did good, kid," a red, one-horned figure added. "Get the girls into the tunnel before more of the damn beasts come. We'll make sure those flying leeches won't bother your men until everyone's inside."

Rapha couldn't understand much of their words. She barely kept her eyes open as they passed through.

When the shamans sealed the pass, she could finally close her eyes and rest knowing that they were now safe.

CHAPTER 12

ANTICIPATORY REVENGE

In the eastern parts of Pàrras, sermons sounded inside the administrative dome. Both shamans and priests had taken a liking to the grandiose structure and partitioned it to fit their needs.

The innermost sanctum of the spiked building housed the temple of Zeja, and in its depths, Kathaga smiled as she prayed for her people. She prayed for more victories over the bereke menace, and with them, prosperity in the Frontier for years to come.

And even though good news had come, there was still the possibility of the bereke standing at the gates of Pàrras once more. This time, however, a simple distraction wouldn't be enough to fool them.

The people were wary, and the council filled with fear. If only Zeja could come down from the heavens to guide her people once more towards victory.

If only, she wished as she closed her prayer by pouring a few droplets from her flask of meron water over the altar, the last of her supply. *For now, Lev will act as her liberator. Her beacon on this world shines brightly through him.*

She'd had many nightmares about not only her fate, but those of fellow acolytes, along with Lev. Night after night she'd awaken in a cold sweat, gnashing her teeth in fear at the possibilities her visions brought.

Some had been mild, others not so much. After all, a Pyrrhic victory over the bereke is considered mild when one is besieged by visions of Pàrras's streets burning.

She sighed as she stood up from her knees. "Zeja, I promise you Lev will be victorious once more."

"And once victory is secured," she muttered, "I'll make sure to end whatever taints our champion."

"I'll make sure the bogeys rise without a tyrant's strength. There will not be a repeat of Ainshard's ironclad rule," she solemnly vowed as she walked towards a haze lantern.

She lifted it from its support hinge, then walked towards the exit to converse with the other followers.

Before she could leave, though, she heard an intruder's bells echoing throughout the outer sanctum. If not for a certain joyful hum, Kathaga would've mistaken the bells for those announcing a prayer session.

The stone doors in front of her creaked open. A voluptuous belly bounced forwards, attached to a familiar frame.

"By Jom's beard, Bodobert, why are you here?!" she yelled.

Bodobert gave a short bow, almost losing his balance as he did so. "My sincere apologies, high priestess. Nobody knows I've left the Grand Halls."

"Were you followed?" Kathaga inquired with raised eyebrows.

"I wasn't. Besides, I'm the council's fool, remember? Nobody pays me any mind unless I want them to."

Kathaga relaxed her expression. "At least your theatrical abilities weren't lost after the exodus. Always the melodramatic one, aren't you?"

Bodobert flashed a bright smile. "That I am, dear Kathaga. That I surely am."

"So? Any news from our champion on the council?"

"Aside from the war, he's given Kul the title of Chief of Justice," Bodobert playfully answered as he skipped around her.

Kathaga nodded. "Good, then he won't be distracted. Kul's an old fool anyway; let him play his little ex-overseer games."

Bodobert chuckled. "I wouldn't call him a fool. He's already found out about little Servius's nasty business."

Kathaga's expression scrunched up into a sneer. "Don't tell me he's still selling that filth on the streets. He knows my stance on it, doesn't he?"

Kathaga looked at the altar. "After all, Zeja wouldn't want this for the Frontier."

Bodobert knelt in front of the altar. "Oh, great Zeja, please save us from the dargs!"

"Stop it, you fool. I'm not in the mood for it."

He got up and glanced at Kathaga with empty eyes. "Oh? But I thought you liked Zeja's miracles."

"At last, there's the Bodobert I know," she replied. Her compatriot walked into an unlit area of the sanctum.

"Oh, and one more thing," his voice echoed from the darkness. "I've made sure our heroes of Zeja will die heroically for goblinkind when the time comes."

His bells eerily jingled, but Kathaga could not discern from which corner. "It's like you said, priestess. Little Lev needs better odds in the next elections."

A soft chuckle escaped from behind Kathaga before two hands started massaging her shoulders. "As for old Kul, I'll make sure he doesn't get too far. We still need to shift the narrative against Vyrga. An unresolved drug crisis would be ideal, don't you think?"

"I agree," she responded as Bodobert's hands moved upwards to massage her neck.

"Bodo."

"Yes?"

"Don't get me wrong, I appreciate your services, but it's time to go now. Even a fool will be missed when entertainment is needed."

Bodobert's hands retreated, and so did his body, making its way through the door. "Understood, priestess. Until we meet again."

She heard his bells echo once more, as well as his humming. Once she couldn't hear him anymore, she gasped for air.

That damn creep.

Just as she was about to leave the sanctum herself, a shrill screech escaped from the hallways. "M-Master!"

Heavy footsteps followed, and soon the doors opened once more. "Don't you know rats should be caged, Kathaga?" Vyrga said as he threw Bodobert to her feet.

His cold demeanour sent a chill up her spine.

Vyrga gently tapped the doors closed with his foot and smiled. "I wonder how much time it would take the two of you to replace me with Lev."

Both Bodobert and Kathaga recognized the flames of ambition in his eyes. They'd seen the same when they lured him to his father like a butcher to his pigs.

Bodobert shivered as he struggled to form words. He found himself repeating, "How?"

"How? You take me for a birdbrain? It's not a matter of how, it's how long."

Bodobert crawled towards Kathaga and grasped her robes with trembling hands.

"How long, then?" Kathaga calmly replied.

"The moment you crowned Lev as the liberator. All this time you've sat idle in your pretty temple, adored by the meek and hopeless. For years you've prayed, but never did you act until Gherm started calling himself Lev."

"At first I only entertained your betrayal, but after each perished son, I grew more cautious."

Vyrga glared at Bodobert. He shrieked. Deciding not to meet his gaze, he crawled behind Kathaga for protection.

"How pitiful," Vyrga commented. "And to think you were once in charge of the nobility's intrigue. Did you think those bells would distract me from your past?"

After a short pause, Bodobert laughed. He replied with a mischievous smile and a malevolent glint in his eyes. "You got me. Looks like my act won't fool you."

Vyrga tilted his head upwards. "Hmm, I don't think it ever did, Bodo. You may have fooled Heimo back then, but a father never makes the same mistakes as the youngest of his pack."

Kathaga gasped. "So you knew from the start!"

Vyrga glared at Kathaga. "Of course, witch. I know everything that happened in those accursed caverns. The same goes for inside these walls."

Bodobert scurried from behind Kathaga and slowly walked towards Vyrga. "My bells might not have rung loud enough, but Lev's infamy has!"

He threw his arm around Vyrga's shoulder in a fatherly grip. "Who do you think the dargs speak of when they come home to their wives after earning their weight in gold in Pàrras?"

"Let me guess, your little lost soul, our esteemed Chief of Commerce?" Vyrga huffed with a hint of annoyance.

"Correct!" Bodobert maniacally cackled. "Then you can't blame us for betting our cumulative futures on him!"

Kathaga chuckled, but Vyrga couldn't make out if it was out of joy or anxiety.

"Well played, High Chief. It must've taken you a while to pass through my armed acolytes."

Vyrga slapped Bodobert's arm off his shoulder, making him protest with a grunt. "I'm the High Chief, I simply asked them."

The chuckles halted. "Asked? But their loyalty lies with Zeja!"

"And their wages are paid by the council. You've spent all of your allocated budget on repurposing this ancient temple for your war goddess, after all. Not to mention the espionage and subterfuge you commissioned to tail me."

Kathaga scowled but couldn't prove Vyrga wrong. It'd taken most of her funds to rebuild the dome according to Zeja's will, leaving little means to pay tribute to her closest of followers.

Bodobert pointed his finger at Vyrga. "That's an abuse of authority! The council will hear of this!"

Menacing laughter was all the voluptuous ex-clown got in response. "Instead of arguing like swine over wild onions, let me tell the two of you a tale as old as Ainshard."

"A tale?!" Bodobert blubbered but was silenced by the quick draw of Vyrga's haze-imbued sword. He grunted before pushing her blade aside.

Vyrga sneered, "Don't revive your clown act when something inconveniences you, Bodobert."

The noble's eyes sharpened. "Very well, then, no bells and cheap laughs from me anymore. Tell your tale, oh wise one."

With his audience silenced, Vyrga began his tale.

He walked around the sanctum, keenly observing each intricate detail in the walls his council had funded. "It's a tale that happened even before your beloved Zeja. Even Maga wasn't there to witness it."

He rubbed his hand over the altar and continued, "Do you know its protagonist?"

Kathaga pondered for a moment as Vyrga paced around her like a vulture. She said, "If Zeja and Maga weren't there, then only Mal the Exiled remains."

He hummed with satisfaction. "Correct. So you do know your folklore after all. I thought you were just roleplaying as a high priestess. Looks like I was wrong."

"Then you know of her youth, priestess?"

"I don't. Mal's wretched tale doesn't concern the war goddess," Kathaga answered.

Vyrga stopped his stalking. "Oh, but it applies to two souls. And even though they don't want to show it, they're cowering in this very room."

Seeing Kathaga and Bodobert's lowered gazes, he continued, "When she was young, Jom, after learning she shared his gift of creation, pampered her and indulged her in this world's knowledge."

"It's safe to say she was his favourite child, which made his other children envious."

Vyrga closed in on Bodobert and, with index and ring fingers, walked his hand on his shoulder. "They plotted against her and tricked her into burning the tree of providence."

Bodobert felt his cold finger slide over his throat. "As you two know, the tree of providence was Jom's greatest achievement. It'd taken eons to grow, and before its existence, gifting his creations with power proved difficult for Jom."

Kathaga eyed the High Chief as he scrutinised her. "Within its fruits," he said, "he'd grown the souls of the progenitors of all goblinoids. The best among them, and most magically gifted, being the bogeys."

Vyrga sneered, "So how did he feel when his favourite child, as witnessed by her traitorous siblings, destroyed his greatest work?"

Kathaga answered, "He banished her into the dark abyss where she sought revenge. She bided her time and built an army of monsters and demons. Then she ravaged the lands, scarred the gods, and crippled the races; this allowed the invasion of the Void Walker to go on unabated."

With an exaggerated gasp, Vyrga acted perplexed. "So you do know your Mal lore? And here I thought a priestess of Zeja wasn't concerned with trifles."

"I recognize a tale of revenge, you arrogant prick. I also know no one wins in the end," Kathaga scornfully replied.

Vyrga leaned in closer to Kathaga, who stepped back. "Watch your tongue. I've been very patient with you and the sly actor over there."

He walked back to the sanctum's entrance and slightly opened the door. "I'll do the same with the snakes that killed my sons and plan to wrap their slithering scales around my throat. After this war is done, I can afford the instability your deaths will cause."

"And you think we'll sit pretty for you to slit our throats when it's most convenient?" Kathaga bellowed. "The people adore Zeja more than Jom, and her champion will lead them to victory over the bereke!"

She grinned. "Who will take his revenge then, Vyrga? The people's united voice overpowers a thousand High Chiefs."

"I'll make sure to remind those united souls who fought their wars. Zeja merely observed and gave meaningless blessings. Bide your time and scheme to your heart's content, but just like Jotul, you'll never win," Vyrga stated before heading out.

With him gone, a messenger entered the sanctum and whispered something in Kathaga's ear, causing her to scowl.

"What did he say?" Bodobert asked, sweat dripping from his brows.

"All of the other temples have announced that they'll do their best to support both the war and Pàrras. Many are even offering shelter to the settlement refugees and the avians!"

"What's with the change of heart? Most of the high priests of the other temples are scoundrels themselves, and the ones who are not are poor."

Kathaga clicked her tongue. "It's Vyrga. He convinced them to give aid and funded the temples in need just like he did ours. We need to send missionaries to bless the armies before we lose our advantage. Our war isn't just with Jotul now..."

CHAPTER 13

KORRIGAL PRIDE

Leaves crunched under the korrigal as they passed through abandoned roads. Under the leadership of Vreskiven and Baldem, the proud warriors mounted atop their man-sized war rams eagerly marched to war.

They sang shanties and gossiped to pass the time as they trotted slower than preferred so that their supply wagons could keep up. Along with weapons, food, and water, the wagons held a different kind of resource: a group of disgruntled bereke shamans.

Coming from a race of inventors and engineers, Baldem was impressed that the root-covered roads could handle the weight of the oxen-driven wagons despite their age. It was a testament to the ingenuity of their creators.

Ainshard's empire was known for its architecture and logistical prowess, and no sign of that was greater than its vast expanse of ancient roads that cut through the continent. Many roads lead to the previously lost city of Pàrras, and while they'd been reclaimed by nature or long forgotten after centuries, they were still mostly viable to the korrigal thanks to their agile steeds. War rams could traverse rougher terrain than horses.

Baldem's reflection was interrupted by the cries and squawks of various birds. With their abominable sounds having ruined his mood, he disdainfully looked towards the skies, and through the overgrown trees, saw the wretched crimson-eyed birds. They sang their hearts out, heralding the arrival of the Crimson One's judgement.

He groaned. "Can't the stupid things shut up? There's no way the damn goblinoids don't know our location from their incessant noise."

Hearing no reply from his brother, he figured Vreskiven was still brooding on the previous battles. The humiliation and losses they'd suffered at the hands of their adversaries proved too much of a strain.

Baldem couldn't help but frown. He'd wanted to pull his brother's hair to get his attention but knew better. *This isn't the time for shenanigans. Guess I'll need to butter him up.*

In his best attempt to seem amicable, he put on a gentle smile. "Getting lost in our failure won't help, you know."

"What?" Vreskiven growled.

Baldem's smile twitched, yet he tried to uphold his facade. "I'm just saying you win some, you lose some. No one could've predicted that things would end up like that."

"Can it, Baldem. We were winning until those wretched goblins pulled that cheap magic trick. It's not fair," he argued.

Hearing his brother whining like a child made Baldem click his tongue. All thoughts of handling things mellowly were off the table now.

"Calm down, you big baby. All I'm saying is that I know how you feel, but we also played our own tricks. The goblins' tricks were just better. All is fair in war, Vres, and you know that."

Baldem kept going. "Instead of sobbing your little heart out on what can't be changed, keep a cool head so you can keep an eye on the bigger picture. We should make sure not to give them another chance to try that stunt again."

With a sigh, Vreskiven exaggeratedly rolled his single eye. "It seems you're right, brother. I was so lost in that... mishap... that I haven't noticed you finally grew a brain! I thought your mind would always be as tiny as the crimson bastard's pet birds."

A smug smile on his face, Baldem raised his hands to the heavens. "Finally, a quip! Thank our ancestors and the Sky Horde! I thought you'd wallow in self-pity through the entire war! Though you're still an idiot who'd walk into the goblinoids' traps without a care in the world."

Vreskiven grinned. "They can play every little trick they want. We now know better."

"That's the Vres I know! You're still a whiny little sod, but you don't stay down. I still remember that time during a hunt when your bellyaching drove Father mad enough that he tied you to a tree. You kept thrashing 'til we returned at sunset."

Vreskiven's cheeks turned red, and his nostrils flared, but before he could stammer a response, a despicable caw was heard. An ominous crimson-eyed crow landed on Baldem's shoulder, causing him to shudder before ordering his men to slow down.

I'll never get used to this, he wanted to complain.

Neither Baldem nor the crow enjoyed each other's company. The only reason it landed on Baldem was because Vreskiven would swat it away the moment it touched him or his ram.

Baldem found Vreskiven grinning like a buffoon. His eye was twinkling with mirth at his brother's discomfort.

His own eyes hardened when the impatient bird pecked his bald head. Vreskiven couldn't keep it in anymore and erupted with laughter.

Baldem took out an imaginary piece of parchment in his head and penned: *Next time I'll feed you to the corrupted birds, you cheeky bastard.*

Usually, the korrigal considered crows to be a good omen. They believed that the birds were the guardians of souls in life and the couriers of the Sky Horde in death, but that belief changed if their eyes glowed a crimson red. Nothing touched by the bereke's Crimson One was considered a good omen.

Despite Vreskiven's amusement, the two brothers felt an innate distaste towards the corrupted bird. In fact, all korrigal did.

Baldem clicked his tongue. "Seems we'll need to use *his* eyes. Show us what you want, you tainted sky rat."

"May the Sky Horde protect us from the Crimson One's influence," Vreskiven said before the two received the bird's vision from a few hours ago.

What they saw were the goblinoids. The grey ones were building palisades and covering pits with leaves and dirt. The crow couldn't get close enough to see what was inside the pits, but the brothers simultaneously surmised it'd either be spikes or, if their adversaries wanted to keep them alive, oil so that they couldn't climb their way out.

The traps were placed in a clearing not too far from the forest's exit, and there, to Vreskiven's disdain, was the red-skinned bastard he swore to kill.

"Grasha," he hissed with unbridled scorn.

"Calm down, brother. More importantly, I can't find the fancy-stick-wielding bitch and her dense knight anywhere. Who knows what nefarious spells she's preparing right now."

Vreskiven came back to himself. "That's not the only strange thing. Shouldn't there be more of her kind? Where are the rest of their shamans? They'd surely know after our last fight that we're not built for handling magic, right?"

"That's one of the reasons Jotul sent those pompous pricks with us."

Baldem's words reminded Vreskiven of their disgruntled guests.

To prevent a repeat of last time, Jotul had ensured that a squadron's worth of shamans would accompany her brothers' forces.

While the korrigal hadn't been pleased by this, they understood the tactical advantage of having their own shamans. But most of the bereke met Jotul's command with outrage.

The two brothers remembered how a few nobles had childishly stomped their feet and banged the table in the war room. The demeanour of the highborn bereke only improved when heads began to roll.

"I doubt they sent us their best, but they'll have to do," Vreskiven said. With that remark, the vision ended, and the crow puffed its chest with pride.

Baldem glared. "What are you waiting for? A treat? Scram! Go with your fellow contaminated birdbrains and find where they're hiding their shamans!"

The crow squawked and ruffled its feathers before flying away to heed its new orders. More birds followed it and spread throughout the forest and the clearing ahead.

With most of the accursed birds gone, Vreskiven turned towards Baldem.

"Hey, how about a bet? I'll shave my head as bald as yours if the goblins don't attack our wagons the moment we attack their fortifications."

Hearing the word "fortifications" made Baldem chuckle. "You mean their fluke, right? They know we have the crimson bastard's birds, so they have no reason to be so obvious about their shoddy traps."

"We'll still bring down our might on them when the birds return. Shoddy traps or not, they're still blocking our path, and my gut tells me if we don't act soon, their shamans will ambush us in the woods. Vilde had some of the damn birds and they pulled one on her, so I'm sure they're hiding somewhere."

Baldem's brows creased as he contemplated this. His eyes surveyed his surroundings, taking in the gigantic trees in all of their majestic glory, before noticing a branching road concealed beneath their roots. Even though it was overlaid with thick brambles and low-hanging branches, the road was viable enough for their men to gallop through.

He said, "We'll both need to charge from the direction they least expect and bring as many of our men as possible. Including the magical twats."

Vreskiven grinned and yelled, "It's settled, then! To war!"

With their decision made, the two brothers ordered their men to get ready for deployment. The few who were assigned to guard the wagons grumbled, as they too wanted to join their brothers and prove themselves to the Sky Horde.

The bereke shamans were grumbling for the opposite reason. With the exception of a lucky few, most of them were not thrilled that they had to ride behind a magicless race such as the korrigal.

The rams bleated when their riders forced them into formation. Soon enough, all of their chatter and clamour was gone as they awaited their commanders' signal with eager anticipation.

Just as the two brothers predicted, not many birds returned. Out of the mismatched flock from before, only a pigeon and the crow from earlier found their way back.

The panicking birds fumbled their way to the top of Baldem's ram. Much to its annoyance; it shook its head, but they refused to fly away without delivering their visions. What the brothers saw were the woods, the clearest paths, and where the birds had sensed their feathered kin had fallen.

The siblings contemplated pulling back, considering all of these factors, but one of the areas with the heaviest loss of birds was to their rear.

Calculating the odds, Baldem couldn't help but groan. "It seems like there's no way out. The goblinoids have us surrounded. I'm sure they have enough men to wear us out over time."

"Since we can't retreat, we can only break through," Vreskiven said.

"Then what are we waiting for? An invitation?"

Once everything was prepared, they raised their weapons to rally their men.

"For Jotul! For the Sky Horde!"

Trusting their commanders, the men ignored the branches and bristles filling their path and sped ahead. The shamans latching onto the korrigal riders screamed bloody murder at the sudden change in speed.

Their cries and curses were eventually muffled by the sounds of thunderous explosions.

Some of the korrigal patted their rams, trying to allay their own fears as their eyes traced the dancing smoke wafting through the air behind them.

Vreskiven frowned. "Looks like the wagon guards have already engaged with the enemy. Should we have left more of our men to safe-guard the wagons?"

"The lads will be fine! They won't fall to a bunch of snivelling gobs."

Taking one last look behind him, Vreskiven offered his comrades a silent prayer. They were almost out of the woods, and he could see the clearing ahead, but he knew it wasn't over. The sound of horns confirmed that.

Took them long enough. We weren't exactly subtle, Vreskiven muttered in his mind.

Once they arrived, the korrigal's rams slowed down to a trot so that the riders could survey the area ahead.

Their foes nervously readjusted their formation upon noticing the korrigal riders. With no obstacles in their way, and the enemy's cavalry a fair distance off, the goblinoids knew they were at a serious disadvantage.

Viciously grinning, the korrigal let out their ancestral war cries and dashed towards the unprepared goblinoids. The earth rumbled under their rams' hooves as they left behind a cloud of dust.

One look at the goblinoids' pale faces and Baldem could tell that the squirming soldiers were in a bind. Yet a single yell from their grey-skinned commander brought them back to their senses.

With a wave of the commander's hand, their ranged forces began to fire at the korrigal, slowing them down enough for his men to hurry back into formation.

Baldem lowered his head as a bronze bolt bounced off his ram's horns and shot past him. He squinted his eyes, looking at the goblinoids' commander, and frowned when he realised it was the same long-haired grey goblinoid he fought during their ambush.

The enemy commander cocked his head towards him, and his eyes widened before his surprise morphed into disdain. He brought his hand to his belt and grabbed a horn. Once he blew it, the foliage covering the pit traps began to shake.

The korrigal's jaws tightened when earthen pillars emerged from the pits, carrying with them the rest of the goblinoids' army.

Both brothers tightened their grips on their reins. The goblinoid girl from last time and her beefy grey guard were peeking at them from the pillar closest to the enemy's army.

Baldem took a glance at the bereke shaman sitting behind him, noticing that she looked unimpressed.

"Can you handle the green harlot up ahead?" he quizzed.

She let out a disgusted snort and glared at him with narrowed eyes. "Are you comparing me to a mere goblin, tusked mongrel?"

"There's nothing mere about that goblin," Baldem hissed. "If you want us to survive, you better be able to do your job."

She scoffed at his words but refused to elaborate on her tactics. Instead, a white light emanated from her hands and a warm sensation spread out to cover both of their bodies, along with their steed.

Baldem knew from past battles that the sensation was a sign that a barrier had been formed. Even when the light dimmed, he could still feel the warmth hovering a distance above his skin.

The other shamans followed suit; a wave of lights bloomed throughout the battlefield, covering Baldem's brothers-in-arms. Just in time to receive another volley of bronze-headed bolts.

The goblinoids cheered when their bolts flew true and struck the korrigal. However, their joy turned into grimaces when their projectiles seemingly bounced off of their skin and armour.

The enemy's dread-filled eyes brought a toothy grin to Baldem's face. Even though his barrier crackled from each projectile hitting it, he knew it wouldn't break.

"Stop smiling like a dumbass and dodge! Otherwise, we'll die!" the shaman screamed, then tugged on Baldem's ears.

Before he could yelp in protest, a large black fireball headed straight towards him.

With a quick pull at the reins, his ram bleated before making a turn and dashing to the left, narrowly evading the ominous fireball.

The earth rumbled as it hit the soil. Their barrier screamed, resisting the splashing flames.

The bereke cried, "What in the name of the old ones was that? How did the goblins put so much magical energy in a spell?!"

"These bastards shouldn't be underestimated. Hold on tight," Baldem answered before jerking his ram back to the right.

The shaman wrapped her arms around his waist as the korrigal reorganised into an arrow formation.

Baldem tightened his legs around his ram, signalling that it was time to charge. He took out his axe. "Barriers or not, we'll die if their formation stays cohesive. On my mark, use your strongest spell."

She took a deep breath to gather her wits and gave an affirmative; shortly after, she began gathering magical energy like the rest of her kin.

The goblinoids pelted the korrigal with projectiles and spells. Some of their barriers broke and they fell victim to the enemy's attacks, but despite their casualties, the korrigal soldiered on. Once they were less than ten kjäls away from the goblinoids' shield wall, Baldem yelled, "Breach!"

The shaman released her spell and sent a tornado-like gust of wind tearing its way through a section of the wall, followed by a plethora of spells from the other shamans.

The goblinoids immediately tried to patch their formation, but it was too late.

With their opening secured, the korrigal charged into the thick of the fray. It was time for bloodshed.

A korrigal's pride can't be left tainted.

CHAPTER 14

GOBLINOID PRIDE

Unlike the deka, Rak didn't have much experience in mounted warfare, so he wondered why the korrigal riders tended to take the shape of a wedge or arrow whenever they charged instead of a simple horizontal lineup. When he questioned Grasha, he'd told him it was more effective at breaking defensive formations.

The spearmen shivered as the earth rumbled beneath their feet. The stampeding rams' glaring eyes paired with the war cries of their riders shook them to their cores. Their only comfort was knowing their brothers-in-arms would share the same fate.

The goblinoids flung their spears forwards and braced for impact, knowing that even united, the beasts and their riders could never break through, or at least they hoped not.

Rak watched his men's resolve shatter when the bereke shamans unleashed their arcane might. His grip tightened around his axe when a conjured gust of wind sent his men flying and tore a hole in the shield wall. More offensive spells followed while they tried to patch their formation. Alas, under the strain of the adversary's shamans, they weren't able to resume a proper defensive stance, and the first line of riders crashed through the shoddy line of defenders.

With gritted teeth, Rak could only observe as his spearmen were trampled under a hundred hooves. Even though the second line of defenders desperately tried to repel the korrigal, the enemy still managed to widen the gap further yet, trampling more spearmen.

Even if they managed to hit the riders, whether by spear thrust or crossbow bolt, it'd simply bounce off the invaders' magical barrier.

To the greyborns' magically attuned eyes, it looked as if each enemy were covered with a glowing shroud that absorbed their blows. Rak would've blown his retreat horn if not for a few of his men managing to break through a barrier with successive hits.

In the end, what remained of the shield wall broke as men in the back rows were forced to flee by the widening gap. Victory was less important with the threat of being trampled by giant rams looming above them. The rams lost their momentum and slowed down to a crawl. The battle devolved into a bloodbath.

Rak jumped into the fray with a mighty roar. Once his men saw their leader join the battle, they were filled with newfound vigour.

With his axe held high, he ran through the grassy field and leapt off of a boulder. A powerful swing later, he'd shattered an incoming ram's barrier. Its riders dismounted the fallen steed and brandished their weapons. While his tusked foe wielded an axe, the bereke shaman started collecting magical energy in the palm of her hand. Rak knew he had to strike the shaman first, as she was a wild card. Only death awaits those who turn their backs on a magic user.

"What are we going to do?" Hemgall asked Orva as they watched the battle from atop one of the soil pillars. The original plan had been to trick the korrigal into a false sense of security with fake traps. They would have been lured into a gauntlet of Orva's design.

Even though their defences and plan had gone up in flames, Orva was sure they could still come out victorious. Even with the enigmatic magical shields covering the enemy, she knew it wouldn't be too long before the shamans tired out.

She grimaced. *If we had known that, we could've prepared a stone wall between our men and the bastards. As it stands now, how the hell are we going to bleed them out without harming our own?!*

"Orva?"

She couldn't hear Hemgall. *If it hadn't been for Rak joining the fray, the men would've been routed already.*

"Layered spells," she muttered out loud.

"What?"

"Layered spells provide great buffs but come at high costs. Their shamans will be worn out soon enough."

"So all we need"—Hemgall clenched his jaw when he saw Rak brawling against a one-eyed korrigal—"is for Rak to distract them long enough." Weighing all of his options and their consequences, he took a deep breath before turning towards Orva with vexation in his eyes. "Are you sure you can handle it? Shouldn't I be the one to help Rak? I mean, you can stay here and fire at their shamans from above."

Orva showed off a toothy grin. "You think I'll stay here, high and dry, and let you and Rak take all the glory? Who do you think I am..."

"Alright, then. Ready to bury the sheepfuckers alive?"

She gave him an affirmative nod. Hemgall was reminded why he'd been tasked with protecting Orva once he saw a vast amount of magical energy swirling around her.

The wave of energy felt like a gentle stream that danced its way around her staff.

It's more refined than last time, he thought with relief.

His elation was short-lived, as the pillar Orva had conjured to survey the battlefield shook and began crumbling underneath them. The bereke had changed targets, and every pillar was under fire.

The two of them struggled to stay upright. As the pillar's foundation sank back into the earth, Orva, wobbling, directed the energy she'd been building up into the sky.

Hemgall's first instinct was to grab Orva and hold her tight in his arms. Instead, he stumbled as she disappeared into the rising dust cloud. The pillar shook for the last time before it fully submerged.

By some miracle, the two of them were unharmed. Now on the ground, they stood up from the rubble and began coughing their lungs out.

Unable to bear the suffocating air any longer, Orva hastily gathered magical energy in her staff and released a powerful gust to clear the debris in their vicinity.

She wanted to survey the damage and check on her fellow shamans, but her senses warned her of an incoming spell.

Ready, Orva formed a dirt wall to block an incoming spike while Hemgall protected her rear and cut at an approaching ram's front leg.

He'd expected a barrier to block his attack, but to his amazement, his axe had cleaved right through its limb.

With a missing leg, the ram couldn't support its weight and crashed face-first onto the ground. The bereke shaman in the back was flung towards a nearby tree and snapped his neck.

Hemgall snapped out of his stupor when he noticed that the korrigal rider was still very much alive.

The moment he stood up, the korrigal desperately searched for his axe, but it was nowhere to be seen. When he noticed the approaching greyborn, he reached for his sidearm, a curved dagger, and jabbed it at Hemgall so he'd keep his distance.

A grin on his face, Hemgall split his axe into two. He easily weaved past the close-ranged jab before digging both axes into the korrigal's skull.

With his opponent dead, Hemgall turned to the remaining bereke shamans. Most had dismounted the rams and formed a line behind the tree line. A flurry of energy bolts flew past their covered position towards the recovering defensive line. He was astonished to find Rak had managed to restore his men's formation so swiftly.

He couldn't help but chuckle once Rak's focussed gaze met his eyes. *Just like the expedition, heh.*

His merriment was dampened when he saw a giant fireball crash near Rak. Even from his position, he could tell one strategic push from their adversaries could destroy the brittle line once again.

He'd have motioned to Rak for a tactical retreat if not for the diminishing magical energy on the enemy's side. While the korrigal still laboriously forced their beasts ahead, their bereke shamans were sickly pale.

I guess their juice is used up. Just like when Orva used all of her energy to hold back the behemoths.

Hemgall sighed. "I guess I'll let Rak deal with their commander on his own. At least until Orva's cast her signature attack against them."

He turned towards Orva and smiled. "Are you ready to send these dregs to The Cycle?"

Orva channelled lightning around her staff. "More than ever."

With the coast clear, the two stood up and Hemgall turned his attention to the remaining dirt pillars. A third of the earthly towers had collapsed and become their makers' graves, along with those of their entourages.

"I'll be damned if we don't tear them to shreds."

"You don't have to tell me twice." Orva planted her staff into the ground.

It didn't take long for a pillar to start rising under their feet.

Once more, Hemgall carefully surveyed the battlefield from the top. What he saw made him burst into laughter.

"What's so funny?!" Orva whined as she shot a bolt at one of the bereke shamans. Her bolt pierced through their barrier and incinerated the slender bugger.

"Watch and see," Hemgall quipped with a dumb grin.

Out of morbid curiosity, Orva approached the pillar's edge and studied the other combatants. She couldn't understand what Hemgall found so humorous. All she saw was a feast for crows in the making.

She noticed how, thanks to Rak's actions, many goblinoids now zealously faced the enemy.

The tusked ones still had the advantage as their giant beasts slammed and trampled everything in their path. Even with the ever-decreasing presence of bereke shamans, the goblinoids struggled against their barriers.

But if goblinoids were one thing, they were resilient.

The first to adapt to the korrigal's attacks were the greyborn bogeys. Many had gone through at least one expedition in their lives and were used to fighting and dismantling larger, heavily armoured foes such as the hivelings.

The initial shock and fear of fighting against the rams went moot when they instinctively relied on the same exploitable tactics of hiveling warriors.

A ram bleated in fear as it was surrounded on all sides by spears. Its rider lay lifeless underneath its belly.

It kicked around desperately, trying to scare off the bogeys to no avail. "Kill that monster before it goes haywire!" a green bogey yelped.

They circled the creature like a swarm of bees. With each thrust, the ram's barrier grew weaker. Once that was broken, the majestic beast was turned into a bleeding pincushion.

While Orva was not a fan of violence and gore, she was glad their defences were finally pushing back the korrigal onslaught.

Just like the goblinoids' shamans, the bereke had to be cautious when launching close-range spells in order to avoid harming their allies.

With the goblinoids adapting at a rapid pace, the korrigal were finally on the losing end.

"I see why you laughed earlier. The korrigal are done for," Orva said, much to Hem's amusement.

At least their main force is. I wonder how Grasha's handling things on his end.

The sight of Vreskiven's devastated forces was what Hemgall needed to allay his worries. Only a third of the korrigal were left, and their leader, Vreskiven, was locked in a duel with Grasha.

Hemgall would've been worried if he hadn't noticed that Vreskiven's shaman was lying dead on the ground next to him.

Not all was well, however, as Grasha and his steed were covered in their fair share of wounds.

The one-eyed korrigal could barely muster the strength to lean on his ram as he rode. Hemgall was sure his fate was sealed the moment he saw Vreskiven's axe fall from his shaking hands.

He shouldn't have brought a sheep to a horse fight, Hemgall concluded with a grin as he saw Grasha trotting towards Vreskiven.

He squinted when Grasha began to talk to the beaten korrigal. He couldn't make out his words, but he figured that Grasha was giving him a chance to surrender, only to have Vreskiven spit at his gesture in disgust.

"That tusked bastard might've dropped his weapon, but I'm sure he has a trick up his sleeve. Can you shoot him down if he tries anything?" Hemgall asked Orva.

She shook her head. "If they were farther apart, I might've been able to take him out, but now? There's a big chance I hit Grasha."

Hemgall's grip tightened around his axe as he watched in trepidation, waiting for the moment of truth.

To his shock, Vreskiven leapt off of his ram towards Grasha, who retaliated by thrusting his spear, piercing the korrigal's shoulder. Vreskiven still managed to throw Grasha off his horse.

When they struck the ground, Grasha's spear burrowed deeper

into Vreskiven's shoulder, but he shrugged the pain off and pivoted himself to get a grip on Grasha's throat.

The world stood still before Hemgall's eyes. Both he and Orva stared in horror as Vreskiven sank his teeth into Grasha's neck and spat out a chunk of flesh.

Grasha desperately covered the gaping hole with one hand and reached out for his sidearm, a spare xiphos on his belt. At least, that's where it should've been. Vreskiven had taken the xiphos himself on their way down and now held it above his opponent's head. Grasha coldly stared at his blade before it struck his throat, and cleanly cut through the rest of his neck.

Having finally killed Grasha, Vreskiven grabbed his lifeless head and let out a jubilant roar to the remnants of his forces, who let out cries of their own in response.

He hopped on his ram and galloped to aid his brother, who was having his own duel against Rak.

Hemgall gripped his axe so tight that his knuckles turned white.

"Where are you going?" Orva screamed.

"Rak's strong, but he can't deal with the two brothers by himself. I'm going to butcher that pig and make him pay tenfold for killing our old friend."

Orva shared Hemgall's anger. She too wanted to kill Vreskiven with a spell of her own. The sounds of hooves meeting dirt from her rear changed her mind. She raised her staff and met the eyes of a dozen korrigal riders. Dirt spikes burst out of the ground, piercing the giant rams in their abdomens.

She clicked her tongue. Their charge hadn't wavered. It was clear they wanted to distract her long enough for Vreskiven to join his brother. *Sorry, Hem, you have to avenge Grasha for the both of us.*

* * *

"What's the matter, Rak? Are you getting tired already?" Baldem teased his foe, who spat at him in response.

Rak leaned against a boulder. He ached from all of the injuries he'd received, and his arms felt as heavy as lead, but regardless of the pain, he kept a steady grip around his axe.

"Are you going to yap all day or are you going to come at me?" he retorted.

Despite his earlier mockery, Baldem wasn't in better shape. During his bouts with Rak, his armour had become riddled with cuts and dents, and his battered ram had lost its left horn.

To make matters worse for him, the shaman sitting behind him placed her entire weight on his back. The burden of putting up so many barriers and having them destroyed left her pale and on the cusp of losing consciousness.

Even with the recent setbacks, Baldem kept a smile on his face. Unlike Vreskiven, he rarely ever went berserk in a fight. He knew that losing his composure would endanger the lives of his men.

That didn't mean that he didn't enjoy a good fight, all korrigal did, but the battle had turned far worse than he expected. With only a Pyrrhic victory in sight, he was willing to bear the shame of ordering a retreat.

If only escape was an option in the first place. How in the world did the goblinoids surround us?

No matter how much he studied his opponent, Baldem couldn't find out how one goblinoid had been the catalyst for this unfortunate development.

The korrigal were used to the sight of conscripts fleeing for their lives.

The goblinoids, however, were fighting for their survival. Fleeing this battle would only endanger their society.

I don't know what kind of life they lived, but they're not normal. They viciously dismantle our rams like a pack of wolves.

There's only one way to break them.

"It's time to end this," Baldem muttered, his eyes set on Rak.

With a tug on its reins, his ram let out a mighty roar and rushed forwards.

Baldem kept his grip firm on his axe as his eyes traced Rak's every movement. He took a deep breath and prepared himself for when Rak would dodge. What he didn't expect was for his opponent to throw mud into his ram's eyes before scurrying away.

No matter how much Baldem tried to calm his steed, it ignored his every command as it kept hurling itself toward the boulder. He grabbed hold of the shaman behind him and leapt off of his ram before it smashed its head on the stone in a frenzy.

Baldem hugged the bereke tightly and took the brunt of the fall.

He placed her safely on the ground and struggled to get up. The first thing he saw was the horrible aftermath of the crash.

His ram could barely stand on its shaky legs as blood spurted from every hole and wound on its face. With one last cry and a loud thud, it plopped down on the ground.

"My poor girl," Baldem muttered under his breath. He was about to take a step towards it but was kicked from behind.

He tried to roll out of the way, but Rak held him down with his foot and raised his axe to strike.

The two exchanged silent glares until Rak issued his demand. "Tell your men to stand down."

"I heard from the dargs that korrigal are a prideful race, but we both know admitting defeat is the only way to guarantee you and your men's survival."

Baldem chuckled. "Looks like they haven't told you enough about us."

Before Rak could question him any further, Baldem spat towards his face, but his bloody phlegm merely trickled down the greyborn's chest. "Go fuck yourself, you grey co—"

Rak silenced him with a kick before turning him on his back. Baldem tried to stand, but his head was firmly held down by Rak's boot.

And with that, Rak dug his axe into the korrigal commander's neck. He kept digging and digging until he managed to chop off Baldem's head.

After the soft thud of a head hitting grass, Rak collapsed on his knees and observed the ensuing panic. Both korrigal and bereke were panicking at the sight of Baldem's body briefly remaining on hands and knees before joining its head.

Just as Rak was about to announce his victory, his ears twitched at the sound of rumbling hooves.

He instinctively grabbed his axe and jumped out of danger in the nick of time. When he stood up, he found himself face-to-face with a giant ram and its enraged rider.

Despite his severe injuries, Vreskiven thrust forth Grasha's spear.

Rak, tired as he was, dodged Vreskiven's enraged stabs. Every now and then, he found an opening and replied in kind.

Vreskiven's steed wanted to grunt in pain, but knew its master wouldn't care. Instead, it decided to jump a short distance away from the greyborn.

"What?" Vreskiven uttered in disbelief.

"Heh... Looks like even your gallant steed is spent," Rak jested, axe ready.

In an ever-intensifying fit of rage, Vreskiven tugged harshly on his ram's reins, making it bleat from pain. It desperately charged towards Rak, not paying attention to the bloodied soil.

With its frayed nerves, the ram failed to readjust its legs and stumbled onto the ground. Vreskiven held on for dear life as they fell and found himself stuck underneath his steed.

The ram, with its neck half-twisted, let out another pained bleat as it cried out for its master's aid.

"You unworthy beast..." Vreskiven hissed back as he struggled to lift its weight.

With careful steps, Rak approached his fallen opponents. He gently patted the ram as it drew its last breath. Unbeknownst to Rak, his act of mercy gave Vreskiven an opportunity to thrust his spear towards Rak's leg, stabbing him in his Achilles tendon.

With his mortal enemy on the ground, Vreskiven burst into boisterous laughter as he crawled his way out from under the dead ram. He grabbed Rak's weapon and raised the axe into the air. "An eye for an eye, you brother-killing wretch. Prepare yourself for damnation."

Before he could deal the finishing blow and achieve his revenge, he found a glowing axe burying itself deep in his neck.

"Remember me?" Hemgall asked the korrigal as he pulled out his weapon, blood gushing forth.

Vreskiven tried to laugh but could only blubber as Hemgall grabbed his axe with both hands and lifted it up high. Once he was down, his spine let out a sickening crunch. With that, his limp body dropped to the ground.

Hemgall sighed before taking off Vreskiven's chestplate and ripping a part of his tunic off to use as makeshift bandaging.

Small balls of green light illuminated the night sky. "That's their retreat signal, isn't it?" Rak muttered.

Hemgall watched the last one fizzle out. "Looks like it."

With the korrigal and their shamans dead or in full retreat, Orva stormed towards the duo, coming to a halt right before Vreskiven's lifeless body. Satisfied after giving it a kick, she turned towards Rak and pointed her staff towards the gaping hole in his leg. Slowly, new flesh and muscles began to grow.

"Any reports?" Rak asked.

Orva frowned. "Do I look like a scout?"

"Just answer the question."

She rolled her eyes. "If you insist. When the bereke launched their shoddy light spell, a few korrigal fled to the woods with Grasha's men chasing after them. If you want anything detailed, you have to wait. The scouts are doing their job and counting the bodies. The important thing is that we've won."

Rak took a look at his surroundings and rubbed his head in frustration. "I wouldn't call this a victory."

Hemgall picked up Grasha's spear and sighed. "A lot of good men died, especially a lousy but fun drinking buddy of mine."

"We'll give him and the others a proper burial. I'll make sure of that," Orva promised.

"Yeah... We have a lot of work to do."

CHAPTER 15

ONE-UPMANSHIP

"Urgh..." Lev groaned as he stirred from another bleak night of sleep. His cluttered surroundings along with his uncomfortable posture made him realise that he'd fallen asleep at his home desk again.

He wearily got up and stretched his aching back.

Opening his window's shutters, he found himself blinded by the sun's light.

Is it noon already? The council will be furious. Not that those fools were ever calm, especially not with the ongoing war.

Lev let out a loud yawn. *It's not like I'm missing out on much. The council members just come to the Halls to argue and trick themselves into feeling productive.*

He sighed and grabbed one of the scrolls on his desk. "Screw it. If those buffoons don't have anything beneficial to say, I'd rather make better use of my time."

Since the day he had that nightmare, Lev had been dedicating all of his time outside of the war room to uncovering Ainshard's darkest secrets. He'd scoured the city's ancient library to assemble a compendium of myths and legends.

I must not allow the Guides to repeat such a tragedy! he thought before opening the first scroll in his collection.

He nodded in approval; it seemed to have been properly translated from old Ainshardian to the common tongue. Most shaman scribes were deployed on the battlefield, with the latest batch having headed out with Rak a few days ago. Luckily enough, the scrolls had apparently been translated prior to the war.

Lev reclined in his chair. *The war...*

It wouldn't be long before he had to face Jotul and her forces. As a member of the council, he was forced to stay behind to monitor the situation from the comfort of Pàrras.

On one hand, it wasn't all that bad. He had time to think, to reflect. Sure, Jotul's forces outnumbered the goblinoids three to one, but they were fighting on two fronts.

If there hadn't been the bereke civil war, Lev wasn't sure if Pàrras would have come out on top. Though he was sure the Guides would aid him if Pàrras were to fall.

Three days ago, messengers arrived and informed Lev and the council that Jotul would reach one of the fortified outposts in a week. Most of Lev's forces had already departed, with the exception of Raban, Shahn, Gerwyn, and himself. Even Eleric, the human who had only recently assimilated into goblinoid society, had volunteered to join them in this fight.

Knowing that he didn't have much time before his departure to the front line, Lev curiously read the scroll, hoping it contained any information that would ease his tired mind.

It was about one of Ainshard's sons escaping the continent on a ship after the fall. Even though it provided some insight into the lives of Ainshard's kin after his demise, it mentioned nothing of the tall goblins he'd seen. Not even the Guides, Ainshard's most trusted councillors, were mentioned in the scroll.

It was as if they'd disappeared into obscurity.

No wonder nobody knows they exist. Even the avians only knew of Kram.

Lev silently turned to the remaining scrolls on his desk and took a deep breath to collect his thoughts.

Ainshardian mysteries or not, I better head to the council. They're pissed enough already.

He hid the scrolls inside a hidden compartment underneath the fireplace before packing his necessities inside a sack and tying it to the shaft of his glaive.

Master, I'd rather you not use me in such a manner. This is insulting! the glaive complained.

Weren't you the one who said Lev is always right and that we should do as we are told? Gherm snarkily replied.

Under normal circumstances, I'd agree, but that's when our master is...

"Say it, Miss Glaive. His right mind," Lev muttered with a frown as he exited his room and went down the stairs.

Don't mind her, Lev. She doesn't share your memories. But she has a point, this fixation on the past isn't healthy. You should focus on what's ahead.

Lev chuckled. *Gherm, you of all people should know that I'm building towards a better future every day.*

There won't be one if you destroy our body, Gherm argued back.

He gnashed his teeth and tightened his grip on the door's handle. *Lives are at stake here, Gherm! One of the Guides just needs to turn on that abominable orb and—*

Lev was interrupted by the shrill sound of the departure horn.

Looks like the council wants to end this war earlier than I anticipated. We were supposed to depart next week!

He burst out of his house and headed towards the southern gates, which had been christened the Gates of Victory by the people ever since the first goblinoid army had marched out to face Jotul.

He found the main route blocked by cheering onlookers and took a detour, rushing past the masses.

Once he reached the gates, he found the area crowded by civilians and soldiers alike, then joined the throng.

At the head of the gathered army, he saw Vyrga, decked in full gear. He addressed the crowd with a confident grin.

"Another threat invades our lands and dies by our hands."

"We have toiled and rebuilt what had been lost to the aeons, hoping to bring about a new dawn, and yet, vile serpents fear our rise."

"An agent of death holds her blade at our throats. Her god, known as the Crimson One, is a wicked butcher whose only goal is calamity. Truly a maddened war god. Any being that desires bloodshed should be purged from this world."

Vyrga made sweeping gestures before the gathering. When Lev turned to look at them, he was surprised to see that not only goblinoids had gathered, but also avians.

"The bereke and korrigal thrive on hatred. So much so that they even hate their own species."

"Rak's scouts personally informed me about their civil war. Now is the time to deliver the final blow."

A few disgruntled council members in the crowd wanted to protest against Vyrga's hastiness. After all, they'd all agreed on the various battle plans and their timing. It'd taken lengthy discussions to draft them.

Vyrga didn't give them room to argue as he fervently continued his speech. "Our beloved council has pleaded with me to hasten our plans. It was through their wisdom that I came to realise the enemy's infighting!"

The council members remained silent.

Lev smirked. *Still the same old Vyrga.*

He raised his arms like a concertmaster leading his violins. "The enemy saw our progress and shuddered in disgust and fear."

The crowd gasped collectively, awaiting Vyrga's next words with bated breath.

He melodramatically hissed, "In a short time, we built their antithesis, a society that values unity!

"While we haven't thrown our blades aside, we gave our hand to those in need. We communicated with, traded with, and accepted others." As he lectured, he pointed at the avians.

The crowd turned their attention to the birdlike creatures. For once, they looked at the poorest of Pàrras with commiseration instead of intolerance.

Vyrga gestured, cutting a hand across his neck. "For that, he sent his craven hounds to tear our throats, but I, as the first High Chief of the Frontier, shall not allow the vermin to besmirch our path of progress. I won't allow them to harm our people!"

Lev noticed some people starting to cry, but didn't know whether it was out of admiration for Vyrga or fear of Jotul. Then again, he remembered he'd used actors to sway the mob in his favour in the cavern days.

Vyrga pointed at the southern gates. "Our brave men and women are dealing with her pawns as we speak." He raised two fingers. "Two of them, a greyborn and a goblin, already slew one of her hounds and are making their way back home. Should I, your chosen leader, do any less? You chose me to lead you, so it is my duty to sacrifice myself for you."

"This is outrageous!" a man cried out from the crowd. He was wearing the robes of a priest of Zeja. "It was already planned that Lev, Zeja's champion, should lead the war against this god and his emissary! The champion of *the* war goddess should be the one dealing with the champion of a false war god!"

Vyrga sneered. "How foolish."

The priest was furious. "And what part of what I'm saying is foolish, High Chief? Heeding the goddess's command? She chose him for a reason, and he alone has her blessing!"

Vyrga threw his cape open. "That Zeja put that entire burden on Lev and blessed only him? Is he not a mortal man?"

The priest's eyes widened. "W-What do you mean?"

"I'll admit that he is a genius," Vyrga said, pointing at Lev, his voice rising into a yell, "but isn't this burden too much for one man? Are you saying we should burden Lev more than we already have? Have you seen his state lately?!"

What are you planning with all of this, Vyrga?!

"This man threw his life on the line multiple times for the people and helped build the foundation of our society. He invested time, effort, and money to make Pàrras recover. He reinforced our trade routes and played a crucial part in planning for the war effort. All of this, and you want to throw this weary soul into the furnace of war?"

The priest was speechless.

"Lev has done a lot and will do more, but a society can't survive on the back of one man. We need to fight against this threat together. With every proud soldier's aid, I'll join the fray, and we'll face this enemy together! I'll face Jotul the Mad One and put a stop to her encroaching darkness."

Vyrga took out his blade, and the wolf-pommelled sword let out a powerful glow. "I'll be the light that protects our people from the dark! I'll draw my sword to cut off the serpent's head. I'll bring justice to those who fell to the bereke's wanton massacre!"

The ground trembled under a hundred stomping feet. "Vyrga! Vyrga! Vyrga!"

Lev approached Vyrga from the crowd, which caused the cheers and stomping to quickly subside. They wondered if Lev truly had gone mad. Was the warrior of Zeja finally at wit's end? Maybe it really was time for the High Chief to take the battle reins and show Lev his place. Vyrga had been fairly elected, after all, or so they'd heard.

"Can we have a word in private?" Lev muttered as he walked past the esteemed High Chief.

With a dramatic wave of his hands, Vyrga ended his speech and motioned for Bolo to follow the two of them to an empty guard barrack.

Once there, Lev shut the door behind them all and thumbed through the desolate weapon racks until he found a folding table for them to sit at.

"What's all of this, Lev? Have you truly gone mad?! You better have a good reason to disrupt my speech," Vyrga yapped.

Bolo nodded as he fiddled with his mace. "Your lordship had the people at his feet, Lev. You do realise his only goal with all of this was to keep morale high?"

Lev clapped his hands, startling his guests. "And I applaud you for that, oh great High Chief. But a little bird told me you're trying to claim all the glory for yourself."

Bolo narrowed his eyes. "Don't take this the wrong way. Those priests of your beloved Zeja were trying to do the same. Many of our people sacrificed their lives for us to reach this point, so what makes you think you deserve all the acclaim?"

"We share the burden, and its reward," he added.

Vyrga shushed Bolo. "That's enough. You've got a point, Lev. You are Zeja's chosen one and the people adore you. You deserve all of the credit."

Bolo rolled his eyes as Vyrga mellowly continued, "You're the rebellion's poster boy while I was a villain, or so they say."

As Bolo was about to protest, he felt the air in the barrack change, and sure enough, Vyrga slammed both of his fists on the table. "But you're becoming dangerous, boy! Ever since we arrived in Pàrras, your actions have been taking a turn for the worse."

Lev retained a calm facade. "Dangerous? I think our common enemy poses a bigger threat than my so-called lunacy."

With open palms, Lev stretched his arms towards the two. "What are you going to do? Arrest me?"

Vyrga grunted and took a glance at Lev's glaive, which sat neatly behind his chair. "Arrest you?"

He wondered if Lev might have lost enough of his mind to attack him in a last-ditch effort to save face. If so, Lev would have the advantage in both range and speed. With luck, Vyrga would be able to get a stab in, but not after suffering a few jabs himself.

Then again, were he to survive the clash, he'd have the backing of the people and a traitor to be hanged in the plaza. He'd come out on top, with nobody in his way. A sly smile crept on his face at the thought of Zeja's servants grovelling at his feet for forgiveness.

Nonetheless, he had to choose his next words more carefully. "Far from it. You've grown complacent with all of your antics and it's our fault for blindly allowing you to do as you see fit. If not for your ignorance, I would've allowed your games for a tad longer."

The former gang leader pulled his chair uncomfortably close to Lev. "Your excuses might fool the council, who believe you to be Zeja's chosen one, but they don't work on me."

Lev raised an eyebrow. "Excuses?"

"What else can they be? You've always thrown valid arguments behind your ideas, but after appointing Kul as the Chief of Justice, you ignored your duties and hoarded scrolls related to Ainshard in your house like a madman. Let legends rest in their tales."

Lev stood up and walked behind Vyrga's chair. "While I do agree that I've been absent from recent sessions..."

He leaned in over his shoulder. "I'm not crazy. You say Ainshard is dead, but we see Ainshard every day."

"When you walk through Pàrras," he went on, approaching Bolo, "you see remnants of his marvellous architecture. When you gallop along ancient roads, you flow through his empire's blood."

"An empire which has long since died out," Bolo remarked as his eyes followed Lev.

"I would love to show you the things I've seen, but I can't. You wouldn't understand," Lev continued.

Vyrga chuckled. "We've entertained you long enough, boy. Sure, I'll admit you're an exceptional leader and have proven yourself in battle, but you've finally lost your mind."

He tapped his fingers on the table's wood as he pondered something that had always bothered him. How could a juvenile brat who'd always been so down-to-earth rise to such heights?

Vyrga allowed the thought of Lev being backed by Zeja. Crazy as it seemed, there was a small chance the war goddess had truly lent her strength to him for some grand purpose he couldn't begin to comprehend. For one, it'd explain his sudden change in character and the knowledge that came with it.

"Gods only know what happened to you after that cave-in. Many took it for a blessing, and in a sense, it was, but dare I say you slept with Mal herself to gain these curious insights."

The middle-aged greyborn reclined in his chair. "Enlighten us by whatever means, Zeja's chosen one. I implore you to wash our ignorance away!"

Bolo coughed and covered his mouth yet couldn't fully hide away his smile.

Lev walked back to his chair. Once seated, he grabbed the glaive and vertically planted it between his legs. "A wise man once told me it's better to show than to tell."

He flashed a sly smile of his own. "His compatriots were always too verbose.

"Vyrga, could you take out your relic sword?"

The High Chief stood up and brandished his wolf-pommelled sword. "Have you finally decided to challenge me?"

Unlike his father, Bolo didn't find the situation humorous. He quickly stood up with his mace.

Vyrga looked back at him and cackled. "Calm down, son! I want to see what trick he has up his sleeve. I haven't laughed like this in ages! To think I gave him a position of power!

"Bolo, do me a favour and assemble the men at the river. I'll join you in a bit after neutering this child," he ordered to reprieve his son.

"Vyrga," Lev maintained a calm tone. "Look at the blade of my glaive."

Bolo tightened his grip around his mace. "I'll stay. It's better to see how this plays out."

"Fine. Show us"—Vyrga dropped his sword as intense magical energy surged from the glaive. It overpowered all of his senses and grasped his mind like tendrils—"Lev!"

Bolo's chair clattered on the ground as he took refuge behind a weapon rack to shield himself.

With squinting eyes, Vyrga grabbed for Lev. "What is this?"

Using the glaive's ability to slow down his perception of time, Lev got up from his chair and leapt behind Vyrga.

Vyrga had sworn Lev was in front of him, but seconds later, he heard Lev's voice from behind. "I'm here."

"By Jom's beard!" Bolo yelped in anguish. "Make it stop! I can't feel my body!"

The magical energy only increased, forcing Vyrga to fall on his knees. "Answer me, Lev! There's no relic like this! What is this power?!"

I implore you to stop, master. You've released most of my energy! the glaive whined in Lev's head.

"Ainshard's power," Lev answered as the energy in the room faded.

He glanced at the weapon racks and saw Bolo's unconscious body slumped against them.

"You still haven't answered me! Even if this is Ainshard's power, how did you obtain it? Was it the key that K-35 mentioned?" Vyrga demanded with a snarl.

"Like I said, High Chief. If I were to explain, we'd be sitting here until Jotul comes banging at the gates."

Vyrga wearily stood up and patted the dust off his mantle. "Fine. You can play your game, and I'll play along. I'll allow you to retake control of the remaining forces."

Lev hung his glaive around his shoulders and grabbed his bag of belongings from the ground. "The lunacy you speak of is the price of this power. There are higher beings that rule over this world, Vyrga."

"Higher than Zeja?" Vyrga asked as he sat down to catch his breath.

"Something like that, I guess," Lev replied with a toothy grin, and left the barrack.

Didn't you go a bit overboard? Gherm quizzed.

I agree, Master. Showing them the empire's power so blatantly will make Vyrga warier of you.

"They had to be reminded. This was the only way."

If you say so, master.

Gherm remained silent, but Lev could feel his ever-growing despondency.

CHAPTER 16

FEATHERED FRIENDSHIP

At the tail end of noon, the city was bustling with activity. The merchants peddled their wares, children played in the streets, and the creaking of carriages rumbled across.

All of this noise stirred Abelarda from her sleep. The moment she took off her blanket, she was assaulted with a powerful headache. It felt as if a blacksmith had been hammering her brain.

The door to her room creaked open, and inside walked Volker, a cup in his hand.

"Seems like someone's finally awake," he said with a smile. He placed the cup on the bedside table.

Confused, she looked around and realised that she wasn't in her own home. She was in a guest room at Volker's place.

She felt another pang and grabbed her head. "What happened?"

Volker shook his head and replied, "You drank too much during the celebrations."

Her eyes widened as her cheeks turned red.

Yesterday was her brother's triumphant return. An invisible weight had been pulled off her chest when she'd seen her younger brother walk through the eastern gates.

He'd been flustered by all of the cheers as he walked upon the road of heroes. Rapha, on the other hand, took the cheers in stride, grinning.

Back then, Abelarda couldn't help but push her way through the crowd and tackle him with a hug. The crowd gasped in shock while Volker's men burst into laughter.

She vaguely remembered how Vyrga had ordered for a feast to be arranged in the Grand Halls, to celebrate the first victory amongst many.

Cloudy memories of bountiful food and drink from every race resurfaced.

She'd scarfed down meals she wouldn't have dreamed of during the cavern days. And being the sister of a champion, she'd drank drinks meant for kings.

Her last returning memory involved her downing an entire keg of deka ale. Everything afterwards felt like one hazy blur.

"If it weren't for Ghorza and the girls dragging you away, you might have woken up in a barrel like last time. Father wasn't happy at all."

"It only happened once," Abelarda yelled as her face turned a deeper shade of red.

Seeing how flustered she was made Volker burst into laughter. His merriment ended when she banged him on the head.

"Jeez, you didn't have to go so far," he mumbled while rubbing the bump.

Abelarda cracked her knuckles with a sneer plastered on her face. "Laugh at me again and I'll remind you of the *good* old days."

Volker raised his hands in mock surrender and backed away. "Just drink the medicine. Hermut made me pay an arm and a leg for the herbs."

Hearing the name of that obnoxious witch doctor brought a bitter taste to her mouth. She gingerly examined the contents of the cup; her left eye twitched at the bubbling green liquid swirling within.

She didn't know if it was her hangover or the vile goop, but her stomach began to turn.

"Come on, Abel. You have to drink it if you want to feel any better," Volker urged her sternly.

Knowing he was right, she hesitantly reached for the cup before bringing the foul concoction near her lips. Her nose scrunched from the smell, but she knew Hermut's medicines were the fastest way to cure her pounding head.

With one fell swoop, she downed the accursed remedy.

Volker shuddered as Abelarda's face turned sickly pale. She could feel the liquid bubbling its way up her throat, so she brought her hands to her mouth and fought the urge to vomit. Yet, despite her apparent nausea, she let out a relieved sigh.

"What in the name of Mal does he put in his remedies for them to turn out so awful?" she complained.

Volker shrugged. "At least it works."

"I'll never drink deka ale again in my life just so I never have to try this again."

He rolled his eyes at her proclamation. *Sure you won't.*

"Volker. Food's ready!" yelled a feminine voice from down the hall.

When he turned towards the door, Abelarda noticed a goofy smile on her brother's face.

"So Varra lives here now?"

Volker scratched his head. "Y-Yeah. I was thinking of taking her to our parents' place today."

He yelped when Abelarda pulled him close and began to aggressively rub his head.

"Look at you go! My little brother's becoming a man now," she teased.

No matter how hard he tried, Volker couldn't get out of her grasp.

"Please knock it off! We're not kids anymore!" he cried in despair.

"As you wish."

With a grin, she complied. Once she let go, Volker lost his balance and wildly swung his arms as he fell on the floor, the carpet softening his fall.

Once he got up, he grumbled, "Abel, you're an asshole."

"I wouldn't be a good older sister if I didn't tease my little brother every now and then. Now, if you'll excuse me, get out so I can freshen up. I have to meet up with the girls and I can't waste a single minute."

"Since when did you turn down meals?" Volker exclaimed, much to Abelarda's indignation.

"Are you trying to imply something?" Abelarda demanded with a growl. "And for the record, Ghorza's in a bad spot, so we're planning on cheering her up."

"I noticed. When I asked her if she's okay, she tried to play it off and smile, but it was obvious. I'm sure she's worried about Lev."

More than you can imagine, Abelarda thought.

All three girls could tell that after they'd moved to Pàrras, things had turned icy between her and Lev. On many occasions, it felt as if he were distancing himself from her.

When Abelarda had tried asking Thorst, he told her that when he was called Gherm, his original name, he was a much different person.

Ghorza's hiding something, Abelarda decided before letting out a sigh. *But as a friend, it's not my job to pry into her secrets. She'll tell us when she's ready.*

"I'm glad that she found some good company. You have no idea how much Lev's worried about her. Can't you make some room for lunch before you go? You've already slept through breakfast."

"No, Volk. My stomach's still turning from Hermut's shitty..."

"Abel?"

"Varra made lunch, right? So that means it's afternoon."

"Yeah?" Volker hesitantly replied.

At those words, she burst out of the door, much to her brother's surprise.

She made a quick turn to the washroom to scrub her face. With that task done, she ran past a shocked Varra and made her way towards the entrance.

"What's wrong?!" Varra yelled while chasing after her.

"I'm late, that's what's wrong! Lore will kill me!"

Much to the darg's confoundment, Abelarda exploded out of the door and onto the crowded streets.

Many passersby stopped in their tracks to look at the weird spectacle, but Abelarda didn't pay them any mind. Her eyes darted around the road, trying to figure out the best shortcut to Ghorza's house, and once she made her decision, she rushed as fast as she could.

* * *

"Thanks for helping me out. My family's been putting me in quite the bind lately," Lore told Ghorza.

The two of them, along with Reeza, were hauling large crates across the northern district. Despite their size, the crates weren't heavy, and at Lore's insistence, they marched on with almost no breaks.

"What are friends for if not for hauling?" Ghorza replied with a grin.

"Tell that to the slacker. We could've carried a few more if she was here," Lore grumbled.

Reeza came to Abelarda's defence. "You've seen how much she drank. The poor thing must be having the worst time of her life. I hope Volker's taking good care of her."

"That beanpole is pretty close with his sister. There's no brother who'd just leave his—" Lore shut herself up. She immediately eyeballed Ghorza, and seeing her disheartened expression made her curse herself for her careless words.

Reeza suddenly stumbled forward. Both Ghorza and Lore looked on in horror as she seemed about to fall, only to sigh in relief when she managed to regain her footing just in time.

Ghorza put her crate down and ran to check on her. "You're not hurt, right?!"

Reeza gently placed the crate on the ground and twirled to show that she was unharmed. "It's okay, I just tripped on a pebble."

Hearing her words, Ghorza couldn't help but hug the girl. She smiled kindly as she squeezed the younger, but much taller, brunette. It looked as if a child were hugging her older sister.

"We should get a carriage, so nobody gets hurt again. Isn't that right, Lore?" Ghorza suggested whilst still hugging Reeza.

Lore didn't respond. She absentmindedly stared at the two before surveying the road. Her eyes widened when she had an epiphany. *I don't see any pebbles for her to trip on.*

She grinned when Reeza winked at her. *She must've intentionally done that to change the topic.*

"Lore?"

In order not to waste this newfound opportunity, Lore responded as the hug ended. "Sorry. It's just that, other than the dargs and the guards, not many people are willing to take their carriages to the northern part of the city, especially with the recent drug incident."

With furrowed brow, Ghorza eyed the street looking for help from the locals. "Then can't anyone help us?"

Some avians stared back with wary curiosity while others averted their gaze.

"Don't waste your time. Many avians fear we'd drag them into an incident with Kul and the guards. One of the reasons my family wanted to help them in the first place is to build a relationship with them now that the dargs have blown their chance. They can make quite the partners if we get them on our side."

Ghorza bit her lip. "Thorst wouldn't like that."

"Trust me. It's better for everyone if they get work and a shoulder to lean on instead of us leaving them to the mercy of merchants and corpse-eaters. Now, will you two laggards pick your crates up or leave it all to poor old me? If you do, you'll be missing out on a sweet reward at the end."

Ghorza wanted to protest, fearing that Reeza would harm herself again, but the brunette patted her on the back.

"I'll be fine. We should finish this before it gets dark," she said before picking up her crate.

Ghorza sighed and followed suit. With that, the three girls picked up the pace.

The avians couldn't help but stare at the odd trio trudging deeper into their territory. Normally, goblinoids didn't go beyond the Heart of Edorai, especially not now.

The three girls didn't mind the uncharted slums, though.

We've carried heavier mushrooms back when we lived in the caverns. These crates are nothing, Lore noted.

Halfway towards their destination, Lore had a change of heart. The box almost fell from her shaking hands, and her veins felt as if they were about to burst.

She sighed when she regained her bearings. *I should've brought a carriage! I don't care if I have to beg the purple asshats for one. If we don't arrive there soon, my arms will give out!*

Seeing the pitiful sight that was Lore, some of the masked birds moved closer in order to help, but their companions held them back. None of the girls could understand what the birdfolk whispered to their friends, but afterwards they all eyed the crates suspiciously and backed away from the girls.

Their actions left her livid. "The nerve of leaving us like this! Don't they have any form of chivalry?"

Annoyed by Lore's whining, Reeza reproached her. "Weren't you the one saying how they don't trust us, and thus, likely won't help us? Looks like you're right, and I can't blame them.

"From their perspective, we're three weird greyborn girls barging straight into their neighbourhood while carrying large mysterious boxes. I wouldn't trust us with my life."

Lore sighed. "I just wish I was wrong. My arms are killing me."

"Another reason as to why you should exercise. I'm doing fine and Ghorza isn't even breaking a sweat."

She realised the brunette was right. Ghorza wasn't having any issues at all. She couldn't help but stare enviously at her friend, who was carrying the largest of the crates with ease.

Oblivious to Lore's troubles, Ghorza gawked at the makeshift architecture. With their support dwindling due to the war effort, the avians had taken renovating the northern district into their own hands.

The buildings lacked the finesse that came from having the shamans sculpt the stones, but they compensated for that with a wide assortment of wooden homes and support structures.

From conical houses built on top of the flat, decaying roofs to short towers connecting walkways across the various structures, the district was a marvel. Ghorza even heard some avians had decided to turn their basements into communal quarters.

All of these structures were adorned with symbols that Ghorza had never seen before.

Along their walls, she saw droves of avians gathering around cooking stands.

Her heart wrenched when she saw the skinny form of a child. The child had lost most of their feathers, so Ghorza couldn't tell if they were a male or female. What she could make out was how they desperately held out a bowl, only to receive watered-down gruel.

"Don't worry, we'll help the snotty chicks soon," Lore assured as they passed the crowds. "Maybe then they'll help us next time we pass through."

From the way she squirmed in discomfort, Ghorza noticed that her heart was also pained, but still Lore soldiered on.

Before they knew it, they found themselves at their destination. It was a small plaza surrounded by avian lodgings. Most of the city had been restored, making it surprising to see that the council had neglected a plaza. Sure, it wasn't as grand as the main one but restoring it would surely boost the district's social cohesion and bring some coin to their empty pockets.

The moment they reached the centre of it, Lore spitefully threw her crate on the ground and used it as a stool.

"Watch it! What if you broke the box?!" Reeza told her angsty companion.

"Don't worry, my family wouldn't be good smugglers if they cheaped out on containers. And the insides aren't fragile either."

Having answered the brunette, Lore tried to take her water gourd off of her belt, but her clumsy hands wouldn't comply.

She wanted to scream when the bottle slipped from her fingers and broke on the ground.

"My arms wouldn't hurt as much if that drunkard made it on time."

Reeza shook her head. "There were only three crates. Unless you wanted her to carry yours, I don't see why it would've mattered. Isn't that right, Ghorza?"

Ghorza didn't respond. She was still thinking about what they witnessed on their way.

What's wrong with Lev? I thought he was acting strange because of the suicidal bird attacks, but to take it as far as ignoring the avians? He brought them here. What's happening to my brother?

Her thoughts were interrupted by a squawk from an avian child. Despite their parents' warnings, a few kids had approached the crates with piqued curiosity.

Ghorza chuckled when she saw the youngest run a few laps around the wooden containers.

"What is box? Food?" questioned one of the children in broken common tongue. The dark blue plumage on his neck swayed in the wind making it easy to tell that he was a boy.

Ghorza felt a pull at her heartstrings when he looked at her with those inquisitive eyes hidden behind that mask.

"They're..." Not knowing what to say, she turned to Lore for help.

Seems like their little beaks are keener than I expected, Lore thought.

Finally able to feel her arms, she complied and opened one of the crates.

She picked up a cloth bundle and threw it towards the kid.

Once he caught it, the little avian boy sniffed it, and his eyes widened. The feathered creature eagerly ripped the cloth away, spilling the foodstuffs inside on the ground. He lifted his mask and began devouring a roll of bread stuffed with meat.

"Tha biadh ann!" one of the other kids exclaimed. With his words, more avians, both young and old, paid attention to the three greyborns.

When the crowd noticed more vegetables and rolls had fallen on the ground, they began to caw in glee.

Ghorza was stunned by the sheer number of birdfolk that approached her. The first kid hastily grabbed what he dropped and ran towards his family while she faced the incoming hungry horde.

She could only stutter when they waved their arms demanding food.

Thankfully, Lore came to the rescue. "Hey! Birdbrains, can't you see the girl's confused? If you want to eat, then settle down and wait in line!"

The crowd stared at her in confusion until an avian with a green mask began explaining the situation to his kin.

Lore's shoulders sagged in relief when the birds arranged themselves in three neat columns.

Seeing the avians following her orders put a smile on Lore's face. She turned to her two companions and clapped her hands.

"Now it's our turn. Each of you, open your box and start giving the birds their meals."

Looking in the eager eyes of the avians made Ghorza gulp. "That's a long line of birdfolk. Will the three of us be enough?"

"Trust me. That blonde brute won't take too long to arrive. Besides, like I said earlier, there's a nice reward at the end."

Reward? Lore's second mention of it sparked Ghorza's interest, but before she could ask any questions, she was interrupted by a loud baritone squawk.

She immediately grabbed a sack and put it into the giddy avian's hands. Even if she couldn't understand him or his masked facial expressions, the grateful bow he gave conveyed his gratitude.

Soon, the next avian came forward, and the one after that, but Ghorza didn't mind. She found herself falling into a rhythm as she gave away the food. She entertained herself by studying the fascinating birdlike creatures from closer than she ever thought possible.

Ghorza marvelled at the subtle cues they gave and felt as if she began to understand some of the chirps and squawks that accompanied their mystical language.

Before she knew it, a third of her box had been emptied. That's when she heard some alarmed cries from the avians and saw a yellow blur approaching from the distance.

"You're late!" Lore grumbled at Abelarda's arrival. She narrowed her eyes as she scrutinised her tardy companion.

"If you were going to take your time, you could have at least changed your clothes."

Unable to look Lore in the eyes, Abelarda turned away and mumbled, "They're still clean… enough, and I was already late. It's not like I covered them in vomit!"

"Vomiting over your clothes would have been the least of your worries."

"You really went all out yesterday," Reeza added with pompous side-eye.

Abelarda stomped her foot on the ground and growled. "Hey, don't judge me! With this stupid war, when will we ever drink or eat like that again?" she argued. "I was taking in the fleeting moment of joy to the fullest extent!"

Lore opened her mouth, but no words came out. Failing to come up with a valid argument, she lowered her head in defeat.

"I can't deny that. Food prices have been increasing lately. The war has taken a huge toll on us all."

Since the start of the war, priority supplies had been given to the army. Most consumables were being sent to the soldiers on the front lines, leading to the ever-worsening food shortage, which especially hurt grain, meat, and spices.

The biggest saving grace was that the bogeys didn't find it as bothersome as the other races. They were used to a narrower diet due to their earlier life in the cavern, where they had their fair share of food shortages.

With all of the girls distracted by Abelarda, a few disgruntled birdfolk chirped loudly to catch their attention. To Lore's appreciation, they were reprimanded by their kin, who had already formed a fourth queue column.

"Let's talk while we work. Neither us nor the avians will get any less hungry if we dawdle," Reeza suggested before going back to her crate.

Now that they had Abelarda, the division of work became more bearable, and the four girls kept at it until the late hours of dusk.

Ghorza reached into her food crate and found one remaining packet, which she promptly passed to the next avian in her queue.

"Does anyone have food packets left?" she asked her companions, only to receive a negative from all three girls.

With a deep sigh, she turned to the remaining birdfolk, then gave them an apologetic smile whilst slowly managing an apology.

She averted her gaze when their shoulders slumped in response. Now that feeding time was over, they listlessly walked away, a few of them giving her nods on their way out.

The end of the hungry crowd meant the girls finally had a chance to rest. Reeza and Ghorza were dragged off by the grateful kids to play with them while the remaining two girls lay on the ground near the empty crates.

"It's finally over," Abelarda blurted out, much to Lore's chagrin.

"You're the last one who should complain," the black-haired grey-born argued.

Before Abelarda could respond, they were approached by an avian with greying feathers: an elder.

Lore wasted no time heading towards one of the crates. She took out a knife from beneath her dress and plunged it inside, right above the bottom edge.

With a soft plop, the fake bottom was removed, revealing sacks full of coloured powders.

Abelarda gasped before approaching Lore with a sneer. "Don't tell me you took a page out of the dargs' book. Haven't the birds suffered enough?"

Lore frowned. "What do you take me for? These are just some dyes from Brizilum. The avians love the stuff, since it's better than what they're used to."

"Why don't they buy it from the dargs, then? Add this food scheme to the check and I'm sure all of this costs your family a fortune."

"It seems you've got a few things wrong." Lore smugly grinned. "Both the food and dyes are investments for a brighter future. And we didn't buy the stuff off of the dargs."

Abelarda crossed her arms. "Ghorza's hubby won't like the idea of you dealing with contraband."

Lore pointed towards Ghorza, who was laughing with some of the avian kids. "Then go snitch on me and spoil her mood. If she hasn't put two and two together by now; she already knows my family is trying to win the feathered ones over."

Abelarda couldn't help but shake her head. "I hope that's enough to protect you. Just in case, make sure not to get yourself in trouble. I've heard the drug trade has been driving our Chief of Justice mad lately, and we both know he doesn't like your business."

"He'll like my family's side hustles more when we lend him a hand. The purple bastards are putting their fingers in everyone's pies. Buying the avians' trust and giving them food is one way to keep them away from the dargs' depravities."

Lore continued, "I never miss an opportunity, Abel. You should know that by now."

Abelarda held back her complaints. "At least we're done for the day."

"Oh, hardly." Lore grinned. "There's still that special reward I told you about, right?"

Though Abelarda wanted to question what Lore meant, she paused when she heard loud noises.

"Are those... drums?"

Pleased by the blonde's confusion, Lore beamed. "If you'd dealt with the avians enough, you'd know that they're a generous people. And they pay back everything in kind."

Ghorza and Reeza rushed towards the duo. The former asked, "What's happening?! Is everything okay?!"

Just as they had started, the drums suddenly stopped.

The four girls noticed a formally dressed avian with an intricate mask had emerged from one of the houses along with a retinue of six younglings. The old avian held an opened box with four masks.

Ghorza's eyes widened; the masks roughly fit a bogey's head.

One of the young retainers handed a mask to each of the girls, and when Ghorza got hers, she stared in awe at its fine craftsmanship.

It was made from white birch and had symmetrical notches on the sides of the beak.

With the masks given, the old avian raised his hand and all of the others began to cheer.

Lore turned towards the confused Ghorza. "You were asking about what's happening, right?"

"Yes?"

"We've sealed the deal my family made with them, and to top it off, the four of us earned their friendship. The masks are a sign of that. I can't promise great things will come to the city, but you did great, *we* did great. Things will look better for the birdfolk, at least."

"Huh, I guess you're right. We did Kul's job for him."

To Lore's surprise, the old avian scoffed at Kul's name.

When she turned towards Ghorza to smooth things over, she was surprised again as her friend shrugged her off.

Ghorza sighed. "It's fine. Lev, no, Gherm hasn't been himself lately, and I can't blame the avians for hating Kul, the so-called Chief of Justice. They don't know what the drug's doing to them, and neither do I, to be honest. If you ask me, Kul's too old to handle this. He's a good man, but he's hyperfocussed on the dargs and neglects the other problems the avians face."

Lore frowned. "Look, I don't know what came between you and your brother, but it's clearly bothering you. We won't pry your secrets out of you, but for your sake, just know that whatever happens, we're on your side."

"We're friends, after all," Reeza added.

"I can always bust his balls if you want. You just need to give the signal."

Ghorza began to laugh. A few tears streamed down her face as she did, and the girls gave her a hug afterwards.

She might not know what the future would bring, but she was thankful she had others by her side.

CHAPTER 17

THUNDER BEFORE THE STORM

In the outer Frontier lands, two slender figures had taken refuge in the wilderness, away from prying ears. "It's been confirmed. More supplies and men will be sent to support all of our fronts."

"Good," Jotul said whilst inspecting her battle plan. She held a small piece of parchment with a crude drawing of the Frontier lands.

Her eyes trailed a red arrow one of her commanders had drawn. "This will lead us there undetected, correct?"

"Yes, we've been able to map out the best route to their capital using your birds and the Crimson One's guidance."

She followed the arrow until it ended at a scribble of a city. "One of Ainshard's ancient vestiges, huh," she said before spitting on the ground. "There'll be nothing left of his accursed legacy once we're done with them."

She briefly inspected the other groups' paths. Those led to the remaining goblinoid settlements whereas hers led directly into the heart of the Frontier: Pàrras. Unlike her brothers, Jotul had to take her men down an unconventional route to avoid Pàrras's fledgling settlements, which had proven quite resilient after their initial skirmishes.

The once-disorganised farmers were now tried-and-tested militiamen who'd fought her armies long before Pàrras's own had arrived.

Despite Jotul's focus on his map, Commander Alram approached his battle-hardened leader. "As you can see, if things go according to plan, we should easily avoid any ambushes from their militias. Can't say the same for your brothers. They're our distraction, after all."

"Well, it's your plan, it better work," she said, looking at the tall bereke she trusted her life with. "I'd normally draft my own maps, but this time it's different."

Alram nodded. "I agree. Who knew that there were still people capable of flushing out our eyes in the skies. I thought only our people had such abilities."

Her lips shivered for a brief moment before she corrected it, pressing them still. "We will someday reconsolidate what Ainshard took from us. The youngest of our kin have even shown signs of greater magical potential yet. His vile curse is waning, and it will break faster with the Crimson One's aid."

"It's been a few hundred years since we were brought down, Jotul. It's not a long time for us, despite our shortened lifespans, but the world won't wait for our recovery."

"One of the reasons we need to deal with Ainshard's spawn, the Coalition, and then Brizilum," she said. "I hope your strategy doesn't fail us. We've lost many good souls already, too many."

"You're talking about Vilde, aren't you? Any news of your brothers? Last time, you told me that all of their birds died with the exception of two. Did the surviving birds report anything back?"

Jotul shook her head. "All of their birds were killed a while ago. If we weren't on the move, I would've been able to establish a connection between us and know what happened to my brothers. None of this bodes well."

"The goblins are strong, but those two alone can make an army bleed, not to mention their korrigal riders have got their backs. If they lost, I'm sure they've escaped and are on their way to rendezvous with us," Alram assured.

"Then we better win this war before their arrival. With the might of the Crimson One, I will lead the charge while you will serve as the brains of the operation."

Alram huffed and crossed his arms. "I must warn you, though. If your brothers are right about one thing, it's your overreliance on the Crimson One's gifts. Indulge too much and it'll hamper your judgement."

Jotul remained silent and kept her attention on the crude battle plan.

"The men are dissatisfied," Alram dryly stated. "With your *god's blessing,* they became used to charging into the enemy and overwhelming them with brute strength."

"Wasn't he your god as well?"

Alram dismissively shook his head. "At one point in time. But life reminded me why our kind, like the korrigal, stopped worshipping gods a long time ago."

Jotul frowned. "Then us bereke should remember why gods are necessary. The men will have to learn that we aren't dealing with measly mercenaries or incompetent conscripts from the Coalition anymore. We're dealing with an unknown force who can detect the Crimson One's messengers."

Alram sighed. "Now they have to fight a war the proper way. Things wouldn't be so bad if only the Coalition hadn't used your recent absence to renew its war effort. I can already hear our *supporters* cursing our names for fighting the goblins and calling more soldiers away from the front lines."

Jotul rolled up the parchment and gave it back to Alram. "As long as they do their job, they can yap to their hearts' content. I would've silenced them, but we still need them to support my legitimacy."

"Doesn't make them less of a nuisance," Alram complained.

"They'll shower us with praise once we march through Pàrras.

We'll be triumphant like we always are and rightfully spill the filthy blood of those goblinoid scoundrels."

Alram could tell that despite her calm facade, Jotul was barely controlling her bloodlust. The death of Vilde and the high possibility of her brothers' defeat had taken a great toll on her psyche.

She's on edge. We better defeat the enemy soon; she'll mistake her own men for goblins if this keeps up. The Crimson One's curse may bring benefits to its hosts, but they come at a great cost.

Not wasting another moment, Alram took an ancient horn, one his ancestors used before him, while Jotul mounted a grazing Enok. His family had been serving the Crimson One's champions for generations, long before Jotul came along.

It had been an easy choice for her to allow Alram to join her ranks. A choice she questioned whenever he shared his own opinion about his family legacy and their master, much to her brothers' delight. Now, though, only he remained to help her keep control over herself.

He took a deep breath and placed his mouth on a hollowed piece of bone, before filling it with air.

Fugheeeeaaaah!

Its sound meant only one thing. It was time to march closer to the gates of hell, to satisfy their leader's desire and, in turn, the Crimson One's.

Jotul's men marched through the woodlands, creeping their way deeper into the goblinoids' territory until their forces neared an unavoidable settlement and found it surprisingly empty.

Confused grunts and murmurs could be heard. The settlement was nothing but a ghost town, littered with rotting food and the decayed corpses of cattle.

Jotul inspected an empty barn filled with dry wood and hay. "They've relocated the labourers to the city, I presume."

Alram frowned. "So much for sneaking our way to their city. The bastards must've evacuated after our first skirmishes."

She smirked. "They're smart; let's hope they'll remain worthy opponents."

"I'd rather they didn't. Why they left so many resources to waste here beats me," Alram said, struggling to make sense of the situation. "We could still salvage what's edible from the remains. Shouldn't they be more cautious?"

A soldier proudly remarked, "I bet their settlers ran towards safety the moment we first passed through this land. I fought alongside Baldem and Vreskiven during one of their raids!"

Others chattered and laughed until they heard a yell from the woods. A dishevelled scout appeared at the forest line and ran towards Jotul.

She looked at the man to see a scared face staring back at her. "What happened?"

"M-My apologies, it's just that I..."

Jotul was getting quite annoyed as the scout kept rambling, so she dismounted Enok and pulled the beast closer to the scout. The giant ram roared in the man's face before baring its teeth.

"That tongue of yours better start making sense, or Enok will be getting an early snack."

With a gulp, the scout gave a shaky salute. "I found an injured korrigal rider, and he claims to be a part of Vreskiven's men!"

Jotul tightened her hands around Enok's reins. "Bring him to me as fast as you can!"

The anxious scout gave her another salute before running back into the woods.

Alram apprehensively eyed his men as they began whispering about what had gotten into Jotul, but she didn't care. News of her brothers trumped any rumours.

It didn't take long for the scout to return, supporting the korrigal with one arm.

The men's eyes studied him as he shambled towards Jotul. His emaciated body was covered in grime and his right ear was missing.

Once he got close, he knelt on the ground and lowered his head.

"If the champion of the Crimson One has any mercy, please cleanse my failure with death," he requested, much to everyone's surprise. Those few words heightened the men's anxiety, especially for the korrigal engineers accompanying Jotul's forces.

She opened her palm, and all noise died down.

"You've escaped with your tail still drooped between your legs and left my brothers, your commanders, to die?!" she hissed.

The flabbergasted korrigal growled. "Are you calling me a coward?"

He staggered on his feet and met Jotul's cold gaze. "I fought with Baldem and Vreskiven against the goblinoids. We foiled our foes' traps and drove them into a corner, only for the tide of battle to return to their favour. Your measly Blood God surely wasn't on our side during the battle, Miss Champion, and my commanders and brothers-in-arms paid for his negligence with their lives."

All of the soldiers' faces turned pale at his insolence. They imagined all the way Jotul could brutalise the man before his death.

Jotul approached the korrigal rider, yet he didn't flinch. Instead, he defiantly assumed a combat stance. As he was about to lunge at Jotul, his vision blurred, and he slumped back onto the ground.

When he came back to his senses, he was on his knees and felt a searing pain in his lower jaw.

His worst fears were confirmed when Jotul casually threw two tusks near him.

"W-Why?!" he cried as he covered his bleeding mouth.

"You fled the battlefield and left your commanders to die, yet you disgraced me in front of my men. You are a cowardly deserter, nothing more and nothing less. Instead of asking others to grant you death, redeem yourself by proving your usefulness."

Jotul could feel the hatred in the korrigal's eyes.

She cocked her head towards the scout. "Drag this oaf to the shamans and continue your duty. We have to make sure that we reach the next village in the coming days if we don't want to run out of provisions and starve."

"About that. Our... tuskless friend here mentioned a hidden outpost halfway to our destination. With us not being able to resupply at the abandoned settlement, it might be a good idea to go there. If we speed up, we'll arrive by nightfall," the scout informed her.

"Then let's not waste any time."

At Jotul's words, the army resumed their march.

Alram observed the soldiers and the morose atmosphere surrounding them. What had caught his eye was the red glint in Jotul's eyes when she'd ripped out the korrigal's tusks. That familiar gaze she had, along with the smile that momentarily crept on her lips, made him shudder.

Her brothers' death left a vulnerability for the crimson bastard's madness.

With a deep sigh, he clenched his fists and turned to Jotul. "Things are tough and will get tougher over this war. Will you be alright?"

"My brothers died, Alram. Vilde alone was a heavy blow, and now my closest companions are gone..."

Alram couldn't find it in himself to reassure her like before. "Those two are now part of the Sky Horde. For now, we can only focus on the battles ahead and wish for the best."

She turned to her assistant. "Wishing would be futile. We will simply claim our victory. The time to hide is over and the time for retribution has come! We'll annihilate the bastards!"

Her men roared at her declaration, raising their morale.

"I just hope the outpost isn't a trap."

"If it is, we'll skin anyone who deserts," she swore.

With her newfound conviction, Jotul led her men to the outpost. A step closer to her ultimate goal.

* * *

By nightfall, Jotul's army finally settled down in the outpost without any serious issues. Jotul and the rest admired the sturdy architecture, and its green-painted walls covered with leaves and shrubbery.

No wonder the Crimson One's scouts couldn't find it, she thought.

Once they had checked the barracks and found them desolate, all her men gathered around their supply wagons to prepare for the night.

Alram rubbed his eyes in frustration after receiving the scouts' reports.

What did we expect? If they were thorough enough to empty an entire village of goods, there's no way they'd leave anything of value behind.

When he heard a cough, he raised his head and found his men patiently awaiting their next orders.

"Alright, split into groups of six and divide the tents among yourselves," Alram yelled at the assembly.

Next to him stood Jotul. Her eyes were closed as birds circled above the outpost. "I don't sense a threat, so we should be safe for the night. Still, it's better to stay vigilant."

"Good, I'll have our cooks prepare dinner for you. A servant will deliver it to your tent once it's been set up."

"That sounds delightful," she listlessly replied, causing Alram to groan.

* * *

Alram sat down in Jotul's tent. "I left one of my guys to keep an eye on our new friend. I'll also take the guard shift for now."

"You don't have to trouble yourself. Just assign two of your men outside, or better yet, don't assign anyone. The Crimson One's flock is ever vigilant."

He rolled his eyes. "Still, you know that it's mandatory for a leader to have some guards. Besides, what better way to pass time than with an old friend? Surely you can't live your entire life through the eyes of birds."

Alram grinned at the slight smile creeping on her lips.

After it faded, Jotul gestured at an empty seat. "Just like the good old days, huh. Just you and me bantering into the late hours of the night."

To her delight, Alram shared some stories about his time serving her father. As much as she wanted a hearty meal to materialise, his tales did grab her interest and curb her hunger. Not to mention that they always helped distract her mind from darker thoughts.

Alas, his tales were cut short once the shouts of her men erupted from outside. Both Jotul and Alram jumped from their seats. The smell of burnt canvas invaded their tent.

Fire? But where?

She closed her eyes once more, channelling her magical energies through the eyes of her birds.

"There's oil on the ground!"

"Where did it come from?!"

"It's encircling us!"

The moment Alram rushed out of the tent, a bolt whizzed past him. Turning to his right, he saw it came from a nearby hole. *Since when were these bastards part mole?!*

"I got one," a soldier yelled as he dragged the body of a dead grey goblinoid forward. "He came from one of the sinkholes with a torch in hand. There's a trapdoor where I found him."

Jotul got out of the tent. Her eyes were glued to the hole. "Cunning bastards. So that's why I couldn't sense them earlier."

But how did they know we'd camp here? Jotul pondered for a second before she was engulfed by rage.

"Where is he?! The man who led us here?!" she demanded.

"We can't find him! He was with us a while ago!" a half-dressed soldier yelled back.

You despicable, tuskless rat! I'll skin you alive when—Her curses were cut short when she felt a pang.

One of her birds crashed near her feet and, as it drew its last breath, gave Jotul one final image of the goblin ambushers fleeing into a field behind the forest, before its eyes slowly lost their red hue.

"They're running towards the forest! Call the birds back, Jotul!" Alram yelled as he deflected an incoming crossbow bolt.

"Where are the rest of my men?" Jotul shouted as she took cover behind a nearby wagon.

All she heard were the whizzing of bolts flying by and the battle cries of both her men and the enemy.

She bit her lower lip. *They started firing as soon as most of their kin had fled to the forest.*

The heavy fighting was soon replaced by an eerie silence as the final bolt landed, hitting the wagon Jotul hid behind.

With the sight of her injured followers before her and the warmth of a wound flowing down her back, Jotul gnashed her teeth and pulled out a bolt.

"Damn you all," she cursed, but no one answered. The bombardment had stopped.

"Alram! Sound the horn and gather our remaining men. We're not letting those bastards escape!"

Swirls of red energy wrapped around Jotul. With a fearsome growl, she ran past the wagon towards the woods. On the way, she grabbed a round shield and unsheathed her blade.

She covered the sword's edge with her red glow, but it wasn't going to drink any blood, at least not tonight. All the goblins along with the korrigal traitor had disappeared, leaving behind the corpses of her men and only a handful of their own. There were more bolts in their bodies than there are quills on a porcupine.

With the attack over, many turned to Jotul for guidance. Many of them regretted it once they noticed the maddened malice that laced her sneer as she stared at the corpses.

I might have spared the youngest and the elderly before, but now I'm going to kill your entire kind for this.

* * *

Jotul and what was left of her men soberly trudged through the woods. Their feet shuffled on the ground, and many were either irritated or jumping at shadows.

"These woods are cursed. Why are we even here? Just to die chasing after runaways and short green men?" one of the soldiers, an old spearman, griped.

"There were even grey ones. I think I saw a blue one, a few deka, and a darg," an archer added.

"Was I asking you for a description? I couldn't care less what their colours are! All I care about is when we'll be done with our oh-so-great leader's stupid quest—"

The archer covered the man's mouth. "Do you want to lose your head?"

The spearman slapped his hand away. "I'm not even allowed to complain after all the hardships we've been through? We keep falling into the goblinoid bastards' traps. They keep us up all night before disappearing with the wind, and their riders keep targeting our supplies. With those rams dead, the korrigal can't even chase them."

The archer shook his head. "In return we've captured a good number of them to use for labour and bait. Besides, this is war. It could've been worse."

"War?" The spearman's eye twitched, "You dare call this a war? I served three years in the Coalition's army before one of their nobility exiled me for protesting against his weak leadership. I know damn well what war means!"

With a sneer, he waved towards his fellow soldiers. "This travesty isn't a war! Since when do wars involve one's enemy crawling out of the arse of earth like cowards? To make matters worse, we can't get near any trees without their crossbowmen piercing our throats. How come the crimson bastard's birds can't tell if goblinoids are lurking nearby?!"

The archer backed away. One look at his surroundings was enough to see that many soldiers devoted to the Crimson Lord were slightly agitated by the old spearman's ramblings.

Their reaction made the old man grimace.

"Fools," he spat. "One insult to your god and you turn on a man who fought by your side and called you brothers."

Their squad leader turned to them. "If you want to live, you better calm down. You're not only making enemies, you're embarrassing yourself by whining like a spoiled brat," he complained. "You mustn't forget how much the Crimson One and his chosen one have given you."

"I should be grateful for the deaths of my comrades?" The old soldier's face turned a fierce red. "If anything, I should've rejected Jotul's jingoism long ago!"

"Don't go any further," the archer yelled. "It's said that the Crimson One can curse your entire squadron if you're bold enough to defy him, let alone anger Jotul."

"We're already cursed! Why are we going through this pointless hell?! Another failed chosen one is leading us to our doom, right in front of your eyes, something her henchman, Alram, promised wouldn't happen after his failure of a father died.

"We should be advancing on the Coalition, not some primitive goblinoid tribe. Seems that your beloved master's curse took over Jotul and drove her mad. The madwoman will lead us to our—"

The soldiers' frustration turned into surprise once the old man's head flew off his shoulders, ushering forth a fountain of blood.

His killer was none other than Jotul herself. Her hair was disheveled and there were black bags under her red, glowing eyes. Some of her more magically attuned men swore they saw a bloodlike miasma surrounding her body.

"Anyone else who can't help but delay our march?" she asked, her tone colder than the iciest of winter winds.

Everyone gave a military salute, and with due haste, returned to their marching positions.

"Mutinous soldiers, the last thing I want right now. We'll find where the goblinoids built their little nest and smoke them out!" she grumbled under her breath before receiving her daily twinge.

Her right eye twitched with the death of another one of her birds. One she'd sent into the forest to tail the goblinoids.

She rubbed her face and took a deep breath to ease the pain, but to no avail.

"Damn it!" she cursed before burying her fist halfway through a tree trunk.

I only have three birds left and none of them are suitable for the night. If only an owl survived...

"Please hold on for a little longer." Alram told her. With her speculations running amok in her head, Alram brought her no comfort.

It didn't take long for the sea of trees to be replaced by sunlight and open fields. The warm feeling kissed Jotul's face as she regained her usual demeanour.

Ahead of them sat the goblinoids' fort. It consisted of tall stone walls, trenches, palisades, and towers, and likely had many hidden traps surrounding it. There were also two ballistae installed on the gate towers. The fort had been built above a river, which passed through the bottom via a narrow waterway dug in the fort's walls.

"Sieging this place will be quite difficult," Alram complained.

Jotul shook her head. "Tell me about it. Even if we find a shallow part of the river, I doubt they'd give us enough time to slip through the range of the ballistae."

"Great. A siege it is, then," he grumbled.

Not wanting to risk the last of her birds, Jotul ordered Alram's men to scout their surroundings. Another ambush was the last thing she wanted.

After finding no hidden tunnels, the scouts geared their attention towards the fort itself. Soon they arrived back and informed Jotul.

"This is a disaster," she muttered.

Over two thousand well-armed soldiers were guarding the fort. They included goblinoids of all races and the traitorous tuskless rat.

"There's also another thousand goblinoids handling their supplies, and about five hundred individuals of all ages, likely refugees from the settlements we raided," one of her scouts added.

She took one look at her men. They were tired and injured, some even riddled with disease and malnourished.

Doubt overcame her rage and began gnawing at her heart. *Can we beat them in this state? The plan will fail. We don't have many resources, and without Vres's forces, we can't siege them for long. They can call for reinforcements and surround us.*

She took a brief look at the supply wagons. *We can hold out for five more days at most.*

Desperation was creeping upon her soul, almost overpowering the Crimson One's influence.

When she was lost in her doubts, a pigeon's cooing reached her ears. The bird landed on her shoulder and rubbed its head against her cheek.

It forced a link between them, and through its memories, Jotul could see inside the fort.

They only have eight hundred men in there while the rest of the soldiers are dressed-up puppets, she concluded with delight.

"You shouldn't have searched without my command," Jotul complained in a stern tone, yet there was no malice in her eyes. She gently rubbed the pigeon's head.

"Yet, if it hadn't been for your sharp eyes, we'd have been forced to retreat," she told her bird, and it let out a soft coo in response.

Jotul had initially led a force of six thousand men while Vilde and the brothers led forces of two thousand each.

With the destruction of her enforcer and brothers, only her forces remained, and they had suffered heavy casualties. Out of her six thousand soldiers, only half were in any state to fight.

The situation felt hopeless, but the recent information gave them a fighting chance.

It all makes sense now. I've been wondering why they were relying so heavily on ambushes. After killing my commanders, I thought the goblins were planning to gather their forces to deal the finishing blow.

With more of the bird's memories flowing into her head, a confident smile crept onto her face.

There are about thirty shamans. Excluding them, half of the goblinoid defenders are spearmen while the rest are armed with crossbows.

Her mind focussed on the image of a single grey goblinoid, one she'd seen multiple times through the eyes of her birds.

Every fibre of my being is telling me that he must be the main driving force who brought that accursed city back to life.

Maybe I don't need to siege their city to crush the goblinoids; all I need is to cut off one snake's head. The resulting power vacuum would break them for me. But how would we even reach him? Jotul pondered.

As if it were a sign from the heavens, a felled tree was swept away by the river, barely making it through the waterway. She grinned and could feel the Crimson One's delight at her thoughts. With a gleeful pulse, his fierce energy coursed through her veins.

Alram nervously eyed the pigeon. "Please tell me it's good news."

"Seems not only the Crimson One is on our side. Nature itself wants the goblinoids gone."

"What?"

"Have the men find a clearing in the woods to build a camp and tell the healers to heal as many men as they can. No matter the cost, we'll get rid of the goblinoid menace at dawn. The nasty buggers have an advantage at night."

"Won't they attack at night?" Alram asked.

Under the Crimson One's guidance, Jotul picked up a short spear off the ground. "Of course they will," she nonchalantly answered while twirling the weapon in her hand. "But we'll welcome them with open arms."

CHAPTER 18

THE MESSENGER

With a twist of her leg, Jotul could've thrown her spear towards a darg riding a horse. He had emerged from the fort's gate with a white flag fluttering in his hand.

The Crimson One's protests reverberated. She could hear his acrimonious voice echo inside her head.

No. Killing their messenger would be a terrible idea, especially a darg. He's likely a hired third party or one of Brizilum's proxy traders. The ambitious fools would risk anything if it meant gold in their pockets.

Alram noticed her struggle. "Keep your master at bay, Jotul. The dargs are linguists by trade, so it's natural for them to offer their services to everyone. The Crimson One won't supply our armies with food and resources if we make them our enemies, especially when our relations with their human masters are far from amicable."

Jotul gave a slight nod and lowered her spear. She could feel the Crimson One's aggravation, but she refused to relent. "I vow to you that we will have our war, but I won't be a damned fool and risk bringing the ire of Brizilum upon my people, not before we're ready. We can still use this parley as an opportunity to either buy time or catch the goblins off guard."

Her commander sighed in relief. "You almost gave me a heart attack boasting that spear. Killing a messenger never ends well, especially not when they hail from human lands."

Jotul nodded. "From his simple tunic, you can tell the purple whelp isn't high on the social ladder, but it's still a risk I won't take. Any rash decisions we make would outweigh our coming victory and future survival."

Alram nodded. "Can't argue with that."

At a tug on its reins, the horse stopped a distance away from Jotul and her entourage.

She smirked as she watched the messenger's display of false bravado. Even from afar, she could see his smile quiver as he nonchalantly patted his steed before getting off.

He knelt down to tie the reins to a nearby tree. Jotul would have applauded his acting if his shaking hands weren't fumbling around with the rope.

Her enhanced sight, a blessing from the Crimson One, noticed every small flaw in his form. His twitching shoulders, the quickness of his breath, and the slight shivering of his ears being among the more obvious ones.

The messenger took a breath and put on a confident smile. He stood up and headed towards Jotul, believing he had them fooled.

Contrary to his expectations, instead of ire, the messenger could only find an amused smile on Jotul's face.

His pace slowed down when he noticed a predatory glow in Jotul's gaze.

Stay calm and remember your training. I just need to give her the list of demands and hear her response. If she'd wanted to kill me, I would've died the moment I got off my horse, he asserted to himself as he was laid bare under her scrutinising gaze.

The messenger breathed in deeply to calm his nerves and straightened his posture, continuing his approach.

Even whilst surrounded by jeering enemies, he kept his cool and respectfully bowed to her.

"Judging by your stoic form and beauty, it wouldn't take a genius to know that you're the mighty Jotul, prophetess of the Crimson One. I come here on behalf of Pàrras to see if both our parties can come to amends."

Jotul grinned. "Impressive. Most messengers I've met would either quake in fear or have their pompous heads so stuck in their asses that they'd forget common courtesy. The latter never end well."

Both she and Alram noticed a minor tremor in the darg's ear, but nothing else.

I'm not surprised that the dargs train their messengers much better than the Coalition. If it'd been one of those louts, they wouldn't have been able to maintain their facade for this long.

Though… the dargs are true traders and politicians by nature, unlike the heads of the Coalition. What's he doing here, this far inland? Resettled or not, is Ainshard's broken husk of a city that valuable to the dargs and their skirt-wearing masters?

Jotul's guards pointed their weapons at the messenger after the darg took a box from his pocket.

"Stand down," she commanded. "Its magical energy is dormant. The Crimson One would've warned me if it weren't so."

The guards begrudgingly lowered their weapons, one of them retrieving the box.

It was stylized and silver with a copper latch for a lock. Jotul set her spear down before the guard placed the box in her palms. She studied the engravings in detail before nodding in approval and unlatching it.

What she found inside was a droplet-shaped amulet made of silver, and in its centre, a glowing green crystal.

Jotul felt the Crimson One's excitement surging at the sight of it, causing her to chuckle. *Now I know why the dargs are working with the other goblinoids.*

"Is our gift satisfactory?"

"Saying it was satisfactory would be an understatement. I thought I was ready for any nasty surprises my enemies could throw at me, but a darg messenger offering me a valuable magic focus wasn't one of them. Eloquence is hard to come by in these parts," Jotul admitted.

The messenger's lips curved into a sly smile. "And you've surprised me with your praise. Our way of combat isn't what many of our military advisors would call honourable."

Hearing the word *honour* rubbed both Jotul and the Crimson One the wrong way.

Under his influence, she couldn't help but sneer. "Such advisors are nothing but fools. What good would honour do when your enemies refuse to play by its rules? Especially if they win. Honour and justice belong to the victors."

Seeing the shocked messenger and her nervous men, Jotul suppressed her master's will to calm everyone down.

"My apologies. There are times when our inner thoughts won't allow themselves to be hidden."

"I—I understand," the darg replied with a nervous smile. "I'll keep that in mind for future discussions."

"And I wish I could be a better host in future discussions," Jotul half jested. "I wanted to return the favour for the amulet and invite you into a tent to treat you with proper etiquette. Despite its plentiful bounties, the wilderness doesn't provide much in terms of luxury during a parley."

The messenger nodded in appreciation. "That would be too much for me. I'm just a simple messenger who came here to relay my people's offer and deliver that parcel. If you agree to peace, then proper diplomats will arrive to handle further negotiations."

Jotul and Alram exchanged looks before she returned her gaze to the purple goblinoid. "Then lay the terms on me. If they're not too outrageous, I find no reason not to discuss this matter further."

The messenger smiled. "That's all we'd hoped for."

He slowly took out a small brown scroll from behind his back.

That's not papyrus. Is that... paper? Isn't that product exclusive to Brizilum?

Once the scroll was unfurled, the goblinoid messenger cleared his throat. "We hope that this message safely reaches Jotul, champion of the Crimson One and true leader of the bereke. We hope for the possibility of further negotiations to end further aggression between our factions. We only wish for mutual prosperity."

The messenger took a glance at her before his eyes shifted back to the scroll. "After much deliberation and discussion, we have all agreed to offer an olive branch to prevent further bloodshed upon these lands.

"Neither of us is a stranger to warfare. Both of us know the risks that come from a Pyrrhic victory on either side."

His eyes widened as he continued reading. He nervously turned his attention to Jotul to study her expression, only for his breath to catch as he found a mirthless smile on her lips.

He gulped and continued reading, "W-War is costly, and manpower is scarce. If you continue on this path, I assure you that by the end of it, those pesky rats nipping at your heels might be able to reach your throat..."

"This isn't a threat, it's reality. We won't end up unscathed but will survive and watch as a brilliant flame gets reduced to a flickering candle."

Her men grumbled, with some throwing insults at the messenger. The darg paid them no heed. Even without looking up, he could feel Jotul's eyes on him.

Despite his pounding heart, he kept his eyes glued to the scroll in his shaking hands and continued.

"Do not prolong this pointless war. While we cannot raise the dead, we will compensate both you and the families of the men who died in haze crystals and rare metals. Furthermore, we will return the well-kept bodies of those you hold dear. Good things will come if you leave quietly and never encroach upon our lands again."

The messenger eyed the bottom of the scroll before rolling it up. "I believe that I have delive—"

"I'd assumed you were a professional, yet you didn't deliver the entire message. What did your dear leaders say in the end? You better not lie," Jotul remarked, her narrowed eyes sending a shiver down the messenger's spine.

He hurriedly unfurled the scroll once again but paused and bit his lip.

Finding his indecisiveness unbearable, Jotul brought her spear near his throat. "With your hesitation, you've already shown how insulting the rest of the message is. Do your job properly or death will be the least of your worries."

The messenger's shoulders slumped at her provocation. She retracted her weapon and massaged her forehead.

With a heavy heart, the darg continued reciting the message. "We hope you listen to reason. If you insist on a conflict, we won't hide. If you challenge us, we'll gladly oblige.

"You'll be greeted by our axes and spears. Your men will never return home as their bodies become dwellings for worms and maggots while hanging from the trees. Your generals will be the ground we sow our future on, and worst of all, you... will never be remembered."

The messenger's ears drooped and his hands stopped shaking. Jotul could tell that he'd made amends with whatever gods he worshipped. "You won't go back to your fledgling kingdom," he said. "It will crumble as your enemies devour its corpse. Your people's story will end with you being removed from the annals of history. Your only legacy will be a folktale to warn ambitious people never to bite off more than they can chew. Choose wisely," he concluded, morose.

Feeling that Jotul and her followers had reached their boiling point, he simply rolled up the scroll and uttered one last prayer.

Having made his peace, he closed his eyes and exposed his neck. "Please remember that I'm just a messenger; I beg you to make it painless."

He twitched at the sound of an unsheathed blade.

One of Jotul's men slowly approached the shaking goblinoid and waited.

She turned towards the fort and could already imagine the small grey goblinoid she'd seen from the eyes of her birds grinning. *If only I was as simple as you think I am.*

To the darg's surprise, instead of the sound of steel cutting through muscle and bone, he heard Jotul's erratic laughter.

"Your master's message would've been more amiable without the threat. Don't you think?" she jested.

It took a while for him to gather his wits. *Shouldn't she be livid and putting my head on a stick?*

The tall bereke woman grabbed a fistful of the messenger's hair, lifting his head up. "I didn't get this far by playing by other people's rules."

"I... I'm..." the messenger tried to utter.

"Now, then." Jotul let go of his hair. "Off you go. We need time to discuss this... proposal."

The weary darg retraced his steps. A spear poking at his rump turned his cautious pace into a sprint with bereke laughter filling his ears.

One of Jotul's men shot an arrow which landed right in front of the messenger, almost tripping him.

The way he managed to stand after rolling on the ground, only to sprint faster than ever before sent the laughter of Jotul's men to record heights.

"Oh, and thanks for the horse! We'll put it to good use," Jotul shouted.

Once the messenger was out of sight, she approached the darg's horse and gave it another look. "Interesting," she muttered. "Good equipment can make a world of difference, especially when it comes to riding. We need to capture some of their cavalry and find out how they got their hands on those stirrups."

Alram let out a deep sigh. "I guess peace is off the table, then."

Jotul sneered. "Peace was never an option. They forsook that chance the moment they killed my brothers. If I relented here, their lives would be in vain. I don't want my enemies to think I give up that easily."

"I guess that settles that. You won't change your mind," Alram concluded in a gloomy tone. "I suppose it was inevitable, considering we came here to lay siege to them."

She grinned. "I'm sure the rewards will brighten your mood. We might even find some secrets that'll help us against the Coalition."

"I need you to gather all of the qualified shamans and korrigal craftsmen," she commanded.

Alram turned to her, flabbergasted. "Why in the world do you need all of them?! It'll be hell setting up camp without them! And if you take our best carpenters, it'll be hell to build our siege ladders and battering rams!"

"All of these hindrances will be necessary for our victory. You'll see," she muttered.

With a final look at the goblinoids' fort, she raised her sword and declared, "In a matter of days, we will burn their fort to the ground. For the Crimson One!"

"For the Crimson One!" her men roared in unison.

CHAPTER 19

SWEET INSOMNIA

Lev observed his men as they clambered on top of the stone walls to join him. They had all seen what transpired between Jotul and the messenger; the soldiers made no attempt to hide their outrage. While the darg had survived, the treatment was nothing short of scandalous.

Their aggravation calmed down when the messenger passed the halfway point, far and safe from enemy fire. A few men rode out of the gates to help him calm down and bring him back into the fort.

Lev made a mental note. *Things went as expected.*

Gherm was unnerved by his satisfaction and chided, *I don't know what came over you to write a proposal like that. The poor man could have been killed!*

Lev clicked his tongue. *I don't think his victims would share your outrage. You know as well as I that poor man of yours was part of the dargs' drug circle. The only reason he wasn't exposed and in chains is to bring more of his kin to our side. If Jotul was foolish enough to kill a messenger over some disrespect, I'd be surprised that she managed to grow her faction in the first place.*

He felt a tap on his shoulder. When he turned to look, he found a concerned Volker.

He'd been surprised when Volker had arrived at the fort a week ago, considering it hadn't been long since he beat Vilde.

At the time, Lev had been waiting for the darg barges to arrive with much-needed supplies and troops.

Primitive as they were to his eyes, the large rectangular boats and their darg crews were truly marvellous. During Lev's journey, they'd avoided a myriad of wayward rocks through the narrow rivers that connected Parràs and its strategic outposts.

One of the finely crafted riverboats had slowed down when it neared the fort. He covered his eyes as light reflected off of a bronze statue placed on the boat's bow.

He had barely made out two forms near the statue giving him a salute.

His jaw had almost dropped when his vision cleared. The figures were Volker and Varra.

Lev had welcomed the two and received a report that Rak and his men were on their way, accompanied by Gozzag and Ban. There weren't enough barges to transfer their horses, so the two deka chose to bring the entire might of their cavalry through a land route.

Volker and Varra had quickly adjusted to the fort, and the former kept Lev company while Varra helped with the logistics.

"Are you okay, sir? You seem very agitated," Volker hesitantly asked, bringing him back to the present.

Gherm scoffed when Lev put on a forlorn expression.

"I am. You've seen how they treated our messenger. If they treat someone of interest in such a manner, I shudder to think how they're treating the captives under their care."

Much to Lev's curiosity, no words came out of Volker's wide-open mouth. His intrigue was further piqued when his second-in-command nervously looked away.

"What is it, Volker?" Lev asked his tense companion.

At first, Volker shuffled his feet and kept his eyes away from him, but at his superior's insistence, he mustered the courage to say what was on his mind. "Couldn't it have been due to the contents of the letter you wrote? From what I saw, Jotul was amiable until our messenger began reading the letter. And the more he read, the more fraught the atmosphere became. Were you intentionally trying to rile up the enemy?"

Lev groaned when he felt Gherm's satisfaction and simply asked, "And pray tell, why would I do that?"

"It's easier to take down an enemy that isn't thinking straight. And from what we've seen with the carnage in the settlements, I doubt any of our men would want a truce with them in the first place."

"I doubt even the bereke want peace. From what we've seen, any truce we propose would just be us giving them a chance to lick their wounds and wreak further havoc on our lands in the foreseeable future," Lev muttered.

"So I was right in assuming that your goal was to rile them up," Volker concluded with a grin.

It was Lev's turn to avert his gaze. "I might have gotten a bit too carried away when I was writing the letter. If things went wrong, our poor messenger would have lost his life."

Poor messenger? Why, you hypocritical piece of—

Before Gherm could finish, cheers erupted from the wall as the leaders of the Frontier appeared from their barracks and joined Lev and Volker at the top.

Eleric was the first to speak. "Seems an attack is inevitable. The real question is when will they begin?"

Lev turned his gaze back towards the woods and found the area devoid of his enemies. He surmised Jotul and her men had retreated deep into the woods after the parley. The only signs of their persisting presence were the sounds of hammers and falling trees. "They need time to build their camp, so I presume the assault will take place in less than three days."

Volker contemplated Lev's words. "Would three days be enough? Doesn't she need time for her men to build the ladders and siege engines?"

"She does, but with her birds, she probably figured that Rak and the others are on their way, so I doubt she would be resting on her laurels. They don't have the luxury of time to prolong their siege. Things might take a surprising turn."

"With the additional shamans that Volker brought with him, I doubt the bereke are capable of breaking through our gates," Gerwyn scoffed.

"We shouldn't underestimate them. They still are a magic-attuned race and have their own repertoire of skills," Volker commented.

Gerwyn sneered at the reminder. "They're a disgrace! They waste their magical potential on convoluted techniques that merely empower their bodies. Why use magic like an animal when you can bury your enemies in a mountain of rubble?"

"I'm sure that's not the only trick they'll use," Lev said. "Never underestimate a cornered animal, especially not on a battlefield."

"I don't. Most of them are fools, but I have to admit that their so-called shamans are frightening adversaries."

Eleric rolled his eyes. "I don't doubt that."

Even from a young age he'd heard about the unpredictability of their kind. It was said that at one point in time, the bereke were even able to rob living beings of their souls.

"They were?!" Volker yelped.

"That's what the rumours say, but if it was true, we'd have seen it in previous battles."

"More importantly, we should probably place more barrels filled with pitch and boiling oil," Eleric added, then turned to Gerwyn. "Even with the extra shamans, there still aren't enough to cover all of our bases."

"You're not wrong," Gerwyn begrudgingly admitted. "If only we'd had an extra year or two, we would have had a legion of shaman bogeys."

Shahn shook his head. "Sadly, time waits for no one. Bogeys wouldn't be the only ones who'd improve if we had such a time frame."

"For now, we can only use what we have," Volker added. "We've already set up some ballistae and there are enough supplies and craftsmen to assemble a few onagers. They might not rival korrigal engineering, but they'd go hand in hand with pitch."

Varra suggested, "We need to throw more caltrops on the surrounding terrain. That'd slow the attackers down enough for our ranged troops and shamans to deal heavy blows."

"That's a popular tactic in Brizilum. I'm sure our crossbowmen would appreciate it," Eleric pitched in.

Lev grinned when he saw his five companions exchanging ideas and discussing what further additions would help bolster their chances.

Having observed the bereke's activities, Volker couldn't help but wonder. "It's getting late and they're still going at it. Aren't they worried that we'd launch a night raid?"

Shahn turned his gaze to the forest line that surrounded the fort. "I'm sure they are. While we can't see their camp, I bet a leg that they didn't skimp on patrols. Whatever we throw at them, they've likely prepared for it."

He turned towards Lev and smiled. "Unless we have a new trick up our sleeves."

His eagerness fizzled out when Lev gave an apologetic shrug. "Sadly, I'm no miracle worker."

Eleric snapped his fingers. "It's sound, isn't it?"

Shahn looked at him. "Come again?"

Eleric cleared his throat. "We could use their wariness to our advantage and harass them from the safety of the fort. All we need to do is have some of our men stand on the walls at dusk and wreak havoc on horns and drums until dawn."

"There'll be mayhem among their ranks," Volker concluded, earning him a pat on the back from Eleric.

"Exactly! They're already exhausted from labouring on their siege equipment, so why not exploit that until they break?"

Shahn crossed his arms. "The risk is too high. Remember, we're not dealing with your average army. Do we really want to bet everything on horns and drums? The best option is to prevent her men from building siege towers in the first place. We should wait until Rak and his men arrive. Only then can we chop off the snake's head."

"That might look like the safest option, but it's also the costliest in the long run. We can reduce our casualties if Jotul's soldiers are worn out," Eleric argued.

Shahn raised a brow at Gerwyn. "Is it true that shamans can rejuvenate one's stamina?"

During the expedition, Shahn had noticed shamans casting healing magic on their strongest warriors. He'd seen battered men turn into vicious beasts.

Gerwyn pondered for a moment before speaking up. "Yes, because most of our shamans use a focus. The haze crystal within drastically enhances the effects of whatever magical energy we expel. It makes the process faster and more efficient."

Shahn started pacing around the group. "Now, tell me, how many bereke have you seen using them or any such medium?"

"I suppose hardly any. Servius told me they abhor haze crystals. The prideful fools believe too much in their own might. Most of their shamans seem to rely on..."

Gerwyn's eyes widened. "Most bereke choose to empower themselves by spreading their power internally, and if it becomes unstable..."

Lev grinned. "They go boom. Their shamans have to conserve their magical energies for battle. It seems we've got ourselves a sound plan."

"We should still prepare for the worst outcome," Eleric warned. "A good commander always keeps a few tricks in reserve. I'm sure her birds aren't the only thing in her arsenal."

"She can throw as many tricks as she wants at us, but we won't lose," Lev affirmed. "Whether we wear her out or stay put until Rak's forces arrive, we'll emerge victorious. Jotul is already doing us a favour by delaying the fight."

"More importantly..." His eyes traced his compatriots. "Inform the men who aren't assigned to the night watch that they need to sleep early. Make sure to have them sleep in their armour with weapons by their side. I doubt she'll use our tricks against us, but it's best not to take any chances. They might want to chop our heads instead of trees if we keep them awake long enough."

"What about the equipment you put on the puppets? It'd take time to dismantle it all," Volker asked.

Lev remembered how nervous Volker was when he first saw the puppets. His nervousness had even caused Varra to chuckle.

As a smile crept on his face, Lev turned towards his second-in-command. "I should have told you back then, but we don't need to. It's all smoke and mirrors, Volk. Most of the equipment is defective trash that the blacksmiths wanted to melt away, so I've decided to put it to good use."

Volker uneasily scratched his head. "I'm sure she's already found out, sir. She would have retreated or acted differently during the negotiation if it were otherwise."

Lev's ears drooped. "Sadly so. It's the price of not being able to get rid of all of her birds. She outnumbers us by a large margin. Our best option is to conscript whoever can fight amongst the refugees and give them supportive roles."

"If we're going to use civilians, might I suggest you take up the stage?" Eleric advised. "Some words of comfort would definitely boost their morale."

"Gather everyone at the break of dawn and you will have your speech," Lev answered as he started to descend the wall's stairs. "I'm heading to bed, I suggest you all follow suit."

Once inside his bunk, a familiar albeit concerned voice nudged in his head.

Even with all the fortifications, can we win this fight? Be truthful, Lev.

Of course we'll win! the glaive interjected. *We've prepared for this fight and made sure there aren't any vulnerabilities. No matter how many winged pests she sends, she won't find any openings, meaning she only has two choices: get crushed once our reinforcements arrive or run with her tail between her legs.*

You seem to have forgotten they outnumber us three to one, Gherm countered.

The glaive let out a stream of unstable energy that made Lev's ears ring. *Laying siege is never easy, greyborn. Her men might end up as cadavers on the river's shores. If I were her, I wouldn't be focussing on the goblinoids in the first place. Those Brizilum upstarts are far more dangerous if left unchecked.*

"She'll risk a fight," Lev blurted out.

You... want her to initiate an attack? Gherm questioned. Lev could feel his confusion as he struggled to wrap his head around the idea.

Would I want her to both waste the lives of our soldiers and see many of those who pledged their lives to me die? Of course not. But that doesn't change the fact she declared war on us.

Wouldn't it be better for her to just give up and leave?

She can't, Gherm. It's already too late for that. She had many chances, and our master would be a fool if we allowed her to escape now. Even if she did, it'd destroy her reputation, the Glaive explained.

Gherm was flabbergasted. *He's not our master, and how would losing one battle ruin her reputation? It'd be dumb to turn against her because of one loss.*

Jotul lost her commanders and the best of her forces against us, Lev replied, *and her rivals will make use of that if she allows for another blunder. Once someone gains their position through force, they can't let their grip slip. While I don't fully trust everything they say, we heard from the captives how Jotul rose to prominence. Remember?*

He felt a fog clear from Gherm's mind. *Strength, faith, and fear are the foundations of her rule,* Gherm said. *She built herself up to be an indomitable force, capable of bringing the korrigal to her side. Her supporters, especially Vilde, made sure the naysayers chose death over opposition. I remember now, Lev. The captives kept talking about a city named Briecka.*

Lev closed his eyes. *Then you're aware of what happened to those who rebelled in Briecka.*

Death, the glaive and Gherm answered in unison.

* * *

The next day, as the sun sank below the horizon, Eleric's plan commenced. A hundred horns and drums atop the fort's walls echoed throughout the woods. With nothing but thin fabric and ever-diminishing trees protecting their ears, the bereke would soon grow tired of it.

Lev gritted his teeth as he waited for Volker to check the barracks. Even though the horns and drums were pointed towards the forest, sound leakage was inevitable. Living in the overcrowded cities of Eurasia had proven that time and time again.

It didn't take long for Volker to join Lev. "It's barely noticeable, sir. I'm sure the men won't lose sleep over it."

Lev nodded to himself. "Good. Now all we have to do is wait for them to attack us."

Once he climbed up the stairs to the ramparts, he was greeted by the sight of armed volunteers. With their settlements in ruins, there was nothing left for them but revenge. Many of them had gathered in the fort in the days prior to Jotul's arrival. After all, this could very well be their last chance to save Pàrras from a similar fate.

He was pleasantly surprised when the volunteers mimicked the soldiers and gave him a salute. Disregarding their sloppy execution, it brought a smile to his face.

Lev cleared his throat. "War is upon us once again."

He solemnly gazed at the crowd, causing a few to gulp in anticipation.

"We're no strangers to the hardships of war, and nor were our ancestors. Many of you came to Pàrras to avoid the ravages of the past."

People in the crowd began to nod and whisper their approval.

"We all wanted peace, a chance to start anew and build up our lives and the future of our kin, but..."

With a contemptuous sneer, Lev turned his head towards the woods. "A new threat came to burn down our hopes. Marauders worshipping violence and despair saw the signs of a budding utopia and made it their goal to quench its flames. Many of you experienced their abhorrent acts firsthand."

Lev raised his voice before his audience could react. "The foul locusts of the Crimson One will stop at nothing to spread their madness, but my men and I will be the line that they shall never cross!"

"Those who stand before me replaced hoes and seeds with spears and shields in order to protect what is most dear to you, your freedom. Be proud, for you shall be the guardians of the future."

"Hail the liberator! Zeja's blood flows through him!" a priest of Zeja yelled from within the crowd.

"Hail the liberator!" they cheered.

CHAPTER 20

THE CRIMSON ONE

Deep in the woods, Jotul's craftsmen were hard at work building her engines of war.

The foreman supervising them kept a firm hand on the construction operation. His ears twitched when a loud plop hit the ground, craning his neck towards the perpetrators, he could only gnash his teeth when he saw two of his men having a hard time assembling a ladder.

"You call that shoddy mess a ladder?! Are you trying to help your brothers climb the walls or help the goblins kill them off?!" he erupted in the workers' faces.

His fury didn't stop there, however, as his eyes met with the form of an incomplete battering ram. One look at the waste of timber was enough for a guttural growl to escape his lips.

The workers were gobsmacked when the foreman's fists met the timber, resulting in a crack echoing through the forest. "The wood's hollow! Hollow! Is this supposed to destroy the gates or shatter on impact?"

Before the flabbergasted workers could open their mouths, the livid foreman knelt down to its wheels. After just a glance, he turned towards them with a scornful stare and hissed, "Where are the iron rings? You're dragging this ineffective abomination on rocks and hard dirt, not paved roads! Do you want to tire yourselves out halfway through the battle? Because I'm sure the goblinoids' archers would appreciate that."

Unable to bear his critique any longer, most of the workers gathered around him to hurl insults and complaints. "We didn't sign up for this! We've been slaving away to the best of our ability while enduring your bullshit, but enough is enough!" one protested.

"You expect us to work efficiently with those darned drums and horns? They've been blasting them every night!" another threw in as he rubbed his eyes.

The foreman wasn't intimidated by their numbers. He crossed his arms and huffed. "And I didn't sign up to babysit a bunch of amateurs! Three days of poor sleep was all it took for you to lose the ability to tie a few sticks together."

Just as the conversation heated up, the foreman felt a hand on his shoulder. He whirled around to confront the aggressor, only to turn meek when he found out it was Alram's.

"S-Sir," he whimpered, much to the delight of his workers.

They eagerly waited for the foreman to receive his comeuppance, but their hopes were deflated when Alram decided to calm the situation instead.

He carefully eyed the messy grounds of the construction site and the sleepless faces of the workers. "You've got yourself a bunch of insomniacs. Why don't you move your men's tents away from the construction?"

The foreman coughed and stared at the ground. "We won't be able to build them in time if we have to walk back and forth."

Alram's sigh turned the foreman sickly pale. "If we face the goblinoids with contraptions of such quality, we'll be giving them an easy victory. Move the tents out or face the consequences."

"Being a master of your craft, it must be painful seeing such simple works, but time is of the essence. We need to cut corners if we want to beat the goblins, especially now."

"But that'd be the height of stu—"

Alram shot him down with a stern glare.

Utterly defeated, the stupefied foreman lowered his head and whispered an apology. "Excuse my insolence."

"It's fine," Alram responded. "Sacrifices must be made, but please, be a bit more lenient with the lads and try to guide them instead of scolding them to oblivion." He patted the foreman on the shoulder once more. "The sooner this is over, the sooner we can sleep like conquerors again."

Despite his confident appearance and jovial act, Alram was groaning on the inside. *We fumbled the bag this time. If our men lose faith, I doubt they'll be able to fight even if the plan goes through.*

To lift their spirits, he swallowed his distaste and yelled, "The Crimson One finally answered our calls!"

This sudden outburst stunned the foreman and his workers. It took them a while to process what he said, but mumbles and whispers soon replaced their silence. Some were sceptical, taking into account his usual stance towards the Crimson One, but many were blinded by their excitement, especially the most ardent of the Crimson One's believers.

"Really?" a worker asked. He could barely hide his enthusiasm.

"Why else would Jotul take the korrigal if not to turn the tide?" Alram pointed out.

"Then why was she so indecisive before now? We stood by her side from the beginning!" yelled another voice.

He hid his distaste once more. "Because the Crimson One demanded patience. Like a farmer waiting for harvest season."

"She's a fool who doomed us all with her sick god!" a rather short korrigal replied.

"And you're a worm," Alram curtly answered.

"Unlike worms like yourself, she persevered. When we're done here and we've reached the enemy's capital, the Crimson One will reward the faithful and punish those that sowed doubt. You can be assured of that," Alram promised.

"What a load of bullshi—" the disgruntled korrigal yelled before he was restrained by Alram's personal guard.

He couldn't finish his sentence, as Alram stabbed him in the throat with a dagger. "Let this be an example."

The man hacked and coughed, gurgling on his own blood, and before long, the life in his eyes was extinguished.

Alram cleanly wiped his blade and turned to the apprehensive crowd.

"Once we crush the goblinoid menace, it'll be the Coalition," he yelled. Despite the earlier macabre display, many of his men responded in cheers. At first, Alram noticed, the chants felt forced, but gradually they turned to genuine adoration as the pool of blood beneath the fallen protester grew.

Hearing his comrades' ovation put a smile on his face. Even the most suspicious of his men were swept up in the mood and cheering for their eventual victory.

I've bought us some time, Jotul. I reignited the fire in their hearts as best as I could. You better end the fight before it goes out again.

With their hopes rekindled, Jotul's men worked themselves to the bone, only stopping once the first rays of sunlight pierced through the forest line. Shortly after, the drums and horns ceased their insomniac orchestra.

During the entire debacle, Jotul had spent her time inside her tent, only allowing a select few individuals inside.

She could usually be found sitting behind her desk, brooding over her battle map.

At least when her mind was busy, she could focus on the task at hand. When it wasn't, she could be found in what Alram called her less ideal state. Some of her guards had heard a scratching sound coming from within her tent. Those who dared to disturb Jotul during those moments emerged from the tent in a daze. Those were the lucky ones.

When the Crimson One's influence was at its worst, it spread to the unfortunate few like an infectious disease and turned them into beasts wearing bereke skin.

The only warning of that accursed hour was when Jotul let out manic cackles accompanied by eerie hymns and gleaming red eyes.

Now, though, her head lay on a fur-laced pillow.

Pitch-black beads gazed at her from atop the war table. The bird let out a loud caw.

She got up from her bed and patted the bird's head. "Be patient, and I'll promise you a feast for the ages."

The sound of wind chimes announced another presence within her tent, bringing an end to her revelry.

Her face morphed into a menacing sneer. "Who is it now?"

That expression softened the moment she realised it was Alram who'd entered. "Oh, it's you."

He paused his steps and scrutinised Jotul's spindly form. The madness of the Crimson One had done its work on her. The crimson light swirling in her pupils had intensified since his last visit, confirming his greatest fears.

She won't be able to recover from this. After this battle, another one will fall to your influence, you monster! Alram silently lamented as Jotul grew more restless.

"What is it, Alram?! I was having a dire discussion with our master!" she frantically yelled, gesturing at the crow.

Despite his grievances, he steeled his heart. "It's almost time,

Jotul. The spymaster sent us a report. Despite their sleeplessness, the korrigal will be done with the siege equipment you requested in two days."

She stared at him with unblinking eyes. Her antipathy sent a chill up his spine. Once he took a step back, she chuckled with glee.

"Good. It's time to end them! How I've waited for this day! To increase our chances, we need to prepare the captives for their redemption."

"You want to use them as meat shields? I doubt they'll be cooperative."

"Oh, Alram, there are better ways to make use of their flesh. We'll use the ancient ways," Jotul snarkily replied.

Alram shuddered. "You can't! Our ancestors swore off such techniques for a reason!"

Jotul flashed a vicious smile. "Someone as experienced as you should know it's the Crimson One's will to annihilate the Ainshardian menace, and for good reason."

"They are a threat, Jotul, but converting their life force into energy is going too far. It would damn both them and our shamans. Even the influence of the Crimson One is less corrosive than soul magic!" Alram desperately yelled.

Jotul clicked her tongue. "The Crimson One himself ordered for it to happen. Sacrifices must be made for us to succeed, Alram, or do you have another way?"

Seeing her second-in-command averting his gaze was the only answer she needed.

"I wish we had time to starve the goblinoids out," Alram uttered.

"And I wish my brothers had survived. We've done all we can, yet even his miracles by themselves aren't enough to grant us victory. I won't allow us to delay the inevitable even longer!"

"Blood? If we killed them all, it'd be in vain. The most prudent option is to capture their leader and keep him as a hostage until we make our escape," he advised.

"Capture... yes. We need to capture their leader," she replied with a manic grin.

His eyes twitched. *Just like my father's, her mind finally fell to your will. We're doomed.*

As if to oppose Alram's verdict, the crimson light in her eyes began to dim, and with it, all of her earlier revelry was quelled.

With a weary sigh, Jotul plopped down on the seat behind her desk, and gestured at an empty chair in the corner.

Once both were seated, she opened a drawer and brought out two cups and a bottle of mead.

Despite being younger than him, she was his superior, so as custom demanded, Alram reached out for the bottle to fill the cups.

Jotul tapped her long nails on the desk. "Consider this an apology for my earlier... eccentricity. You're right about capturing their leader alive. Our survival will be in vain if we don't."

Alram uncorked the bottle and poured the golden liquid, and the two drank in silence.

Her loyal general placed his empty cup on the table. "Speaking from experience, this battle will be the end of you as an individual, won't it? You might even fully lose yourself to the Crimson One halfway through."

Jotul shrugged. "Who knows? I could lose myself before the battle even begins or I might last until the Coalition is crushed. If my lord wills it, I might even go berserk in my sleep."

Alram looked down, holding his head in his hands. "Remember, most of us joined the fight to rid our lands of the traitorous Coalition and avenge our fallen king. If you lose yourself prematurely, every-thing we worked for will collapse."

He lifted his head and gazed at Jotul. "My earliest memories are of my father teaching me how to offer sacrifices in your god's name; he was somewhat sane back then. Once the Crimson One no longer needed us, he left my kin to rot after my old man's death."

"You've told me that tale a million times," Jotul retorted.

"Then you know that your father, the king, gave me a chance to redeem myself in the aftermath and I vowed to protect you."

A mirthless chuckle left his lips. "If I can't protect you, those Brizilum dogs will have the last laugh. The whole continent will wave their banners."

Jotul hissed as the red glow reemerged in her eyes. In a swift motion, her blade disappeared from her scabbard, only to find its way near Alram's throat. "If you want to protect me, then quit your whining. Get out of my tent and take action!"

Alram gulped before nodding. The glow subsided once again as she let go of her blade.

He plopped down on his knees. "Yes, my queen."

Having regained his bearings, Alram stared up at Jotul with soulless eyes before leaving through the tent flaps.

She dug into her desk work once again. "It was always a possibility, wasn't it?"

The crow landed in front of her, on top of the battle map.

"I wonder what I'll become," she muttered as she stared into the crow's uncaring eyes.

CHAPTER 21

THE DAMNED

A few days had slipped by since Jotul's arrival, and now, at the break of dawn, the fort hummed with activity. Amongst the goblinoids, the earliest stirrings were from the soldiers on guard duty.

On top of the walls, a spearman stifled a yawn. He'd kept his gaze on the woods since daybreak, hoping for another uneventful day, but the lack of activity from the enemy was worrisome.

He warily scanned the tree line for signs of Jotul's infamous crimson-eyed birds, but eventually decided rubbing his drowsiness away was more important.

Afterwards, he lazily stretched his back, only for a voice to startle him from behind. "Haven't had much sleep?"

He stumbled as he turned around, half expecting it to be one of his superiors. A chuckle escaped his lips as he greeted the newcomer—a crossbowman from the third squadron.

The newcomer pointed at the tallest tower of the fort. "I hope the boss hasn't seen you. He's already on the signal tower."

That turned the spearman's stomach. He cocked his head towards the tower and noticed Lev standing amidst the billowing smoke, his solitary figure keeping its vigilance through the grey haze.

The crossbowman sighed. "He's quite a sight, isn't he? Lesser grey-born would avoid taking on that task."

The spearman shook his head. Though every soldier understood the tower's importance for communication, he didn't envy the duty it entailed.

It was known that Lev had devised the system of signals himself, ensuring swift communication between Pàrras, the fort, and surrounding settlements.

The use of smoke columns to convey the level of danger was ingenious. The tower had three beacons. Lighting one beacon meant that the fort was active and unconquered. The second told of the enemy's presence, and the third that their invasion had begun.

"Light the third beacon!" Lev ordered from above as the shrill cries of a horn and the thunderous beatings of drums emanated from the surrounding forest.

The crossbowman readied his weapon. "Like it or not, the bastards are coming, and they're dragging something heavy."

His words were proven true when Jotul's army emerged from the foliage, their approach heralded by ram-like steeds dragging a variety of loaded mangonels.

"Shit..." the spearman whispered. Just as he reached out for his horn, the sound of a carnyx erupted from the signal tower.

Twhuuuuuuduuuuu.

With the alarm sounded, the two soldiers ran to their battle stations as more joined them on the walls.

Lev couldn't help but smile as he watched his men execute their duties with remarkable efficiency, a testament to their unwavering dedication. Under the guidance of Volker and Varra, the soldiers soon stood along the top of the walls, ready to repel the invaders.

They're improving faster than I expected.

His merriment was interrupted by footsteps climbing the signal tower's stairs, and before long, he was confronted by Eleric, Shahn, and Gerwyn.

"Glad that you could make it to the party," Lev quipped. "I would've prepared some drinks, but we need to lead our forces soon."

"W-We..." An out-of-breath Gerwyn incoherently mumbled before grabbing his water gourd and downing it.

"For someone ready to engage the enemy in combat, you seem to be in a mood for jokes," Eleric mused.

Lev turned his gaze down to Jotul's ever-encroaching siege equipment. "Can you blame me? We don't know what Jotul has in store for us, but it's reassuring to see how much our men have grown."

Shahn watched the approaching force and groaned. "If only discipline could scare her army away."

Eleric nodded. "We've done all that we can to wear Jotul out, but those siege engines remain a problem."

Lev patted him on the shoulder. "Look on the bright side. They weren't able to muster more than mangonels. Sure, they are dreadful, but they need to get into our shamans' range if they ever hope to fire anything over our walls."

Eleric pointed at the back of the enemy formation. "Regrettably, artillery isn't the only thing we need to worry about. It seems that bereke witch took a page from my people when it comes to siege tactics."

Lev glowered at Jotul's forces once he understood. "Sappers," he hissed.

Apart from the usual ladders, battering rams, and mangonels, Lev found a group of heavily armoured soldiers near the tail end of the infantry. Instead of swords and axes, they were carrying spades, picks, and hammers.

I didn't think siege warfare had developed to this degree around here, he said to himself.

His gaze turned to a group of rams being led by the sappers. The beasts of burden were carrying ropes and barrels. *Are they trying to build a pontoon bridge?*

"I don't see the big deal; it's just some miners and sculptors posing as warriors," Gerwyn jeered.

Lev rolled his eyes. "Then burn them to a crisp before they reach our walls," he commanded. "We need to deal with whatever tricks Jotul has in store for us. She hasn't even shown herself yet."

"We'll deal with whatever she throws at us," Shahn assured.

Before Lev could respond, a horn blew from deep in the forest, signalling the enemy's advance.

At the second blow, Jotul's men foolhardily rushed towards the fort.

Lev tightened his grip around the glaive. "It's time," he declared, receiving solemn salutes from his companions before they made their way to their respective positions.

Gerwyn directed most of the shamans to the other towers while Shahn and Eleric took control of a few squadrons of reserves—refugees from the surrounding settlements—and made them guard the bailey, protecting the walls against any tunnels or breaches.

Lev descended the signal tower's staircase and sprinted his way atop the manned wall above the gate. His arrival was greeted by silent cheers and muffled grunts.

The men held their breath, silently awaiting the approaching bereke.

Some soldiers were absentmindedly fiddling with their weapons. Others were praying to Jom to return them to their families.

Even with death staring at them, creeping ever closer, none had broken off from their formations.

Lev raised his hand, and the crossbowmen took their aim, dutifully awaiting his signal.

Yet just when he was about to give the order, all of the bogeys felt an ominous surge of energy swirl around the assaulting bereke.

A chill went up Lev's spine as he witnessed their transformation. *This feels like when the birds bombarded the city!*

His suspicions were confirmed when the bereke let out bestial cries.

With the enemy rushing at a breakneck pace, Lev commanded the crossbowmen to unleash a volley, firing hundreds of projectiles onto the approaching tide.

Bolts whistled through the air towards the bereke, with only a disappointing third hitting their mark.

The defenders shuddered at their lack of reaction. Most of them didn't seem to care as the bolts flew past them. Those who were hit showed a lukewarm response at best.

"Rocks!" one of his men screamed.

Lev clicked his tongue and tackled a stunned soldier to the ground as a boulder flew over the adjacent merlon and almost smashed his head into pieces.

Surveying the field, he found that the mangonels were positioned farther back than expected. Their handlers were operating the trebuchets with alarming efficiency.

"Brace!" he yelled once the operators released their second volley of stones.

Gerwyn watched the situation from atop one of the towers through narrowed eyes. *The bereke haven't reached the fort and we're already in this state. It seems we need to play our part early.*

He tapped his haze-laden staff on the ground. It was a recent design he made in hopes of rivalling Orva's, one that allowed him to gather magical energy faster at the cost of harder manipulation.

With a powerful burst of magical energy, he unleashed a fierce blast of wind that swept away the incoming stones, curving their path past the wall.

Gerwyn puffed his chest. "There! Mere pebbles can't compare to the power of magic."

Lev groaned, as the blue shaman's boasts hadn't escaped his glaive-enhanced ears. *Then keep us safe from the mangonels while we handle Jotul's soldiers.*

He turned his attention to the glaive. *Do you sense any nasty surprises Jotul or her Crimson One might have in store?*

Nothing, master. All I can sense is my disappointment at these failed specimens' misuse of their gifts. It's a sad sight how far their race has regressed, the glaive answered.

If their race had truly fallen, they wouldn't have managed to gain momentum early on in the fight, Lev pondered.

And that's where you're misguided, master. For you see—

Can it wait? Not wanting to waste precious seconds on the glaive's inane prattle, Lev brought his attention back to his men. His crossbowmen were at the front, hiding behind the fort's battlements as they safely rained hell on the maddened berserkers through arrow slits.

Lev grinned when he saw significant casualties finally befall the enemy ranks. *No matter how much her god enhances their bodies, he can't make them immortal.*

The deaths mounting amongst the bereke dissipated the goblinoids' fears of their presumed invincibility.

"We'll survive," vowed one of the soldiers.

"No, we'll win!" bellowed another.

"It won't be different from fighting Gelmar, nor the Jiira."

"We've got this!" the soldiers clamoured.

Hearing their optimism left a wide grin on Lev's face. *Good.*

Broken and doubtful men can never win a war. Whatever Jotul throws at us, we'll be ready.

Gherm was stirred up in support. *We won't lose, Lev. We won't let them harm Ghorza and the others.*

Lev nodded.

Once Gerwyn deflected another round of stones and the winds subsided, Lev turned to Gerwyn's tower and raised his glaive.

With a single swipe at the air, Gerwyn's shamans drowned the bereke in flames.

The bereke's vanguard screamed. Their shields proved ineffective against the raging fire, only buying them a few seconds before they were engulfed by the magically enhanced flames. The enemies behind them fled into the river under the cover of the resulting steam.

Lev watched as a single ladder bearer clung to the walls in desperation, ready to take his chances with the defenders.

By some miracle, he had survived the shamans' spell and the bolts. He wasted no time on the climb up, and for all his bravado and zeal, received a bolt to the head. He fell headfirst onto the ground, leaking a concoction of blood and brain matter onto the ashen soil.

The bereke who survived the flames reemerged from the dispersing steam and tried their luck in climbing up the walls.

"Hold the line and shower the bastards with bolts!" Lev commanded before slicing the neck of an ascending bereke.

A surprised yelp came from the far side of the eastern wall as a large, heavily armoured bereke pushed his way on top of the rampart. The runes on his pauldrons shone brightly while a barrier protected him from the goblinoids' spears.

Just as he was about to unleash terror on the desperate defenders, a ballista bolt broke through his barrier, fizzling his runes out. As he regained his bearings, Volker and Varra rushed towards him.

He narrowly blocked Varra's xiphos, subconsciously taking a step back. This let Volker unceremoniously kick him off the wall. The armoured bereke let out a wail of despair as he plummeted to his death next to his compatriot's oozing brain matter.

Volker and Varra proceeded to push the ladder off the wall, sending many pleading enemies to their doom.

More armoured bereke joined the ranks of the attackers, a good number of them targeting Lev.

Where did these bastards come from?! Gherm complained as Lev broke through another soldier's barrier.

Once the runes powered down, he swung his glaive at the noble bereke's helmet, staggering him, before grabbing a misericord attached to the man's belt and plunging it through the helmet's slit.

Drenched in bereke blood, Lev surveyed his surroundings and the numerous armoured corpses. *That's the last of them... for now. Guessing from their equipment they're probably knights, or whatever knight equivalent the bereke have.*

Despite the odds, his men maintained control of the walls and disposed of the bereke's multiplying siege ladders.

Lev sighed in relief when he saw the pontoon bridge burning and the mangonels being bombarded by fire. *Looks like the shamans are doing their job.*

When he checked on Shahn and Eleric, he couldn't help but shudder at the condition of the bailey. The ground was littered with holes, each filled with mangled corpses soaked with boiling blood.

W-What's happening?! Gherm yelped when a sapper broke through the soil. The moment he reared his head from the ground, Eleric's hammer met his skull. Afterwards, Shahn filled the hole with hot oil before more of the bereke could come out.

Even after death, Lev could feel the Crimson One's energy emanating from the boiling sappers. *I guess Shahn and Eleric would love playing whack-a-mole.*

As the bereke placed another ladder, Lev resumed his onslaught.

Throughout the battle, his men managed to keep the bereke outside the fort, and before they knew it, the fight had been prolonged to the early hours of noon.

Lev was confused as to why the bereke hadn't retreated yet. Wave after wave, they'd displayed the same degree of fanaticism, even as they rushed past the dead.

And even though the goblinoids' confidence hadn't wavered, he felt a familiar itch. One he remembered from his past life. *Shit always hits the fan when an operation goes too well.*

"Jotul still hasn't shown her face," he muttered.

After the shamans burnt down the last mangonel, a pitiful horn blew from the woods, and with it, the bereke retreated.

Lev's men gleefully jeered at their fleeing foes. Some crossbowmen even took potshots at the humiliated soldiers.

"This is beyond wrong. It was too easy. None of it makes sense," he muttered to himself, only to hear a groan from his left.

"Easy?" Gerwyn growled, having descended from his tower. "I've been holding those curs' contraptions for far too long, and you dare say the battle was easy?! The walls would've already fallen without me!"

Lev furrowed his brow. "Still, what in the name of Zeja is Jotul thinking?"

It didn't take long for him to get his answer. The earth started shaking. Volker rushed towards him, pointing upriver, with Varra behind him. Lev felt a chill go up his spine when he saw the panic in their eyes.

"The river! It suddenly dried up! The scouts report that Jotul and her elites are marching through the river!"

Gerwyn was about to retort but swallowed whatever words he had in his mouth when he turned to face the dry stretch of riverbed.

Yet the water hadn't dried up. Even further away, out of sight, it had been dammed by magic.

Everyone felt the tremendous force approaching before a terrifying flood sprung forth.

Many of their defenders fled the scene. Those on the ground pushed and shoved each other, desperately trying to open the gates, while others dropped down from the ramparts, breaking their legs on impact.

Gerwyn raised his staff, and with an immense display of magical energy, he and his shamans tried their best to hold back the flood.

Countless earthen walls rose from the riverbed. None were able to hinder the flood's path.

Eleric and Shahn climbed up the signal tower before the fort shook from the river's wrath.

The wall facing the river crumbled, the screams of those still in the bailey silenced in an instant.

Everyone stared in horror as the water splashed off the other side of the fort, but miraculously, the walls there were still intact.

Before long, the river's magic vanished, and the now-crimson water swirled as it drained itself out of the goblinoids' ward. They could only stare in silence as the water level dropped, revealing debris and the floating corpses of their brethren.

Whether they were bogeys, goblins, or dargs, none exchanged words as their minds processed the tragedy and the sight of the draining fort.

Whatever remained of the shamans' dirt walls had acted as a stopgap dam which slowed the draining process down. If not for that, it would have been harder for the goblinoids to know what lay in the water.

"No!" one of the soldiers cried as he hugged the corpse of a civilian woman.

Volker turned towards Lev for aid but shuddered when he found him seething with unbridled rage.

Master, calm down. Anger won't help, the glaive pleaded. *Those who volunteered to help the soldiers knew what they were getting into.*

You don't understand, Gherm hissed with surprising animosity. His fury and vitriol even surpassed Lev's. *That monster killed them.*

Indeed. We fell for her trap and our casualties are immense, but—

No! These aren't just the victims from Jotul's flood. Many of the corpses belong to her hostages!

The glaive went silent after Gherm's cry.

Assessing the corpses, she found they contained the same magical signature as the flood.

Gerwyn knelt and, with a shaky hand, inspected the slit throat of a young man.

"How could those animals defile both magic and our people in such a way? Wasn't their crimson god one that valued honour?" he spat out.

"Honour is the right of the victors, Gerwyn. I'll be damned if we don't put Jotul in chains for this," Lev swore.

As if to deny he and his men their solace, the sound of yet another horn resonated in the distance.

Everyone broke out of their stupor and turned to where the shattered earthen walls lay.

Behind the carnage, hundreds of killigs away, Jotul was approaching with her reassembled army at her back. She held the horn casually, as if to mock them, a maddened grin plastered on her face.

Once she saw the desired effect in her enemies' eyes, she licked her lips and, with another blow from her horn, ordered her revitalised army to charge. Their bodies glowed an eerie red from the blessing of the Crimson One.

Lev and his men solemnly turned to face their wretched foes.

Though their bodies were tense, there was no fear on their faces. They calmly adjusted their formation, revenge the only thought on their minds.

CHAPTER 22

HOUR OF RECKONING

Jotul grinned as she saw her enemies repositioning themselves for the battle's next phase. As rain began to fall, she turned her head skywards, welcoming the storm's arrival.

Under the heavy shower, her army eagerly stomped their way across the muddied soil.

Their march could have been impeded had Enok slowed down. The beast developed a fear of loud sounds after the battle against Hakan, but under Jotul's firm hand, it maintained its pace in the centre of their formation.

A light flashed from the heavens, followed by a rumbling boom which caused Enok to bleat.

Jotul gently rubbed its crimson fur.

"Don't worry. It'll be over soon," she assured her noble steed as she brushed its head and muzzle.

With a wave of Jotul's hand, the bereke stopped four hundred killigs away from the fort. Puzzled murmurs spread among the troops, but their questions were answered when they heard a loud caw coming from the woods. A crow emerged from the tree line, letting out another cry to herald its arrival before landing on her mistress's shoulder.

"I assume Alram's departure was successful," she asked the

crimson-eyed corvid. It flapped its wings, spraying both Jotul and Enok with water droplets, before opening its beak.

"Depart. Depart." It mimicked her words in its hoarse voice, earning a rub under its beak and a snack before flying away.

Jotul let out a sigh of relief. *Good. If I fall, there's no better man to train future champions. Forgive me, old friend, but they need your guidance if we want to achieve our dream.*

With no more worries on her mind, she turned to the fort and grinned. *It's time.*

The wall facing the river now lay in ruins, with the goblinoids standing tall in front. Her enhanced sight caught every sign, from their shaking shoulders to the way their white knuckles gripped their spears, that the goblinoids were waiting for her army's arrival. They wanted blood as much as she.

It's a miracle they're able to keep themselves together, Jotul thought as she witnessed them standing in lines, staying in form despite their apparent aggravation.

She felt budding excitement, seeing the scorn in their eyes, but that feeling wasn't just hers.

A multitude of bombastic voices shrieked in her head.

Glory will come with the blood of our enemies! Let us pave the future with their ashes!

They felt alien yet familiar, as if they had been with her since time immemorial, bearing witness to her rise.

But they're nothing more than fakes, an undesirable result of relying on soul magic, she assured herself.

Their shrieks grated at her nerves as they banged against her sanity.

She tightened her grip around Enok's reins in a vain attempt to retain control, but the silent screams intensified.

The voices promised her victories at any cost.

But that's a line I've already crossed and will cross again, Jotul told herself. She raised her spear and ushered Enok and her men forwards.

Her forces complied, eager to bring further anguish to the goblinoid defenders. Their enemies' torment was cathartic after so many of the bereke's comrades had died under the goblinoids' schemes.

With each step they took towards their fated enemies, the heavens grew more erratic, booming louder as if to keep pace with the hastening steps.

Enok sped up to a canter, moving to the front of its master's army. The goblinoids responded by tightening their formation, standing shoulder to shoulder with their shields held high in defiance of the encroaching horde. Their crossbowmen eagerly awaited the order to shoot.

Both sides' anticipation grew stronger, both knowing that they would finally settle their score.

With one final roar from the heavens, Jotul twisted Enok's reins, forcing it to a full gallop. With a war cry, she charged with her men at her back. They screamed her name and that of the Crimson One. The goblinoids retaliated by letting loose a rain of crossbow bolts.

The earth rumbled under the bereke's feet as they raised their shields overhead to block. When they crossed the halfway point, the goblinoid spearmen responded by bracing for impact, pointing their spears towards their encroaching foes.

Jotul's grin widened at the enemy's impressive gallantry. She felt remorse, since recruiting the survivors into her ranks would be impossible now.

Her connection with the Crimson One grew stronger when all three remaining crimson-eyed birds flew above the army and let out an unnerving, unified cry.

The goblinoids stared in shock as a maroon glow surrounded the bereke and refined their magical energy even more, hardening their bones and strengthening their muscles and tendons. The bereke soldiers felt unprecedented amounts of adrenaline pumping into their veins.

In their newfound bloodlust, they discarded their shields just to reach their enemy faster.

The goblinoids' bolts struck the maddened soldiers, but to the crossbowmen's horror, they didn't slow down the warriors in the slightest.

Jotul laughed. Under the Crimson One's blessing, nothing less than a headshot could stop her men now, especially now that combatting the flood had drained most of the goblinoid shamans of their magical reserves. It'd take hours for them to recover.

The shamans who remained desperately unleashed their strongest spells on Jotul and her galloping ram. Only her demise could turn the battle in their favour.

To their astonishment, Enok nimbly dodged the magical barrage. Whether it was stone, ice, or fire, none could graze its fur, let alone its rider. It only stopped when it sensed an intense gathering of energy ahead, the most powerful yet.

Jotul turned towards the source: a blue goblinoid standing atop the remnants of a tower near the broken wall.

She scoffed when she noticed the peculiar staff in his hand, along with a look of haughty disdain in his eyes. Gerwyn's arrogance turned to surprise when she took no precautions against the spell he charged. Instead, she urged Enok ever forward.

Gerwyn shook his head at her rashness, and with a disgruntled huff, he pounded the end of his staff against the remnants.

A powerful torrent of lightning snaked its way towards Jotul, only to clash against a red swirling light.

Just as Hakan's ram had done, Enok borrowed the powers of the Crimson One, and a barrier formed around it and its rider.

Jotul ignored the intense whirring sound of Gerwyn's assault on Enok's barrier.

The voices in her head cheered at the prospect of drawing first blood, only for their hopes to be dashed and their joy turned to indignant screams when the earth in front of Enok rose, blocking their vision.

Enok huffed at Gerwyn's petty tricks and crashed through the earthen wall, dashing towards the fort. Jotul coated her spear with energy and thrust it at the last remaining wall blocking their path.

As her spear pierced the wall, cracks formed, followed by a boom.

With its path cleared, Enok galloped towards the shield wall. Soon after Jotul made contact, a tide of bodies slammed into the goblinoids' shields, only to be pushed back by the defenders and their spears. And while most of the bereke ignored the pain and continued their rampage, others succumbed to their wounds and joined the many bodies littering the battlefield.

Despite their fatigue, the goblinoids fought back as hard as they could.

Even those who were dragged out of the shield wall took out their blades and thrashed Jotul's men as their allies replaced their positions in the wall.

Yet despite their efforts, the wall finally fell, and the goblinoids faced the bereke in mortal combat.

Jotul's inner voices became muffled when she sensed the Crimson One's power flooding into her veins. A feeling of ecstasy was building up inside her at the sight of the goblinoid slaughter.

Merely facing the empowered bereke head-on turned the enemy into nothing more than impediments.

But she found her eyes wandering to a goblinoid being horizontally cleaved in half. It should've been an instantaneous death, yet he was still breathing, clinging to his killer's feet before chewing off a piece of ankle. As the bereke tried to overpower the dying goblinoid, another stabbed him through the ear with a dagger.

Despite the Crimson One's blessing, the bereke warriors were being shaken by the goblinoids' resolve. All except for Jotul.

With rising bloodlust, her maddened eyes wandered from foe to foe, searching for a worthy opponent. Just as she settled on a burly goblin, her eyes met those of a grey, then a purple goblinoid.

From the pair's exceptional synergy to the armour which spoke of their high positions, everything about them urged her to jump in.

She was caught off guard when Enok thrashed against the stones forming around its feet. Jotul cocked her head towards an exhausted Gerwyn and noticed another figure on what remained of the fort's ramparts.

Looking at her was none other than Lev. Seeing her primary objective brought some clarity to her mind and reminded the maddening screams of her true goal.

With one last pat to Enok's head, she whispered a final command into its ear and tightened her legs around its sides.

Then, with a cry, Enok expanded its barrier, and at that moment, Jotul struck at the stones with her spear, crumbling the shackles surrounding Enok's feet.

Gerwyn hurled whatever was left in his arsenal their way.

Enok narrowly avoided the lightning barrage, taking a sharp turn midair by forming a barrier below its feet and jumping off. When it landed, Jotul infused her body with energy and leapt on top of the ramparts.

Once there, she rolled to the side, just dodging Lev's glaive.

She grinned. "You missed, false Ainshard."

Not wanting to waste more time on pleasantries, she readied her spear and lunged with inhuman speed at the disgruntled greyborn.

Even with the glaive enhancing his strength, Lev had no chance to dodge Jotul's attack. He opted to block it instead.

What resulted was a clang so loud that it reverberated across the battlefield, travelling far enough to capture the attention of the soldiers on the ground.

Lev was grinding his molars as he struggled to hold her off, but Jotul was just astonished that someone managed to block her attack.

Her surprise became more palpable when he managed to push her back enough to disengage, then countered with a stab of his own—one Jotul thought she dodged until she saw a nick on her arm.

Lev readjusted his stance and warily awaited his opponent's next move.

What are you waiting for, take Jotul down while she's stunned! Gherm yelled.

That monster isn't perplexed anymore, she's excited, Lev responded as his grip tightened around the glaive.

He took a deep breath when he saw an unnerving grin on her face.

We'll slay this rabid beast, master. Even the mightiest of predators is prey for our cause, the glaive uttered, and Lev responded with a slight nod.

Before long, Jotul rushed towards him once again, and thus their duel began.

* * *

All of the combatants felt the weight of impending finality as the battle reached its zenith, and neither side knew who'd come out on top.

With ragged breaths and a bleeding shoulder, Volker roared as he dispatched yet another bereke soldier. The maddened berserker thrashed wildly on the muddied ground as he tried pulling Volker's spear from his throat.

When he was about to grab hold of the spear's shaft, Volker

shifted his entire weight onto the weapon, digging it further into the wound.

Volker strengthened his grip and kept his stance until the hatred in the bereke's eyes dimmed.

He let out a sigh of relief and turned his eyes to the ramparts.

It was eye-opening to witness the Crimson One's champion repelling Gerwyn's magic. *No wonder the bereke call her a war goddess.*

To the people of Pàrras, Lev held a similar position. The chosen of Zeja, the liberator of greyborns, and an undefeated champion on the battlefield.

Will Lev be safe? Volker questioned, apprehensive.

A powerful wave of magical energy bombarded his senses, followed by a thunderous boom. With one empowered kick, Jotul shattered a chunk of the wall. A kick that Lev fortunately managed to dodge.

The soldiers closest to the wall, bereke and bogey alike, fled in terror as a large slab of stone crumbled upon their heads. Only a few were lucky enough to avoid the collapsing structure while their comrades were buried under the debris.

With gritted teeth, Volker instinctively rushed to the ravaged stairs leading up to the ramparts, only for another shockwave to shatter the stairs at the last minute. Just when he was about to search for another way up, he heard a scream. Once he turned to face the sources, he saw that the shaken conscripts were being overpowered by the berekes.

Volker hesitated for a moment before rushing to their aid. He rallied some of his men and thrust his blade at the stunned bereke, gouging his neck.

"Maintain your offensive and make the bastards bleed!" he roared at the top of his lungs, and the men followed.

Sorry, sir, but the people need me. If someone doesn't rally them, Jotul won't be the only bereke you have to deal with.

Once again, Jotul thrust her spear at Lev. His back was against the wall, but using the glaive's power, Lev managed to duck away. Instead, her spear split a merlon behind him, sending it falling on top of the soldiers below.

Lev panted heavily as the glaive's power took a toll on him.

Even with his body screaming for respite, he valiantly thrust the glaive at Jotul's head, only for her to take a step to her left, leaving a nick on her face.

Master, don't let her hit you, the glaive started. *Her blessing isn't the only thing coating her spear. Her attacks can harm the soul. The only reason we're unharmed is due to my powers.*

It's not fair, Gherm yelled in his head.

Can't argue with that. We can only wear her down 'til her blessing is at its weakest, Lev responded.

Can you two hold on until then? Gherm sounded worried.

It's tolerable, the glaive answered, *but if this goes on much longer, I fear my powers will corrode Lev's body.*

Just peachy, Lev snidely commented before blocking a kick with the glaive. He flew a killig away before rolling on the ruined crenellations and standing up again, only just managing to maintain his grip on the weapon.

It's like fighting a pulse rifle with a butter knife.

The world seemed to slow down before his eyes as Lev channelled more of the glaive's power. Jotul's movements were still quick, but at least he could follow them.

He took a step to his left, barely dodging her spear. Jotul followed up with a slash aimed at his torso, which Lev parried with the spikes on his gauntlet.

She kept laying down her onslaught, Lev trying his best to hold his own against her brutality.

When he fell for a feint and was about to be sliced in two, he commanded the glaive to let out an overwhelming glow, blinding Jotul.

Not wasting the opportunity, Lev swung his glaive at her neck, but she sacrificed her left shoulder to avoid the fatal blow.

Jotul hissed in pain as he pulled the blade out, then thrust it at her torso. Luckily, she wasn't able to heal herself without her shamans. The deep cuts in her chest and shoulder were gushing out blood.

Enraged, she thrust her spear to create distance.

As he was backing away, Lev felt a minute gathering of magical energy. Eyeing the source, he could barely hide his amusement.

This will be tough, but when I give you the signal, blind her again, he ordered the glaive. When he received her affirmation, he rushed at Jotul once more, this time aiming at her waist.

Instead of blocking him, she tore off a piece of battlement with her injured arm and kicked it towards him.

Lev dodged to the left, only to be met with her glowing spear.

He half knelt to block the attack with the glaive, but winced from the reverberating pain, legs beginning to shake from exhaustion.

Jotul cackled. "It's impressive how long you've managed to stand against the might of the Crimson One. But—"

A new, sanguine light wrapped around the tip of her spear, and Lev could sense it distorting the other magical energy surrounding the weapon.

"Not impressive enough!" she bellowed.

Now! Lev screamed in his mind, and the glaive shone as bright as the sun.

"This won't work again, goblinoid!" Jotul closed her eyes before shifting more power to her spear.

Yet she was startled when she sensed magical energy suddenly gathering above her.

She disengaged and retracted the crimson energy.

"You again?!" Jotul shrieked. The source, now on the wall, was Gerwyn.

She cursed as he struck her with a barrage of lightning, almost sending her falling off the rampart.

Exhausted, Gerwyn fell to his knees.

"You did well, leave the rest to us," Shahn replied, standing next to Gerwyn. He swirled iron-cast chains like a lasso and wrapped them around Jotul.

"Eleric, now!" he yelled.

Eleric aimed his crossbow at Jotul and pulled the trigger.

The bolt flew true and pierced her chest armour. The malevolent energy around her began to fade; she collapsed on the ground.

He lowered his weapon. "For all her prowess, that wasn't so hard."

Easy for you to say, Gherm wanted to complain. *Isn't that right, Lev?*

Lev didn't answer. Instead, he vigilantly stared at his downed adversary. With a twist of his wrist, he signalled Eleric to reload while Shahn helped Gerwyn to his feet.

He had a look at the situation below. Some of the disheartened bereke began to flee once they saw their leader had fallen while others kept fighting, believing Jotul to be invincible.

A pleasant surprise was the sight of cavalry in the distance.

Took Rak and Gozzag long enough. Lev wanted to complain but paused.

Is something wrong? Gherm asked.

We've already won, master, there's nothing left in her, the glaive reassured.

Lev shook his head. *Something feels off.*

His brow furrowed. *Where are her damned birds?!*

Then it dawned upon him. "Eleric! Get away from her!"

An explosion erupted from behind Eleric, throwing him a few killigs away like a rag doll.

At the same time, a falcon clawed at Gerwyn's eyes. In his panic, he'd dropped his staff, causing all of its remaining energy to discharge.

"No... Shahn! Keep her down!" Lev yelled before rushing towards Jotul.

The moment she opened her eyes, her once-dormant aura flooded the battlefield.

Before Shahn even had the chance to tug, Jotul grasped his chains and sent him flying off the wall.

Once Lev got into striking range, she scraped past the glaive, grabbed it, and used his momentum to slam him into a merlon.

While blood gushed from his mouth, Jotul tossed the glaive aside.

To Lev's surprise, Eleric jumped towards her with a hammer. A faint magical glow surrounded his body as he swung the hammer at her head.

Before he could hit her, Jotul dislocated Eleric's jaw with a single punch.

"Brizilum filth," she jeered.

"Gerwyn! Run—" Lev started to scream, but Jotul had already thrown her blade.

The old shaman let out one last gasp before the sword tore its way through his guts.

He couldn't utter a single word before he fell to his knees.

When she turned her attention back to Lev, she couldn't help but grin. If looks could kill, the hatred in his eyes would have erased her very existence.

"It's not pleasant, is it? Your henchmen robbed me of my brothers, so I understand your anguish. But now I only feel satisfaction," she said as she approached Lev.

"From what? Sowing destruction or killing my people?" he spat in defiance.

"From reaffirming my decision to deal with you before the Coalition. You showed me a battle those leashed dogs couldn't even imagine. I doubt I would've won if you had more time to grow. All that's left is to kill you and prepare a larger army to burn down your city."

Lev couldn't help but let out a contemptuous chuckle.

Seeing her bemusement made him laugh even harder.

Jotul raised an eyebrow. "Are you done?"

"Do you really think by killing me you'd win? Pàrras has others besides me. Better leaders and better warriors will rise to the occasion. You'll die with me, Jotul. The others won't let you leave."

She shook her head in disappointment. "And here I thought you were smart enough to understand me. Do you think I care about my life? Even if I fall, my dream will survive, and my successors will accomplish my goals."

"My people's enemies will burn. No matter what happens, I'll be the victor in the end, especially when I give them Egon's key."

"Egon?" Lev muttered as more blood spilled from his mouth.

"Surely you know about his kind. I'm surprised you've only used their power to unlock relics from bygone times."

Lev glanced back at his glaive. "They're using us, Jotul. It won't be your dream anymore if you keep using their powers."

She cracked her knuckles and grinned. "It will be realising the full potential of their powers to shatter your spine like a twig."

He slowly got back on his feet. "We'll see about that."

Once he'd assumed a combat stance, Jotul cackled. "Pick up your relic, goblinoid. Least I can do is give you an honourable death."

Lev's battered body screamed in agony, each movement sending shockwaves of pain through his nerves. Dodging was no longer an option; he had to attack. As he picked up his glaive, he commanded her to forego numbing the pain and focus on enhancing his abilities.

A tide of pain crashed over him, accompanied by a surge of strength. With reckless abandon, he charged at Jotul, their weapons clashing in a final dance of steel and blood.

Each strike sent jolts of torment through Lev's ravaged nerves, but he held on, his attacks leaving bloody gashes in Jotul's flesh. Fatigue weighed heavily on her, and she struggled to block his relentless assault.

Their blood painted the ramparts crimson as the glaive strained to block the soul magic infused in Jotul's fists, but even the enigmatic polearm had its limits. Lev could feel their connection fraying with each successive blow.

Leave everything to me, he instructed the glaive.

I... can't... let you... die... the glaive muttered, her voice barely coherent in her damaged state.

Lev smiled gently. *I won't. I haven't left a big enough impact on this world yet, and we both know she's reaching her limit.*

As you wish, the glaive answered.

"I think it's time to end this," Jotul whispered, facing his attacks head-on.

As the glaive sliced through her damaged shoulder, her crimson energy-wreathed nails plunged into Lev's right eye. He howled in unspeakable agony as his essence and nerves felt the shredding of countless blades. His shattered form rolled on the floor, his vision fading to black.

Jotul, impressed by Lev's tenacity, lowered her head in respect, only to be surprised by the flicker of life still burning in his left eye.

"A lost soul..." she whispered, realisation dawning on her. "No other way your soul would have survived the Crimson One's raw power."

She let out a laboured sigh, retrieving Eleric's hammer. "It's a shame to kill you, Lev. You're simply too dangerous."

As the greyborn stirred, he looked at his hands in confusion. "Wha? Lev, where are you? M-My hands... I can feel them."

Jotul laughed at his reaction. "I'll make this quick and save you the embarrassment."

She rushed towards him, hammer raised to cave in his skull, but as he grabbed the glaive, magical energy gathered within it. Expecting a blinding flash, Jotul covered her eyes, but instead, a blazing inferno erupted around him.

Jotul focussed all of her aura on defence as she approached her target. And even as he released everything, he had to deter her, she kept advancing.

Suddenly, he felt a tug from the glaive, and he knew what he had to do. He gave control of his magical energy—his birthright as a grey-born—to the glaive. Sparks erupted, dyeing the flames a deep, unnatural purple.

Jotul felt an instinctive fear when her barrier began to crack from the scorching heat. With a desperate scream, she was engulfed by the inferno, her charred form falling from the rampart into the river below.

That wasn't Lev was her last thought before hitting the water.

Silence fell over the battlefield before the goblinoids erupted in cheers. "Lev! Lev! Lev!"

But their leader felt no joy. "Forget about that! Go capture her and recover Shahn!" he yelled.

As his men obeyed and rallied their captives, he collapsed, taking a deep, shuddering breath. Tears welled up in his eyes. "I'm back...

The target has been neutralised, Gherm, the glaive informed,

having recovered some energy from his magical boost. *It won't be long before our master recovers, so enjoy it while it lasts. You've earned it.*

Gherm stood up. "Once we're done here, I need Lev to see Ghorza."

To his dismay, the battle's aftermath took longer than anticipated. The soldiers discovered Shahn unconscious in the riverbed, but Jotul and her ram, Enok, were nowhere to be found.

CHAPTER 23

DISHONOURED

Jotul's rasp echoed in the musty cave. "Have I been abandoned, my lord?"

Since her defeat against the goblinoids, she had been unable to communicate with the Crimson One.

Alone in the cave, Jotul lay surrounded by insects swarming around the glowing moss, her only company in the darkness.

Enok, her faithful companion, had not returned since it saved her from the river. Her memories of the events following the battle were hazy, but Jotul was certain that Enok had never left her side throughout the ordeal.

In the dim light of the moss, a trail of blood and hoofprints caught her eye. As she strained her neck to follow the trail, a shining stalactite caused her to freeze.

"A haze crystal..." she gasped.

The shock quickly disappeared upon seeing her reflection. Hoarse laughter escaped her charred lips. Death on the battlefield would have been a blessing compared to her current state.

Her once-long, raven-black hair was now singed, and her formerly gallant face had become a molten mess with but a single functional eye. Waxy, white bits of flesh sloughed off her skin, revealing a crimson layer beneath riddled with bubbles and blisters.

Suppressing the rising bile in her throat, she followed the bloody trail up a steep climb leading to the cave's exit.

"Enok could still be alive," she muttered, her chest burning with each exhale.

A familiar, rough voice whispered in her mind, *Pathetic.*

"They're back," Jotul sneered.

As she closed her eye, she took a deep, painful breath, and steeled herself against the impending insults from her warped psyche.

The voices poured out their contempt, jeering, *We could've won! We had the runt right in front of us, but your hubris made you slow to respond!*

All you had to do was spill more blood!

Your dreams have fallen, false prophet. Our ambitions are no more.

They continued to taunt Jotul. *That lamb is dead, you know. A failed pet for a failed master. It could've served you one last time by offering its lifeblood to quench your thirst. Now it, along with your birds, will be nothing more than decoration on the goblinoids' plates. Your god was a fool to choose you.*

"Enough!" Jotul's frail voice echoed through the cave, silencing her critics. A familiar warmth enveloped her body as a crimson glow wrapped around her, the bond with the Crimson One burning anew. Though weaker than before, his light spread across her body, alleviating the pain from her injuries.

A semblance of a smile formed on her deformed face. "So you haven't abandoned me."

Suddenly, the soothing sensation vanished, replaced by a sharp awareness of a new presence in the cave. Jotul's skin crawled at the clicking emanating from the depths. Turning to face the presence, she was greeted by a swarm of glowing eyes.

"Hivelings," she hissed, recalling the tales sung by bereke bards of the ancient bugs' dark past. Even Ainshard had been unable to fully eradicate these monsters.

Instinctively reaching for the dagger at her waist, Jotul found that her blade had melded with its sheath. Undeterred, she grabbed a rock and willed her scorched legs to stand.

Confusion replaced wariness when the creatures stopped a short distance away, clicking their mandibles and shaking their feelers without displaying any aggression.

What are they waiting for? Jotul pondered, her legs beginning to shake. She leaned against the wall for support, her body barely able to bear its own weight.

The Crimson One pumped more strength into her veins, yet with his diminished power, the blessing felt incomplete, hardly enough to combat her current predicament.

Turning her focus inwards, Jotul felt the Crimson One's energy flicker like a candle in the wind. "My lord, are you..."

We call it Hollowing. It's a bane to our kind, an ominous, machine-like voice whispered in her mind, yet she felt that it came from the direction of the hivelings.

Their eyes glinted with a purple spark. "The damn insects are...

"My puppets," the mechanical voice added.

A hooded figure materialised above the monstrous ants. "Beware the masked crow, Ainshard's scribe, misfortune's herald, the ruinous guide."

A beaked mask appeared as the figure grew more visible. "Beware the deceiver, the knowledge eater."

The mask's goggles burst into two distinct purple lights. "The masked corvid, Kram the Wise.

"My brother choosing birds is understandable," Kram continued, "but surveillance cannot match the power of absolute efficiency."

Jotul's eyes narrowed. "Your brother?"

The hivelings' eyes flared with an eerie glow. "Egon, the Crimson Guide, and Ainshard's former Minister of War."

Her grip on the stone tightened until her knuckles turned white. "He was one of Ainshard's decrepit Guides?"

"We ensured your kind could sense it, yet it seems you've somehow taken him for a god."

Jotul felt the Crimson One's agitation at Kram's words.

"Egon's silence speaks volumes," Kram sneered as he floated closer towards Jotul.

She felt Kram's energy resonate with her own blessing, and worse yet, with the purple flames that had shattered her barrier and seared her flesh.

Kram anticipated her quivering at the revelation, as countless others had before her, but she defied his expectations, meeting his gaze with unwavering solemnity.

"Why have you come?" Jotul demanded, her voice rough as gravel.

Kram deliberately delayed his response, scrutinising her from head to toe. "To comprehend why my failure of a brother chose you. We presented him the opportunity to join us in supporting Lev, yet he chose to resist. Now he has lost everything, save for his connection to you."

Her eye widened. As she prepared to denounce his deception, Kram raised a gloved hand. Egon erected a mental barrier to shield her, but in his weakened state, he was no match for Kram.

Jotul stood paralyzed as a torrent of visions inundated her mind, each depicting the Coalition's conquest of her territory.

Cities crumbled as its armies and their allies breached the border. Initially, her forces held their ground against the traitorous tide, but the stalemate shattered when they could no longer harness their god's power.

"This was the moment you succumbed to Lev. Egon invested too much of his power in you, and your defeat fractured his domain," Kram's voice whispered in her ear.

Jotul's heart pounded as she helplessly observed the aftermath. "Even without the Crimson One's blessing, this wouldn't have transpired!"

A magical boom silenced her protest. She gnashed her teeth at the Coalition's armaments. Many of its soldiers wore fine steel and employed tactics reminiscent of their greatest rival.

The sight of the banner of the Coalition's allies confirmed her suspicions. Though many were not human, they bore the regalia of Brizilum.

A mirthless laugh escaped her lips as she glared at her enemies. "Insects, the lot of them! They usurped the throne with human outsiders' aid, and now they grovel for their assistance in waging war? The whoresons have blindly sold our people to the butchers!"

"Why has Alram allowed the infidels into our..." Jotul froze, her body trembling as the next vision unfolded.

"Spare your lackey the blame. He did his utmost," Kram remarked as she witnessed Alram's demise. He hung from one of Briecka's gates, Brizilum's symbol carved into his bare chest. His arms and legs, slathered with honey and seeds, made a sumptuous meal for vultures.

Kram chuckled. "Your pet fared no better."

The final vision depicted a decapitated Enok, slain by Rak, the same man who had killed her brothers.

The rock she'd grabbed earlier to defend herself slipped from her hand. "How did it all go so wrong?"

Kram shook his head. "Egon's arrogance and poor judgement are to blame. He lost his wager and refuses to pay the full price. If not for our little game, you two would have served a higher purpose: the dawn of a new empire."

Jotul pondered Kram's words, her voice a hoarse whisper. "You would slay… your own brother?"

"Regrettably, he is inefficient. A liability like him has failed us for the last time, and the cost of reversing the Hollowing outweighs any value he possesses. I have no need for such a brother. My only mercy is granting you two a swift end.

"Farewell, Egon and his pet." With those parting words, Kram vanished.

The hivelings' eyes dimmed, their bodies shuddering before releasing a piercing screech as they descended upon Jotul.

She snarled like a wild beast, her eye blazing crimson.

"I have failed you," Egon's once-thunderous voice whispered, devoid of its usual gravity.

"We have failed each other. You may have guided me to my doom, but I chose to follow, and I would have likely perished much sooner without your aid. I refuse to be a part of Kram's world, and if we must die, we die standing. We can only hope the goblinoids possess the wisdom to avoid repeating history," Jotul replied.

With nothing left to say, she brought the rock crashing down on a hiveling worker's head and ripped off its mandible to wield it as a makeshift blade.

Despite her injuries, she tore into the hivelings, drenching herself in their blood.

The violence drew the attention of numerous corpse-eaters, their emerald eyes gleaming at the sight of carnage.

Jotul's moves grew increasingly sluggish as Egon's strength waned.

A hiveling warrior tackled her, its mandibles finding purchase. With a defiant roar, Jotul mustered the last of her strength, plunging the severed pincer into the warrior's thorax, decapitating it with a sickening pop. In its death throes, the giant ant's mandibles tightened, splitting her in two.

As her upper half tumbled to the ground, her vision dimmed.

Have I served you well? she asked in her final moments.

She could no longer feel Egon's presence, nor could she feel pain as the hivelings tore at her.

While her only eye turned murky, Jotul heard gruff voices speaking in the korrigal tongue accompanied by the drums of the Sky Horde.

Four gentle hands picked her up, and as her vision returned, she stared at an army of korrigal marching in the clouds, riding their rams. Her body felt renewed, mended.

"The Sky Horde is a marvellous sight, isn't it?" said one of the two who held her. Jotul shuddered at the familiarity of his voice. She nervously turned to face them and gasped once she realised that it was Baldem's.

"Colour me surprised. I never expected your asshole god would let you join us," he said with a cheeky grin.

He turned to the other man, Vreskiven, and yelled, "It's a miracle, you raggedy bastard. You won a bet for once!"

Vreskiven sneered. "Don't make me rip your tongue off, you belligerent buffoon. Jotul, once you get acquainted with the others, come help me teach this milk-drinker a lesson."

With a shit-eating grin, Baldem pulled on his hair before running towards the horde. "Try catching me first, dung-breath!"

With a furious roar, Vreskiven gave chase.

Flabbergasted, Jotul stared at the two before erupting with laughter as she chased after her brothers.

BONUS CHAPTER 1

THE SELECTION

"How many kingdoms are in the Empire?" a female voice asked Lev as the two sat in one of their hideout's many repurposed storage rooms.

"Three," Lev replied, his voice steady. "The Kingdoms of North America, Central America, and South America."

Maria's lips curved into a knowing smile. "Correct."

She pressed on. "Then how many noble families govern the Kingdom of North America?"

Lev started, "Five—" but quickly corrected himself. "No, it's four. The Ruxgans, Webfields, Von Mitternachts, and the Vincards."

He paused as a thought struck him. "Gabriel, the one we met at the banquet. He's a Mitternacht, isn't he?"

"Indeed," Maria affirmed, her eyes gleaming with recollection. "I met him during my early days in the Empire. I'm their retainer now, at least until the next selection concludes."

Lev shifted uneasily. "You should've mentioned you joined forces with a noble house."

Maria's expression softened. "Listen, I've outmanoeuvred the Imperials at their own game," she replied with a hint of pride in her voice. "I'm sure you'll do great in the selection and join the Ruxgan house."

"Maybe you can even start your own house, if the emperor allows it."

"Is something troubling you, Lev?" Maria inquired when he didn't reply, her head tilting.

Lev frowned slightly. "Why am I serving the Ruxgans? If the Mitternachts were your stepping stone, why can't they be mine?"

Maria let out a sigh. "Remember, the Ruxgans are currently vulnerable. When I ventured to the Imperial lands, the Mitternachts were in a similar plight."

"The Mitternachts had lost the emperor's favour, and with each failed military venture, they spiralled towards obscurity. Even the retainer before me couldn't save face in court."

"And the Ruxgans' Achilles' heel is Lucian, right?" Lev probed, aware that Maria disliked repeating herself. While the flavours of the banquet's cuisine lingered vividly in his memory, he struggled to remember all the new faces that had accompanied it.

Rolling her eyes, Maria conceded, "Yes, Lucian's reckless behaviour is eroding their influence in court prematurely. He foolishly believes the emperor owes his family."

"Anyhow." Maria gestured to Lev's documents. "I'm surprised you still use paper records."

"It's the Eurasian way," he explained, bracing himself for the next question.

"Would you like a digital tablet? It's more efficient for sorting information. You can even ask its integrated AI to create a quiz."

"I'm fine, thank you," Lev replied with a grin. "Please, continue."

I'd rather have her quiz me than some soulless device.

Maria nodded and asked, "What are the two Imperial powers in the Empire?"

Lev hesitated, contemplating the various influences within the Empire, from noble duties to the emperor's commanding presence.

"Those who protect the realm and those who administer it?" he guessed.

Maria shook her head. "Almost, but not quite," she said. "Think, Lev. You know the two powers."

She leaned forwards, whispering, "Here's a clue: the selection."

The selection. Lev reflected for a moment. In a system where military achievements dictated social standing, the selection served as a gatekeeper to the Imperial court. Historically, royal courts encompassed the extended royal household, yet this emperor permitted only a choice few to enter his inner circle.

"The emperor's eyes and hands!" he exclaimed.

"Precisely! Now, differentiate between them for me."

"The eyes and hands both shape the emperor's decisions, yet they also serve to balance each other's power. The eyes continuously monitor what the hands enact and ensure coherence is maintained."

Lev's gaze shifted to the pile of still-unanswered questions. "But there's something that confuses me."

"What is it?"

"I remember seeing Lucian with the Imperial Court eagle insignia at the banquet. If the selection is what grants a family's retainer access to the Imperial Court, then why is he involved? He's not a retainer, right?"

"Well, yes and no," Maria began. "An Imperial family is allowed to select one of their own to act as a retainer, but it's highly frowned upon."

"It's not surprising he was the only Ruxgan invited to the banquet. It's bad optics." She chuckled, startling Lev.

"So they'd rather have a nobody like me act as their retainer," he muttered as he crossed his arms, slightly annoyed at being a third wheel.

"Correct, it's better that way. You see, once you've been part of the emperor's court, you can't participate again. The emperor is wary of those who've been close to him for too long, especially the nobles. He believes power can corrupt."

Tell me about it, Lev mused.

"If you can cycle through retainers acting in your name, you can stay in court virtually forever," Maria added.

"So... is that the reason why the other American kings under the emperor are excluded from joining his court?"

Maria pondered for a minute. "Exactly. The court is restricted to retainers or members of noble families within North America, the emperor's de jure domain."

"The other kings are essentially figureheads, appointed to maintain the illusion of autonomy among the Empire's citizenries."

"Were you ever a part of the Imperial court?"

She exhaled slowly. "I still am, but not for much longer. I'm hoping you'll succeed me as one of the emperor's hands after the selection."

Lev remembered what Brutus had said about her *stellar* military achievements. "You must've paid a steep price for the emperor's trust."

Maria stiffened momentarily before regaining her poise. "You have no idea. Anything else you're curious about?"

He sensed the tension in her demeanour. The weight of countless lives, both Imperial and Eurasian, lost in the immutable war, must burden her conscience. Back in Eurasia, he'd waited for signs of life from Maria, but it was only now that he understood the reason behind her prolonged silence.

"Yes," he said. "I was wondering about the Imperial System. It not only enables commoners to become Dukes, Counts, and even Kings, but also reshuffles the existing hierarchy to accommodate these newcomers."

Maria looked puzzled. "Your point?"

"With such a system promoting social mobility, why aren't there more uprisings? Surely the disgruntled masses could pry their way into their ranks like us and rebel once the emperor least expects it."

Her brow creased in thought; indeed, the Empire sustained a delicate equilibrium of power, held together primarily by the allure of military glory. It only takes one person to bring down a house of cards.

Then she remembered how Imperial nobility meticulously groomed newcomers before passing the torch to ensure they assimilated seamlessly. They'd made sure to integrate Maria as well, with various background checks before the selection. Lev was lucky he could use Moritz's identity to bypass the latter, whereas Maria had to prove her feigned loyalty from scratch.

"There's always the chance a few might resist the glamour of their newfound status. We will be those exceptions, Lev. As outsiders, we aren't entangled in their obligations or too fearful of jeopardising our families."

Don't you consider me and Brutus your family, then? Lev quizzed to himself.

"A benefit of being orphans," he replied with a hint of sorrow.

He recalled similar scenarios in Eurasia—ambitious leaders, once defiant, ultimately falling just short of their aspirations, and crushed under the weight of the council.

Maria glanced at her wrist device's digital clock. There wasn't much time left before they had to leave for the selection. "Let's talk about this later, after the selection."

Her gaze intensified. "Remember, you're not some nobody. You're Moritz, a decorated veteran and one of the emperor's keenest spies. You'll need to impress the Ruxgans and the emperor himself."

Lev nodded. Passing the selection wasn't just about survival; it was about securing a role in shaping the Empire itself.

Maria leaned forwards. "I'll go over the selection process one more time."

"The Imperial families stake their prestige on the selection. It's an annual contest where each family's chosen retainer competes to determine their representation in court.

"A retainer," she continued, "must navigate the subtleties of Imperial society and demonstrate their valour in a duel."

"The first part of the selection is akin to an examination. All retainers participate simultaneously. It's a test of wits, strategy, and knowledge of Imperial customs and history."

"The physical duel," she went on, "is more complex. It's a series of stages where opponents are matched based on their abilities. So, Moritz," she said, "you'll face someone with similar combat skills."

Lev lowered his gaze. His Eurasian training and his years of service might not be enough to match Moritz's renown.

Maria sighed, a hint of empathy in her voice. "I must warn you that without an MCS enhancing your movements and reflexes, you're at a significant disadvantage."

He felt a twinge of concern but masked it quickly with a determined nod. "I'm aware. I've sparred with Brutus and Maik these past two months."

Her wrist device beeped. "Looks like we need to go now. Time to meet the other retainers."

* * *

Not long after Lev's arrival, all of the contestants were gathered together before the guards escorted them to the examination area. The walk there was short, but it still gave him enough time to study the other three retainers representing the noble houses of North America, and they did the same. They warily eyed each other, and even this early, the atmosphere was already tense and charged with anticipation.

Their fervour climaxed once they reached their destination. Lev squinted his eyes, as he could barely make out the silhouettes around him with the few dim lights emanating from the machines in the centre of the room. When he looked up, he could feel dozens of eyes scrutinising him through what seemed to be a giant one-way mirror. He wasn't sure, but it'd make sense for interested parties to observe the other houses' retainers.

He found himself envying Brutus and Maik. Despite starting their journeys as military logistics managers, they weren't burdened with the constant pressure of performing under the probing gazes of both the emperor and his nobles.

The emperor's spokesperson, a stern figure in ornate robes, stepped forward. "The selection begins now," he announced, his voice echoing through the room.

A massive digital display descended from the ceiling, illuminating the once-dark area and its machinery.

You have one hour to strategize. Please go to your assigned battle stations.

Confusion washed over Lev. Maria had informed him that the first part of the selection would be an examination. He'd assumed it would be like the ones in Eurasia, and he'd be required to answer open and closed questions. However, the instructions on the screen suggested something entirely different.

He nervously observed the other retainers striding to their designated stations. Lev scanned the room until his eyes settled on an unoccupied table with a small display embedded in its centre and approached it.

Welcome, Retainer. Tap the screen to continue.

The other retainers seemed to be engrossed in their own stations, tapping and swiping at their screens with purpose. Lev wondered if they had received prior information about this part of the selection process, or if they were simply more skilled at adapting to unexpected situations.

Taking a deep breath, he reached out and tapped the screen. The display flickered to life, presenting him with a complex interface.

Yeah, this is definitely not like public school.

Aside from the options and menus, the screen displayed a detailed map of a fictional battlefield, complete with terrain, resources, and opposing forces.

So that's what Maria meant by wits, strategy, and knowledge.

With only an hour to strategize, Lev began to analyse the map.

His eyes were drawn to the symbols representing destroyed resource depots scattered across the battlefield.

Lev also spotted stationary red, orange, and blue dots in each corner of the map, with his own forces represented by green dots.

When he tapped the screen, the view zoomed into the collection of green dots.

Each individual in his army was distinct, unique. The level of detail was astounding, far beyond any technology Lev had encountered in Eurasia.

Furthermore, the resemblance to Eurasian troops was uncanny—from their distinctive military combat suits to the blue visors on their helmets. It was a mirror image of his own comrades.

He watched as two soldiers huddled around their own map, discussing strategy and pointing at locations.

This technology is light-years ahead of Eurasia. Do we really stand a chance against the Empire?

Lev zoomed out slightly, taking in the broader view of his corner of the map. Empty trenches snaked through the terrain, providing cover and strategic positions for his troops.

His eyes darted to the other retainers, who were still absorbed in their own battle stations.

They must be the other colours.

Lev focussed his attention back on the screen and zoomed out, the camp shrinking back into a sea of green dots on the map.

His brow furrowed as he moved the camera to the red dots, zooming in to get a better look at the enemy camp. To his surprise, all the details he had observed in his own camp were obscured by a thick fog.

A literal fog of war, he thought, *how fitting.*

Curious, Lev shifted his focus to the orange dots, only to be met with the same impenetrable fog.

However, when he turned to the blue dots, he was taken aback. Instead of the expected fog, he was greeted with the same level of detail as before. As he zoomed in, labels appeared above each soldier.

Allied Forces.

Those in the blue camp shared the same distinctive Eurasian appearance.

Could it be? he wondered.

It seemed like he and another retainer were controlling the Eurasian army in this battle simulation while the red and orange dots represented the Imperial army.

Who's controlling the blue dots?

He glanced up at the large display's countdown.

45 minutes remaining before battle phase.

Lev scanned the room once more, hoping to catch the eye of whoever might be controlling the allied blue forces, but the other retainers remained fixated on their own displays.

Then he noticed a small icon in the corner of his screen. As he tapped it, a transparent circle appeared beneath his finger.

Tap to ping.

So this is how I communicate. Interesting.

With a few quick taps and swipes, he selected a quarter of his forces and directed them towards the trenches. Sure enough, the green dots began to move across the virtual battlefield.

Lev arranged the remaining troops into battle formations. He positioned his infantry behind the trenches, with artillery and support units behind them.

0 minutes remaining before battle phase.

Commencing battle phase.

He deftly manoeuvred his troops towards the closest supply depot and noticed the blue dots were rushing towards the same one.

Let's see if they understand this.

A quick tap and swipe, and Lev positioned a ping above a depot further ahead. The blue dots responded much faster than he'd expected and moved past the depot he was still aiming for.

Once Lev's forces reached the destroyed building, they automatically began repairing it. A trench was near the structure. In a few taps, he ordered half of his troops to occupy the trench while the other half focussed on repairs.

He shifted his attention back to the blue dots. They had reached the other depot, but were now under heavy fire from enemy artillery. Red circles on the map indicated the origin of the enemy bombardment.

After he rained down hell on the red circles with his own artillery, the enemy barrage ceased; his allies safely reached the other supply depot.

A frustrated groan from a nearby retainer caught Lev's attention.

So you're Red. Got it.

As his depot reached full repair, a new menu appeared on Lev's display, offering three reinforcement options: ground attack planes, tanks, or assault infantry.

If Orange is Red's ally, and still has their artillery intact, tanks will be sitting ducks, and infantry will get shredded. Air support it is.

With a decisive tap, Lev selected the ground attack planes and directed them towards the orange positions. Their jet engines roared as they closed in on Orange's fortifications.

The fog of war momentarily dissipated, revealing a detailed view of the enemy fortifications.

Lev zoomed in to assess the damage. The ground attack planes unleashed a barrage of bombs and missiles, striking the orange artillery positions with surgical precision. Explosions erupted across the landscape, sending plumes of smoke and debris into the air. The enemy's defences crumbled under the relentless assault, their once-formidable artillery reduced to smouldering ruins.

Having confirmed the carnage, Lev took a deep breath as his heart rate gradually slowed down.

He pondered the significance of the supply depot he had just repaired. In a real battle, such a structure would take days to restore, but in this virtual world, it had taken mere moments.

If this were real, this phase would take days, if not weeks.

As he surveyed the battlefield once more, Lev noticed that the blue dots, his apparent allies, had begun to regroup near their own repaired supply depot, and had called in a dozen tanks to reinforce it. The red and orange forces, however, were still largely in disarray.

This is just the beginning, he thought. *There's still a long way to go before I can replace Maria as one of the emperor's hands.*

He glanced at the other retainers, their faces a mix of concentration and frustration as they navigated the simulated battle.

I can't fail now.

BONUS CHAPTER 2
SURVIVAL OF THE FITTEST

Lev's forces continued their advance, capturing and repairing supply depots with ruthless efficiency. Both he and the retainer controlling the blue forces had been pinging his troops. Both of them now coordinated in almost perfect synchronisation. With the last depots almost in their grasp, and the enemy's defences crumbling under their combined assault, they had the upper hand.

Just as Lev was about to call in another wave of infantry reinforcements, his display flashed a new message.

Final Stand initiated.

Orange and Red have been granted defensive buffs for the remainder of the game, a last-ditch effort to turn the tables.

His eyes widened as he noticed a previously greyed out reinforcement option had now turned green on his display.

Tactical Nuke.

Even during his time on the battlefields of the neutral zone, he had never encountered such a weapon.

As his finger hovered over the option, he noticed how his points had grown substantially from repairing the supply depots and controlling them.

This ammunition would cost him most of his points, but what choice did he have? They had to secure their victory before anyone mounted a counteroffensive. He selected the bomb and aimed it at the remnants of his enemies' positions before they had a chance to re-inforce themselves.

As soon as Lev confirmed the nuke's target, the display zoomed in on the incoming ICBM as it released its warheads.

The warheads glowed hot as they re-entered the atmosphere, plummeting towards the enemy trenches.

The resulting explosion was so intense that Lev had to shield his eyes from the blinding light emanating from the display. The virtual environment shook, its air seeming to ripple with the force of the blast. When the dust settled, the scene that greeted him was one of utter devastation.

Under a mushroom cloud, he could spot scorched bodies littering the battlefield. A few surviving soldiers dragged themselves out of the trenches, only to collapse moments later from their wounds.

Blue and Green have emerged victorious.

"What have I done," Lev blurted out, causing the other retainers to stare at him with confused looks.

A retainer approached him with an outstretched hand and a friendly smile. "You must be Moritz Antonius. I'm Gerard de Bruce, Maria's replacement."

Lev shook his hand, trying to mask his surprise at the mention of his assumed identity. "How do you know my name?"

"Maria told me you'd be here. You're a retainer for the Ruxgans, right?" Gerard replied casually.

"That's right."

Gerard pointed at his battle station, which still showed the famil-iar blue dots on its map. "She said we'd make a great team, which is probably why we were paired together in the first phase."

"I see. Well, it seems like Maria was right. We worked well to-gether out there."

Gerard grinned, patting Lev on the shoulder. "Indeed we did.

That was some impressive strategizing on your part. You should've seen the look on Albert's face when your nuke detonated!"

Lev forced a smile. "Thank you. I just did what I thought was necessary to win."

"And win we did." Gerard's eyes gleamed with admiration. "Are you ready for the next phase? It should be starting anytime now."

"I hope so."

"Oh, by the way," Gerard began, gesturing at a retainer complaining to the spokesperson. "The pissed fella over there is Albert. He's a retainer for the Vincards."

"Then the girl staring at us is from the Webfields, right?" Lev asked. "I think I saw her at the banquet."

Gerard nodded. "That's right, I forgot her name, but Maria said she's well-versed in martial arts. Wouldn't wanna mess with her."

The emperor's spokesperson cleared his throat, interrupting the two. "The second phase shall now commence. Proceed to the next stage."

With a sudden *hiss,* a seamless door slid open, prompting the retainers to enter.

As Lev stepped into the room alongside the others, his eyes were drawn upwards, searching for a ceiling that seemed to stretch endlessly into darkness. The room was compact, yet the absence of a visible roof lent it an air of vastness. At the chamber's heart stood a circular platform.

The Imperial spokesperson's voice cut through the silence. "Please step onto the platform."

Lev exchanged glances with his fellow retainers before they collectively moved forward. As soon as they had all taken their positions, the platform beneath their feet shuddered to life, and a low hum filled the air.

Higher and higher they climbed, the platform's ascent accompanied by the growing sound of drums and the roar of a massive crowd. Light began to filter through from above, growing in intensity until, with a final surge, the ceiling parted, and the arena was revealed in all its glory.

The platform locked into place, and Lev found himself standing at the centre of a grand spectacle. Loges teeming with spectators lined all six walls of the hexagonal arena.

As the crowd's roar rose to a deafening crescendo, his gaze was drawn to the largest of the loges, undoubtedly reserved for the emperor himself.

It was then that Lev noticed the black, slitted outline bordering the platform on which they stood. Before he could ponder its significance, the announcer's voice boomed through the arena.

"House Von Mitternacht and House Ruxgan, stand aside."

Gerard stepped to the lowest row of seats without hesitation, with Lev following suit.

A massive holographic display hovered a few feet above the platform, glowing in a mix of red and orange.

House Webfield and House Vincard. Please step into the arena.

Once the two losers of the first stage made their way onto the platform and stood opposite each other, a translucent barrier rose out of the outline, imprisoning the two retainers.

The barrier stopped, and the crowd's roar died down to a hushed whisper.

"Esteemed retainers, the emperor himself will now address you," the announcer's voice declared, echoing through the arena.

All eyes turned to the holographic display above the circular platform. The hologram transformed to reveal the emperor in his resplendent Imperial regalia. A crimson cloak draped over his shoulders, fastened at the neck with a golden clasp bearing the Imperial crest. Beneath the cloak, a tailored suit of the finest black silk hugged his frame, adorned with intricate gold embroidery that glinted under the arena's lights. Upon his head rested a crown of polished obsidian, studded with crimson rubies.

The emperor's voice filled the arena. "My loyal subjects, I stand before you today, proud to oversee this glorious ceremony. The old guard will soon retire, untainted by the possibility of corruption that so often follows authority."

Gerard, Albert, and the female retainer gazed up at the emperor's loge with unwavering devotion, their eyes straining to make out his regal figure.

"This selection will determine your fate: whether you will become my hands…" He raised his hands before the crowd, fingers splayed. "Or my eyes." He brought his hands upwards and gestured towards his face.

"But know this," the emperor cautioned. "Should you fail to prove yourselves worthy, you will be relegated to the role of either my left eye or left hand. Only the best among you deserves the honour of serving as my right eye or right hand."

As the emperor's image vanished from the holographic display, the crowd erupted in a thunderous chant.

"Glory to the Empire! Death to Eurasia!"

The hologram shifted, its pixels rearranging themselves into a vibrant display of red and orange. The colours danced across the screen, their hues pulsating with an almost hypnotic rhythm.

Gerard leaned towards Lev. "Funny, isn't it? How they use the royal houses' colours to represent the players in the selection."

Lev felt a flush of embarrassment creep up his neck. He had assumed the colours were randomly assigned, a mere aesthetic choice. "Yeah, right… funny."

The announcer's voice overwhelmed the din of the crowd. "Esteemed guests, the battle between the losers of phase one will now commence!"

The arena fell silent, and all eyes turned to the circular platform, where the two retainers from House Webfield and House Vincard stood trapped within the barrier.

The hologram shifted once more, this time showing the spectators a detailed map of the arena floor. The platform itself began to transform, sections of it rising and falling to create a complex terrain of obstacles and cover. The barrier stretched to accommodate.

As the stage of battle took shape, Lev couldn't help but marvel at the intricacy of the Imperial selection process. Every detail seemed meticulously planned, designed to test the retainers' skills and resolve in the most gruelling of circumstances.

The announcer's voice rang out once more with the final countdown. "Retainers, prepare yourselves. The battle begins in three... two... one..."

The barrier shimmered, and the two retainers sprang into action, their movements a blur of speed and precision. The crowd leaned forwards in their seats, their eyes locked on the unfolding spectacle.

Lev glanced at Gerard, who was clapping his hands in excitement as the two on the platform duked it out, using the terrain at their disposal to create every possible advantage.

Unlike Albert, the woman moved with a grace and fluidity that belied her skill. She launched herself at Albert, her body twisting in midair as she delivered a series of rapid-fire kicks to his chest and head.

Albert stumbled back, arms raised in a desperate attempt to defend himself. But the woman pressed her advantage with a flurry of punches that seemed to come from every angle at once. Albert mustered his all to block her attacks, desperately withdrawing until he found himself backed into a literal corner. His eyes widened when he realised that he had no room to escape.

She dropped low, sweeping his legs out from under him with a swift kick. As he fell, she leapt onto his chest, her fist poised to strike. Albert's eyes widened in fear; he tapped the ground frantically.

The woman stood, her chest heaving with exertion. She wiped the sweat from her brow with the back of her hand as her eyes scanned the loges.

"Webfield! Webfield!" the crowd chanted.

The platform's terrain reconfigured itself into its previous circular shape. A group of medics rushed forwards from behind Lev and Gerald to haul Albert onto a stretcher as the woman stepped off the platform. She briefly made eye contact with Lev before disappearing with the medics.

Gerard nudged Lev with his elbow. "She's the perfect fit, don't you think? Deadly and passionate!"

* * *

Lev and Gerard stood on the platform, their eyes locked as they faced each other. The platform expanded and again transformed into an intricate battlefield.

"I won't hold back, Moritz. I want to become the emperor's right eye, and I'll do whatever it takes to get there."

Lev remained silent, controlling his breathing. The announcer's voice rang out, signalling the start of the battle. Gerard wasted no time, rushing at him with a fierce determination that caught Lev off guard. Despite his bewilderment, Lev held his ground, his body poised and ready.

As Gerard closed in, time seemed to slow. Lev's muscles tensed, and he smoothly countered the charge with a well-timed throw. He redirected Gerard's momentum and sent him tumbling onto the ground.

Gerard quickly regained his footing, but Lev was already on the offensive. He delivered a series of precise strikes, each one finding its mark with devastating accuracy.

A few strikes later, Gerard lay on the floor, gasping as he struggled to catch his breath. Lev reached out his hand, and he grasped it, pulling himself up with a grunt.

"I have to admit," Gerard panted, "I didn't take you for a fighter. I thought you were more of a tactician."

Lev shrugged. "Sometimes, the best tactic is to be unpredictable."

Gerard grinned. "I'll be unpredictable from now on as well, Moritz. Let's see how you handle this."

The two retainers circled each other, their gazes locked, searching for any hint of movement. Gerard lunged forwards with his right fist aimed at Lev's jaw.

Muscle memory kicked in. He swiftly dodged the blow, countering with a sharp jab to Gerard's ribs.

Gerard grunted but recovered and launched a series of quick strikes. Lev's training took over as he deflected and parried each attack with precision. The crowd watched in awe as the two retainers engaged in a deadly dance.

Lev saw an opening and seized it, delivering a powerful kick to Gerard's chest. The impact sent his foe stumbling backwards into a pillar, but he managed to quickly regain his balance and evade a punch to the liver. A smile crept onto Gerard's face as he wiped a trickle of blood from the corner of his mouth.

"Not bad, Moritz."

Gerard charged forwards, feinting to the left before striking with his right fist. Lev barely managed to block the blow, the force of it reverberating through his arm. Gerard followed up with a solid punch to his jaw.

Lev's vision blurred for a moment, but he quickly regained his focus. He shifted his stance, adopting a more defensive posture as he waited for Gerard's next move.

Gerard advanced once more. He saw the surprise in Lev's eyes when he jumped off a ledge and gave him a flying kick. Lev had to alter his posture to dodge it, then gritted his teeth when he narrowly blocked a spinning whip kick the moment Gerard's feet touched the ground.

Gerard kept up the offensive and threw several jabs, testing his opponent's defences. Lev deflected each strike, biding his time until he saw an opportunity to counter.

As Gerard threw a hard right hook, Lev ducked under the blow and delivered a swift uppercut to his chin, snapping his head back.

He pressed his advantage, forcing him onto the defensive. Gerard managed to block most of the blows, but Lev's relentless assault was taking its toll—one that Gerard couldn't afford.

With a deep bow to the audience, Gerard signalled his defeat, tugging Lev along to bow with him.

Once reconfigured, the platform hovered towards the far end of the arena, where a seamless giant door slid open to grant them exit.

As they walked, Lev turned to him. "Why did you end the battle? You still had some juice in you."

Gerard sighed. "That first move of yours... it told me everything I needed to know about someone like you."

"Someone like me?" Lev asked.

Gerard's eyes narrowed. "Someone with real combat experience."

* * *

As the two ascended the staircase leading to the emperor's loge, they encountered the woman and caught her smiling.

Someone's in a good mood, Lev mused.

Once at the loge, they saw two armed guards in tailored three-piece suits. One guard, after checking his earpiece, opened the door and gestured towards Lev. "Moritz, you go first."

Lev stepped inside and the door slammed shut behind him. His heart pounded as he caught sight of the emperor's back, the man still facing the now-empty arena. "Leonard, you've come far to see your archnemesis."

Shock coursed through Lev's veins. He opened his mouth to question the emperor but was swiftly silenced when the emperor turned around to face him.

"We don't want the others to hear our little secret, do we?" The emperor motioned for him to take a seat.

As Lev settled into the chair, the emperor leaned forwards with an intense gaze. "Now, Leonard, I have a proposition for you. Which position would you like to have in my inner circle? After all, your grades are beyond exceptional for both phases of the selection."

Lev swallowed hard, his voice barely above a whisper. "Your Majesty, I don't understand."

The emperor chuckled, chilling Lev to the core. "Oh, Leonard, I know more about you than you could possibly imagine. But that's not important right now. What matters is your answer to my question."

When Lev remained silent, the emperor spoke up again. "So? What will it be?"

Lev's hands clenched into fists, his heart hammering against his rib cage. He knew he had to choose his words carefully, for the fate of his mission and the lives of his comrades hung in the balance.

"Your Majesty, I..."

The emperor raised a hand, cutting him off. "Choose wisely, Leonard. Your decision will have far-reaching consequences, not just for you, but for the entire world."

Afterword

And that's all, folks! At least for now. Once again, we've done our best to balance writing this book with the demands of producing the webtoon.

We can't thank our readers enough for joining us on this amazing journey that started all those years ago. Your support means everything to us!

As always, we salute the incredible MoonQuill team for their dedication and hard work.

Please consider writing a review on the book's Amazon page.

Thank you very much for your support!

About Michiel Werbrouck

Michiel Werbrouck was born in Oxford, UK but grew up in the Belgian city of Leuven. He has a bachelor's degree in applied computer science and currently works as a graphic designer, and author.

He started out writing short sci-fi stories on various online platforms before finally taking the next step. Since then, he has improved his craft, honing his writing skills.

In his free time, Michiel enjoys playing grand strategy games, hanging out with friends and reading fantasy novels. As a tech fan, he spends lots of time developing apps and games of his own.

In the future, Michiel sees himself developing games based on his books, working on software/web IT solutions, writing more novels and traveling the world.

You can connect with Michiel Werbrouck at:

Twitter: @MichielWerbrou1

Subreddit: r/lordofgoblins

Discord Server: WG4d4pg

ABOUT HADI Y. BENDAKJI

Hadi Bendakji has always had an overactive imagination. Fueled by his love for mythology, fantasy, and science fiction. He always dreamt of worlds and the sagas they held. Since childhood, these interests spurred a desire to create his own works.

Sadly, due to familial obligations and the need to focus on his education, he's been unable to spend his time on creative pursuits until his graduation.

With minor bouts of procrastination and self-reflection here and there, he constantly pushes himself to improve his skills in order to achieve his aspirations.

On top of his passion for creative writing and gaming, Hadi likes listening to metal, reading books, and watching historical documentaries.

You can contact Hadi Bendakji at:
Twitter: @DarkSerenos
Subreddit: r/lordofgoblins
Discord Server: WG4d4pg

Thank you for reading a MoonQuill original novel. More exciting stories can be found on at www.moonquill.com and on our platform, www.moonquillnovels.com

We would greatly appreciate it if you could take a moment to leave a review. Every review helps the author and supports their ability to continue writing fantastic books for everyone to enjoy!

Want to get more great books? Scan the QR code below to join our mailing list. You'll get 4 books for free!